say that this is the best of the lot.
Highly recommended."

– SF Crow's Nest

PRAISE FOR *THE PANTHEON SERIES*

"Intelligent and provocative, it's yet more proof that Lovegrove is one of the UK SF scene's most interesting, challenging and adventurous authors."
– *SFX* on *The Age of Ra*

"A compulsive, breakneck read by a master of the craft, with stunning action sequences and acute character observations. This is the kind of complex, action-oriented SF Dan Brown would write if Dan Brown could write."
– *The Guardian* on *The Age of Zeus*

"5 out of 5. I finished it in less than three hours, yet have pondered the revelations found within for days afterwards and plan to reread it soon."
– *Geek Syndicate* on *Age of Aztec*

"A fast-paced, thrill-filled ride... There's dry humour, extreme gore, tension and large amounts of testosterone flooding off the page – and a final confrontation that leaves you with a wry smile."
– *Sci-Fi Bulletin* on *Age of Voodoo*

"A love poem to both comic books and the Hindu faith... As always, Lovegrove's style is easy going and draws you in quickly. A fine addition to one of the best series in urban fantasy available today. "
– *Starburst Magazine* on *Age of Shiva*

"Lovegrove has very much made 'godpunk' his own thing... *Age of Anansi* is enormous fun; *Age of Satan* is entertaining and thought-provoking at the same time; I loved the pace and energy of *Age of Gaia*. Another great example of James Lovegrove's skills as a writer of intelligent, fast-paced action adventure stories."
– *SF Crow's Nest* on *Age of Godpunk*

THE AGE OF ODIN

THE AGE OF ODIN
SPECIAL EDITION

JAMES LOVEGROVE

SOLARIS

This edition published 2015 by Solaris

First published 2010 by Solaris
an imprint of Rebellion Publishing Ltd,
Riverside House, Osney Mead,
Oxford, OX2 0ES, UK

www.solarisbooks.com

ISBN (UK): 978 1 78108 422 9
ISBN (US): 978 1 78108 408 3

Designed & typeset by Rebellion Publishing

Printed and bound by
CPI Group (UK) Ltd, Croydon, CR0 4YY

If it's not raining we're not training and if it's not snowing we're not going.
— modern British military motto

FOREWORD

"I DIDN'T SEEM to be creating, but rather relating events that had occurred," said Robert E. Howard in a letter to Clark Ashton Smith, dated 14th December 1933. He was talking about writing the exploits of his best-known fictional creation, Conan the Barbarian. "The character took complete possession of my mind and crowded out everything else in the way of storywriting... [It was] as if the man himself had been standing at my shoulder directing my efforts."

I can't claim to have had quite the same experience, but I came pretty close with the writing of *The Age of Odin*.

The novel was the third in my *Pantheon* series, following on from *The Age of Ra* and *The Age of Zeus*. Having dealt with the Ancient Egyptian gods and the Ancient Greek gods, it was time to turn my attention to the Norse gods, that squabblesome, roisterous bunch. I knew I wanted to set the book in winter, specifically the three-year-long Fimbulwinter which presages Ragnarök, the final battle, the end of all that is. I knew I wanted to make the gods – Odin, Thor, Loki, Frigga, Heimdall, Skadi, Bragi, the Valkyries, Hel, the whole temperamental, tempestuous lot of them – as real and as tangible as could be, as credibly humanised as they are in the *Eddas*. I also knew that I needed a lead character who could match them for earthiness and relatability. That was where Gideon Coxall came in.

Gid didn't exist in my original proposal for the novel, which was a somewhat different beast, centred around a pair of rival families, the Easons and the Vanians, who live in adjacent valleys in a remote corner of the Rockies in Colorado and feud constantly with one another. A professor of comparative religion stumbles across them and soon becomes convinced that he is in the company of the Aesir and Vanir of Norse myth and that the end of the world is here being played out in microcosm.

Little of that one-page outline remains in the novel you're holding in your hands right now. Really all there's left is the opening scene – a driver trapped in a crashed car, in the middle of a snowy nowhere, with wolves closing in – and the tagline "Every death is a kind of apocalypse," which I ended up putting in the mouth of wise old, foolish old Odin. And much of the blame for this lies with Gid.

I chose to use first-person narration in the novel mostly because I hadn't done a first-person narrative at novel length before. I'd used the form in several short stories and it seemed an interesting and valid challenge to try it across 100,000+ words rather than just 5,000. Once I'd decided that the protagonist would be an invalided soldier – a good man who's had some very bad luck and who's looking for another shot at life, a second chance – the character of Gid just sort of appeared fully-formed in my mind. The moment I sat down and wrote the opening few paragraphs of the book in his voice, Gid took over. He had a story to share. He was standing at my shoulder, telling me what was going to happen next. It was like taking dictation. All I had to do was listen.

I'm not for one second suggesting that in Gid I have dreamed up a character as dynamic and as durable as Howard's Conan. That would be laughable, not to mention all too easily refuted. I can, though, understand now what Howard meant when he said he was "relating events that occurred."

Howard must surely have known, as I know, that writing fiction is just making stuff up. It's not real, any more than the statement of one's finances that one puts in one's tax return are real. It's a fabrication woven from a combination of necessity, the desire to make sense of things, and the wish to give people something to read that's worth their time, with just enough truth in it to make it plausible. Just like a tax return.

All the same, when as a writer you fall into the storytelling, so deep that the story seems to be telling itself, it's a wonderful sensation. It's a gift from the muse (or from your subconscious if you insist on being rationalist about it). It's the compensation for the hours, the weeks, the months, the years you've spent racking your brains on other stories, other novels, working out the fine details, wrestling with the plot, struggling to get all the crucial elements in the right order, driving yourself half-mad in the pursuit of a decent, workable narrative. It's a freebie, a cashback offer, an upgrade to business class, the payoff for all that regular outlay, that credit card use, those frequent flyer miles.

When Gid started speaking to me, everything else just fell into place. Something bigger than I'd first envisaged, and funnier, and more profane, and more sincere, emerged.

Here it is now, in a nicely spruced-up new edition, the text very slightly amended, a few typos and tiny inconsistencies cleared up, all ready for you to read. Gid's story. He told it. I just typed it out.

JMHL
Eastbourne
March 2015

ONE

So there I was, driving through the worst snow storm I'd ever seen, in a crappy rental Vauxhall Astra, with Abortion in the passenger seat offering useless advice and trying to get the stereo to work and, when he wasn't doing that, rolling up joint after joint and smogging the car up with skunk fumes. Our rate of progress was roughly ten miles an hour. It was getting dark. We didn't know exactly where we were going.

At what point, I asked myself, was I going to accept the fact that this was the worst plan in the entire history of mankind?

Knowing me, never. Stubborn, I was. Pigheaded, Gen used to say. "Except," she would add, "that's an insult to pigs. Compared to you, they're quite reasonable animals."

The snow filled the windscreen like static on an untuned TV. The Astra kept slewing and lurching, its wheels somehow finding every slippery patch on the road, despite my best efforts. Every half mile or so we'd pass another abandoned vehicle whose driver had had the common sense to admit defeat and dump their ride by the roadside and head off for shelter on foot rather than blunder on. This storm wasn't letting up any time soon. The forecasters predicted it'd last at least another twenty-four hours and maybe longer. Blizzard conditions. Batten down the hatches, Britain. The future's white. No one with any brains is going anywhere.

"Can't be much further now," said Abortion. His eyes were pink and glassy from the weed.

"How can you be so sure, if the place isn't even on the map and all you've got to go on is a bunch of written directions?"

"Dunno, just am. Call it a feeling." He offered me a pull on the joint he'd just sparked up. Abortion's joints were unique. To save on Rizlas, he used segments of pages from a Bible he'd been given by a maiden aunt for his confirmation, so each one had little lines of text running round it. He'd started doing this when he left school. The paper was thin and slick and could be sealed with a lick – just right for the job. Now his Bible had about a hundred pages left in it. He was nearly through the New Testament and coming up to the Book of Revelation.

"Bit of herbal mood elevation?" he asked.

"No, ta."

"Come on, Gid, one little toke won't hurt."

"I've got to concentrate. Need a clear head."

"This clears your head," Abortion insisted through a blur of exhaled smoke.

I was tempted. But those days were gone. The booze, the spliff, the hazy mornings, the lost nights... They belonged in the past, with the pain. I'd taught myself to live in the present, not to do everything I could to escape it. It had been a hard-learned lesson.

I was probably half high anyway just from breathing in Abortion's second-hand smoke.

We ploughed on. Literally, almost. Drifts were building up across the road. I could just about make out the tramline indentations where other traffic had gone before us, but they were becoming silted up with snow. The Astra was carving a fresh furrow, as best its underpowered engine and poxy front wheel drive could manage. Not for the first time I found myself wishing we'd sprung for a 4x4, something decent like a Range Rover or a Shogun. But fourbies were at a premium these days, and the rental companies were charging more for them than Abortion and I could hope to afford. With the cash we'd been able to scrape together between us, this fucking heap-of-shit hatchback was the best we could do.

Then the heater packed in.

"Oh fuck me rigid," I sighed once it became clear that the vents were blowing nothing at us but freezing cold air. "Does this cunt of a car hate me or what?"

Not that it made much difference because the heating hadn't exactly been doing sterling work beforehand. Abortion and I both had put parkas, hats and gloves on shortly after setting off, having sussed that the Astra itself wasn't going to be much help in the keeping warm department.

By now the sky was so dark grey it might as well have been night-time, although it was barely four in the afternoon. I hit the headlights. The snow flurries became a bright swirl of stars, galaxies in fast motion.

Another three miles on, something under the bonnet began to hiccup and whine.

"Ever get the impression someone up there's got it in for you?" I wondered.

"Everything in the universe happens for a reason," Abortion replied.

"Sorry, didn't quite catch that," I said, cupping my left ear, the one that was genuinely hard of hearing. "Did you just say, 'Hippy bullshit, blather blather, hey wow man bollocks'?"

"Just don't stress. We'll get where we're going to, if that's where we're meant to be."

"Thank you, Mr Dalai bloody Lama. In the meantime, I'll be busy making sure we don't stall and break down in the middle of fucking nowhere in subzero fucking conditions, if that's all right with you."

Definitely a problem with the motor. I could feel it through the accelerator pedal, all misfiring and stuttering, struggling like an asthmatic donkey. We were still going forwards, but the power kept sagging. I was no expert, but the car wasn't going to take us much further unless we stopped and had a look under the bonnet. Stopping, though, was bonkers in a storm like this. Driving in snow, as I knew from doing arctic-weather training in Alberta, you had to keep going, slow and steady. It was the only way. Stop, and you might not be able to regain traction when you started up again, even if you stuck the car in high gear. "You park," as our instructor so bluntly put it, "you're screwed."

So we hobbled on, and I was hoping against hope that the engine trouble would just somehow sort itself, and I was mentally composing the extraordinarily sweary letter of complaint I would be sending the rental company if and when we ever got out of this situation, and of course the engine trouble didn't sort itself, it just got worse. The periods of power lag became longer and more frequent, and I started scanning around for signs of human habitation, the lights of a distant farmhouse, the glow of a far-off town, something to indicate there was somewhere we could take refuge if need be, but there was nothing, fuck all, just blackening sky and the endless thickly spinning snowflakes and the road that was disappearing, becoming buried, merging into the countourless whiteness all around.

We were out in far-flung hilly countryside, north of most of the cities I knew of, the furthest north I'd ever been without ending up in *Och-aye-the-noo*-land – where they painted their faces blue and called chips salad – and there was nothing like civilisation any more, not here. We'd left that behind us in this half-arsed venture of ours. Half-arsed venture of Abortion's, to be precise. It was all his idea, and I'd just gone along with it for want of anything better to do, any other viable option, and honestly, a bloke whose nickname was Abortion... He'd been christened that by a sergeant major on his very first day of basic (because, apparently, he looked like a foetus – and he did, to some extent, in certain lights, all bulging-eyed and big-foreheaded) and he hadn't been able to shake it off since, and why the hell had I listened to *him*, of all people? A man who measured out his life in quarter-ounce wraps. Which of us was the bigger fool for embarking on this journey, this wild goose chase, in the face of the worst bout of weather anyone could remember? The addled dope head, or me, the supposedly sane, normal guy?

And then, a miracle, hallelujah, out of the blue, a petrol station appeared. A BP garage. Lights on. Open. With a covered forecourt that was more or less free of snow. The sign even promised a café, just above the orange digits displaying the eye-wateringly high prices for a litre of diesel or unleaded.

"See?" said Abortion, stubbing out his J in the ashtray, which could be found just below the THIS IS A NO SMOKING CAR sticker. "All that flapping for nothing. The universe is telling us it's on our side, it wants us to make it."

I held up two fingers in a peace sign, then flipped them round.

"Make war not love, man," I said.

AT THE BP, I had a squint under the bonnet. The spark plugs were all carbonised. When was the last time someone serviced this fucking banger? I gave the plug heads a clean with some paper towel. Fingers crossed this had been the source of the problem, but for good measure I fiddled with the distributor and wiggled various vacuum hoses, checked the oil, made sure the battery connections were secure. The full extent of my auto mechanic expertise. Watching *Top Gear* religiously didn't make me Jeremy Clarkson. After that I topped up the fuel tank, and joined Abortion indoors. He'd gone in for a slash, and now he was sitting at one of the tables in the tiny café, watching telly in the warm, huddled over a hot drink.

"What's that? Coffee?"

He nodded.

"And you didn't get me anything."

"Didn't know what you wanted."

"Tea. Never go anywhere without a brew inside me. How can you not know that? Some friend you are."

He frowned, distracted. The news was on.

I credit-carded the petrol, then paid cash for a tea and a jam doughnut. I had a dig at the girl behind the café counter about the price. "Three quid for a cuppa? And three ruddy fifty for a doughnut? I know petrol station mark-ups are a rip-off, but..."

She looked blank, like she just didn't care. She was a scrawny young thing, with her hair scrunched tight back in a Croydon facelift and a jewel stud in the dimple of her nose. Okay-looking, but just not my type.

"It's the grain shortages, en't it?" she replied.

"Even so. I can remember a time when doughnuts were, like, thirty pee."

She looked me up and down. "Yeah, I bet you can."

Thoroughly put in my place, I handed her the money and moseyed on over to the seat opposite Abortion. The room was empty apart from the two of us, the girl at the counter and another sales clerk, an Asian kid with a sorry excuse for a moustache, working the main till. He looked as stupefied with boredom as she did, and there was a forlorn air about them both as well, the way they kept throwing glances towards the window. They weren't sure they were getting home tonight and the prospect of kipping down in some backroom here was not an appetising one.

I drank the extortionate tea and savoured every last overpriced morsel of the doughnut. On the TV, the weather was making the headlines. Again. What a surprise. The weather had been making the headlines for months on end. The telly news people never tired of telling us about it, as if we didn't already know. Three of the coldest years ever, in a row. Three of the longest, fiercest, snowiest winters since they first started keeping records about such things. With cooler than usual seasons in between – chilly springs, lukewarm summers, quick autumns – a brief bloom of green soon turning brown, then over and done, the white returning. And not just in the upper latitudes of the northern hemisphere but everywhere, all over the world. Wintry around the equator. Arctic in Africa. Little black kids chucking snowballs at one another, still enjoying the novelty while the tribal elders, wrapped up in every item of clothing they owned, muttered darkly and stamped their sandalled feet. Snowfall in the rainforests. Frost on the palms in Saudi Arabia. Ice floes on Lake Victoria. The Panama Canal frozen and impassable for half the year. Groves of Caribbean pineapples festooned with icicles. Kangaroos in the Outback letting out huffs of misty breath.

Three years of this, and still the climatologists could only shrug their shoulders and say, "We haven't a clue what's happening or why."

Some blamed global warming, stating that this freak cold snap proved somehow that our carbon footprints had fucked the ecosystem, things would be steaming up again soon but we could expect to see a continual seesawing between extremes, higher hot peaks, deeper cold troughs, the planet not knowing what to do with itself, fiddling with its own thermostat in a desperate effort to balance things out.

Others claimed it was obviously the onset of a new ice age. Ice ages came along every eleven thousand years, and seeing as the last one was eleven thousand years ago, the next was due, even overdue.

Most, though, were pointing the finger at the recent spate of volcanic eruptions worldwide. Etna, Mount St Helens, Stromboli, Kilauea, Piton de la Fournaise on La Réunion, Eyjafjallajökull and its bum-chum Katla – all of them had blown their tops big-time during the past decade, shoving up billions of tons of soot and ash into the atmosphere and increasing the Earth's albedo, whatever that was, creating a haze of cloud that reflected away the sun's rays. Result: bit of a nip in the air.

Whatever the cause, people were worried, no two ways about it. Not only had the crop harvests had been consistently poor three years running, meaning food shortages, but the old folk were dropping off their perches by the thousand. Most hospitals, you couldn't move for the sick and dying elderly that were clogging up the corridors, stricken with pneumonia and hypothermia, rattling their last. Everywhere, the wheels of industry were grinding slower and slower. Economies were suffering. Not to mention the infrastructure of certain nations, including our dear own United Kingdom, was falling to pieces.

Prime Minister Clasen had been trying to keep a lid on it all and failing significantly. The more the plummy-voiced, baby-faced buffoon insisted in his cod-statesmanlike way that everything was under control, the less anyone believed him. All those floggings, fagging and buggery at public school hadn't moulded a man capable of coping with a nation in crisis. Daddy couldn't open the chequebook and get him out of this one. He was going to have to handle it himself. Or not, as the case may be.

Clasen said how much he was looking forward to putting heads together with America's President Keener in a few weeks' time and having a full and frank exchange of ideas about the crisis, and it just so happened that the very next item on the programme featured the luscious Mrs Keener herself. It was coverage of her State of the Union address which she'd given the previous evening and which she claimed was directed not just at Congress or even the American people but at "all the citizens of the world."

What it boiled down to was some guff about not panicking, digging in and seeing this through. The usual bromides from the First Lady, delivered in that honeydew Deep South accent of hers.

God, though, she could always make it sound good. Plausible. Like there was no reason why you shouldn't trust every word she said. No reason to doubt her.

Helped that she was so fit, too.

"I'm from the state of Georgia," Mrs Keener said, "where we normally know it's winter 'cause I see my grandmother maybe wearing an extra sweater. Before I came to Washington, I had no idea what cold was. But I got used to it once I was here, and learned to bundle up on those days when the Potomac turned white. And if I can do that, we all can. This ain't no ice age, that's just fool talk. No global warming neither. This is just some funny old weather cycle, a little jape the Good Lord has seen fit to play on us, and it'll pass. Long as we wrap up warm and look out for each other, we'll be fine."

"I would," said Abortion, gesturing at the screen.

"Her?"

"Absolutely. Wouldn't you?"

I looked again at Keener. Those cheekbones. Those lips. That voice. That figure, which her tailored suit did nothing to disguise and everything to emphasise.

"Yeah," I admitted. "If she wasn't a happily married mother of two."

"Even then," said Abortion. "Especially then. Happily married mothers of two don't get any at home. She'd be gagging for it."

"The first ever PILF," I said.

"PILF?"

"Politician I'd Like to Fuck."

Abortion chortled. "PILF." He chortled again. "I'm going to remember that one. For use later."

AS WE HEADED back out to the car a massive yawn ripped through me like an earth tremor. I was knackered. Been driving all day, without let-up, and on my mettle every inch of the way.

I didn't want to ask him – it went against every instinct I had – but I couldn't see a way out of it.

"Abortion, will you drive?"

"You sure?"

"No, but I don't think I can go on without catching some rest."

"You said you didn't trust me behind the wheel."

"Fucked-up as you are, I still don't. But I need to get my head down, and we need to get back on the road while there's still a road to get back on. Just be careful, don't go fast, don't get fancy. Half an hour's shuteye, that's all I want, then we'll swap back over."

Abortion snatched the keys from my hand and bounded over to the Astra.

Honestly, it was like being with a kid, not a grown man the wrong side of thirty.

Which reminded me.

As Abortion got the car in motion, I fished out my mobile. Shouldn't be calling Gen's but wanted to. Wanted to speak to Cody, just hear his voice, make contact before Abortion and I disappeared into whatever it was we were about to disappear into.

One bar of signal, flickering. I gave it a shot.

"Gid."

"Gen. How you doing?"

"You're very faint."

"Reception out here's being knackered by the snow, like everything else."

"Out here? Where are you?"

"Fuck knows, frankly. Somewhere way north. Just passed a sign saying 'Beware – Wild Haggises Ahead.'"

"You're travelling? Are you mad? Have you not heard the Met Office warnings? It's going to hit minus twenty in some parts tonight."

"Since when have I ever paid attention to warnings?"

"Seriously, they're saying people could die out there."

"It sounds like you almost care," I shouldn't have said but did.

Gen's voice went rigid. I could imagine her eyebrows puckering, that way they did when she was annoyed. "Would you like me to put Cody on?"

"Go on then."

Some clattering, feet on stairs, Gen saying "Your father," and Cody groaning, which broke my heart.

"Yes?"

"Hey, boy. What's up?"

"Not much."

"School today?"

"No."

"Snow day."

"Yeah."

"Did you get outdoors? Make a snowman?"

"No." Like: *Why would I do something so lame? I'm twelve, you know.*

"Sledging?"

"Stayed in with my Xbox. Roz bought me this awesome new game. *Bushido Midnight*. Roz's cool. She played it with me for hours. She's better at being a samurai but I kick her arse when I'm playing as a good vampire."

"Don't swear."

"What's that? Dad, I can hardly hear you."

"I said don't... Never mind. It's great that you had a nice time with Roz. She's a good bloke."

"Da-a-ad," he sighed.

But I'd meant it as a compliment. Sort of. "Anyway, look, Codes, you take –"

"Dad?"

"You take care, and –"

"Dad? You there?"

"And do your homework –"

"Mum, I think he's gone."

"And –"

Nothing. Silence. Disconnected.

"And," I said into the ether, "tell your mum and that butch bitch girlfriend of hers to stop making me out to be some sort of idiot monster you should forget about. Just because I don't ever see you doesn't mean I don't love you. I'm still your dad, for fuck's sake."

I slapped the phone shut. Slumped disconsolately into my seat.

"That's got to suck," said Abortion, bent over the steering wheel. "Your wife's turned into a rug muncher and your kid barely knows who you are. Bummer."

"Abortion..."

"Just saying, bad enough you put Gen off men for life, but now you don't even get to visit the child you fathered with her and he's being brought up in a household of dykes, which is surely going to warp him for life. Can you imagine what it's like when the pair of them are on the blob? A normal household, the dad's there to balance things out and take the flak when it's rag week, but –"

"Abortion," I growled, "shut the fuck up."

"Okay."

"Just drive."

"Okay."

I folded my arms, leant my head against the side window, and closed my eyes. At least the Astra was chugging along all right now. We had plenty of petrol, and according to the directions Abortion had downloaded we weren't a million miles from our destination. I felt the vibration of the engine through the cold window glass. The muffled crunch of snow under our tyres was oddly soothing. One thing I knew how to do, one really useful trick I'd picked up in the army, was being able to nod off in any circumstances. In the belly of a roaring Chinook, in the back of a jolting troop transport, in a bivvy bag, basha or bedroll, on bare ground under starry skies, it didn't matter. I was never bothered by insomnia, never lay awake wishing I was asleep. I could just shut myself down like switching off a computer.

Blip.

Gone.

"*SHIIIIIIIIIIIIIIIIT!*"

Abortion, almost screeching.

And then a tremendous bounce, a brief throat-filling sensation of weightlessness, followed by an immense thundering *kerrrump* that shook the entire car.

My eyes snapped open in time to see the landscape veering in the windscreen, then bands of white and black switching places, ground and sky pivoting over each other like tumbling clowns, and glass shattered, shards sprayed, and Abortion was pleading-screaming, and there was a series of awesome concussions as though the Astra were a drum someone kept beating, and then we were upside down, and there was snow coming in through holes, and I was aware of blood trickling from my brow up into my hairline, and white faded to black.

TWO

COMING TO WAS a case of admitting unpleasant truths, one by one.

First, I was freezing cold. Skin numb in places.

Second, I hurt. Pain spiking outward from several sources, mainly my chest.

Third, I was suspended from the seatbelt with my head angled against the underside of the car roof, neck cricked horribly, boxed in, unable to move.

Fourth, it was pitch dark.

Fifth, help wasn't coming. Because I must have been unconscious for several minutes, maybe as much as half an hour, and if help had been coming it would have got here by now.

We'd crashed. Come off the road. Rolled down a hillside. Fetched up in a snowdrift at the bottom. That much I could figure out. And if anyone had witnessed the accident they would be down here trying to see what they could do for us. And there was no one out there, no voices, no footfalls. Outside the car there was only silence. Dead silence.

So, all in all, not good.

But I was awake, I was coherent, I'd assessed the situation. Now to do something about it.

"Abortion?"

"Uhh."

Better to use his proper name. "Carl. Carl Hill. It's Gideon. Speak to me."

"Gid?"

"Can you understand what I'm saying?"

"Uh-huh. Yeah. Jesus, what happened?"

"You tell me. What's the last thing you remember?"

"Umm, driving. Then... skidding."

"Anything immediately before the skid?"

"No." In tone that said *Yes, maybe, but I'm not telling.*

It didn't matter. Wasn't relevant right this moment. "Okay, Carl," I said, "first things first. We're upside down in a crashed vehicle. I don't think there's a danger of explosion. I can't smell fuel or smoke. Still, we need to get out. I'm kind of stuck. My seatbelt's locked and I'm squashed in on all sides and can't reach the buckle. Can you?"

"Dunno."

"Well, will you try?" Striving to keep my voice under control and not bark at him. Because this was his fault. I'd no idea what he'd done, but he'd done something. Something stupid. Something that validated his nickname.

"All right. Here goes."

I heard him fumbling. Grunting with effort. Then there was a click, and a thump, and an "owww!"

"You okay?"

"Yeah," came the sore reply. "Just undid my belt, not yours."

Some kind of genius. "Have a go at mine, then."

More fumbling, another click, and I felt myself coming loose, legs sliding around and down, and suddenly the places where I was hurting all expanded at once, merging, joining forces so that my body became a single solid mass of pain.

"Gid? Gid?"

Abortion's voice came distantly to me, as though through fog, getting louder as the pain slowly lessened.

"Gid, you're injured."

"No kidding," I gasped. "What gave it away?"

"Uh, the way you were yelling?"

I had, admittedly, been screaming like a girl.

"I think I've got a couple of broken ribs," I said. "Maybe a broken ankle too. Done something to my shoulder. And I've banged and gashed my head – don't think it's any worse than a cut, don't think there's skull fracture, but even so, it throbs like a bitch." Quite an inventory. "Apart from that, just super-duper."

"Look, I'm going to get out of here. My side window's gone. There's snow filling the gap but it can't be too thick. I reckon I can dig through and crawl out. Then I'll phone for help."

"Good plan."

"Stay put."

"Not going anywhere."

It took him several minutes to claw a hole through the snow. As he burrowed his way out, a dim gleam of light crept in, revealing just how badly trashed the Astra was. My side had taken the worst of it. That was why I was all banged up and Abortion was unscathed, and why I had so little room to manoeuvre. The roof was dented down at an angle, to the extent that the passenger-side windows were crushed flat, almost nonexistent. The glove compartment door stuck out like a tongue from a shut mouth. The dashboard was cracked wide open, instruments popping out like eyeballs. The steering column was twisted almost to vertical, the airbag which had saved Abortion from serious harm dangling off it like a used condom.

I didn't think we'd be getting our insurance deposit back.

It was agony to laugh, so I stopped.

Abortion's ugly face appeared at the end of the snow tunnel.

"Can't pick up a signal," he said. "'No network coverage,' display says. Fucking Orange. Future's bright? Future's shite, more like. I'll head off and find help. There must be someone living nearby, and they'll have a landline."

"No," I said.

"No?"

"No, you can't leave me. In these temperatures, I won't last long. Pull me out and I'll come with you."

"Think you can walk?"

"No, but I'll have to. As long as I'm moving, I stand a chance. If I just lie here, by the time the emergency services reach me I'll be a freezer pop."

"Won't pulling you out be painful?"

"Almost certainly."

IT WASN'T PAINFUL.

It was ten times worse than the worst pain I'd ever known.

And I'd known pain.

At the end of it I was mewling like a distressed kitten. I felt like a human-shaped bag of toxic waste. I just wanted to curl up in the snow and die.

But of course, with my reputation for pigheadedness, that wasn't about to happen.

While sat up gathering my strength, getting ready to rise, I dug out my phone to see if I could obtain a signal even if Abortion couldn't. But my poor little Nokia wasn't going to be calling anyone ever again. It had snapped along the hinge, and the screen was split in two by a zigzagging fissure. Nothing more pathetic than a piece of dead technology. I sent the phone, both bits of it, cartwheeling off into the snow.

Abortion then helped me to my feet. Or rather, foot. My left ankle was like splintered celery. It could barely take any weight on it. If he supported me, though, I was able to limp along.

And we set off. We laboured upslope, following the trail of huge gouges and scrapes the Astra had left in the snow during its bouncing somersault descent. There was debris: a wing mirror here, a taillight there, sprinkles of glass. The contents of our overnight bags had been tossed out of the boot of the car and burst open, all our clothes and toiletries strewn down the hillside, soaked by the snow and beyond salvaging. Finally we reached the top, and the road. Tyre tracks showed where we and the public highway had parted company, the Astra punching through the flimsy wire fence that ran along the verge.

I blinked snowflakes off my eyelashes.

"Not having a go at you or anything, Abortion," I said, "but those don't look like skidmarks to me. They don't swerve suddenly. They're almost straight. They look more to me like someone either didn't read the road properly, or someone's mind was on something other than driving."

Abortion's expression resembled a guilty dog's. "I'm sorry, Gid."

"What was it? You were skinning up, weren't you?"

"Only a small one. I've done it a million times before. Mostly I use just the one hand, but for crumbling the grass into the paper you need both, and I waited for a straight stretch to do it, and what you do is you hold the wheel steady with your knees... and... and then you..."

My look told him not to continue.

"I'm sorry," he said again, feebly.

"Abortion," I said, "when this is over I am going to smack you so hard, your balls will still be jangling like bell clappers a week later. But until that glorious moment comes you're the person I need most in all the world. Without you, I'm dead. Do you understand?"

"I get it. I keep you alive so that you can kill me later."

"That's pretty much it."

"You're not a balanced individual, you know that, Gid? Your soul is all out of alignment."

"Like your face if you don't stop talking and start walking."

WE WALKED. To be precise, Abortion walked, I stumbled alongside him. No cars passed. That would have been asking too much, to have someone drive by for us to flag down and cadge a lift from. It wasn't likely anyway, not on an evening like this, so far off the beaten track. Even a farmer on a tractor would be too much to expect.

Two things we had going for us. One: we had warm clothing on. We were dressed for the weather, just about. That was a lucky break.

And two: we had Abortion's directions. They'd been in his pocket. And they informed us that two or three miles up the road, perhaps a little more, was the place we were aiming for.

Asgard Hall.

All we had to do was keep our eyes peeled for certain landmarks. Specifically, a set of black rocks which were supposed to resemble a sleeping giant.

What I didn't want to consider right then was that, with nearly a foot and a half of snow freshly fallen and more coming down by the second, a set of rocks was going to be hard if not impossible to make out, however big they were. That was a thought I had no wish to address, or share with Abortion. Us not being able to find Asgard Hall simply wasn't an issue. We had to find it. Otherwise we were screwed.

Instead of contemplating future unknowns, I directed my mind onto past knowns. To keep me from dwelling on the pain as much as anything. Every lurching step I took jarred my ribcage and made it feel as though talons were digging into my side. Rather than wallow in the misery of that, I decided to wallow in the misery of rehashing the conversation Abortion and I had had that led us, ultimately, to the SNAFU we were now in.

We'd been down the pub. That was where we always met, at The Seven Bells just off Battersea High Street. It was neutral territory for both of us. Nearer Abortion's flat than mine, but then I'd been barred from almost every drinking establishment in my area owing to, ahem, past infractions, so it wasn't as if I had much choice but to board the bus from Wandsworth and head Battersea way. Abortion himself was a regular sight at most of his local boozers but The Seven Bells was the only one he didn't do any work in. He'd reserved it as recreation only, so he always kept his mobile off when he was there, and he wasn't pestered by a constant stream of scabby teenagers coming up to him to score. It was an old man's pub, traditional, a relic: no jukebox or fruitie, snug, dark, with flock wallpaper and horse brasses, the air still retaining a faint whiff of tobacco even though nobody was allowed to smoke there any more. Above all it was quiet, the background conversation seldom rising above a murmur. A lot of the clientele just sat on their own, nursing beers and bitter memories.

"So I've heard this rumour," Abortion said. We'd been silent ourselves for a while, eyes not meeting, two blokes who had less in common than they'd care to admit but very few others to call friend.

"Oh yeah? This the one about Beyoncé and Prince William again?"

"No, although I swear that's true. Heard it off a man who knows someone who works at the palace. Apparently the guy, he's a valet or something, and he's got the condom to prove it, and he's going to flog it on eBay."

"Ooh, a used condom with dried royal spunk in it. What's the reserve on that going to be? Twenty pence I'd guess."

"You could clone your own royal baby out of it."

"Like *Jurassic Park*, you mean?"

"Something like, only without the dinosaurs. No, I'm talking about another rumour. A whole new one. One that's got to do with people like you and me."

"Losers?"

"Ex-service. Discharged. Looking for work."

"I'm not looking for work. I have work. I have a job selling reconditioned printer toner cartridges and it pays handsomely, thank you very much."

"No, it doesn't."

"All right, it doesn't, but with that and my half pension I get by."

"And what about the child maintenance?"

"Okay, so I don't get by. I can barely makes ends meet. So what? Anyway, you have work too, so why would you be looking around for something else?"

"I sell dope. That's not work. That's a hobby with benefits. And the money's shit, actually. There's hardly any product coming in right now, what with the crops getting hammered by the bad weather, but people still aren't prepared to pay more than they're used to. Never mind that I tell them about supply and demand, they just won't wear it. So who's getting squeezed? Who's barely able to turn a profit? The middle man, that's who."

I refrained from pointing out that he would up his income if only he stopped smoking so much of his own stash and kept more of it available for purchase. No great shakes as a businessman, Abortion, bless him.

"But this," he said, downing a gulp of his Scrumpy Jack, "this is an opportunity. A solid gold opportunity to make some serious coinage. That's what I've heard. They're after blokes like us, you and me. Former servicemen. Government-trained. Still got all the skills, all the moves, but surplus to requirements. Old soldiers but still young enough to fight."

"*Who* is after us?"

"Dunno. Some people."

"And to fight in what?"

"Again, dunno. But like I said, and this is the main point: for a lot of money."

"How much?" I hated myself for asking it. Hated myself for feeling a scintilla of interest in what Abortion was saying. Not just interest. Stronger than that. Eagerness.

"Couple of grand a week."

"No fucking way."

"That's what I was told."

"Who by?"

"Bloke. Customer. Not a regular. Don't see him often. But he's ex-army too. The Regiment."

"Which regiment?"

"*The* Regiment."

"SAS."

"So he says. Well, not so much says as hints. You don't say 'The Regiment' unless you're referring to *The* Regiment, do you?"

"Or unless you're a prize bullshit artist. The SAS I've met don't speak about it at all. That's how you know they're SAS."

"Look, this fella's kosher, I'm sure of it. He acts like an SAS guy acts, all hard and gruff and a bit psycho. And the other day he came round to my place to buy an ounce of black, and we were just having a little test of it, you see, a little sample taste, and he let slip about these people, the Valhalla Mission. He read about them in a comment posted on some ex-servicemen's forum, which linked to a blog entry.

It's a word of mouth thing, apparently. The blogger didn't put down much more than I've told you, a few lines about the job offer plus a location, how to get to wherever it is they're recruiting. Somewhere way up north, some castle or what-have-you. SAS guy said he was thinking about going there himself. Bit short of the readies, he said."

"What, he left the Regiment and didn't manage to wangle himself a fat juicy publishing contract? How's that possible?"

"Funnily enough, he said he'd written a book about his Spec Ops experiences and he showed it to a literary agent but the agent told him the SAS memoir market's all but dried up."

"Who Dares Loses. My heart bleeds. Another one?"

I bought him a fresh Scrumpy Jack and a Theakston's Old Peculier for myself. My second pint of the night, and my last. I never took it further than the two, not any more. That was my limit. Exceeding it led to trouble. Anger. Flare-ups. Punches. Bruises. Police. Holding cells. Cautions. I'd been down that road too many times. I'd even done a short stint at Her Majesty's pleasure. Never again. The pleasure had been all hers.

"What d'you reckon, then?" Abortion asked. He was Devon born and after a drink or two his West Country burr always got thicker. The "r" of his "reckon" dragged while the "ck" in the middle all but vanished.

"I *rrre'un*," I said, "that blogger's pulling everyone's leg. Two grand a week? For washed-up non-coms like us?"

"The impression I got is they're not too fussy."

"They'd have to not be. I mean, there's me with eighty per cent hearing loss in one ear and a titanium plate in my skull, and there's you with your, well, habit. We're hardly what you'd call prime soldiering material. They'd have to be pretty desperate to take us on, and if their standards are that low then what sane person would want to sign up with them anyway?"

"Do you miss it?" said Abortion. It sounded like a non sequitur but wasn't.

"The army? What's to miss? Low pay. Appalling housing. Getting shouted at all the time. Getting shot at. Going round the world to visit the dingiest shitholes there are, putting your life on the line fighting a war some nob-end in Whitehall thinks is a good idea but no one else does, saddled with shoddy uniforms and shonky kit that doesn't work properly half the time..."

"That's a yes, then."

He had me bang to rights. "You know I miss it. Every fucking day. I'd give anything to pull on a uniform again, pick up an assault rifle and get out there again, mixing it up with the bad guys."

"You can't explain it to civilians, can you?" Abortion said. "They just don't get it. Having your mates around you the whole time. Ripping the piss out of each other at every opportunity but knowing you trust these people with your life. Being part of a unit, feeling part of something that's big and strong and organised. Like being a member of the best gang ever and no one's going to mess with you. You don't have that in civvy street, that sense of belonging. Here, everyone fucks everyone else over. It's all about yourself. Me, me, me. What can *I* get? What can *I* grab? Never happens in the army."

"I always used to think it's like being at school again but being a grown-up at the same time," I said. "All the benefits of school – order, schedule, hierarchy, someone cooking your meals for you – with none of the bollocks. Rules and regulations that keep things in line but don't interfere with you having a good time. And even the combat... Shit, you don't get a rush like that anywhere else. Fucking hairy-arse scary while it's happening, but afterwards – woo-hoo! And I speak as someone who got blown up by a fucking IED."

"Yeah, if *that* couldn't put you off enjoying active service, what could?"

"Well, it's like they say. If you can't take a joke..."

Abortion chimed in: "...you shouldn't have volunteered."

"So you think this is on the level, this Valhalla Mission whatnot?" I said.

Aborted teetered his hand in the air. "You can't know 'til you've tried. Suck it and see. But two grand a week's nothing to sneeze at. And the minimum contract term is three months."

I did some mental arithmetic. Twenty-five-thousand-odd quid. What could I do with that?

Actually, the question was what *couldn't* I do?

Clear the backlog I owed Gen, for starters. The Child Support Agency was chasing me up for arrears of near on ten K, the total sum I'd "neglected" to hand over during my more difficult periods after the divorce, plus interest. I'd have my rent on the flat sorted for a few months in advance. I'd even have enough left over to take a decent holiday, go somewhere nice, find one of the few warm spots on the planet down near the equator and catch some rays.

But it wasn't even about the money, I knew that.

It was about a second chance. To do what I did best. To do the only thing I really knew how to do.

When I got home I did a web search for "Valhalla Mission" to see if anything came up. Not one worthwhile hit other than the blog entry Abortion had talked about. Same with "Asgard Hall," the name of the castle the blogger mentioned. Nothing of any use. I assumed, if it even existed, it was some old crumbling pile that used to be called something else and new owners had taken it over and rechristened it.

Of course I had huge doubts and misgivings about the whole enterprise. It all seemed unspeakably dodgy. A hoax, even. We'd rock up at this place and either there'd be no one there or a camera crew would be waiting and it'd turn out to be some reality TV stunt or a game show or what-have-you. I had no desire to be an ordinary person bumped up overnight to celebrity class and be made a public laughing-stock and whipping boy, however much dosh was being dangled in front of me. I didn't want to be famous for fifteen minutes or even fifteen seconds. Those stories never ended well.

But if it was legit...

Well, obviously it wasn't legit. This was someone recruiting for a private army. This sounded like mercenary or private security work, and very much at the iffy end of that particular scale. Proper "risk management" agencies operated out of swanky offices in Mayfair and were run by ex-Sandhurst Ruperts with tight haircuts and tailored suits. They advertised properly; they didn't wait for word of mouth to bring in employees. They also didn't hire blokes like me who were technically disabled, who'd been invalided out. They liked their meat to be in tiptop condition, ace fighting machines with a thirst for blood and a barrel-scraping of scruples.

Whereas for the Valhalla Mission, the blogger wrote, "clean history and health are not a priority." In other words, we don't care, we'll take anyone. Like Abortion had said, not too fussy.

So the alarm bells were well and truly ding-a-linging in the back of my head, but it was surprisingly easy to ignore them. There was more involved here than me just clearing my debts with Gen and removing that rather large bone of contention from our relationship (if it could even be called a relationship any more). No doubt about it, if I paid that money off there was every chance I'd get my visitation rights to Cody restored. I'd be able to see my son again, take him out, go to the park and the pictures with him, re-establish myself in his life as his dad, actually get to know him and allow him to get to know me so's he could learn that I was more than just a voice on the phone he was obliged to talk to every now and then.

That was one hell of an incentive.

But to be a soldier once more – that was the really *big*, shiny, orange carrot.

So I phoned up Abortion and I said, "Let's do it."

And he said, "I knew I could count on you, Gid."

And I said, "This could be the biggest mistake I've ever made."

And he said, "Mistakes are just opportunities in disguise."

And I said, "What fortune cookie did you get that from?"

And he said, "It's not wisdom to mock the wise."

And I said, "But clocking smartarses round the earhole is."

And he said, "Wednesday. We'll go next Wednesday."

And I said, "I think I can sort my affairs out by Wednesday," knowing that my affairs wouldn't take much sorting out beyond asking for time off at Tony's Totally Toner and getting a neighbour to go in and water my spider plant while I was away. And I didn't even care if Tony said no or my spider plant died. I'd still go.

And Wednesday came around, and it was Wednesday now, and recalling Abortion's remark – "Mistakes are just opportunities in disguise" – as we trudged through the snow storm, I couldn't help but think, *You couldn't be much wronger, mate.*

Two MILES? THREE miles?

Distances were hard to judge. So was speed. So was time. In the midst of that whirling whiteness you couldn't be sure of anything. How long had we been walking? How fast? How far? No idea, no idea, no idea. The snow baffled your senses and your instincts. It seemed to leech all certainty out of you and replace it with cold emptiness. It made you as blank as it made the landscape. There was so much of it coming down that the night sky scarcely seemed black any more; it was just one huge tumbling curtain of snow. Snow everywhere. White everywhere. Inside and out.

"Can't be much further," Abortion kept saying, over and over, like some Buddhist chant. "Can't be much further. Surely can't be."

But maybe we had passed it, I thought. The landmark. The giant-alike rocks. Maybe we'd blundered straight by, missing it in the storm, and Asgard Hall was behind us now, and we were staggering onward into nothingness, with the pure resolve of idiots. They'd find us tomorrow frozen stiff beside the road, buried to the waist in snow, conjoined statues of men, a work of sculpture with the title *The Triumph Of Desperation Over Logic*.

And then, lo and behold, there it was.

At first neither of us could quite believe our snow-stung eyes. It loomed before us, and it was almost too perfect, too obvious. Hulking great rocks protruding up, so sheer-sided and sharp that the snow could not easily settle on them. Huge, too, some of them, black spires and hillocks dotted across a shallow valley. A natural formation, had to be, but together they described a distinct shape. There the brow, there the nose, there the hands, there the knees. A supine, slumbering giant. The valley was his bed, and he filled it from end to end, and the snow, which according to cliché was always a blanket, *was* a blanket. It draped him smoothly, covering all but the bits that poked out.

It was a remarkable sight, and Abortion let out a whoop of joy, of vindication, while I grimaced a smile and felt, if nothing else, we were going to survive this ordeal after all, even though we didn't really deserve to.

Shortly after we spotted the giant we came across a turnoff, a track that ran perpendicular from the road, down into the valley. We took it, and crossed the sleeping giant's midriff, and climbed the slope on the other side, and found ourselves entering dense pine forest.

The track bored straight through the trees, and was broad and clear to see, for a while.

Then it narrowed and became winding. Either that or in the darkness we mislaid it. The tree trunks seemed to close in on us. We threaded between them, convinced we were still going the right way, or convinced enough at any rate, but in our heart of hearts far from sure. The grinding pain inside me was beginning to wear me down. My brain said I could carry on but my body was arguing otherwise. Each step was becoming a supreme effort, an act of teeth-gritting willpower.

Finally Abortion halted. "I hate to say this," he said, "but I think we're going to have to retrace our steps. Find the track again."

"I hate to say this," I said, "but I don't know if I can."

"We can't just keep going forward if it's only going to get us more lost."

"Mentally, I can't go back. It would be too much to take."

"Corporal Coxall..."

"Don't try that."

"Corp, we are turning back. That's an order."

"You can't pull it off, Abortion. Natural authority – it's just not you."

"No?"

"No."

"Okay," he said, "so where does that leave us? What should we do?"

As if in response, there came the eeriest sound I'd ever heard.

It rose, rose a bit more, then fell.

I stared at Abortion. He stared at me.

Seconds later, the sound came again.

And, from somewhere else, was answered.

A howl.

The howl of a wolf.

THREE

"No FUCKING WAY," said Abortion. "That isn't... That's just not..."

But we both knew it was.

I dimly recollected that there'd been a program a few years back to reintroduce wolves into the wild in the Highlands of Scotland. It had seemed a pretty daft idea to me – *let's let some dangerous predators loose in the countryside and see what happens* – but a bunch of conservationists had lobbied hard to be allowed to do it, on the woolly-headed reasoning that wolves had once been native to the region, so why not again? They'd seemed surprised when local farmers started complaining about losing livestock, as if they'd been too busy hugging trees and crocheting pashminas out of mung beans to anticipate such an outcome, and eventually the Scottish parliament proposed a cull, but by then it was too late. The wolves were well bedded in and proliferating fast.

With the run of cold weather the animals had gone from strength to strength. A snowy climate suited them, and over the past three years their population had grown exponentially, as had their territory. They were now known to roam south of the border. They'd hurdled Hadrian's Wall, and packs of them had been spotted as far into England as Cumbria and the Pennines.

So, all in all, it perhaps shouldn't have come as a shock to me and Abortion to discover that there were some just here, in this area.

Especially since Sod's Law was so clearly in effect already.

The howls grew numerous. They were coming from several directions at once. Excited. Keen. Spreading some kind of good news – and I had a feeling in my gut I knew what it was.

"How many of them d'you think there are?" Abortion said wonderingly.

"Who do I look like, David ruddy Attenborough?" I shot back. "All I know is they sound hungry to me, and even if it's not us who's on the menu I don't want to stick around. Just in case today's the day they fancy varying their diet."

"But they don't attack people... do they?"

"Again, you're not talking to a wildlife expert here – just an ignorant twat who really doesn't like the idea of coming across a pack of wild carnivores in the middle of a dark forest in atrocious weather, and who thinks we'd be better off getting a wriggle on and seeing if we can't locate *some* sort of building around here to take shelter in, even if it's just somebody's shit-smelling outhouse. Generally I'd consider that our best course of action, wouldn't you? Instead of standing around like a pair of lemons while those howls get louder."

Which they were, and it didn't take an Einstein to work out that this meant the wolves were getting nearer. I simply couldn't believe that it was us they were zeroing in on. From the little I knew, I understood that the beasts were shy of humans and avoided us wherever possible. Set against that, however, was the fact that Abortion and I were the only other creatures at large in this forest, as far as I could tell. And one of us was bleeding. Not badly – the gash on my forehead had sealed itself – but clotted blood clung tackily to one side of my face, and the wolves would surely have smelled it. And maybe, once they had the scent of blood in their nostrils, it didn't matter where it came from – prey was prey.

We started to move as fast as we could, which was faster than before but, thanks to me, not the flat-out sprint that both of us would have preferred. A surge of panic damped most of my pain down and lent me renewed energy, but my either-busted-or-else-severely-sprained ankle was a hindrance that no amount of adrenaline could overcome. We lumbered in the opposite direction the howls were coming from, or so we hoped, but it was impossible to be sure. The trees confused things. So did echoes. Sometimes the bulk of the wolf pack appeared to be on our left, other times on our right. Once or twice it even seemed as though a lone wolf was ahead of us, an outrider, scoping out our positions and relaying the information to the rest. We'd seen nothing yet, not a glimpse of fur, a glint of an eye. Not even a shadow. And that was the most unnerving aspect of all. The howling was chilling enough, but worse, the animals making it were invisible. It was almost as if our surroundings themselves were the source of the noise, woods and landscape and snow all baying at us, taunting us, driving us on, quickening our pulses, shortening our breaths. The stormy night, toying with us. Nature itself our enemy, one we hadn't a prayer of defeating or evading.

I was flagging. The adrenaline had done its best but there were more cracks in me than it was able to paper over. I was barely holding myself together. Abortion kept dragging me along, a superhuman effort on his part, and I regretted every nasty thing I'd said to him this evening, justified or not. He'd fucked up – so eager to get wrecked, he'd wrecked us – but when it really counted, he was coming through. I was just so much dead weight. He could have dropped me. Perhaps should have. If the roles had been reversed, there was no saying I wouldn't have dropped *him* and scarpered off on my own. Every man for himself and all that. But Abortion held on to me by the scruff of the neck and propelled me onwards, virtually carrying me, while I added whatever pathetic impetus I could with my one functioning leg and the feeble strength that remained in it.

Those wolves, however... Neither of us was in any doubt now that it was us they were after. The howls encircled us on all sides, a shifting perimeter that tacked and jinked with us whichever way we went. I could hear yips and yelps in the mix, unmistakable expressions of glee. They were having a high old time, our unseen pursuers. They'd got us surrounded. They knew we were frightened and exhausted and one of us was in rough shape. They outnumbered us. They had every advantage, and they were loving it.

"I swear," Abortion wheezed, fighting for breath as he forged on, "I swear to God... if I get out of this... I'll give up the weed and be an... honest citizen the rest of my life."

"Don't," I heaved, "make promises... you know you won't... keep."

We burst into a glade. There was an outcrop of tall rocks at one end. The rest was a flat amphitheatre, almost perfectly oval. As soon as we got there I realised this must be where the wolves wanted us to be. They had herded us to this spot like sheep. I could tell because the instant we reached the clearing, the howling stopped. Abortion and I likewise stopped. We had to. Abortion was utterly drained. He couldn't go on. And me, I was long past going on. We both slumped to our knees in the snow, him a trembling, winded mass, me groaning helplessly.

The silence was expectant. Terrible.

I noted that the snowfall was slowing, thinning. The air was clearing. And I waited. We both waited. It was all we could do.

Then: eyes.

In the dark column-like spaces between the trees, pairs of eyes blinked alight. Peering at us. Dozens of them. Yellow in the snowlight. All around.

And now I could make out puffs of exhalation beneath each pair of eyes.

And now the silhouettes of the wolves themselves. Ears pricked. Heads high. Stock-still.

They were waiting, too.

For what?

A shimmer of movement atop the rocks, and into sight loped a wolf, larger than any of the others, padding proudly to the summit of the outcrop and taking up position there. A grizzled alpha male, leader of the pack. Imperious on his vantage point, like a Roman emperor at the Coliseum, presiding over the Games. His the decision who lived, who died, and how, and when.

I hadn't the wherewithal to do anything but peer bleakly up at him and hope for mercy. As if that was even a remote possibility.

The snow dwindled away to a few meagre flecks and wisps, and then all at once the clouds above parted and a ferociously bright full moon shone down. Its glow drenched the glade like brilliant water, and everything came into detailed, pristine relief. I could see the wolves, the dark and light shades of their pelts, their skinny legs and muscular flanks. I could see the rugged ribbed bark of the pine trunks. I could see the diamond-field sparkle on the surface of the fallen snow. I could see it all with a clarity I'd never known before. It was as though up until this moment I'd never really *looked* at anything, glancing at the world without taking any of it in properly. Now a veil had been lifted. Everything had meaning and purpose, right down to the tiniest item. The individual hairs on the wolves, each needle on the trees' snow-bowed branches, the speckling of white on the alpha male's muzzle – nothing was there without a reason. Everything belonged. Even me and Abortion.

I realised then that I was about to die. Why else this flooding of my brain, this overwhelming tide of sensory input, if it wasn't my final moment? A revelation at the very fag end of life. A brief, parting gift of insight to make up for three and a half decades of muddle and incomprehension.

The alpha male lifted his head. He opened his maw. He let rip with an almighty howl, a great cascading, crescendoing ululation.

To me, looking up from below at an acute angle, his jaws framed the moon and were gaping wide enough to swallow it, as though it was some sort of celestial dog biscuit. The optical illusion was perfect. All it would take was for those two sets of wickedly serrated teeth to snap shut and the moon would be gulped and gone and nights would be empty and black forever after.

The howl was an instruction. An invitation.

Thumb down from the emperor.

The wolves around us padded out from the trees, into the glade. Time to die.

FOUR

Not that I was prepared to go out meekly. Neither was Abortion.

We tottered upright together. We were weaponless. We were shagged out. But we had our fists, our feet. Our teeth too, if need be. The army had spent time and money teaching us hand-to-hand combat. Not much use against wolves, perhaps, but better than nothing.

Instinctively we positioned ourselves back to back, to cover each other. The wolves closed in, forming a tight ring around us. A couple were wagging their tails, others had their tongues lolling out, and I thought to myself, *Tossers. This is all a bit of fun to you, isn't it? You big bunch of bullies.*

Righteous indignation gave me focus. And fire.

"All right, Abortion," I said over my shoulder, "you take the dozen on the left, I'll handle the dozen on the right."

"My left or your left?"

"Does it matter?"

"Fair point. What about the big bastard on the rock?"

"Prize. For whoever finishes off their lot first."

"Gotcha."

"One thing, though. I can't quite figure it out. Is this situation something the universe wants for us or not?"

"The universe," Abortion admitted, "is sometimes a bit of an arsehole."

"That's what I thought. Consider me enlightened, O Master."

"Better late than never."

One wolf came at me. It was a feint. A quick nip at the air in front of my knee, then the wolf backed off.

Another darted in from the side, and I turned and bellowed – "Yaahhh!" – which seemed to intimidate the thing. It retreated, curling its rump round.

I should have known that I was just being set up. A third wolf darted in from behind and bit my leg. Fortunately its teeth latched onto my jeans, not the leg itself. The wolf bent its back and tugged, growling, and I swung round and gave it a thump on the snout. It yelped and let go.

I heard Abortion shouting, "Go on, you fuckers, gerron out of it!" He was aiming kicks left, right and centre at the wolves. None of his shots actually connected but they were enough to see off his attackers and hold them at bay. For now.

But the wolves were getting bolder by the second.

Two sprang at me at once, and more by luck than anything I managed to grab one of them by the forelegs, mid-leap, and swing it like an Olympic hammer against the other. Both rolled in the snow in a heap, then disentangled themselves and started snarling and barking at each other.

Before I could regain equilibrium another wolf leapt, crashing into me. Next thing I knew, I was on my back and staring up into the beast's face. Gust of foul breath. Glint of triumph in yellow eyes. Then the wolf lowered its head, teeth bared, lunging for the throat.

How I got my arm in the way, I wasn't sure, but I did. Instead of soft, tender neck the wolf buried its fangs in bony, sinewy wrist. The pain was excruciating, but all I could think was: *It's only my wrist. As long as that's getting bitten, not my throat, I'll live.* This was the kind of calculation I was reduced to making. The wolf could gnaw my hand off, but that was a survivable wound. If it kept me alive a little longer, okay by me. Any loss was acceptable, even part of a limb. That was how much I didn't want to die.

The wolf's jaws bore down. Pressure mounted. I felt something splinter and crack in my wrist. Worse, heard it.

Then: Abortion to the rescue. He appeared beside me and, without pausing, without hesitation, rammed a thumb into the wolf's eye. The eyeball burst wetly open. The wolf screeched and let go of my arm. Half blinded, the beast danced away, rubbing at the empty socket with a frantic forepaw.

"Reckon that makes us even," Abortion said with a grin –

– and then a wolf pounced onto his back and buried its fangs in the side of his face, while another sneaked between his legs at the same time and bit upwards.

Abortion didn't even have a chance to scream.

The wolf on his back peeled half his face away with a single, twisting wrench of its head. The other yanked down, tearing off the crotch of his trousers and much of what lay within. His blood sprayed me like rain. He stood there twitching spastically, one cheek and ear gone, his groin a ragged ruin. His eyes rolled upwards. He let out a zombie-like moan, a tragic, pointless sound.

Then other wolves were on him, six, seven of them. He crumpled under their weight, collapsing like a demolished factory chimney. The rest of the pack dived in. There were ghastly moist noises of crunching and feasting. Abortion's booted feet juddered, then lay still.

I watched, dazed, appalled. Then self-preservation kicked in and I rolled onto my belly and started crawling away, hauling myself through the snow by elbows and knees. With the wolves preoccupied with their kill, if I could get to the trees... maybe find a broken-off branch to defend myself with... or else find somewhere to hole up where the wolves wouldn't be able to reach me...

The alpha male planted himself in my way.

He was wilier than the others. He wouldn't be distracted by the presence of an easy meal. Nor was he about to let the pack's second victim escape scot-free.

His eyes were full of nothing but cold greed as he stalked towards me.

I struggled up onto my haunches to greet him. My hand was hanging off the end of my arm at an ugly angle, and blood was pouring from deep teeth marks. My ribcage was like a corset of fire. My skull throbbed. This would all be over very soon, I knew. Big old Mister Wolf here wasn't one to muck about. I was as done as a Christmas turkey.

A thread of drool twinkled in the moonlight.

I thought about Gen, and about Cody. Mostly about Cody.

Cody – the only thing in my life I was genuinely, unambiguously proud of. The only thing I hadn't messed up. At least, not as badly as I'd messed everything else up.

I wished he could know how sorry his old man was. How much I would have loved to be a dad worthy of him. How great I thought he was.

"Come on then, you furry wanker," I told the wolf. "Get this over with. Just make it quick."

The alpha male tensed. I could see him eyeing up which part of me to go for. All set for the kill.

Then his head cocked. His eyebrows arched quizzically. He glanced to the side.

A moment later, I heard what he'd heard.

A mechanical buzzing.

Like a chainsaw, but lower, deeper.

Coming from the depths of the forest, but growing in volume rapidly.

All of a sudden a patch of snow at the alpha male's heels erupted, with the *crack* of a gunshot. The wolf leapt to one side, alarmed.

Someone rode into the glade on a snowmobile. In the blaze of its headlight I caught a silhouetted glimpse of the rider: goggles, fur-trimmed parka hood, long hair trailing from beneath a helmet. And a hunting rifle, held one-handed. The snowmobile slewed to a halt, and the rider swung the gun down, sighted, and loosed off another round at the alpha male. He, however, was already on the run, skedaddling for the cover of the trees as fast as his legs could carry him.

Some of the pack were sensible enough to follow their leader's example, but others, although startled by the snowmobile's roar and the rifle reports, were reluctant to abandon the tasty snack that was Abortion's corpse. The snowmobile rider levelled the rifle at them and picked off three in swift succession.

Two more snowmobiles arrived in the glade, and the riders joined in the gunplay, taking potshots at the pack. The remaining wolves finally saw sense and scattered, but several more perished before they could get out of range. The slaughter couldn't have lasted more than half a minute, but it was brutally efficient, and in all a good fifteen of the animals were despatched to wolf heaven. Grey bodies littered the clearing, pelts reddened with their own blood and Abortion's, and as I surveyed the carnage – ignoring as best I could the mangled remains of my friend – I thought *good riddance*.

The first snowmobile rider dismounted, shouldered the rifle, and strode over to me. A woman. I'd guessed that already from the hair. The gait confirmed it. She was stocky, sturdy, with a confident posture. I gazed dumbly up at her.

She pulled down the scarf that covered the lower half of her face and demanded, "Are you all right?"

I replied, "Honest answer? No."

Then passed out.

ROCKING. JOLTING. THE blare of a two-stroke engine drilling my eardrums.

I was lying sideways across the saddle of the snowmobile. The woman was leaning across me to hold the handlebars, gripping me in place with her thighs.

Not dignified. Or comfortable. Or even the remotest bit arousing.

But I passed out again before I had the chance to grumble about it.

THE SNOWMOBILE HALTED. Engine off.

Voices.

"Who is this?"

"We found him out in the woods. There were two of them. Wolves got the other."

"He's in a bad way."

"Sharp-eyed as ever, Heimdall."

"All that blood."

"It may not all be his."

"I'll radio the castle, get them to bring down a stretcher."

"Good idea."

"Think he can be saved?"

"How should I know? Not my department. But if you ask me, this one looks pretty resilient. I don't think he's a candidate for Hel."

Hell? I thought. *I should damn well hope not.*

Then again...

A STRETCHER CAME. I was hoisted onto it. People carried me across a bridge, a wooden one. I heard their footfalls tramp resoundingly on planks. I felt weirdly snug and warm, detached inside myself, like I was in a cocoon. Things that were happening to me seemed to be happening to someone else. I was merely along for the ride. A curious bystander. Intrigued to see where this was going, how it would all pan out.

My bearers crunched over snow. Above, branches of some huge tree passed, so thickly interwoven they blotted out the stars. Then there were lights, windows that glowed a deep buttery yellow. Walls of ancient stone towered. Turrets, battlements reared against the night sky.

Ah, I thought.

There was only one place this could be.

I'd made it.

Abortion – God rest his dope-addled soul – hadn't, but I had.

Asgard Hall.

FIVE

IT WASN'T ME that trod on the Improvised Explosive Device, it was someone else. My oppo, Private Davies. I had no memory of the event itself. I could remember everything leading up to it, and fragments of what came straight after, but simply nothing about the actual *kaboom*. Total blank. Perhaps the morsel of grey matter on which it was recorded happened to belong to the small section of my brain that leaked out through the hole in the side of my head. Gone for ever. And better lost, I'd say.

We were foot-patrolling through a remote village not far from Sangin in Helmand province. Six of us on a routine little meander. The village wasn't a hotbed of insurgency or militancy. Not according to the intel, at any rate. Supposedly friendly, and nothing we'd seen so far had given us cause to doubt that. Usual deal for an Afghan village. Flyblown, dust-ridden. Low drab houses in walled compounds. Market area with stalls with corrugated iron roofs. Goats a-go-go. The smells of cooking flatbread, standing water, open-air latrines. No women out and about, only the men, and plenty of kids: skinny little things darting this way and that, yelling, with the brightest of eyes on them, the liveliest of smiles.

A bunch of them knew the drill. They came up to us, holding out battered old packs of Wrigley's Extra which they expected us to buy off them for fifty Afghanis apiece or, better yet, one US dollar. They'd probably been given the chewing gum by the last patrol to pass this way. It was daylight robbery, and we, like mugs, dug in our pockets and paid up, because local economy, spirit of entrepreneurialism, hearts and minds, all of that. And because why not? It wasn't these nippers' fault that British troops were on their turf, was it? They weren't Taliban, were they? None of them was called Bin Laden. So why not be nice and give the saucy tykes something to smile about?

In every eager little face that peered hopefully up at me I saw Cody. He was seven by then. Seven years old, and I'd barely seen him. Maybe spent a year with him all told, in the breaks between tours of duty. Every time it looked like I might be getting a decent dollop of home leave, weeks if not months to spend with wife and son and try to be a family unit with them, boom, along came another compulsory call-up and I'd be off back to Hell Manned, back to Camp Bastion and the tents and dust and heat and mess cuisine and my trusty SA80 and the same old army bollocks all over again.

Letters, photos, emails, phone calls, a few minutes of webcam interface here and there, these were a substitute for the real thing – for contact – but not enough. As each tour stretched on, one after another, I could feel it slipping away, what lay between me and Gen, what lay between me and Cody. My two main relationships, cracking apart slowly in different ways. Gen becoming cooler towards me by degrees, more distant. Couldn't blame her for that. Cody becoming blanker, less comprehending. Couldn't blame him for that either. He was just losing a sense of who I was, what I meant to him, this man he called Daddy but barely saw, this man who wasn't like most of the other kids' daddies, daddies who dropped them off and picked them up, daddies who were home in the evening and at weekends to play footie with them and read them stories and kiss them goodnight. His daddy was a ghostly, uncertain presence, a voice, a pixel-blurry face who sounded like a Dalek, a signature on a card. A stranger.

So those Afghan kids, I loved to meet them and at the same time it broke my heart. Set me longing for home, pining for my crappy two-up-two-down on the estate near the barracks. Where Cody was. Gutted that I couldn't simply walk into his bedroom any time I liked, with its *Star Wars* wall border and SpongeBob duvet cover, and find him there messing about with his action figures. Couldn't snuggle up on the settee next to him and endure *Toy Story* for the kazillionth time or tootle along playing *Mario* on the Wii with him. The only times I truly resented the army and the government's muddy justifications for keeping us overseas engaged in this spurious conflict with no fixed goal – Enduring Freedom my arse – were whenever I was presented with some reminder of how I wasn't on hand to watch my boy growing up, how I was missing out on those milestones like his first day at school, his first wobbly tooth, his birthdays, Christmases, all that.

Thank God, or maybe Allah, that the village children had left us alone by the time Ivor "Biggun" Davies stepped on that IED. We were making our way back to the Land Rovers, ready to return to forward operating base. The village had checked out, all well, no insurgents lying in wait, no Taliban or Al Qaeda lurking under the beds, just a normal innocent speck of civilisation baking in the gravelly grey foothills of the southern Hindu Kush. We followed the track back to the main road and our waiting transport, Biggun and me on point –

They told me afterwards that Biggun was catapulted a full twenty-five feet into the air. Came down minus both legs, intestines trailing behind him like a kite's tail. Me, I was hurled aside smack dab into a wall. Another of our unit was blown clean out of his boots. Literally, he landed on his backside with his socks on, assault boots standing where he'd left them. He was unharmed. The other three likewise. Perforated eardrums was maybe the worst any of them suffered.

Bomb Disposal examined the site later and figured out that the IED had, as was typical, been cobbled together from all sorts of handy household items. The trigger was made from two hacksaw blades, treading on which completed a circuit that ignited the blasting cap, while the principal component was a common-or-garden pressure cooker packed with TNT. It was a fragment of steel from the pressure cooker that punched a hole in my skull and nearly killed me. Domestic shrapnel.

I was evac'ed to Bastion by Lynx helicopter and a week later airlifted out to Blighty. I then spent two months at Selly Oak hospital, off my tits on fentanyl most of the time. The ward there was nice, if you don't count the poor sods in the other beds worse off than me, the ones with the missing legs or the missing eyes or, saddest of all, the missing minds. Plump, bosomy nurses with hooting Brummie accents bustled around us the whole time. I couldn't understand half of what they were saying, between the drugs and one ear not working and them speaking like drunken milkmaids on a hen night, but they were kind to me and kept throwing the phrase "war hero" my way, which sounded great even though it was utter crap. *Heroic* wasn't getting yourself laid out by a bomb made in someone's back kitchen from a saucepan and a couple of saw blades. The only word for that was *unlucky*. Or *stupid*.

But I got better. Slowly, like a car struggling uphill on an icy road, going forwards, slithering back, but I made it in the end. They got me upright and walking once more, although for a while my sense of balance was fucked and I'd keep lurching to the left, into the occupational therapist's waiting arms. Which would have been deliberate if the occupational therapist had been a gorgeous babe, only she wasn't. She was five two, fourteen stone, built like an All Blacks prop forward, and only slightly less intimidating. They also got me thinking straight again, because I'd lost just a tiny amount of brain but enough to give me some "cognitive function issues." Probably this was down to me not having that much in the way of brain to start with. Couldn't spare any of the little I'd got, ha ha. I cracked that joke quite a lot during the speech and language sessions. Amused me, if no one else. Anything to alleviate the arse ache of vocabulary tests, spatial reasoning tests, comprehension tests, logic tests, oral tests – *aargh!* Like sitting my school exams all over again, but more of them, and harder.

I fought my way back to normality, or as near there as I was ever going to get. I thought I'd made it.

But if so, why was I in bed again, being tended to by people? Why was my head bandaged again? Why did bits of me hurt? It didn't make sense.

Obviously I'd had some kind of relapse. I'd been ambulanced back to Selly Oak. How soon after I'd last been there? How much time had passed?

All very perplexing. Not helped by the fact that the place I was in didn't actually look much like a hospital. Not even private medical facilities stuck you in a comfy feather bed with a heavy brocade counterpane in a room with a fireplace, a flagstone floor and a bona fide fucking tapestry hanging on the wall. And the people who came in to see me didn't wear scrubs or uniforms or white coats. They wore everyday clothing. They looked ordinary. The one who was in charge of taking care of me was quite old, too. In her sixties at least, past retirement age for a healthcare professional. Well preserved, though. Looking pretty good for an old bird, actually. A lady of advanced years who'd lived right and enjoyed herself and wasn't afraid to let it show. She had ash blonde hair with a few streaks of white in it. A round, jolly face, laugh lines, bright eyes. I liked her the moment I saw her. She reminded me of my mother, but in a good way. My mother as I preferred to remember her, the warm cuddly creature of my childhood, not the bitter-to-the-point-of-dementedness divorcee she became after my dad walked out on her to go and play housey with a receptionist at one of the hotels where he worked as a lift service engineer. The girl was all of nineteen, just five years older than his son was at the time.

I couldn't stop laughing when the old woman told me her name, though.

Frigga.

I mean – Frigga!

How could I be expected *not* to laugh?

She took it well. Wasn't the first time, clearly. She just smiled at me, fondly, like you would a child who'd just fathomed how hilarious the word "bottom" is.

"You'll get over it," she said.

And surprise surprise, she was right. I sniggered the next couple of occasions I used it, and then that was that.

I slept a lot. At odd hours, for odd lengths of time. I ate whenever someone brought me food. I relieved myself in the chamberpot provided, which would invariably be emptied and rinsed out when I next needed it. I let Frigga put poultices and bandages on my various injured parts and I drank the medicine she gave me, even though it tasted like boiled sweatsocks, because it took away the pain better than any pharmaceutical I'd ever known and because I could almost feel it and the poultices fixing things inside me, knitting bones, calming contusions, patching torn flesh back into place. I tried to piece it all together, where I was, how I'd got here, and gradually random thoughts surfaced, memories returned in snippets, and it was maybe my fourth day of recuperation when I finally got everything straight. Of course this wasn't a hospital. The snow storm, the car crash, the forest, the wolves, the women on snowmobiles... Asgard Hall.

And Abortion. Poor old Abortion.

Made me quite sad, remembering him and what he'd done, saving me from that wolf at the cost of his own life. I blubbed. Proper crying, tears and all. He was a useless tit but still, he'd been a mate, and I didn't have many of those. Arguably, I didn't have any now.

That time when he spent half an hour chatting up this German girl in a nightclub just off the Reeperbahn in Hamburg, and came back to us boasting about how he'd pulled, and he couldn't understand why we were all pissing ourselves laughing until eventually someone explained that his ladyfriend wasn't as much of a she as she looked like, and he went back to check, and then spent the whole taxi journey back to barracks muttering about a shim, a fucking shim, you all knew and you never told me...

That time in Belize when he went into a seedy bodega in Cayo West to score some dope off a man there, and we'd told him beforehand that the phrase "*hijo di puta*" was considered the height of politeness, the Spanish equivalent of "my dear sir" in English, and he came running out five minutes later with two massive great moustachioed Mestizos chasing after him with machetes...

That time on base when he crashed out drunk and we got a black marker pen and wrote "SERGEANT MAJOR PHILLIPS" on his forehead, "IS A" on his right cheek, and "CUNT" on his left cheek, and he spent half the next morning frantically trying to scrub it off before parade at noon...

God, we were mean to him.

Abortion.

Carl.

Mate.

SIX

FIFTH DAY, I had a visitor. I woke up from a snooze to find this bloke had pulled up a chair beside my bed and was sitting there, hands laced together on his lap, studying me.

He was old, like Frigga, but wore his age less well. It seemed to hang heavily on him, the weight of years, bending his neck, stooping his shoulders. The lines on his face turned the flesh into little separate pouches. He had long white hair and a bushy white beard, like Santa Claus, but a Santa with manic depressive tendencies.

I could only see his right eye. The left, if it was there, was hidden beneath the brim of a big battered leather hat. The hat was cocked and the wide brim bent so that most of that side of his face lay in shadow.

The other eye shone brightly enough for two, however. It was grey like the North Sea, and there was intelligence in it. The deep, sad kind. Wisdom. I had the feeling that eye had been looking at me a long while, and I imagine that that was how it looked at everything. Steadily, for a long while. With care.

"Good evening," the old man said.

JAMES LOVEGROVE

"Yeah, is it? I try to keep track, but..." Outside the window it was dark and snowy. For a change.

"You are on the mend?"

"Getting there. Things are sore, but I feel like I've been fixed up well."

"You have. My wife is an excellent nursemaid and a gifted healer."

"Frigga." The corners of my mouth twitched, but that was all.

He nodded. "She tells me you came in with quite a litany of woes. Three cracked ribs. A dislocated shoulder. A cut to the head. A torn Achilles tendon. And of course that chewed and broken wrist."

"I was going for the record. World's most beaten-up man."

"You're lucky to be alive."

"I know."

"Had the Valkyries not found you when they did..."

"The who?"

"Valkyries."

"The three snowmobile birds? That's their name? What, are they in some kind of band or something?"

"You're surely familiar with the term Valkyrie."

I racked my brains. "There's that boring Tom Cruise movie. Oh, and a piece of music, isn't there? The one in *Apocalypse Now*. When the helicopters come. Wagner, 'Ride Of The Valkyries.' Dah dah-dah D<small>AH</small> dah, dah dah-dah D<small>AH</small> dah..."

"Indeed."

"They took their name from that?"

He didn't answer, only grinned. There was something about it, that grin. Something I didn't entirely warm to. Reminded me of the wolves. Yeah, that was it. Definitely a wolfish look about it.

"Tell me," he said, "you were searching for us, were you not? You and your companion."

"If this is Asgard Hall..."

"It is."

"And the Valhalla Mission..."

"It is."

"Then yes, we were."

58

"It was an effort to get here."

I flashed him a stating-the-bleeding-obvious smile.

"I'm sorry that it was," he went on. "It does seem that many of you have to suffer in order to fetch up on our doorstep, and a few don't make it at all. Wolves in the forest are a perennial problem, of course, but there *are* worse things."

"Really? Such as?"

"You'd laugh if I told you, so I won't."

"No, go on."

"I could mention the word trolls."

I laughed.

"See?" he said with a shrug. "I'd have been better off keeping my mouth shut. My name's Odin, by the way. Odin Borrson."

"Gideon Coxall."

"Pleasure to meet you, Gideon."

"I prefer Gid. Less of a mouthful."

"Gid," he said, musingly. "Almost 'God' but not quite. Missed it by a vowel."

"Never thought of it that way."

"Whereas I am forever prone to spotting such things. Perhaps over-prone. Looking for patterns and connections and concordances which may or may not exist. It's a failing of mine. A burden."

He slapped his thighs and stood.

"Well, I shan't take up any more of your time, Gid," he said. "I just thought I'd drop by and make my number with you. I try and see all the new arrivals as soon as I can. We'll talk further when you're more rested and recovered. There's much to show you, much to explain. But in the meantime, anything you require? Anything that might make your life easier?"

"Any way I can phone my ex, just to let her and my kid know I'm all right?"

"No phones. Not here."

"Oh. How about internet, then? I could drop them an email."

"Ha. Such things are... not possible at Asgard Hall. We lack the necessary sophistication."

"Broadband not reached here yet?"

"Something like that. If you're bored, I could arrange for someone to bring you something to read if you wish."

"I'm not much of a reader."

"A book does help pass the time."

"Really, not much of a reader. Last time I opened a book was at school. *Great Expectations*. It didn't live up to them. Oh, and *David Copperfield*. I was expecting a bit more magic in it than there was. He didn't even make the Statue of Liberty disappear once. The only thing I can really remember about that one is the first line. 'Whether I shall turn out to be the hero of my own life, or... something, something, something...' Obviously *can't* remember it so well, can I?"

Odin chuckled and left the room.

And I thought, *Nutter*. Not in a condemning way.

Well, not completely.

But Odin Borrson was clearly not a hundred per cent sane.

Eccentric, that would be one word for it.

After all, trolls.

Trolls!

And he'd seemed serious when he said it. As though he sincerely believed things like trolls existed.

DESPITE WHAT I'D said about reading, a book did appear. It was lying on my bedside table when I next woke up. Big fat hardback that looked like it had been read several times. Bumped around a bit. Jacket creased and torn at the edges.

I peered at the large gold lettering on the spine.

Only President Keener's autobiography. Her life story, her small-town-girl made good saga. *From Wonder Springs To Washington*. Last year's big bestseller. I'd heard she got a ten million dollar advance for it.

I left it well alone.

For about an hour.

Then curiosity – and/or boredom – took hold. I grabbed the book. There was the prez, gazing winsomely out from the cover. Off to some fancy function, some Republican party fundraiser maybe. Hair all coiffed. Evening dress on, showing a hint of cleavage but not enough to be trashy. Clutch bag. Diamond necklace and earrings. Teeth all sparkly white like only an American's could be. Belle of the ball.

That face – so wholesome. So shiny and corn-fed and true.

But you could tell. You could just tell. She was a dirty bitch. It was in her eyes. Get her behind closed doors, down under the covers, she'd be all filth and knickers. She'd do stuff no good girl ever would and not every bad girl would either.

Or so it was nice to think.

I started flicking through. Scanned a paragraph here, a page there.

Soon, in spite of myself, I was engrossed. Engrossed as you might be by a glossy soap opera or a grade-Z slasher flick.

SEVEN

Passages from *From Wonder Springs To Washington*:

IF SOMEBODY ASKS me where I come from, I always tell them, "I come from where you come from. I come from a small town where the people are kind to each other and look out for each other and go to church on Sunday and bake stuff like there's no tomorrow and always have time for a 'good morning' and a 'how do you do?'"

But should this person press me, I'll say, "I come from Wonder Springs, Georgia. Location: thirty miles south-west of Savannah. Incorporated: 1936. Population: Just right. Weather: Never less than perfect."

I was born there. Raised there. Have kin there. Still own a home there. I'm a Wonder Springs girl through and through. The name of that burg is tattooed on my heart. Whenever I can get back there, I go, and whenever I'm wandering down Main Street, that wide old avenue where the cottonwoods are draped with Spanish moss like chiffon accents on a gown, everybody greets me as though I've never been away. It isn't "Oh, lookee here, if it ain't Miss Grand High Mucky-muck, come down from Washington to see how us ordinary folks are gettin' on with our lives." It's "Hi there, Lois!" and "Long time no see, Lois!" and "You drop on by for some iced tea, gal, y'hear?"

Wonder Springs exists. You'll find it on a map. You can visit. You'll be welcome.

But for me, it's way more than just a place. It isn't even home.

It's goshdarn Heaven.

I WAS ALL the things a woman of my age and social standing was expected to be. I was a mom, a homemaker, a baker of cakes, cookies and cobblers, a supportive wife to Ted, a good friend to my gal pals. I was on the PTA at Bryan and Carol Ann's elementary school. I volunteered as a parishioner at the First Baptist Church on Mulberry Drive, helping hand out the hymnals and straighten the hassocks. I worked one evening a week at the soup kitchen down on Okefenokee Lane, doing my bit for the homeless. I drove Bryan and Carol Ann to more soccer games and cheerleading practises than I care to recall!

I don't think it occurred to me even once during the first thirty-one years of my life to have ambitions beyond the world of Wonder Springs... to have dreams whose scope extended past the town limits. I was happy to be what I was, content with small-town life and my part in it.

As you doubtless already know, a vision from the Lord changed all that.

Now, there's some as would be embarrassed to admit to having received an honest-to-gosh visitation from the Almighty. Ashamed of it, even, like it's a dirty secret they'd not want others knowing.

Not me. I'm proud of it. So proud I'll state it here again.

I had a vision from the Lord. He came to me in a blaze of light and glory, and He said to me, "Lois, you have been chosen. Here's what I want you to do for Me..."

FOR WEEKS AFTERWARDS I discussed it with Ted, and with Reverend Johnson, and I thought long and hard about it, and I prayed for guidance. All along, though, I knew deep down what course I should take. In my heart of hearts I was sure. What else could I do?

There was no mistaking the Lord's message to me. I may have been sitting in my kitchen when it came, doing nothing more extraordinary than fixing grilled cheese sandwiches for the kids, but the splendor and righteousness the Lord filled me with were overwhelming and the feelings I had at that moment have never gone away. I can see now in my mind's eye, as clearly as when it happened, that image of the White House hovering before me, superimposed right in front of the fridge with all its magnets and shopping lists and the kids' drawings on the door – the White House, and myself standing outside on the lawn, ready to walk in, assume my place in the Oval Office and take command and set this country back on the straight path.

The Lord had been explicit in His instructions. America, His chosen country, His most favored nation, was in trouble. It had become a land of incompetence, impotence, immorality and iniquity.

But I could, with His help, get it back on track, make it a land that was strong, noble, feared, respected and confident once more.

WHEN I PUT myself forward for governor of Georgia, people said I was crazy. I didn't have a hope. The incumbent, Jerry Forbush, was a shoo-in for a second term. The state loved him. Local businesses loved him. His approval ratings were astronomical.

Was it pure chance that that videotape of him came my way? Did it just happen to fall into my lap?

I'd say the answer was yes, if I didn't know better, if I didn't believe that whoever sent it to me had received an inner prompting to do so from a Higher Power. Just as I experienced an inner prompting from a Higher Power to take the tape to the *Atlanta Journal-Constitution*.

Now, a sex scandal is one thing. A governor getting caught on camera with his pants down in the company of three women of ill repute – in this day and age, sad though it is to say, that's not unusual. Politically it can be survived. State-level officials have bounced back from worse, national-level ones too.

Not the use of the n-word, though. There was Jerry on the tape hollering it at that trio of busty African-American ladies he was cavorting with, all "Take that, you n***** b****" and "I'm gonna spank that hot n***** a** of yours." White men can't get away with talk like that except, maybe, if they're paying for it.

And Jerry Forbush surely did pay for it. With his job.

Which then became mine.

I CAN'T SAY I was surprised when a consortium of certain rich and powerful Republican individuals approached me about throwing my hat into the Presidential ring. After all, these were all churchgoing men and women, God-fearing folks. They may not have realized it but the Holy Spirit was moving within them, steering them towards me.

They told me they'd been impressed by my gubernatorial sass and savvy, and they wanted to see me go further and felt I had the, pardon me, balls to. They said they had people who could oversee and organise my candidacy. They had financial backers up the wazoo, a whole bunch of them, including a couple of *Fortune* 500 CEOs, all ready to bankroll me. Was I willing?

Little old me, willing to run for the top job in the land? The girl born Lois Lynchmore, now Mrs Edward Keener, soccer mom and car dealer's wife turned state's governor... president?

Well of course, what else I could say to those guys but "Sure!"

I'LL NEVER FORGET the day of my investiture. The first female President of the United States of America! I appreciate that that is of great significance to some people, and I'm no feminist, but I can see that it's a giant leap for womankind.

But more important than any of that were the proud, teary-eyed looks my Ted, Bryan and Carol Ann gave me as I strode up to the podium to deliver my inaugural speech. That, to me, meant more than anything – my family being so overjoyed at what I'd done, what I'd achieved in just a few short years, how far I'd come.

I'VE HEARD A lot from the carpers, the naysayers, the critics, the commentators, all the heathen so-called intelligentsia who talk down my policies time and again. They say my pro-life and anti-gay-marriage bills – passed through both Senate and House of Representatives with scarcely a murmur of dissent, I'd like to remind you – are an affront to human rights. They say my giving increased powers to the police to stop, search, arrest and robustly interrogate whomsoever they like, as a means of preventing Terror, infringes civil liberties. They say my proactive approach to overseas military intervention is hawkish, anti-UN, inflammatory, and possibly illegal under international law, and that my doubling our annual defense spending budget to two trillion dollars is unsustainable and threatens to derail the economy.

I have a number of counterarguments which I will set out below. But mainly, in response to the people who make these accusations, I have three words.

Get. A. Life.

WAS IT WRONG of me to send US troops to Venezuela to root out political corruption there? Was I mistaken to invade Iran in order to put a stop to their uranium enrichment program and head off the prospect of nuclear conflict in the Middle East? Was the bombing of North Korea an act of warmongering?

As far as I'm concerned, these aren't even questions. They don't merit addressing. The answers are obvious.

Growing up in Wonder Springs, I used to hear this saying a lot: Good fences make good neighbors.

I would add to that.

If your neighbors misbehave, sometimes you gotta aim the garden hose over the fence and give 'em a darned good soaking!

I'M JUST AN ordinary girl still, even after all that's happened to me. Come the evening, when the workday's done, all the paperwork's been gone over and signed, the staff have been dismissed for the night, I check on the kids, make sure they're keeping up on their homework and not just goofing around on Facebook, and then Ted and I curl up on the sofa together with a glass of Chardonnay and catch up on TiVo'ed *Judge Judy* and watch *Fox News* (which always gets it right, unlike the biased left-wing liberals at CNN and CBS). We devour DVD box sets of our favorite series. *Leno* is the late-night chatshow we like to round off our evening's viewing with – I adore Jay's jokes, and he's been kinda sweet on me ever since I went on the show and launched the old Lois charm missiles at him.

I'm usually worn out by bedtime, but never so much that I'm not up for a little cuddling and canoodling. Ted and I are still very much active in that respect, thank you very much, even after nearly twenty years together. In fact, since I got sworn in Ted's been even more of a tiger in the boudoir than before. They say power is the ultimate aphrodisiac, and boy, are they right! Ladies, if your husband's letting you down in the divan department, let me tell you – just get yourself elected to high office and those he-turns-out-the-lights-rolls-over-and-starts-snoring nights will be a thing of the past!

I STILL FEEL I have much to offer, and if it is God's will that I get a second term – and I know it is – then I'll gladly show the American people that their First Lady has plenty of fresh schemes bubbling away on the back burners of her stove, plenty of fresh ideas keeping cool in the pantry. Some of them'll surprise you, some of them might give you pause for thought, but I guarantee, none of them'll bore you or make you regret re-electing me.

But this book isn't a manifesto. I'll leave the promises and the pledges for the actual election campaign. The one pledge I'll give you now is that if you thought my first term was a wild ride, well heck, mister, you ain't seen nothin' yet!

EIGHT

A COUPLE OF days later Odin returned. And he brought a walking stick with him. Nice-looking chestnut one with a crook handle.

"For you, Gid. Time you got up and stretched those legs. Don't dither. This is the grand tour."

The castle was well lit, airy, with bare beams, white plastered walls, and little in the way of decoration apart from tapestries, usually showing a forest or a hunting scene. All the furniture was solid oak, the chairs richly carved and adorned with images of animals and helmeted warriors. Spiral staircases wound everywhere, and Odin took me on such a twisty turny route through the building that within about five minutes I'd completely lost my bearings. I couldn't have found my way back to my room if you'd paid me to.

There was a huge kitchen, and next to it a splendid banqueting hall with a high vaulted ceiling and tables and benches to seat a couple of hundred. These were arranged in long rows leading to a top table dominated by a single massive chair, a kind of wooden throne, backed up next to a large open hearth.

"Yours, I take it," I said, with a gesture at the throne.

Odin twisted his mouth. "I preside at mealtimes, yes. Someone has to. Things can get rowdy. Someone must very evidently be in charge, to maintain order."

We went outside. It was a crisp, clear day, the sky bluer and the sunshine brighter than I could remember them being in a long time. Snow lay knee-deep all around, but a series of paths had been cut through, tidily spaded out.

We followed one of them towards a vast tree which stood a couple of hundred metres from the castle. It was, honestly, the biggest fucking tree I'd ever clapped eyes on, and – surely an optical illusion, this – it seemed to expand as we approached, the squat, gnarly trunk thickening, the branches increasing in number and spreading, the leaves multiplying into infinity, the whole of it rising higher and higher from the ground, arching up further and further into the sky. I didn't think I was imagining this, but probably I was. The tree was growing, swelling, right before me. From a distance it had looked as though it would have given a Californian redwood a run for its money, but up close, absolutely no contest. It was the daddy. The mother of all evergreens. The three roots anchoring it in place were the size of buses, and you could have built a house inside that trunk – not just a house, a ruddy great mansion – and still had room to spare.

"That," I said, gazing up, "is reasonably large. What is it, a cedar?"

"An ash," said Odin.

"That was going to be my next guess." I shivered. It was chilly in the tree's shadow, chillier than elsewhere. Barely a chink of sunlight penetrated its maze of bare branches. But that wasn't the only reason I shivered. No form of plant life had any right being so enormous. It was wrong. Unnatural.

"It has a name," Odin said.

"Thing that size, it bloody well ought to. What's it called, then? Treezilla? Humong-ash? King Conifer?" I was quite pleased with that last one.

"Yggdrasil."

"Come again?"

"Yggdrasil."

"Bless you."

"I suspect however many times I repeat the name, you'll keep pretending to mishear."

"Try me."

"Yggdrasil."

"About a quarter to eleven."

That wolfish grin. "You have quite an... insistent sense of humour, Gid."

"Keeps me sane," I said. "Just about. Yggdrasil, eh? Well, it's better than Bert or John, I suppose. Tree like this, an ordinary name just wouldn't cut it. How old?"

"As old as the world."

"No, but really."

"Really." Odin winked – or maybe blinked. With that left eye of his hidden, it was hard to tell. "Yggdrasil sprang up at the moment of creation, when the Nine Worlds were formed."

"The Nine Worlds? You mean the nine planets of the solar system?"

"No, the Nine Worlds. Earth, also known as Midgard, is one. The others are Muspelheim, the world of fire, Alfheim, the world of the elves, Svartalfheim, the world of the gnomes, Niflheim, the world of –"

"Whoa, whoa, whoa." I tapped the fingertips of one hand against the palm of the other to form a T. "That's it, Odin. Time out. Let's stop right there. I don't mean to be rude, but this is starting to get ridiculous."

"Ridiculous? How so?"

"Granted, I'm not the sharpest tool in the box. Hardly what you might call Oxbridge material. But I'm not stupid either. I've worked out that there's a theme going on here. Asgard Hall. Valhalla Mission. Your name – Odin. Took me a while to piece it all together but I got there in the end. The Norse gods, the Norse myths, whatever. *That's* where all this comes from. The Valkyries too, and old Iggy Pop here. All based on old Norse stuff. I'm not that familiar with the legends, but I did read a few Marvel comics when I was young. You know, the Mighty Thor. He was always popping off across the Rainbow Bridge to Asgard and getting into trouble with Odin, his dad. Wasn't my favourite superhero, with his girly long hair and all those 'thous' and 'verilys' and 'forsooths.' I was more of an Incredible Hulk fan myself. But some of the Thor stories had their moments. And you've borrowed from the same legends, kitted yourself out with the old names, and that's all fine and well if you're into that sort of thing. It's just..."

"Just...?"

"It's... I don't know what it is," I said, lamely. "I'm finding it a bit of a struggle to take in, that's all. There's you going on about nine worlds, and gnomes, and trolls, let's not forget the trolls, and you're doing it absolutely straight-faced and... and I just don't get what it's all in aid of. What's the point? It's like some weird, obscure game you're playing, and I have no idea what the rules are. I came here – me and my friend came here – because we thought, we were led to believe, that you lot were looking for a few good men, as the saying goes. We had the impression there was soldiering to be done, for money, decent money, and you'd take almost anyone who applied, never mind their track record. Now, maybe we were mistaken about that, maybe we misread the signs, maybe we got entirely the wrong end of the stick, but what I wasn't expecting, the last thing I was expecting, was to find that the person running this place is some old geezer who spouts Dark Ages storybook stuff like it's true and has even named himself after the king of the Norse gods. It's – it's confusing. And that's putting it mildly. I feel like I tuned in to watch *Where Eagles Dare*, and *Lord of the Rings* is on instead, and there was no warning on the TV listings page about the change to the schedule."

"I understand," Odin said. "I sympathise. If it's any consolation, disorientation like yours is quite common. You'll adjust. Everyone does. Please be assured that I am not mad."

"Did I call you mad?"

"No, but you're thinking it. Doubtless you'll think it all the more when I tell you that, when I was much younger, I hung myself upon this very tree." He slapped the ash's silvery, honeycomb-like bark.

"Hung yourself," I echoed.

"Nailed myself in place, for nine days and nine nights." He winced. "It was not a pleasant experience. An act of sacrifice, so that I might gain knowledge."

"Knowledge. Right. And did it work?"

"I like to think it did. I observed the patterns Yggdrasil's fallen twigs made on the ground. I perceived that they made letter shapes, spelled out words. That was how the runic alphabet came about. I was the one who discovered it, and with it the magic of written language, the power of ideas expressed in a form intelligible to all. This made me wiser than my brothers Hoenir and Lodur, which in turn elevated me to the position of All-Father, head of my family, the Aesir. A fair exchange, I'd say, for those many long hours of suffering."

"Bargain."

His eye narrowed. "If you want proof, look." He pointed to something about three metres above us on the trunk. "See? Up there? Those stains. Bloodstains. Mine. My blood."

I squinted. Certainly there were a few streaks of discolouration running in long thin lines down the bark. Some dark, sticky substance had trickled there once. Long dried now.

"Sap," I said. "Trees do that, you know. Leak sap."

Odin stared at me for a moment.

"I can see," he said, "that you're not going to make the leap of faith today. One good look at Yggdrasil usually does the trick, but not in your case. That's fine. A shame, but it's still early. You'll come around in time. You would prefer, I imagine, to be shown something more concrete. Something more in line with what you envisaged when you set out on your journey here. Very well. This way."

He set off at a fair old pace, slightly faster than I and my still sore ankle could keep up with. If Odin was miffed with me, which he seemed to be, there was sod-all I could about it. I wasn't prepared to indulge his whims and fancies, this bizarre blather of his. Norse god? The All-Father? Nine days nailed to a tree? Do me a favour! I followed him out of curiosity alone, to find out if there really was any more to this place than a crazy man and his wife and their castle and a handful of equally deluded followers. I didn't think there was, and already I was planning, like the undercover journalist in the brothel, to make my excuses and leave. Soon as I was fully mobile again, I was out of here. The whole thing was a bust. A waste of time. London beckoned, and the ordinary life. Nothing on earth was going to convince me to stay.

NINE

AROUND PAST THE castle Odin went, sticking to the paths dug out in the snow, and I limped after him, quick as I could manage.

Soon the paths petered out and we were forging across open countryside. Ahead on the horizon I could make out a huddle of low buildings. A dozen log cabins, each with a smokestack chimney sending up a pencil-grey plume into the air. Cosy-looking, despite – or maybe thanks to – all the snow heaped high on their roofs. Chalet-like, the sort of thing you might find up in the Alps or on the shores of a Norwegian fjord.

Through the hut windows I spotted metal bunks. Each cabin slept perhaps twenty. The beds were made, and I glimpsed enough clutter and clobber around them to tell me that *somebody* was resident here, even if no one was actually at home at this precise moment.

The sound of voices came pealing across the roofs, dulled somewhat by the snow. Men yelling, roaring, cheering, jeering. Beyond the last of the cabins Odin had halted, waiting for me to catch up. As I joined him I found myself confronted with a field full of people dressed in extreme cold weather gear. Uniforms. Grey and white snow-pattern camouflage. Scores of them.

An army.

Some were at trestle tables, stripping down and reassembling firearms. A few were being given skiing lessons by a pixie-like woman bundled up in animal furs. Others were exercising – star jumps, sit-ups, burpees – their faces pink with effort, their breath coming in sharp bursts of white, their boots churning the snow and the mud beneath to chocolate mousse. The fitness instructor who strutted around bellowing at them was also a woman, tall and blonde. She was too far away for me to make out her features distinctly but she was, from her figure alone, striking, and I knew I'd like to see more. The guys doing the workout certainly seemed to be doing their best to impress her.

The majority of the soldiers, however, were gathered in a large crowd focused inward, and from their cries and jostling and the avid looks on their faces, it wasn't hard to guess on what. Not to mention, money was changing hands. Bets were being placed, and argued over.

"A fight?"

"A sparring match," said Odin. "Useful for morale, every so often. Vents steam. And if I don't miss my guess, one of the participants will be my son."

"Your son. Don't tell me – Thor."

"Naturally. Of all my offspring, he is the most combative. Loves a good brawl, does Thor. Nothing he likes more. Come on, let's go in for a closer look."

The crowd parted to let Odin through, and I trailed along in his wake. The men might have been caught up in the fever of the fight but as soon as they recognised Odin they gave him a wide, respectful berth. Anybody who didn't see him coming was alerted by a sharp tap on the shoulder or a nudge with an elbow, either from a neighbour or Odin himself, and instantly stepped aside.

At the centre of the throng were two men, grappling and trading blows. One was more or less my size, young, black, with peroxided cornrows and a terrific scar down one cheek. Seriously hard-looking sort. While the other was... well, a giant. Seven feet tall, and proportionately broad and brawny. Long red hair, huge red beard, and yes, because this was Thor, could only be, he had a hammer lodged into his belt. A short-handled, square-headed mallet, a stubby affair, looking more ornamental than functional but heavy enough to do some damage all the same if used offensively.

They were going at it with gusto. Scarface I could tell had done some proper boxing in his time and looked fairly tasty. He bunched his fists just right, thumbs alongside rather than in front, and kept a good guard up. Tight but limber, and he danced like a demon, his back foot up on its toes so he could throw his whole mass behind a punch. Wasn't so hot in the clinches, but when he could keep space between him and Thor he fired off solid hits that connected well and gave the bigger man something to think about.

Thor, on the other hand, was a wrestler. He preferred the bear hugs, the holds, the grabs and tussles. He wasn't quick on his toes like his opponent, so he was forever looking to close the gap and hem Scarface in. Once he had him in his clutches, then he was able to bring his superior bulk and strength to bear. He could crush and smother, and Scarface's only possible response was to slug away at his flanks from point-blank range, which didn't have much effect. Thor's frame was meaty enough to absorb the impacts.

After engulfing Scarface for a minute or so Thor would let him go. Maybe throw him away, maybe just release him. Scarface would stay out of his reach for a while, getting his wind and dander back, then weave in sidelong to resume the fight.

It was obvious to me – to anyone with eyes – that Thor was toying with Scarface. He never looked in danger of being beaten. He was just too huge and hefty for that. It would have taken a lot more to topple him than a few punches, however well aimed and executed.

But that didn't appear to bother Scarface. It didn't even seem to be the purpose of the contest. This was about something else, and judging by Scarface's expression, that something else was pride. He kept coming back at Thor – even though he must have realised he didn't stand a chance of defeating him – because he had a point to prove. He was getting the worst of it. One of his eyes was puffing shut and there was blood dribbling from one of his flared, near-vertical nostrils. As I watched, a rogue swing from Thor decked him, splitting open his lower lip. But Scarface got straight up again. He wasn't going to back down or throw in the towel. He was going to continue at it for as long as he had bones in his legs.

"Go get him, Cy!" some of the crowd were shouting. "Show him what a man can do!"

But even as they egged him on, all of them were wagering on Thor to win. The bets weren't about *who*, they were about *how*. Fall, knockout, submission, one of the three.

Scarface – Cy – was starting to wobble, and I felt sorry for him. He'd been doing sterling work, but Thor was easily soaking up the punishment he was dishing out, and giving it back twofold. At one point he had Cy by the neck and I honestly thought he was going to throttle him unconscious. Cy was choking, his eyes rolled up, and if Thor hadn't relaxed his grip in time he'd have gone under. I looked at Odin, thinking that this was taking things too far and he should step in and stop the fight. But he either didn't notice my look or else ignored it. He was wrapped up in the spectacle like everyone else in the crowd, relishing it nearly as much they were.

Cy lurched at Thor one final time. He gave it all he had, a last-ditch effort. Some nice combos battered Thor's head – an uppercut followed by a pair of roundhouses, some jabs with the left finished off with a thumping right hook. Thor simply spat out a trickle of blood and chortled.

Then he seized Cy by the head, with both hands, shook him around for a bit, then just kind of tossed him to the ground, as though he was an inflatable doll. Cy tried to rise. Mentally I begged him not to. He made it to his knees, and the crowd were roaring encouragement, but kneeling was as far as he managed to get. With a croaky sigh he slumped down face first into the snow, and lay there in a writhe of soft groans.

It was over. Everyone howled their joy and dismay. Thor raised his fists above his head and let out a gloating bray.

"See?" he said. "*See?* Challenge me by all means. Feel free. But never expect to best me in a fair fight. I am a god! Thor, whose name means thunder! I've waged battle since time immemorial! Do not think that any mere mortal can overcome *me*."

He bent down to the semiconscious Cy.

"A noble effort, my good fellow," he said. "But next time perhaps you'll think twice before questioning my authority. If I say you are going to rehearse a manoeuvre again, then you are going to rehearse that manoeuvre again, and again, and as many times as I tell you to, no ifs, ands or buts. Got that?"

Cy was in no fit state to "get" anything. At Thor's command, a couple of his fellow soldiers picked him up and carted him off.

"Frigga will have him back on his feet in no time," he said. "My stepmother is a miracle worker."

Now Odin stepped forward. "My son."

"Father." Thor bowed low.

"Leading by example, as ever." Just the tiniest hint of mockery in Odin's voice.

"They are keen to see combat, these men," Thor replied, bluffly, "but discipline is in short supply. Some of them have not known active service in a long while. Every now and then they need reminding who is in charge and how the command structure works."

"As long as showing them who's boss doesn't mean killing them."

"It would never come to that, father. And who is this?" Thor said, frowning at me.

"This is Gid," said Odin. "He turned up a week ago."

"Ah yes. The wolf attack man."

I detected a sneer on Thor's face as he said this, but I let it pass.

"Waylaid by a few stray dogs, were you?" Thor went on.

I held his gaze. Thor's eyes were small and dark and if they had been set any closer together, he'd have been a Cyclops.

"Wolves," I said carefully, "are not the same as dogs."

"A few measly pups. Me, I'd have just patted them on the head and told them to be off."

"Thor..." warned Odin.

But son paid father no heed. "What happened, did one of them lick you a little too hard? Is that why you require a walking stick?"

Keep a lid on it, Gid. Calm and cool. Don't let your goat be got.

"I was in a car crash as well."

"Ooh, a car crash!"

"And for your information, sunshine, it wasn't a few wolves, it was a whole pack."

"Still, if it had been me, I'd have sent them away with their tails between their legs."

"Well, aren't you the big beefy macho man?" I retorted. "Look, Thor, or whatever your real name is, I don't care what you think of me and I've no idea why you're trying to get a rise out of me. I'm just not in the mood, so give it a rest, eh?"

I turned and started walking off.

"And your friend didn't make it," Thor said to my back. "He must truly have been some kind of weakling. Was it even worth the wolves' while eating him, I wonder? I can't imagine someone so lacking in substance would have made much of a meal for them."

That wasn't the final straw.

"Oh, scared to face me, are you?" he bellowed. "Coward!"

That was the final straw.

I halted in my tracks and spun round.

"What did you just call me?" I snapped.

"You heard."

"Say it again. Say it to my face."

The crowd, which had been dispersing, rapidly un-dispersed. They sensed what was brewing.

Thor very slowly and very deliberately repeated the word.

"Coward."

Oh dear.

TEN

THIS WAS WHAT always used to get me into trouble, back during the bad days, post-discharge, post-divorce. Someone only had to say the wrong thing, look at me in the wrong way... Hell, they didn't even have to do that. All it needed was me *thinking* they were saying the wrong thing or looking the wrong way, and I'd bristle.

Alcohol played a part, but by no means every time. I didn't have to be drunk to lose my rag, although, let's face it, drunkenness made a flare-up a lot likelier. Mostly, though, I was just looking for any excuse to start a scrap, and finding it. I was like a balloon in a roomful of porcupines. Only had to float a few inches in any direction and *pop!*

Coward was the one word that could be absolutely guaranteed to set me off. It, of all insults, really rankled. I had a short fuse as it was, but *coward* nipped it to the quick. No idea why, unless it was simply that I'd been a soldier, I'd fought for queen and country, I'd faced enemy fire, heard bullets whizzing past my ears, seen mortar rounds turn men to mince, and I'd never once flinched – so what the fuck would you know?

I'd believed it was all behind me now, that period of easy aggravation and overenthusiastic readiness to ruck. I'd believed I had that hair-trigger temper of mine under control.

Apparently not.

I flicked a glance at Odin. He gave the slightest of shrugs: *Please yourself. I'm not going to stop you. On your own head be it.*

"You shouldn't have said that, you big fat twat," I said to Thor. "Now I'm going to have to kick your arse."

"Come on then, dog's dinner," he replied. "Give it a try."

He beckoned to me.

I limped over to him. The crowd clustered around us.

It was insane. I was in no shape for this. I'd only just risen from my sickbed. An anorexic dwarf could have mopped the floor with me.

But that didn't matter. Consequences were irrelevant. Just as in the old days, the bad days, this was about me hurting someone else in order to make myself feel better. And if the other person managed to hurt me back, that was almost a plus.

I made a show of leaning heavily on the walking stick, looking like I was in dire need of it. The hope was that Thor would underestimate me, and the crowd would sympathise. A couple of them did give me a grin and a thumbs-up, but cash was already changing hands again and I could make a pretty good guess which way the odds were going.

"I shall be gentle," Thor said.

"Don't patronise me, you great nonce," I said. "You're the one who's started this. If you're not going to follow through in any meaningful way, why bother?"

"Very well. Then this won't take long."

"Ooh, you've really got me cacking in my Calvin Kleins," I said, and then I hit him.

Or rather, before I'd even completed the sentence, while he was under the impression we were still in the trash-talking phase of the fight, I hit him. Hoicked the walking stick up between his legs, and the *thwack!* it made brought a collective sharp intake of breath from the men all around.

Thor's eyes bulged, his cheeks too, and as his hands flew to his tender parts I followed up with a heel stamp to the inside of his ankle bone, then clouted him round the head with the stick.

He reeled, and from the crowd's reaction – *oohs* of surprise – I knew that it was the first time anything like this had happened. Someone had actually staggered Thor.

I myself was a mite disappointed. I'd been counting on him falling, but he stayed upright. Worse, once he'd got over the initial shock and the pain had started to fade, he looked across at me with eyes ablaze, and I realised all I'd managed to do was piss him off.

"This is supposed," he said, "to be hand-to-hand."

I shrugged. "Nobody told me. Not my fault if you didn't lay down the rules at the beginning."

"Were I to draw Mjolnir now, that would be the end of you." He patted his hammer. "But I, at least, will play fair. Besides, that stick is no real weapon at all."

"Oh yeah? It's done pretty well so far. You're just jealous because mine's longer than yours."

The audience liked that one, although Thor didn't. He growled and lumbered at me.

He wasn't a fast mover, but it was something to see so huge a man come barrelling towards you like a fucking freight train, hands outstretched, teeth bared, bent on pulverisation. I did have a nanosecond of *Now you've gone and done it, Gid*, but then adrenaline and combat training kicked in. I sidestepped, and at the same time flipped the walking stick over so that I was holding the end with the rubber ferrule. The crook then became a handy tripping device. I snared Thor's shin and down he went, sprawling full length and sliding along in the snow like a bobsledder without a luge. His momentum was such that people in the crowd had to skip smartly aside to avoid being bowling pins.

I shot the briefest of glances at Odin, to see what Thor's dad was making of my treatment of his son. The old man's expression gave nothing away – except was that a twinkle of amusement in his eye?

I pressed on with my attack. Thor was pushing himself up off the ground, but while he remained on all fours I still had the advantage.

I darted in from behind, aiming the stick at his side, hoping to give him a healthy smack in the kidneys.

Somehow, with an unexpected turn of speed, he got a hand up and caught the stick. He yanked it from my grasp distressingly easily.

I knew then that I was buggered. The stick had been my only real edge. Without it, with a bum ankle and a bad wrist, I stood the proverbial cat's chance in Hell.

To make that absolutely clear to me, Thor got to his feet and casually, as though it were made of balsa wood, snapped the stick in his hands. He chucked the broken halves aside and ran at me again.

There were two ways I could play this. Stand my ground and meet him head on, or evade and try to find a new angle of attack, and maybe a new weapon. The risky option or the sensible one.

I went for the risky. It meant a greater chance of being clobbered, but also more opportunity for locating a vulnerable spot, some chink in Thor's armour.

I'd braced myself, but Christ, it was like getting slammed into by a rhino. I managed to grab his wrists, but the force of his charge, with all that bulk behind it, was tremendous, and I found myself being driven backwards. My feet scrabbled for traction on the snow but couldn't gain any. He shoved me along, I slithered helplessly, and his face was right in my face, his reddened features filling my vision like an irate moon, his breath gusting hot on my skin.

We must have travelled twenty yards like this, me a kind of human snow plough, him the engine pushing. I kept my body rigid so as not to crumple and fall, and that was murder on my traumatised ribs, not to mention my poor old shoulder, ankle and wrist.

What eventually stopped us was one of the trestle tables. We crashed into it, and it did what trestle tables did best; namely, collapse. We fell, Thor on top, amid a scatter of gun parts. Springs, screws, feed port plugs, barrels, trigger shoes, sight assemblies, all flew everywhere.

As we hit the ground I felt one of the ribs that had been trying so hard to mend break again. I might have cried out – I wasn't really paying attention to the sounds coming out of my mouth just then. Thor, straddling me, pinned me down. He lodged one forearm under my chin, putting pressure on my throat. With his free hand he started cuffing my head.

It wasn't pleasant. He was holding back, a little. The blows were loose-handed. But they rocked me nonetheless, reverberating like seismic waves through my skull. With each thump I could feel myself becoming more remote from the world, gradually tuning out, getting stupefied. Being choked didn't help matters.

I would not give in, though. Or at any rate, I would go down fighting. Some honour had to be maintained. The humiliation must not be total. Thor was bitch-slapping me, after all. That could not be allowed.

My hand groped around and found something in the snow. I prayed that it was a gun part, and it was. Better yet, it was a rifle stock. An object with a bit of heft to it.

I swung the stock up at Thor, ramming it butt plate first into his temple. He didn't see it coming, and was startled by the impact if nothing else. The weight of his arm pressing onto my larynx eased a fraction. It was all I needed. I thrust upwards with all my might, screaming at the pain this caused – definitely screaming, so loud it made my own ears ring. I threw Thor off, and then I was scrambling away on hands and knees, dazed, wheezing for air, desperately trying to get from horizontal to vertical even as the ground underfoot kept being treacherously diagonal. Meanwhile a part of me was thinking, *Hey, you know what, this is the first fair fistfight you've had in ages*, remembering all the scuffles I'd had previously with loudmouthed knobheads in pubs, slouch-shouldered gangsta wannabes in the street, flabby nightclub doormen, and even, ye gods, that skeletal crack addict in prison who'd fancied himself the big swinging dick of B Wing and needed taking down a peg. For once I was up against someone I wasn't stronger and fitter than, someone who knew how to handle himself and didn't mind fighting dirty. I was on the losing end, which was a novelty to say the least, and almost, in some strange way, gratifying. I'd met my match. I was outclassed. And about time too. Better late than never.

I felt a presence behind me. Thor, come to finish the job. I heaved myself round to face him, teetering to my feet. I had a fist clenched, even though I doubted I had it in me to punch with any great force or accuracy.

It wasn't Thor, though. It was the tall blonde, the drill instructor. Thor was behind her, but she was warding him off with a hand.

"Enough," she said. "That's enough."

"Freya!" Thor bellowed. "Out of the way! This is none of your business. Let me settle it."

"No, young cousin. This ends now. The mortal has acquitted himself well. Hurting him further is a waste of time and beneath your dignity."

"Isn't it up to me what I do with my own dignity?"

"Maybe, but I'd hate to see you squander what precious little of it you have."

It took Thor a moment to understand that he'd just been royally dissed. His face boiled. Then, rage subsiding, he spat onto the snow. "Pfah! Well, if he's happy to let a woman determine the outcome of the contest..."

Frankly, looking at Freya, I'd have been happy to let her determine the outcome of anything she liked. She was a steely beauty. Slim hips, broad shoulders, sharp cheekbones. An Amazonian Grace Kelly. Haughty too, the way she held herself and spoke, but I couldn't have cared less. I was in love. Well, maybe love was too strong a word for it, but besotted for certain. Being semi-concussed was probably a factor, but even in my full senses I'd have found her unutterably, irresistibly gorgeous. She was straight out of a dream, or a not-safe-for-work website.

I tried to speak, say something about carrying on the fight if Thor wanted to, I wasn't afraid of him. All that came out, however, was a jumbled burble, nothing that made much sense. Thor looked all set to push Freya to one side and polish me off regardless, but then Odin intervened.

"Freya Njorthasdottir is right, my son," he said. "You've demonstrated your superiority yet again, and Gid for his part, if I may say so, hasn't fared too shabbily. Why not call it quits and resume your proper business, which is the training and preparation of these fine warriors of ours."

Thor grumbled but relented. You didn't, it seemed, fuck with the All-Father. There was a smattering of applause from the soldiers as he extended a hand to me, a peace offering, and the applause doubled when I, having given it some thought, grasped the hand and shook it.

Thor crushed my fingers in his grip, grinding the knuckles together. I just gave him my biggest, cheesiest grin in return.

Then I turned to Freya to express gratitude, and hopefully more, but already she'd swanned off to resume abusing the men she was drilling. I watched the tossing of her blonde ponytail as she strode away, and also appreciated the pert, toned buttocks moving beneath her tight white sweatpants. Arse man. Always was. I'd never been able to tear my eyes from a decent bum, and hers was way better than decent.

I'd no doubt have stood there all day, tongue lolling, mesmerised by the motion of Freya's behind – like a pair of balloons alternately inflating and deflating – if Odin hadn't taken me by the elbow and suggested we go back to the castle. He wanted Frigga to take a look at me and check I was all right.

All right?

In a world where magnificent-bottomed honeys like this Freya roamed wild and free, how could a bloke not be all right?

Then a surge of nausea hit me, and I bent over and threw up.

After which I passed out. A-bloody-gain.

ELEVEN

Two MORE DAYS in Frigga's tender care. Two more days of poultices and vile-tasting but remarkably effective medicine. Two more days of Frigga clucking and fussing, only this time with added apologies for Thor's behaviour.

"My stepson," she said, "is a brute. Uncouth, shallow. Mud for brains. But then what would you expect with an earth goddess for a mother? What Odin ever saw in that Fjorgyn I will never know. A pair of plump fertile breasts will turn any man's head, I suppose. It certainly couldn't have been her conversation. 'Oh look, a flower! Oh look, a pebble! Oh look, another flower!' And those are among her more intelligent utterances."

I laughed. With Frigga *and* at her. It was clear to me that mass delusion was the order of the day at Asgard Hall. Odin was at the centre of it, a sort of nucleus that the rest of them orbited around – his wife, the Valkyries, Thor, even the delectable Freya. He'd drawn them all, family members and outsiders alike, into his Norse-god fantasy. Like one of those lunatic-fringe evangelical types, a Jim Jones, a David Koresh, only instead of extreme Christianity he was peddling another faith, this one long defunct.

He had the charisma. He had the willing acolytes.

He also had soldiers. And guns.

So what was he planning? What was the point of it all? What the fuck *was* the Valhalla Mission?

I couldn't guess, and I wasn't sure I wanted to know anyway. My main imperative was leaving. Quick as I could. Get back out into the real world, where the sane people lived. My set-to with Thor was a setback, but Frigga had me on my feet again in a jiffy. By the third day I was feeling hale and hearty. Had some beautiful bruising – chest like a sunset, ankle purple from heel to calf. But over all I was perky. Everything in basic working order, even my wrist. So I headed out into the grounds to recce an exit strategy. It didn't take me long to discover a main drive that led down from the castle, curving smoothly through the contours of the landscape. Snowmobile and tyre tracks pointed the way. I walked along the drive for a couple of miles past silent white forests and a tinkling ice-encrusted stream, until I came to a guardhouse next to a bridge.

A man stepped out from the guardhouse as I approached. He wore a parka and a fur-lined hunting cap, the kind with the earflaps, and he had a walkie-talkie clipped to his belt and a gun strapped to his back – an AK-47, weapon of choice for guerrillas, pirates and bongo-bongo-land paramilitaries everywhere, the Big Mac of assault rifles. He also had a thermos in his hand, and was in the midst of pouring himself a cup of steaming hot chocolate.

"Want some?" he said, proffering the cup.

Taken aback, I said yes. I'd anticipated being challenged. *Who goes there?* and the business end of the Kalashnikov being shoved up my nose. But a glug of hot choc went down a treat.

"Heimdall, right?" I said.

He gave a comical salute. "That's me. Watchman of the Aesir and Vanir. Guardian of the Rainbow Bridge. And you, if I'm not mistaken, are the fellow the Valkyries brought past me the other night. I must say, you're looking a lot better than you did then."

"I'm a new man."

"Good old Frigga. I wouldn't be astonished if my dear stepmother could raise the dead."

"In my case she virtually did." I liked Heimdall already. He was the most down-to-earth of anyone I'd met so far here. He made good hot chocolate, too. I held out the empty cup for seconds, and he obliged.

"So what brings you all the way out here to my humble sentry post? Mere curiosity?"

Said genially, but it was a loaded question.

"Just getting the lay of the land," I said.

Heimdall peered at me. I'd not noticed before how piercing his eyes were, or how blue. They were the icy blue of glaciers, of arctic skies. They were eyes that missed very little.

"If you're looking to leave," he said, "I must advise you, you have a considerable walk ahead."

"If I'm leaving here," I assured him, "I won't be walking."

"Sensible man."

"And you, I guess, won't be stopping me." Partly a question, mostly a statement.

"Not my job to. It's what's coming in that I have to keep an eye on, not what's going out. Would you like to see Bifrost?"

I dredged the name up from my memories of those old *Mighty Thor* comics. "The bridge?"

"None other. Come on."

He led me past the guardhouse, through whose open door I saw a glowing gas heater, a chair and, hanging from a hook on the wall, a long, curly trumpet-type thing made of brass.

"Its nickname may be the Rainbow Bridge," Heimdall was saying, sounding much like a museum tour guide, "but in truth it has only three colours, one for each span."

And so it did. It was a suspension bridge which traversed a deep, sheer-sided gorge in three sections divided by a pair of support towers. Its boards, scrupulously swept of snow, were painted red for the nearest section, then green, then blue. As I set foot on the first of them I heard a low, forbidding creak and felt a wobble and a bit of give, which made me step back sharpish. The drop beneath was something like a hundred metres but might have been more. Snow could make distances, especially vertical ones, hard to gauge.

"Don't worry, appearances to the contrary it's quite secure," Heimdall said. "We've had all sorts of traffic over here, even up to five-ton trucks, and Bifrost, anyway, is destined to remain standing for all eternity. After all, it's built out of fire, water and air – the three elements of creation."

Looked to me like the only materials involved were metal, timber and emulsion, but I kept shtum.

"This is the only way in or out of Asgard other than cross-country," Heimdall said, "and I couldn't recommend that. You know yourself what it can be like out there for the unwary traveller. And it isn't just wolves you have to watch out for."

"Yeah, I know. Trolls, right?"

"Or simply getting lost," he said, probably not spotting the cynicism. "Plenty of space out there to get lost in. The forests are vast and trackless. Unless you know your way around them, as the Valkyries do, you could wander there in circles 'til you die."

I gestured to the far side of the bridge. "But that-a-way, over the bridge, that'll definitely get you back to, er, Midgard. Right?"

He nodded. "Long way, though. Very long way. Bifrost is the only link between Asgard and Midgard, but many Midgardian roads lead to Bifrost and you may take the wrong one and end up far from where you'd wish to be."

"Like I said, I won't be walking. I'll –"

All at once, Heimdall's head snapped round. He squinted, eyes narrowing to glittering pinpricks.

"Did you hear that?" he whispered.

"Nope. But then I've got shit hearing."

"I haven't. Quite the opposite. I can hear wool growing on a sheep in a far-off field. I can hear a blade of grass pushing up through the soil in the next county."

"That's quite a talent. Maybe you should –"

"Shh!" he hissed. "There it is again."

He whipped the Kalashnikov off his back, switched the selector to semiauto, and racked the charging handle. His gaze was focused on the woods lying beyond the gorge. I saw him slow his breathing to the bare minimum, scarcely a trickle of vapour coming from his nostrils. He stood rigid. Only those eyes moved, scanning the gloomy darkness beneath the distant trees.

A minute passed.

Two.

I didn't say a thing. Heimdall was scamming me. There was nothing out there. He hadn't heard a sound. He just wanted to spook me, for reasons best known to him.

Only, the intensity with which he was staring...

And, I couldn't be sure, but he seemed scared. Alarmed, at any rate. Genuinely. Not faking it. There was a strain about his face, a tightness to his jaw. Whatever he'd heard, or thought he'd heard, wasn't something he'd been keen to hear.

And then it stole over me – a sense of being watched. Someone out there hiding among the trees, surveying us. A definite presence.

The hairs on the back of my neck crackled. I could see no eyes, but I could feel them. The dead weight of their gaze, looming from the shadows.

Five whole minutes passed, and then, with a "hmph," Heimdall lowered the rifle. "Yes. Well. Gone. A scouting party, sneaking around, reconnoitring. They're starting to get bold."

"Who is?" I couldn't help but ask.

"The enemy. They were well concealed, so I couldn't tell if it was frost giants, trolls, or the other enemy – the one we really have to worry about."

"Oh. So the frost giants and the trolls aren't so bad, then."

"Not to be underestimated, but a nuisance more than anything. Certainly not worth blowing the Gjallarhorn for."

I worked it out for myself. "Your trumpet? The one I just saw in the guardhouse?"

A sombre nod. "That's reserved for one very particular occasion. The day we're all dreading. The day we're preparing for but hoping will never come. When I blow the Gjallarhorn... Well, let's just say you'll wish I hadn't had to."

He left that hanging ominously in the air for a moment or so, like a bad smell. Then his mood lifted and he said, "Still, that's in the future. Now's now, eh? Cherish the moment. Speaking of which, I understand there's going to be a feast this evening. Big celebration."

"No one told me. What in aid of?"

"No special reason. Odin just likes to hold feasts every once in a while. Helps everyone get along. Cements solidarity. You should be there. They're terrific fun. All sorts of roistering goes on."

"Blimey, really? Roistering? I haven't had a good roister in, ooh, ages. You going?"

"Oh no. Never abandon my post. That's my duty and my curse as Heimdall, born of nine mothers, gatekeeper of Asgard. I'm on watch here at all hours and in all weathers. Can't relax my vigilance for a second. I did let my guard down once, you see. A long time back. Allowed a witch called Gullveig to pass. Granted, she was disguised as a beautiful maiden, but even so. Caused all sorts of bother among the Aesir, did Gullveig. They quarrelled over who could give her the most gold. Odin had to sort it out by burning her at the stake. Three times."

"Nice."

"After a slip-up like that, I've had to be extra careful, as you can imagine. So no time off, no fun and frolics for me." A tiny sigh as he said this. "But you must attend the feast. You won't regret it."

Won't regret it? I was regretting everything about the Valhalla Mission. Regretting I'd ever heard about it, regretting coming here most of all. As I followed my own deep footprints back to the castle, I mused on the fact that even the people at Asgard Hall who seemed normal at first glance, like Heimdall, weren't. Every one of them was infected with Odin's obsession, to the extent of spouting gobbets of mythology as though they were pure gospel truth.

It was way past time for me to go. Earlier, I'd spied out a lean-to where the Valkyries' snowmobiles were kept. It nestled against the castle's western wall. Now I ambled past it again, closer this time, noting that all three vehicles had keys in the ignition and there were jerry cans of fuel stacked nearby. A snowmobile was all but begging to be borrowed.

Once back in civilisation I would contact the authorities and tell them about Abortion and let them know roughly where his body might be found. I doubted there'd be much left of him by now. The wolves would surely have returned to finish what they'd started, once the Valkyries had gone. What remained, though, should be retrieved and given a decent send-off, a proper funeral. For the sake of Abortion's relatives, such as they were, and my own sake as well. A cremation ideally. Going up in smoke – it was what Abortion would have wanted.

A feast? Sounded all right to me. Then tomorrow, first thing, I'd be snowmobiling my way across Bifrost to freedom.

TWELVE

Whole roast suckling pigs sat on platters on the banqueting hall tables, apples in their mouths, beds of parsley all around, the works. Their skins glistened like gold in the light of the torches burning in sconces on the walls. There were pies, heaps of root vegetables, tureens of broth, a stew which I was reliably informed was made of wild boar, and more forms of cooked herring than the mind could bear. Serving staff ferried it all in from the kitchen, and two hundred or so bods tucked in avidly, helping themselves to whatever came to hand, reaching, gnawing, munching, slurping.

Odin at the top table looked down on the scene with approval. On his shoulders a pair of large black birds were sitting – ravens was my guess. They perched there like a pair of bulky epaulettes, preening themselves and occasionally riffling their beaks through Odin's hair and beard. In return he fed them titbits from his plate with an indulgent smile.

Flanking him were Frigga and Thor, and lined up on either side of those two were other members of the Aesir and Vanir families. I couldn't see any sign of Freya, however. I looked, but she wasn't anywhere in the room.

Me, I was placed somewhere far down one of the long tables, and by coincidence – or perhaps not – the bloke next to me was Cy, the black guy I'd watched Thor beating up shortly before the thunder god turned his attention to me. Close to, Cy's facial scar was impressive. A jagged line that started just below the eye and ran down his cheek to his jaw. One of those scars that didn't disfigure, didn't ruin your looks, just made you look mean and cool.

Never one to mince around, I asked him how he'd come by it.

"Fight. When I was fifteen. You should have seen the other guy, though."

"Ugly?"

"He is now."

"And don't tell me, you got put on probation and they gave you the choice – prison or the army."

"Bingo." Cy grinned. "You too, man?"

"Not quite. Me, it was army or what the fuck else are you going to do with shitty qualifications like those?"

"Nothing? No GCSEs?"

"Failed them all. I'm not thick. I just don't get on with writing essays or working out equations or remembering who signed the Magna fucking Carta. One look at an exam paper and I freeze."

"Snap."

"South London, yeah?"

"Bermondsey. You?"

"Wandsworth," I said. "And I've got a scar too, we've got that in common as well. Right big fuck-off one, only you can't really see it because my hair's grown over."

"Give us a look."

"All right. As you insist." Like I needed asking twice.

I pushed up the hair on the left side of my head. Cy peered, then whistled. It always impressed people, my scar, once it was exposed. A rough hexagon shape, about the diameter of a ping-pong ball, with straggly lines forking off it in various directions. I tapped it with a finger. "Ding-ding. Titanium underneath. Sets off airport scanners everywhere I go. Which, of course, plays havoc with my millionaire jet-set lifestyle."

"Where'd you get it?"

"Afghanistan. Gift from the Taliban. One of the 'roadside flowers' they planted for us."

"Shit, bruv," Cy said, with feeling. "Harsh."

Some of the other guys around us nodded in sympathy.

"Tell you what I heard about you, though," Cy went on. "I heard you gave Thor a run for his money. After he'd knocked seven shades out of me, you went all psycho on his arse."

"You missed a treat, Cy," said the guy opposite. Spud-faced Irishman with a nose flattened sideways and a big black monobrow. "Yer man here had him down on the floor. Got him in the nads as well. The big fella was all a-whimpering and a-groaning. Honestly, it was a joy to behold, Thor getting his comeuppance. Even if it didn't last."

"I take it nobody likes Thor then?" I said.

"Oh, I wouldn't go so far as to say nobody likes him," the Irishman replied. "He's a harsh taskmaster, that's all, and he enjoys throwing his weight around. You cross him, he lets you know about it. All in the name of maintaining discipline, to be sure, but he can carry it too far. Like with young Cyrus here. Who, all he did was suggest our unit had practised this outflanking manoeuvre one too many times and maybe we should try something else for a bit of variety, and Thor came down on him like a ton of bricks."

"To be honest," said Cy, "I was itching to take a swing at him. He'd been riding me all week, calling me lazy and sloppy and slow. Finally I cracked... and Thor schooled me, like I knew he would. But not before I got in a few good licks."

"Yeah, you looked pretty tasty from what I saw," I said, miming jabs.

"Learned to box down the youth centre when I was a kid. Won a couple of junior amateur belts. Coach reckoned I had what it takes to turn pro. Would have too, if I'd been able to keep out of trouble back home."

"Trouble?"

"Only 'cause the gangstas on our estate kept getting all up in my face, giving me shit, dissing my mum and that. Fucker that cut me up, he fancied himself this big ghetto drug-lord, had all the bling, the pimped car, everything, and he'd been after this girl who was my girl, Tanya, and Tanya wasn't having none of it, so he blamed me for that and went for me one morning. Lay in wait in the stairwell outside my mum's flat and hacked me with a machete as I came out to go to school. I wasn't carrying or nothing. Still, I learned him never to do that again."

"You got the better of a guy with a machete, and you were unarmed?" Cy kept going up and up in my estimation.

"Yeah, well, funnily enough the fuzz didn't see it that way, did they? On account of all I got was a slashed-open face, whereas him – he doesn't look anything like he used to any more, and doesn't think straight or talk so good any more either."

"Fair's fair," I said. "He asked for it. I'm Gid, by the way. Gid Coxall."

"Yeah. Cy. Cy Fearon."

Other introductions followed. The Irishman was Colm O'Donough, although everyone called him Paddy because, well, why wouldn't they? Next to him was a chunky chap with a handlebar moustache. He answered to Ian Kellaway, or "Backdoor" Kellaway if you preferred, and his greeting was to hold up one hand, thumb and little finger extended, heavy metal devil's horns fashion.

"'Backdoor'?" I said. "Should I ask?"

"It's 'cause I'm crafty," Kellaway replied. "Sneaky. In all sorts of ways."

On my right was a Yorkshireman, Tim Butterworth, whose nickname was Baz for no reason I could see other than it started with the same letter as his surname. On the other side of Cy sat a quiet-spoken mixed-race Asian who was Dennis Ling, although he'd been rechristened Chopsticks. Apparently because it was the only tune he could play on the piano, although I doubted that was all there was to it.

I got to know a little about them over the course of the meal, their back stories, their reasons for being at Asgard Hall. Cy had wound up in 2 Para but unfortunately for him it turned out that taking orders wasn't his strong suit, and after a couple of years he and the regiment agreed to go their separate ways. O'Donough had been in the Grenadier Guards, Kellaway the Light Infantry. Butterworth had been a Marine, and Ling was TA but had seen combat in the Middle East owing to our government's sheer desperation to boost front-line troop numbers. O'Donough and Kellaway had both been called up so many times they'd come down with battle fatigue and burnout.

Butterworth, meanwhile, had been officially diagnosed with PTSD after an incident in Iraq when he and his squad were ambushed and captured by insurgents, who'd then set about decapitating their prisoners one after another and videotaping the executions for the internet, or maybe simply so as to have something fun to watch of an evening when there was bugger all else on the telly. American Marines had come to the rescue, in time to save Butterworth but none of his comrades.

"The fundy-jundies forced me to watch as they carved my mates' heads off with a ceremonial sword as long as your arm," he said. "And I'd have been next if the septics hadn't turned up and blown them all to Allah. I have nightmares like you wouldn't believe."

"But still you've signed up with the Valhalla Mission?" I said.

"Aye, well, it gets into your blood, doesn't it?" Miserable yet philosophical. "I think I speak for all of us when I say that. The military is like women. Can't live with it, can't live without it."

I recharged everyone's tankards from the jug in the middle of the table. Beer was apparently not on the menu and we were drinking, no word of a lie, mead. The first gulp of which had made me gag – sickly-sweet and potent at the same time, like Golden Syrup laced with meths. After a couple more swallows, however, I'd got used to it, and now I even quite liked it. Liked the buzz I was getting from it, anyway.

"Listen," I said, "not being funny, but can any of you tell me what exactly is going on here? What's this about? The training, everything. What's it all for? I've been puzzling it over and not got anywhere near an answer."

"Yeah, well, that's the phone-a-friend question, innit?" said Cy.

"You mean you don't know? You don't even know why you're

running around in the snow doing drill and learning to ski and the rest?"

"Odin's told us we'll find out soon enough. I mean, some of us have a vague idea, but mostly we're taking it on faith."

"Faith? Isn't that just a bit, well, wishy-washy?"

"I'm getting paid," said O'Donough. "The cheques are piling up, and I'm not complaining about that and I'm certainly not going to start rocking the boat. As long as the money keeps rolling in, I'm onside with the big man Odin. That's yer faith right there."

"But who *are* those people?" I said, nodding towards the top table.

"The Aesir, and some of their elder cousins from Vanaheim, the Vanir, who are the race of gods who came before the Aesir," said Cy. "Which of them don't you know? Those three to the right, yeah? The younger ones? Those are Odin's other sons, Tyr, Vidar and – what's the last one called again, Baz?"

"Vali," said Butterworth. "They're all half-brothers. Same dad, different mothers. Odin used to put it about a bit. A lot, actually. And the pretty golden-haired lass over on the other side, that's Sif, AKA Mrs Thor. She's wasted on him. Far too nice to be saddled with a bonehead like that. And next to her, the boyish one with the short choppy hair who looks a bit like the pop singer, Björk. That's Skadi. She's a Vanir. Freya's auntie, believe it or not. You'd think they were more like sisters, to look at them, nobbut a year or two apart, but that's the thing with gods, they don't age the way we do. Skadi's into skiing. She's a right little speed demon on the snow. And then –"

"This is all very interesting," I said, "but it's not what I was getting at. You're telling me who they *say* they are. Who are they really? Any idea?"

Blank looks.

"The Norse gods," Ling said eventually, as if it was the most obvious thing in the world. "Who else? The great pantheon from the Sagas. I studied them at school, in Comparative Religion."

"Chopsticks got privately educated," Cy confided.

"*Ohh,*" I said. "Eton?"

"I have, thank you, full up now," Ling said. "Arf, arf. No, my teacher made us read much of the *Prose Edda* and the *Poetic Edda*, so I know what I'm talking about here. All the tales about the gods and the Nine Worlds and how creation came to be and the Aesir's struggles and rivalries and vanities, and... those are them," he said, pointing to Odin and his associates. "They are. I'm convinced of it. They can only be."

I looked at him. Was he serious? He was serious.

"Take Tyr, for instance," Ling continued. "See he's missing a hand? Lost it to a wolf."

I rubbed my bandaged wrist. I had some idea how that might feel.

"Not just any wolf, either. *The* wolf. Big bad Fenrir. And Vali next to him? Him and Vidar are war gods. Tyr likewise. They're helping with our training, under Thor's overall command, and they're going to head up separate units when the time comes. I can see how sceptical you are about all this, Gid."

Sceptical? That was putting it mildly. More like a massive case of chinny reckon.

"I was too, at the outset. But then..."

Ling's voice trailed off.

"We've seen stuff," said Cy, picking up the thread. "All of us. Since coming here. Stuff that... It in't easy to put into words."

"Stuff that would make a convert out of an atheist," said O'Donough. "And unless or until you've seen it for yourself, you'll never believe, and why would you? It reminds me of my granda, my ma's pa, old Padraig MacBride, God rest him, who'd swear blind the Little People existed. Said he used to see them regular-like as a kid, fairy folk and leprechauns all cavorting in the copses and peat bogs around the village. Mind you, this was County Sligo before the war. His ma was probably slipping poteen into his milk to keep him docile, or else he was taking sly nips from the jar himself when the grown-ups' backs were turned. But Granda would become all het up and outrageous if you suggested he was making it up or pulling your leg. 'What one's own eyes behold,' he'd say, 'is never a lie.' And it's the same here, so 'tis."

"Okay then," I said. "I'll bite. What *have* you all seen that's convinced you? Give me a rough idea."

The four of them exchanged glances.

"There was this one time," Cy began, "it was earlier this month, actually..."

But before he could get any further, Odin thumped the table three times and stood up. Everyone shushed everyone else.

Speech.

"My warriors," Odin said. "Tonight we dine heartily, we drink deeply, we laugh and joke and boast and banter, as we ought. I have seen your delight in this repast and in one another's company, and it pleases me. I cannot, however, promise many more such occasions of merriment as this one. Enemy forces are gathering, like storm clouds amassing on the horizon. I have consulted with the Norns today, and the omens are grim. A war is coming. I have warned you of this before, and now do so again, with deeper certainty and sorrow. A war is imminent, and we must make ready for it. We have skirmished with opponents already, frost giants and the like, in order to hone our skills and foster solidarity among us. But our true adversaries await, and they will be like nothing we have hitherto faced. Henceforth we must gird ourselves for attack. It may not come tomorrow, but it will come soon. So enjoy yourselves tonight. Shortly you will be pitting yourselves in combat against an enemy of daunting might and numbers, and not all of you will survive these clashes."

With that, he resumed his seat. The banqueting hall was quiet for several moments.

"Well, that's chirped everyone up, hasn't it?" I murmured to Cy, who gave a silent laugh.

Then, just as conversation was juddering back into life, a man at the very end of the top table got to his feet.

"That's Bragi," Ling whispered to me across Cy. "Another of Odin's illegitimate sons. The poet."

"Is he going to – ?"

"Afraid so. He's actually not that bad."

Bragi cleared his throat, stroked his long, lank ZZ Top beard, and said, "An ode."

There were groans.

"A short one."

There were cheers.

"It's brand new. I call it *The Besting of Thor*."

Louder cheers, and a number of gazes turned my way. I had a bad feeling I knew what was coming.

In a voice that resounded to the rafters, Bragi began his recital:

For all his strength and all his thunder,
Our big, brash Thor had made a blunder.

He'd challenged Gid, a perfect stranger,
To brawl with him. To most, a danger;

For Thor in combat was undefeated.
This, though, had left him quite conceited.

What's more, his foe, whilst seeming game,
Was injured, ailing, wounded, lame.

An easy win, one might foresee
For Thor, but this was not to be.

Swifter than rainwater falls
Gid did strike him in the... place where it hurts.

There was laughter at that.

Then a head blow fast did follow,
Striking Thor where he's most hollow.

And more laughter, louder.

Cries of shock! Gasps of wonder!
Down he went, the god of thunder.

Who'd have thought, who could know,
He would end up eating snow?

Not for long – but long enough –
We saw that Thor was not so tough.

Then up he rose with raucous shout.
The outcome now was ne'er in doubt.

Thor was mad. He flipped his lid,
And started beating up poor Gid.

The man was lost, and suffered sore
'Neath the pounding fists of Thor.

He needed help. Who'd save his skin?
Vanir Freya then stepped in.

She stopped the fight and stayed her cousin
From hitting Gid another dozen...
...times.

"This isn't as easy as it looks," Bragi excused himself.

Still, now we know vain cocksure Thor
Has less to boast of than before.

The lesson taught us by this rumble?
Even gods should be more humble.

"Ye rulers of the earth and sky,
Look up, not down, when man walks by."

He sat down to a roar of applause. Odin seemed amused, while Thor – undecided. He scowled at Bragi, and then across the room at me, then finally, reluctantly allowed himself a wavery smile.

Tankards were raised my way. People leaned over to give me a slap on the back. I just kept my head down and tried to ignore it all. I didn't want to be anybody's hero or the centre of attention.

In the end the fuss died down, and I saw an opportunity to leave. Mumbling something about needing to siphon the python, I made for the exit.

THIRTEEN

I'D BINGED A bit on the mead. Gone over my self-imposed four unit limit. Fresh air was in order.

But Christ, it was *cold* fresh air. The moment I hit the outdoors, the outdoors hit back. My first in-breath, I could feel my throat start to ice up. My teeth ached. My eyes smarted and the tears immediately started to crystallise.

All of which helped sober me up in no time flat.

The sky was amazing. Clear, which explained the shockingly low temperature, and masses of stars. So many stars, they seemed to crowd out the blackness – more light than dark up there. The snowy ground glowed in their brilliance and the gibbous moon's.

Across the way stood Yggdrasil, casting a huge silver shadow. I tramped over to it, curious to see if it would do that weird growing thing again, that optical illusion or whatever it was. Apprehensive, too. But the tree remained a tree, even when I got right up close to it. A fucking huge tree, yes, but still acceptably sized. Not skyscraper big, as it had become that other time. Believably big.

My reason for leaving the banquet – needing a slash – hadn't been completely an excuse. I unzipped and took a long, hard piss against one of Yggdrasil's mighty roots. Ah, relief! Steam rose in clouds. It was one of those wees that went on and on, that made you marvel at the capacity of the human bladder. I started to get bored, in fact. I half-closed my eyes. Come on, finish already. I felt like I was draining the contents of a watermelon.

A noise right in front of me snapped me out of my piss trance. On a low-hanging branch, just inches from my nose, there was a red squirrel, and it was chittering at me, angrily. Its brush of a tail kept flicking and twitching back and forth, and its little black pushpin eyes flashed. It was having a right old go, yammering and squeaking, the whole branch vibrating with the intensity of its movements. If I hadn't known better, I'd have thought I was being told off for widdling on Yggdrasil.

I tucked away and zipped up, chuckling at the squirrel, which only seemed to agitate it more.

"Calm down, you fluffy-tailed rat," I said. "You'll give yourself a stroke."

"Ratatosk is offended," said a voice in my ear.

I swung round, bringing a clenched fist up. Pure reflex.

Big mistake.

Next instant, I was flat on my back in the snow. I'd barely felt it. A hand grabbing my shoulder, a foot hooked behind my knee, and *bam!* Gid Coxall laid out like a frog on a dissecting slab.

To make matters worse, a sheath knife was being held at my throat, tip poised over my Adam's apple.

To make matters very slightly better, the person on the other end of the knife was Freya. The lovely Freya.

Only, the expression on her face was not lovely at all. Her features were fixed in a sneer of contempt. Not even a hint of friendliness there.

"No one raises a fist to me and gets away with it," she said. "Especially not a man."

I wasn't sure if she meant man as in male of the species or man as in mortal being, and I wasn't about to query the point. It could have been either and was probably both.

"Didn't mean to," I croaked. "You surprised me. I reacted.

Overreacted. Don't slit my throat."

The sheath knife didn't move. Somewhere overhead I could hear the squirrel tittering scornfully. There was no other way to describe it. If squirrels could mock, this was exactly the sound they'd make.

"You were so easy to sneak up on," Freya said.

"Was I?" I had to admit the way she'd completely blindsided me was somewhat embarrassing, and I couldn't even blame my knackered ear. She'd come from the right. I should have heard her and hadn't. Talk about stealthy.

"Very easy. Were you a rabbit, or an enemy sentry, your blood would now be reddening the snow."

"Then I'm glad I'm neither of those. Look, will you put that thing away and let me get up?"

"I don't know. Ratatosk, what do you think?"

She was talking to the squirrel, and bugger me if it didn't pause from its tittering for a moment, as if considering, then delivered a stream of chirrups and chitters by way of a reply.

"He thinks," said Freya, "that you're ill-mannered and obnoxious but, after all, only a human and we should take that into account."

More squirrel chatter.

"And he says if you agree to apologise to the World Tree for besmirching it with your waste product, all will be forgiven."

"I say sorry to the tree, and everything's hunky dory again?"

"That's it."

"And you promise you'll put that knife away?"

"Certainly."

"Then you have yourself a deal." Granted, a cockeyed deal with a knife-wielding woman who talked to squirrels, but a deal nonetheless.

Freya got up, slipping the blade into the scabbard on her belt. I stood, brushed snow off me, then bowed my head, solemn as a churchgoer.

"Yggdrasil," I said, "I sincerely regret what I just did. I peed on you, and that was wrong and thoughtless of me. I should have known better. Maybe you could use the moisture and the ammonia to help you grow? Just a thought. But I'll never do it again. All right?"

The "All right?" was directed at Freya, but the tree seemed to think it was being addressed and ought to respond, so it shook its branches.

No, obviously it didn't. A stray wind came in out of nowhere, puffed against Yggdrasil and made all of the leaves shiver, releasing a fine dusting of snowflakes on our heads. That was what happened. The tree wasn't fucking answering me, like something out of an Enid Blyton book. That would have been absurd. It was a random coincidence, nothing else. A gust of wind. On a night as breeze-free and still as any I'd ever known. But still, just the wind.

Ratatosk the squirrel seemed satisfied, at any rate, and scampered off into the upper branches.

"So what brings you out here?" I said to Freya. "Why aren't you inside in the warm, partying with the others?"

"I could ask you the same."

"Not my thing, really." Not these days, not any more.

"Nor mine. I prefer not to gorge and guzzle. My pleasures are simpler, purer. The majesty of a night sky, for instance, and the knowledge that live prey awaits me out in the woods."

"You're going hunting?"

She nodded.

"For what?"

"Deer, rabbit, fox... Any wild game I can find. I'm not picky. The odd human occasionally."

"You're joking."

"Perhaps," she said in a way that implied she was. "I caught *you*, didn't I?"

"True." I was embarrassed enough by that to want to change the subject, so I jerked a thumb in the direction the squirrel had gone. "Anyway, what's up with Ratatouille there? It's dead of winter. Shouldn't he be hibernating and keeping his nuts warm?"

"Ratatosk is no ordinary squirrel," Freya said. "He keeps Yggdrasil free of worms and pests. Normally that's the Norns' job but they're exceptionally busy right now so Ratatosk has pitched in to help."

"Do I count as a pest? Was that why he was so peeved?"

"Very much so."

I was hoping for a flicker of amusement from her at the very least, but there was nothing.

"And who are these Norns?" I said. "Odin mentioned them earlier."

"Three women you really don't want to meet," Freya said. "The Three Sisters know our fates – our futures, our destinies – and it isn't always wise to learn where you're going in life before you get there."

"Oh. No, I suppose it isn't."

She looked at me sidelong. "May I say something, Gideon?"

"Please. Gid."

She shrugged. Made no difference to her. "I find you hard to fathom. You affect nonchalance about everything, yet clearly you are a man of passion."

Was this a come-on? Was Freya flirting with me? I didn't think so, but decided to take an approach as if she was. What did I have to lose?

"I am," I said, "beneath this unflappable exterior, a smouldering volcano. Tap into me and you'll see. Watch the lava flow out."

I added a wink. Few women could resist cheeky chappie Gid with his charm firing on all cylinders.

Freya, it turned out, was one of the few.

"Do you not see," she said, untouched by the waves of sheer sexual magnetism washing over her, "that we are engaged in a vital enterprise here? Nothing less than the fate of the Nine Worlds depends on us."

"Yeah, does it?"

"Of course. Yggdrasil is dying. Do you realise what that signifies?"

I glanced up at the intricate weave of branches. "Looks fine to me. In tree-mendous shape, in fact."

She snorted. Jokes, even the lamest ones, didn't work on her. Seriously hard to crack, this woman, and I was beginning to wonder why I was bothering. Other than she was just plain gorgeous, supermodel-standard, and oh, that arse of hers, and nobody ever said that Gideon Coxall didn't set his sights high. Aim high, and if you failed, you still failed better than if you aimed low and failed.

"Do not be deceived," Freya said. "Yggdrasil may look strong, but it is old, so old. The World Tree has been standing since the dawn of time, and its ancient boughs are tired and its aged trunk is hollow. Those ruptures on its bark, those patches that look as though it has exploded from the inside out? See? Those are cankers. Disease. And sometimes, in storms, battered by winds, you can hear it groaning horribly, in agony. When Yggdrasil falls..."

She shuddered. Faltered.

"But it must not fall," she said. "If it does, all is lost."

"What all?"

"Everything. The Nine Worlds. Destroyed. Utterly."

"Maybe a decent tree surgeon..."

"Oh, forget it!" she snapped, scowling. "You do not understand. You cannot hope to, with a mind as limited as yours. You are as blinkered as any mortal I have met, Gid Coxall. Here, you are being given the opportunity to take part in the most important conflict there has ever been – the only conflict that has mattered or will matter. You have come because fate has decreed it. You are one of the few, the chosen. You are being offered honour and glory the likes of which most men would sell their own mothers for. Yet all you do is snipe and wisecrack and bluster. Ignoring self-evident truths proves nothing except that you are ignorant."

And with that, she stomped off towards the forest.

I didn't take too kindly to being barked at, even if the person doing the barking was, ahem, far from a dog. I raced after her and, abandoning all caution, grabbed her by the arm.

She froze, and out of the corner of her mouth hissed, "Unhand me. Unhand me, or I will unhand *you*."

"No, you just listen to me a moment, Freya..."

"I'm serious." Her palm was resting on the hilt of her sheathed knife. "If you do not remove your hand from my arm this instant, I will cut it off and leave you to bleed to death in the snow."

I yanked her around to face me.

There was a metallic scrape, and an inch of knife blade shone in the starlight.

"You clearly do not value your life," she said.

"No," I said, "what I value is straight talking, and ever since I arrived I've had none of that. It's all been 'Ooh, look at us, we're Norse gods, tra-la-la, we're immortal, we're going to war,' and I've had it up to here with that. I want the honest, unpolished truth. I want one of you, just one, to admit this is pure makebelieve. Poncing around with your myths and legends and your magic trees and your talking squirrels, when you all know deep down it's a load of bollocks. I don't believe in gods, and you people don't either, not really. You're playing a game. All of this, the medieval re-enactment banquets, the daft names, the props like Thor's hammer, it's all a game. Come on, admit it. I'm right, aren't I?"

Freya stared at me. Tight-lipped. Imperturbable.

"And what's more, you know what I think?" She wasn't interested, but I was going to tell her anyway. "I think you're not just lunatics, you're dangerous lunatics. That Odin, he's brainwashed everybody around him. He's got this, this personality cult thing going, and he's using it, using *you*, not to mention all those soldiers stuffing their faces back there in the castle, for some kind of sinister purpose, and if I had to hazard a guess what it was, I'd say it was overthrowing the government, or attempting to. Like those white supremacists in the States, the ones who live in compounds in the mountains and collect small arms and are waiting to rise up against the authorities – when they're not busy screwing their sisters and twiddling on banjos, that is. Far-right redneck fruitcakes who go on about racial purity and Aryanism, and they all want to be blonde and Nordic, don't they? That's the ideal. I think they're even into Norse mythology too, only they don't take it quite so far as imagining they actually *are* Norse gods. Even they're not quite that daft. But that's what I reckon you're up to, what the Valhalla Mission is. You've taken a leaf out of those inbred hillbillies' book, and you've got the prime minister and parliament in your sights because they're all part of some worldwide conspiracy, right? Some Jewish Zionist oppression bullshit which you're going to stand against, you're the last best hope against."

I paused to draw breath. It was a ramshackle theory with holes in it you could drive an HGV through, but it was best I'd been able to cobble together and was, I felt, fundamentally sound.

"Finished?" said Freya.

"Yes. No! So what needs to happen, what someone needs to do, is get the fuck out of this place and report you to the powers-that-be. I'm astonished, frankly, that someone hasn't done it already, but then I guess a hefty wage packet helps seal lips and secure loyalty, doesn't it? But you need to be investigated. Your secret needs to be got out so that the police can come and break this all up and put away the ringleaders, the chief whackos, starting with Odin. That's what needs to happen."

"And you're the man to do it, yes?"

I realised that, in my ranting infuriation, I'd given away too much. I'd announced my intentions, and now I was officially on these people's wrong side. Typical me. Leaping without looking.

No choice now but to brazen it out.

"Perhaps," I said. "Yes. Or maybe not. I don't know. The cops and I don't exactly have a sterling track record together. But somebody at least should blow your operation wide open, even if it's with, maybe, an anonymous phone call. Anonymous tip-off. Something along those lines."

"Well," Freya said, "go on then."

I blinked. "Huh?"

She removed my hand from her, easily, like plucking off a stray hair that had attached itself to her clothes. I'd forgotten I was still gripping her. Then, for the first time in my presence, she smiled. But it was a brittle, lofty smile.

"Go ahead. Leave. Report us to the authorities. No one's going to stop you. Give it a try. See how far you get."

I was taken aback.

"All right then. I will," I said.

"Do."

"Fine."

"Good."

"But don't blame me when it all comes crashing down around your ears," I warned.

"If that does happen, it won't be in the sense that you mean," Freya replied. "Nor will it be your doing."

"We'll see," I said.

For the life of me I didn't know whether I wanted to snog her just then or punch her. Although the latter wouldn't have been a good idea. Not only because It's Wrong To Hit Women, but because she could hit me back just as hard, if not harder. And she was packing a big fuck-off knife and all. Come to think of it, snogging her mightn't have been such a good idea either – for much the same reasons.

And so we had ourselves a little standoff, Freya Njorthasdottir and I. I was six foot, and not many women could meet me eye to eye, especially without heels on, but she could. We gauged each other, there in the snow and the breath-stealing starlit cold, me and this maddeningly cool statuesque beauty, breaths mingling, until finally she looked set to say something, something that meant something, although I didn't have the chance to discover what because that same moment we heard the burp of a snowmobile engine sparking up, followed by two others in quick succession, then all three revving, and a few seconds later the Valkyries veered into view, scooting across the snow.

They were coming our way, and Freya called out "Ho!" and waved, and the three Valkyries returned the gesture as they passed by. Then off they went down the drive in the direction of Bifrost, hunched over the handlebars, weaving to and fro across one another's trails as they chased the cones of their headlight beams into the darkness.

"Huntresses too," Freya said, admiration in her voice. "The Choosers of the Slain. This is probably the last night they'll venture out in search of strays like you, to bring them in."

I wasn't really listening to her. All I was thinking was, *I damn well hope they're back by dawn. One of those snowmobiles is my getaway vehicle.*

Freya gave me a last, long, penetrating look. Then, without another word, she about-faced, loped off to the woods, and was soon lost among the trees.

I didn't follow or try to stop her this time. No point. I'd resigned myself to the fact that this was one woman I was never going to get to the bottom of.

No pun intended.

FOURTEEN

Next day, I was up, dressed, and raring to go before sunrise. I padded through the silent castle. Down in the banqueting hall I found sleeping bodies, revellers who'd not made it back to the cabins and instead conked out on the spot, surrounded by the debris of the meal. I had to step not only over them but over spillages of mead, the odd puddle of puke, even a spattering of dried blood. Things had got pretty rowdy later on, it seemed. Couldn't say I was sad to have missed it.

The sun was just peeking over the treetops as I reached the lean-to. Happily, all three snowmobiles were back home, parked in a row. I topped up the fuel tank of the nearest one, then strapped a jerry can of petrol to the back of it with a bungee cord I found. The machine was too heavy for me to push it away and start it up at a distance, out of earshot of the castle. I just had to hope that the thick stone walls would baffle the noise of the motor so that no one indoors would hear. If that didn't work and I did wake the household up out of their collective hangover, with luck I'd be off and away and far out of sight before anyone got it together to stumble outdoors and see what was going on. The Valkyries wouldn't take too kindly to having one of their vehicles nicked, but if what Freya had said last night was true, they wouldn't be needing them in future, would they? I consoled myself with that thought as I slapped on a helmet and goggles, perched myself astride the snowmobile, and hit the ignition. My guilt wasn't huge but needed soothing all the same.

The snowmobile bucked into life beneath me. The roar of the 1000cc engine shattered the early-morning tranquillity like an atomic bomb. Quickly I engaged reverse and backed out of the lean-to. Then I gunned the throttle, swung the snowmobile round, and aimed for the drive.

I'd ridden one of these things in Canada, and they were pretty straightforward to drive, although rear-heavy and liable to fishtail if you didn't keep your wits about you and a tight rein on the controls. I sped off across powder snow that was streaked blue and pink with shadows and dawn sunlight. With a hundred and fifty horsepower beneath me and the speedo nudging thirty, the castle soon receded behind me. I kept glancing over my shoulder but no doors or windows opened and nobody came charging out looking all startled and irate. Then, all at once, the grey walls and stout turrets were gone, swallowed by a screen of trees.

That was the easy part. Halfway to Bifrost, I swerved off the drive and made for the woods. Heimdall had claimed he wasn't bothered about who or what left the grounds of Asgard Hall, only who or what entered. But if somebody from the castle radioed him in his guardhouse and told him to halt the miscreant on the snowmobile coming his way, by any means necessary, then I'd be heading straight into Kalashnikov fire, and I had no great urge to do that. The plan was I would track perpendicular to the drive for a mile or thereabouts, then resume course until I arrived at the gorge, which I'd follow to where it shallowed out. It must do at some point. After that, I would navigate by the sun, bearing south until I hit a proper road. The tricky bit would be maintaining a more or less straight trajectory through the woods. The rest: piece of piss.

Trees whooshed by on either side. I assumed "posting" position, crouching with knees bent to absorb the juddering from the bumpy, uneven terrain. Snow fanned out behind, kicked up by the caterpillar tread. Blissful heat oozed into my hands from the grip warmers. I felt a flood of exhilaration. I'd done it! I'd escaped! And no one had tried to stop me or anything. A clean getaway with no interference, no collateral damage. I could hardly believe it. Shortly I would be back in civilisation, or what passed for civilisation round these parts. Road signs, fences, dry-stone walls, barns, farmhouses, and not a single self-styled "god" in sight. Gid Coxall was a free man again. And a man with a hell of a tale to tell, if he could only persuade the right ears to listen to it.

Something moved to one side of me. A corner-of-the-eye flicker: a white shape, darting between two trees.

Or not.

It was just a clump of snow tumbling from branches.

I roared on.

Something moved again, there to my right. I had the impression of size, bulk, a bent-over figure hurrying along, shambling but somehow still keeping pace with the snowmobile.

I slowed and stood up straight on the footboards, peering cautiously.

Just trees. Just snow. No figure anywhere. The lenses of the goggles, I told myself, were distorting my vision, creating peripheral phantoms. I hunched down and resumed original speed. The snowmobile's skis sliced smooth grooves. I'd covered my mile, I estimated. I executed a ninety degree turn, heading for the line of the gorge. The machine rumbled obediently. This was good. This was fun.

It reared up directly in my path – this thing, this shaggy white *thing*, ten feet tall.

Polar bear, I thought, even as I yanked sharply on the handlebars to avoid collision. How or why a polar bear would be at large in northern England, I had no idea, but that was the only explanation that made sense. I caught fleeting glimpses of white fur, claws, teeth in a red, red mouth. Then the snowmobile tipped over. On its side it skidded along the ground, with me sliding helplessly in its wake, on my side too. It slammed into a tree belly first, and an instant later I slammed into it, putting a big dent in the engine shroud. The wind was driven out of me. I lay in a daze, tangled up with the snowmobile, wheezing.

Then I remembered. *Polar bear!* And I was up on my feet in a flash, and running, running, sprinting as fast as I possibly could, because *fucking polar bear!*

And it was coming after me. Lolloping, galloping footfalls, gaining. I didn't dare look around. *Just move your arse, Gid.* I dug deep, pounding through the snow, which accumulated on my boots and made each step heavier than the last. Heimdall. That was my best chance. My only chance. Head for the guardhouse and hope – pray – Heimdall saw me coming and saw what was pursuing me and opened up with the AK and blew the beast to kingdom come. Otherwise I was bear breakfast.

But I couldn't outrun it. I knew that. Didn't want to admit it but I knew. The bear was right behind me now. Inches behind. I could hear its snorting breaths. Feel, even, the air it was displacing with its impetus, the pressure wave of its immense physical mass. And I was losing speed. My ankle was yelling in distress. My ribs were sending out the red alert.

A swipe from one paw clipped my calf and upended me. I crashed and rolled. The beast was on top of me. I looked up, and couldn't comprehend what I saw.

Not a bear.

Something else. I didn't know what.

But whatever it was, it was worse than any bear. Way worse.

FIFTEEN

ABOMINABLE SNOWMEN.

They grunted and cavorted around me. Some prodded me with clawed fingertips. Others shoved their faces into mine and snarled. Worst. Halitosis. Ever.

I couldn't move. Spreadeagled on the floor of a huge ice cavern, with my hands and feet bound. Bound by manacles of ice. I'd been held down and water had been poured repeatedly over the ends of my limbs until it froze them to the spot, each under a small rough glistening igloo. The cold burned. If not for my gloves and boots, I'd have been suffering extreme frostbite by now, the kind that ends up costing you fingers and toes.

And still the abominable snowmen, the yetis, these oversized white-furred gorilla men, leered and stamped and yammered. I was some sort of trophy, something for them to crow over and beat their breasts about. A prize. An object of triumph and derision. One of them, to show his contempt, even squatted over me, spread his buttocks and farted full-on in my face – and if I'd thought their breath was bad, it was nothing compared to what came out the other end. I gagged for several minutes and believed air would never smell sweet again.

The whole situation was bizarre, deranged, beyond all normal parameters, yet oddly I was taking it in my stride. Maybe if I'd been thinking clearly I would have been able to see the sheer *wrongness* of it all, and then I would no doubt have begun screaming like a loon. But I was dazed and it all seemed like a bit of a dream, from the moment I trashed the snowmobile onward. Being carried for miles slung over the yeti's shoulders, bumping along across an arctic wasteland similar to the Canadian tundra in winter, descending through the terminus of a glacier into a network of ice tunnels and caves, entering this cavern with its strangely delicate-looking ribbed and scooped surfaces, being manacled with freezing water, the lot of it, nothing more than a fevered delusion.

All at once, the abominable snowmen stopped their gibbering and monkeying about. Someone had entered the cavern, an imposing presence whose arrival commanded respect and hush. I craned my neck. Another yeti. They were all of them tall, none less than ten feet and many taller, but this one the largest by far, fully twice my own height. The others parted ranks to let him through. He was obviously the CO here, the big cheese, the abominable snowman-in-charge. He hulked over to me, long arms swinging. He circuited my sprawled body a couple of times, appraising. Then he bent down and took a long, hard sniff, running his pug nose across me from top to toe, spending longest at my neck and groin.

"Good thing I remembered to shower this morning," I quipped.

The boss snowman acted as though I hadn't spoken. Raising his huge head, he poked me with a knuckle. He probed, soon finding where I had been injured. First my shoulder, still tender from the dislocation. Then his finger moved to my ribs, the broken pair, gentle at first, then digging firmly in. He might as well have been using an electric drill. I gritted my teeth. It took everything I had not to gasp and cry out.

Finally, he stood.

"Not in perfect condition," he said, "but fit enough. He'll do."

They could speak. The yetis could talk.

It was a hideous sound, like gravel and sand going round in a cement mixed, but it was still unmistakably speech.

"The stink of the Aesir is on him," the head yeti went on. "Odin has touched him. Frigga too, and the Valkyries. And the hated Thor."

Thor's name got the rest very worked up. They yowled and hooted in a cats' chorus of disapproval. The echoes batted around among the icy stalactites that hung from the cavern ceiling.

"He is one of their footsoldiers for sure," their leader declared, as the ruckus died down. "Hence we are more than justified in our treatment of him. So then, who will his punisher be? Who volunteers?"

Every hand in the room went up. "Me!" they all cried. "Me, great and fearsome Bergelmir! Pick me!" It reminded me of feeding time at the zoo.

Bergelmir, the boss, bared fangs in a broad yellow grin. "I can choose only one. Hmm. Which should it be?" He stroked the matted fur on his chest. "Hval the Bald," he decided. "You have fought bravely in recent times. You deserve this."

The chosen yeti jumped for joy. "Thank you, oh thank you, Bergelmir. I won't disappoint you. The human shall suffer, and suffer mightily."

Some of the others applauded, some just muttered sulkily at not having been the lucky candidate.

Me, I was not liking the sound of any of this, not at all. My dream wasn't going the way it ought to. Where was my lightsaber? Why did I have the horrible feeling that the part of me which kept insisting this wasn't a dream was right?

"Hang on," I said to Bergelmir. "'Punisher'? 'Suffer'? What have I done, exactly? There I was, minding my own business, riding along through the forest. Next thing I know, I'm the prisoner of a bunch of albino apes, and I'm –"

"FROST GIANTS!" Bergelmir bellowed in my face, voice deafening. "We are frost giants, you insolent cretin, not 'apes'!"

"Oh. Okay. Beg pardon. My mistake."

"And as for what you have done – you have consorted with our avowed enemies. You are an ally of the loathed Odin, he who with his brothers slew my father Ymir. He who drowned all of my brethren in our father's blood, a gory inundation only I and my wife escaped. You are his lackey, and as such our vengeance against him and his relatives may rightly be visited upon you."

"Now hang on there a tick, sunshine," I protested. "I'm no ally of Odin's. Honest I'm not. As a matter of fact, I was leaving Asgard Hall when one of you ambushed me. I'm nothing to do with Odin or any of the Aesir. I just happened to end up at their place after a car crash, and I –"

"Silence!" Bergelmir boomed. "I have no wish to hear your lies. I couldn't care less what pathetic grovelling excuses you try to make. The Aesir's scent is upon you. You are marked with it. That is proof enough for me. For centuries the Aesir have hounded and plagued us. Thor, in particular, has been our most implacable foe. His hammer has stove in the skulls of more frost giants than can be counted. Now you must face the wrath of our race, we who were there long before the gods were born, we the descendants of Ymir, my father who was raised and suckled by the primeval cow Audhumla and from whose flesh and bones Midgard itself was formed."

Briefly an image flitted through my head: the valley Abortion and I crossed, the rocks that resembled the remains of a giant...

"But don't worry," Bergelmir continued, his voice softening ever so slightly. "We're not savages. We shan't simply kill you. That would be too crude. Unlike the Aesir, we still have some principles."

"Oh, that's good to hear," I said, dry-mouthed. Any last vague hopes that I was dreaming had vanished like Royal Navy ratings on two-day shore leave. I was here, in this cavern. The frost giants existed. And I was balls-deep in trouble.

"No," said Bergelmir, "you will face Hval the Bald in single combat. If he wins, you will be slaughtered and eaten."

"Terrific," I said. "And if I win?"

"You will be slaughtered and eaten."

I took this on board. "Doesn't strike me as very reasonable," I said.

Another crooked yellow grin from Bergelmir. "Reasonable? No. But, for us, immensely entertaining."

SIXTEEN

The frost giants shattered my restraints and hauled me to my feet, then retreated to the edges of the cavern, all except Bergelmir and Hval the Bald. Hval lived up to his name, in that the top of his head was completely hairless, although everywhere else he was as fur-covered as the rest of them. Bergelmir clapped his hands, and a female frost giant appeared carrying handweapons, an identical pair of them.

"Thank you, Leikn my dear," Bergelmir said to this floppy-breasted hideosity. His wife.

The weapons looked like an amalgamation of quarterstaff, spear and axe. Nearly eight foot long, they had a thin pointy blade at one end and a flat cleaver-like blade at the other. And they were made out of glass or perspex. Or so I thought until one was placed in my hands.

Ice. They were carved, or moulded, or sculpted, or whatever, out of *ice*.

Well, that's not going to last long, is it? I thought, tapping the axe end of mine experimentally against the cavern floor. *Shatter at the first impact.*

But I banged it a few further times, more and more firmly, until by the end I was whanging it down hard as I could, and the damn thing stayed intact. It even chipped chunks out of the floor.

"Surprising, eh?" said Bergelmir. "Our ice-smiths are master craftsmen. Each component of an *issgeisl* is formed by building up layer upon layer of ice no thicker than a sheet of paper. Long, patient hours of working, smoothing, scraping, binding, fusing together, results in frozen water becoming as hard as diamond. The blades even cut like diamond. The gnomes fancy themselves the great makers of tools and arms, but I'd like to see them forge anything the equal."

I was no expert, but the weapon, this *issgeisl*, felt well weighted too, and so light I could balance it on one finger.

"And remind me again of the rules here," I said. "I lose, I die. I win, I die."

Bergelmir gave an amused grunt.

"Hardly much of an incentive to try, is it?" I said.

"But you will nonetheless. You humans invariably do."

"Has anyone ever beaten a frost giant in single combat?"

"Never."

"Didn't think so. Well, as I'm fucked either way, no harm in doing... *this*."

I whirled the *issgeisl* round, aiming the axe blade for Bergelmir's belly. He wasn't expecting it, no one was, and I'd have gutted him for sure if Hval the Bald hadn't reacted with astonishing speed. He managed to get his *issgeisl* in the way and deflect the blow. The two weapons clashed with a ringing bell-like chime.

The audience of frost giants greeted my little bit of foul play with a near-riot. They bayed for my blood. Some of them rushed forward and grabbed me. They wanted to tear me limb from limb, and began trying to.

Bergelmir calmed them down. "Why such indignation? I am unharmed, thanks to Hval's quick reflexes. We should expect nothing less than dastardly underhand tactics from a human. Did mankind not, after all, start out as trees? Rough-hewn, gnarled, rooted in the earth, 'til Odin endowed them with souls, Hoenir with strong wills, and Lodur with feelings. They are naught but wood granted a semblance of life, so let us not be surprised if they behave like the crude, insensate stuff from which their race sprang." He gestured to the frost giants manhandling me. "Let him go. Leave him to Hval to deal with. I imagine, now, that Hval will make his demise even more lingering and cruel than originally planned."

"You may count on that, Bergelmir," Hval said.

I was released. The frost giants stepped back, again leaving a clear space for me and Hval, an arena. Bergelmir himself took the precaution of joining the crowd, staying well out of my *issgeisl*'s range. For all his big talk, I'd given him a fright, I knew, and I was pleased about that. A small consolation prize for the fact that I was about to meet a very sticky end.

Hval and I started to circle each other warily, doing a spot of mutual sizing-up and checking-out. He twirled his *issgeisl* one-handed and did a few other fancy, flippy tricks with it, showing off how familiar he was with it, how deftly he could wield it. I copied him in the spazziest way I could, waggling the weapon in the air like a commuter with an umbrella, angry that he'd missed his bus. He chortled, and that was good. If he thought I was clumsy and not taking this fight seriously, that was to my advantage. And frankly, I needed every advantage I could get. Hval the Bald was far taller than me, and had a far greater reach. He must be stronger, judging by the size of him. And I'd seen how swiftly he could move. To be honest, the only thing I had going for me that he hadn't was a full head of hair.

"Righty-ho, Hval my old mate," I said. "How do you want to play this? You could just surrender now, or you could wait 'til I've brought you to your knees. Which do you prefer? It's all the same to me."

Hval laughed, and lunged.

Fuck, he was fast. He came like a rocket. I ducked out of his way, slithering on the icy floor. His *issgeisl* whooshed through the air, a shimmering translucent blur. It was a close thing. If I'd been half a second slower in evading him, I'd have been half a head shorter.

I swung my *issgeisl* in retaliation, but I was on the hop, it was a wild blow, and Hval skipped clear of it as smug-casually as though I'd done nothing more than flick a wet piece of spaghetti at him. Next instant he came thundering back at me, *issgeisl* held high. The axe blade end flashed down. All I could do was throw myself to one side and roll. The blade bit the floor with a shivering clang. Shards of dislodged ice rattled into me like hail. Hval inverted the *issgeisl* and stabbed at my leg with the spear end. I somehow got the haft of my *issgeisl* into the path of the blow and parried it. At the same time I kicked out at his heel, hoping to swipe him off his feet.

Fat chance. His leg was so solidly planted, it was like kicking a telegraph pole. His clawed toes, I realised, gave him a further edge over me. He could anchor himself to the floor with those talons. My rugged boot soles afforded me some grip but nowhere near as much.

He jabbed at me again, and I scooted backwards on my bum. The spear tip spiked the floor precisely where my crotch had been a split second earlier. I had time to think, *Nearly lost an inch there*, and, *Not that that wouldn't still leave plenty*, and then he inverted his *issgeisl* yet again and brought it whistling horizontally towards my arm.

No idea how, but I was able to parry a second time. Not as successfully as before, however. Hval's *issgeisl* rebounded off mine and caught me glancingly on the biceps. He'd been intending to take my arm off – at the very least gouge out a chunk – but in the event only slashed open sleeve and skin. Still, it stung like buggery, and the sight of my blood spurting out over the floor raised howls of joy from the spectators.

Hval stepped back with an air of smug satisfaction.

"First blood to me," he said.

"'The first cut won't hurt at all,'" I replied, springing to my feet. Propaganda. Now there was a band. Their album was the first I ever bought, aged eight. On vinyl, no less. Germans who could really do power pop. Whatever happened to them?

Music-lyric references were, of course, wasted on frost giants. I hefted my *issgeisl*. "Now where were we?"

"We were engaged in combat," Hval said, "and I was busy making you look a fool."

"Oh yeah, that's right. Well, I'd better do something to fix that, bettern't I?"

I went on the offensive. About time too. Up to then all I'd been doing was getting hammered on and just barely surviving. If I was going to make anything of this fight, I needed to take it to Hval, not let him bring it to me.

I lashed at him this way and that with the *issgeisl*, using either end of it, just as he'd shown me by example. Swings of the axe, thrusts of the spear. Quantity, if not quality. Not once, though, was I able to hit home. Hval blocked and fended off my every attack. He did this with a big fat smirk on his face all the while, like it was no great bother for him. His *issgeisl* spun on its axis, always there, always intercepting no matter how obliquely or swiftly or powerfully I struck. It was, in all, a pretty dispiriting experience.

Yet I kept it up. I kept it up even though it was hopeless, even though the whole notion of trying to beat Hval was futile, because supposing by some miracle I did beat him, I'd still have a roomful of his frost giant pals to contend with, and they'd easily overwhelm me, through sheer numbers alone, and then – unless Bergelmir was fibbing, and I didn't think he was – I'd be dinner, and I couldn't imagine a worse fate than ending up in the stomachs of these huge, hairy, smelly, ugly monsters. At least, from the sound of it, they'd have the courtesy to kill me first before serving me up with the gravy and the horseradish, but despite that it still wasn't much of a prospect to look forward to.

Obstinate. That was me. That was why I continued fighting instead of simply giving up. Obstinate, and also not willing to go down without securing some kind of victory for myself, recouping some measure of self-esteem, however pathetically small. Even if I just saved face by giving Hval a run for his money, proving I was no pushover, that would be something.

And then he got overconfident. Or rather, his overconfidence got the better of him. Somehow I got past his guard. A lucky shot. A freak statistic. Out of the hundred strikes I made with my *issgeisl*, one finally got through.

The *issgeisl*'s spear blade sank into Hval's thigh. Not deep, but far enough in to inflict some damage and cause pain. Suddenly white fur was stained with a gush of crimson, and Hval let out an agonised roar that stopped the audience noise dead. Where there had been yells of support and chants of glee from the slightly biased spectators, now there was stunned silence. A moment later, boos and catcalls rushed in to fill the vacuum. It wasn't supposed to be like this. The human combatant wasn't supposed to hurt his opponent. That wasn't right!

"Second blood to me," I said to Hval, panting. It was witch's tit in that cavern but still the sweat was pouring down my face. I had to scrape some out of my eyes with my thumb. "How's that feel, slaphead? Not so cocky now, are you?"

Hval looked at me with murder in his jet-black eyes. "You – you dare!?" he exclaimed. "You dare stick your *issgeisl* into *me*?"

I held up the blood-smeared spear tip. "Rather looks like I do dare, doesn't it, chrome dome? By the way, doesn't your scalp get cold? Ever thought about headgear? I can just see you in a beanie, or maybe a woolly bobble hat. Or maybe you like the way it looks. How *do* you keep it so shiny? Mr Sheen?"

That pissed him off. Even though he probably didn't understand half of what I was rabbiting on about.

Which was fine – I wanted him pissed off.

Truth to tell, I was pretty pissed off myself. It was starting to get on my wick, this fight, the entire situation. The absurdity of it, the one-sidedness. It was starting to enrage me, deeply. This was an old feeling, a familiar feeling, one I hadn't experienced in a while. One I welcomed now like an old friend I hadn't seen in ages and forgotten how much I missed. Anger at the inequality of the situation, the unfairness of everything. A sense of having been robbed by life and wanting to get payback somehow, any old how. It gurgled up through me, hot and black as tar. It pulled my mouth into a ferocious grin. It drowned out all extraneous noise. It throbbed in time to my pulse rate. It put a dark frame around everything I was seeing, like the border on an obituary notice in the papers. It left nothing in my sensory field except Hval. Hval the Bald, who was growling like a dog, one hand pressed to the wound in his leg to stem the blood flow. Resentment radiating from his face. Ready to lance and skewer and disembowel and dismember. Ready to kill as savagely and messily as he knew how.

Or was that me?

SEVENTEEN

THERE WAS THIS bloke. Martin Sellers, though I didn't find out his name until after. He had thickish spectacles and kept his hair slicked to the side and sharply parted. Wore a tank top over a checked shirt. Creases in his trousers, turn-ups at the bottom. Weak chin. Rubbery lips. Open-toed sandals with socks. Centre parting. He looked, really, like the living definition of a paedo. Honestly, if you'd searched "child molester" on Google Images, the first picture that came up, after Gary Glitter, would be this fella.

I was at the indoor soft play with Cody. Typical pissy summer-hols day, so I'd taken him off there so Gen could have a bit of a break. So that I could have a bit of a break too, actually, because the soft play was great for that. Let the kids hare off and run wild in the climbing apparatus while Dad sat in a comfy chair with a coffee and a bun reading the *Daily Mail*. Bingo, result for everyone. All I had to do was glance up every now and then, locate Cody inside that huge padded labyrinth affair, make sure he wasn't getting beaten up or beating someone up, and that was that, job done. Tenner well spent.

Cody was nine at the time, looking like a proper boy, all tousled hair and gangling legs. Heartbreakingly handsome lad. Just like his pa.

I'd just finished checking Jonathan Cainer for my horoscope. Apparently I had an unusual stroke of good fortune coming my way owing to a rare conjunction of Saturn and Venus in my House of Total Bollocks, and I'd find out more if I rang a hotline at a rate of £500 per second plus standard network charges. I happened to look round, and there was Martin Sellers snapping away at Cody with his phone camera.

Now, that was exactly how it appeared to me. Cody romping around in the ball pit on the soft play's lower storey, and Mr Couldn't-Be-More-Paedo-If-He-Tried carefully lining up his shots and clicking again and again. I watched him for a full minute, getting more and more convinced that it was Cody he was photographing. He was waiting until Cody dived into the balls so that he could take nice pics of Cody's bare legs and shorts-clad backside poking up. There was this stupid, sloppy smile on his face that told me he was getting off on this. He looked ready to drop his trousers and start whacking himself off right then and there.

The one thought which didn't occur to me, and which might have saved both him and me a lot of agony, was what was he doing here if he didn't have a kid of his own? They'd never have let in a lone adult male. He'd have to have been accompanying a child. Maybe I did think this but dismissed it as unimportant. Maybe I told myself he was a bachelor uncle who'd tagged along on a family outing. The whys and wherefores didn't matter, really. Logic was winging its way out of the window. What I saw, all I saw, was a pervert taking photos of my boy. The rest was just detail.

The black tide surged up. I wasn't aware of much after that. Eyewitnesses said I strode straight over and, without even saying a word to Sellers, started hitting him. Snatched his mobile and smashed him in the face with it a few times, then brought him low with a kind of judo throw and starting pounding on him as he lay on his back on the floor. He was screaming through bubbles of blood. Someone, an employee at the place, ran over and tried to pull me off. I decked him with a single punch. Someone else, a woman, pushed her way between Sellers and me, shrieking at me to stop, what was I doing, get off, that was her husband, he hadn't done anything. I shoved her aside, not listening, and carried on beating the shit out of the guy. The sicko. The perve. The fucking chickenhawk piece of scum.

Three of the burlier dads laid into me, yelling that was enough, leave him alone. They managed to haul me off Sellers, but I struggled free and launched myself at him again. It ended only as I was about to resume *destroying* this kiddie-fiddling dirtbag and, all at once, there was Cody standing in front of me, a look of absolute astonished horror on his face.

"Dad?" he said in a tiny, trembling voice. "What are you doing? That's Tamara's dad. Tamara from school. I was playing with her. He was taking pictures of us in the ball pit. She was being Hermione Granger and I was being Ben 10. We were fighting alien wizards."

Everybody on the premises was staring at me. Martin Sellers lay in a pool of his own blood, making little soft wailing noises like a distant cow mooing. Children were sobbing. I heard somebody on the phone to the police, talking hysterically about a man who'd gone berserk, maybe killed someone. None of it meant anything to me. The only thing that counted was Cody's expression – the fear in his eyes – the way he was looking at me as though I was a monster from a nightmare. His father, on the outside, but inside, something else – a demon, perhaps, that had taken over my body and was still staring out from within, ablaze with fury and hate.

Arrest. Custody. Bail. Court.

The police officer who put the plasticuffs on me knew me. We'd had a couple of run-ins before, normally around pub closing time. He knew I was ex-military, knew about my record, my hospitalisation, my discharge. At the trial he told the judge that I had a history of ABH and public affray, infractions which he and his colleagues had gone easy on because of my "background circumstances." The judge suggested that perhaps if they hadn't been quite so lenient in the past, the distressing incident with Mr Sellers might have been averted. The cop took the rebuke on the chin.

This, after all, wasn't mere ABH, it was GBH. Sellers had needed extensive facial reconstruction surgery. He would never look the way he used to and many of the nerves in his face no longer worked, but fortunately he had suffered no brain damage. He glowered at me throughout every minute of the trial and that was hard to take – if looks could kill and all that – but it was Gen up in the viewing gallery whose gaze weighed the most heavily on me. The hurt and recrimination in her eyes. The set of her jaw, which said, *This is it, Gid, I've put up with it so far, but this is the final straw...*

I got the divorce papers while I was banged up. I signed them, sent them back. She never visited. Why should she? I'd disappointed her once too often. I wasn't the man she'd married. Hadn't been for a long time.

The stretch handed down was surprisingly short, which caused outrage in some quarters: Sellers and family shouting "Shame! Disgrace!" in court, and a handful of indignant letters in the local newspaper. The judge, for all that he'd ticked the cops off for being soft on me, was soft on me himself. An expert witness, a shrink who specialised in the psychology of people who'd suffered major head trauma, stood in the box and said there was every chance I'd not been in full control of my faculties. The injury to my brain could well have upset my mental equilibrium. It was possible I was still suffering the after-effects of the IED explosion, even two years on. "In light of such testimony," the judge said during his summing-up, "you, ladies and gentlemen of the jury, may wish to take the view that Mr Coxall is a man with diminished responsibility for his actions and thus cannot be held wholly accountable for them. You may also wish to take into account his role in Her Majesty's Armed Forces and his service to our country, in the performance of which he suffered most grievously." An eight-month custodial sentence was what I was given.

I'd have got away with serving only six of those eight months, too, if I hadn't had that altercation with the crackhead on B Wing. No time off for good behaviour.

Once out, I made a vow never to let the blackness rise again. If I ever felt it welling up inside, I would simply remove myself from whatever situation was triggering it. I would walk away. All the fights I'd been getting into, the blackness was behind them. It was to blame. I had to contain it, corral my blind rage. It would do me no good.

Except now. Facing Hval the Bald.

Now, the blackness was my great ally. My secret weapon. My ace. It came, and I let it fill me. Consume me. Overwhelm me.

FIVE MINUTES LATER, our duel was over. Hval was on his hands and knees on the arena floor, and I stood over him, *issgeisl* raised. His head was bowed. Blood – his blood – matted his fur and covered the ice in congealing smears, bright red against the glittering whiteness. His breath rattled in and out, thickly, stickily. Punctured lung. He was a goner. We both knew it. Everyone in the cavern did. The frost giants looked on in appalled silence. Out of the corner of my eye I saw Bergelmir clasping his throat, aghast.

"Fancy that," I said, loud enough for all to hear. "The puny human won."

Then I brought the *issgeisl* down with all my might and lopped Hval's head clean off.

EIGHTEEN

In the uproar that followed, two of the frost giants made the mistake of attacking me singly, bare-handed. While I was still armed with the *issgeisl*? When I'd already shown I was at least equal to one of them? Seriously? They learned their error the hard way.

After that, though, pretty much all of them bundled in on me in a huge mob, and I tried my best, but I was on a hiding to nothing. They disarmed me. Then they just started chucking me all over the shop, shoving me back and forth between them, roughing me up, punching, kicking. I pinballed around the cavern, and every way I went it was claws and teeth and flying furry fists and feet. Somehow I didn't blame them. I'd be pissed off too if some little pipsqueak came along and offed three of my relatives.

Bergelmir finally halted the fun with a loud roar. He ordered the frost giants to bring the human to him. I was dragged over and dumped in a heap at his feet.

"Remarkable," he said to me. "Hval is – was – one of our finest warriors. For him to fall to a mere human speaks highly of your prowess. Not in a long time have I seen such pure, perfect battle-frenzy as you have just shown. I am almost impressed. You didn't hesitate, either, when you had him at your mercy. Another man might have attempted to use Hval's life as a bargaining chip, to save his own."

"Wouldn't have worked," I managed to spit out, along with quite a lot of blood, and a molar. "Even if the idea had occurred to me, which it didn't."

"Odin did indeed find himself a valuable asset. Such a shame."

"I told you, I'm nothing to do with –"

"Yes, yes, I know," Bergelmir said with a dismissive wave. "You would have ended up fighting for him all the same. Odin has a way of winning everyone over to his cause sooner or later. An inspiring turn of phrase. An insidious charisma. All true warriors are drawn to him, even if it goes against their better judgement. Does his name not mean 'war fury'? Is it not his allotted role to preside over the Einherjar?"

"Come again?"

"The Einherjar. The Heroic Dead. The army he has been busy raising. Haven't heard the name before? The concept is strange to you? Oh human, how little you grasp of your situation!"

"I grasp that I'm not dead," I said. "I'm not a hero either."

"We could debate the latter. As to the former – well, perhaps you aren't, but it's a situation I'm about to remedy."

He held out a hand, and someone passed him an *issgeisl*.

"Get him into position," he instructed, and frost giants grabbed my arms and twisted them up behind my back, bending me over until my forehead was almost touching the floor.

"In recognition of your extraordinary defeat of Hval the Bald," Bergelmir said, "I shall make your execution as swift and painless as possible. You have won this leniency for the valour and brutality you have exhibited. Not only that, but you have won the honour of receiving the fatal blow from none other than myself. Few humans –"

"Look," I said, with feeling, "are you going to flap your lips all day or are you just going to get on with it? This is boring, and not very comfortable."

"You aren't even going to plead for your life? Beg like a dog?"

"What would be the point?"

"Truly, you are a credit to your species," Bergelmir said, and it sounded like he really meant it. "In other circumstances I might have been proud to know you. Very well..."

The *issgeisl* went up. I heard the *swisshh* it made as it rose through the air.

I'd been near to death in Afghanistan. A gnat's pube away from the Great Beyond. The medics told me it had been touch-and-go for a while when they'd got out to me and were patching me up in the field. Said they'd thought it was fifty-fifty I'd last the chopper ride back to Bastion. There'd been no tunnel of light then, no choirs of angels, no loved ones queuing up to usher me through the Pearly Gates. There'd been nothing except absolute nothingness.

So I wasn't anticipating any afterlife once that *issgeisl* fell. Just an end, that was all. A full stop rounding off the sentence of my life. I braced for the blade to descend.

That was when the shooting started.

NINETEEN

Nothing quite like gunfire to bring instant chaos to any given situation. Within moments of the first salvo, everyone was charging around like headless chickens. I'd been immediately forgotten about. Frost giants were yelling, screaming, and Bergelmir was giving orders, shouting to be heard above the hullabaloo: "To the armoury! Take arms! We're under attack!"

Like, *duh*. As Cody might have said.

Bullets thunked into ice, gouging holes, shattering stalactites, ruining the smooth rounded contours of the cavern. Frost giants blundered into one another. Some let out cries of pain. Some fell.

One landed right on top of me, squashing me flat. I wriggled out from under the corpse, mostly to avoid being suffocated by the sheer bulk of it, although the blood gushing out over me from several bullet wounds wasn't much fun. Crouching, using the body for cover, I took stock of what was going on.

It was more or less what I'd guessed. Odin's forces, attacking. I counted a dozen men spearheading the operation, a first wave of assault sowing death and discord through the cavern. Kalashnikovs and SA80s barked in their hands. Heckler and Koch MP5 machine pistols stuttered.

Once this first lot had done their job, taking the frost giants by surprise, killing as many as they could and scattering the rest, a back-up squad of similar size stormed into the cavern. They fanned out into position, securing the site and checking that all the fallen enemy combatants were as dead as they appeared to be. Head shots accounted for the ones that weren't.

Among the second lot of soldiers I recognised Cy and Paddy. They spotted me at about the same time I spotted them.

"There he is!" Cy said, and he and Paddy rushed over.

"Jaysus, you're alive," Paddy said as they helped me to my feet.

"Don't sound so surprised," I said.

"We were taking bets," said Cy. "Looks like you owe me a fiver, Pads."

"The lad had faith," Paddy said to me. "I was of the view the frost giants would have done for you by now, but Coco Pops here thought different."

"Oi, less of the 'Coco Pops,'" Cy warned. "I just knew you're as tough as bollocks, Gid. No poxy fucking frosties could finish you off."

"Listen," I said, "I don't know why we're talking about breakfast cereals all of a sudden but shall we stow it and concentrate on getting out of here? Guns or not, you lot are going to have your hands full with a hundred pissed-off yetis coming at you waving *issgeisl*s."

"They've got a lot worse than *issgeisl*s," Paddy said. "But you have a point. What use is a rescue mission if the person being rescued gets killed while we're rescuing him?"

"All this, for me?" I said as Cy and Paddy each put an arm around my shoulders and got me moving. After my prolonged duffing-up by the frost giants, walking was doable but not exactly a breeze.

"What on earth gave you that idea?" Paddy replied. "Could it have been my using the word rescue three times in a row just now?"

"It in't just about you," Cy added. "We're having a bash at the frost giants as well. You're an added bonus, that's all."

"A pretext, you might say," said Paddy. "Alive or not, you were a handy excuse for coming and giving the big fellas what-for."

"But how did you find me?"

"Ah well now, you'd have her ladyship Freya to thank for that. She's the one led us all this way. Tracked you from where you crashed in the woods, out of Asgard and across half of Jotunheim to this here lair. Followed your trail like a beautiful blonde bloodhound, so she did. Quite the thing, to see her sniffing her way across the landscape, spotting the tiniest signs here or there that told her where you'd gone – a scratch in the ice, a dislodged pebble, a hair, pieces of evidence so small I couldn't see them myself even when they were pointed out to me."

"We thought you might've been taken to Utgard," said Cy. "The frosties' main stronghold. You're lucky you weren't. We'd never've dared try a retrieval there. Fucking sheer walls of ice you can't get up even with climbing gear. This place, though, it's just one of their gathering places, not nearly as far from the border with Asgard. They weren't expecting us to come after you."

"Well, I can't say I'm not glad you did," I said. "And I'm looking forward to telling Freya how much I appreciate the trouble she's gone to on my behalf."

"I wouldn't bother if I were you, bruv. She didn't want to. Only agreed to 'cause Odin made her."

"Oh."

On that somewhat crushing note, the frost giants re-entered the cavern, all tooled up with *issgeisl*s and more. They emerged from several of the surrounding tunnels like floodwater pouring in, a great shaggy white tide, all of them giving vent to a huge, massed battle-cry. Many, I saw, had put on pieces of armour – breastplates, greaves, helmets. Some carried shields, others had daggers, maces, and what I took to be throwing hatchets, a bit like tomahawks. Everything, of course, fashioned out of ice.

Bergelmir led the repulse. Leikn – Mrs Bergelmir – was right behind hubby. Odin's troops beat a hasty retreat, laying down suppressing fire as they went. They withdrew to the mouth of the tunnel they'd come in by, the one that led back to the outside world. Me, I was already well into that tunnel, Cy and Paddy hustling me along. Rearguards had been posted at all the junctions along the entry/exit route, and they waved us urgently on in the right direction. Guns jibber-jabbered behind us. I longed to seize a spare firearm and turn and have a crack at the frost giants myself, but I knew that the mission wasn't simply about that. Primary objective – me – had been acquired. Now the focus would be on a tidy exfiltration, with minimal casualties. No time for grandstanding or indulging personal beefs. Business, not pleasure.

We emerged from the terminus of the glacier into evening light. The sun hung red and heavy on the horizon. Waiting outside were Freya and Thor, and both looked pleased to see me, but only in the sense that, with me extricated from the frost giants' clutches, it meant the job had been successful.

"Everyone's coming out behind us," Paddy reported. "Including a pack of rather irate frosties."

"Excellent," said Thor. He drew his hammer from his belt and smacked the head of it into his palm. "Mjolnir is hungry to cave in jotun skulls."

"Get him to a safe remove," Freya told Cy and Paddy, with a flick of her fingers at me. "We'll hold off the giants in the meantime."

"Now wait a sec," I said. "I can fight too. I'm up for it."

She looked at the state of me, and her face said she disagreed. "The All-Father wishes you brought back safe and sound. He has entrusted me with responsibility for your welfare. If it were up to me, I'd have you on the front line risking your fool neck in the hope that you might get yourself killed and spare the rest of us a great deal of trouble and aggravation. In fact, if it were up to me, none of us would be here at all. But Odin has decreed, and his word is law. So go!"

"Come on, Gid," said Cy. "Let's do as she says."

As he and Paddy hauled me away from the glacier, I said, "She so fancies me."

They just laughed. "Dream on, bruv," said Cy.

FROM THE SHELTER of a boulder of ice, a titanic chunk that had sheared off when the glacier last retreated and been left stranded a couple of hundred metres from its parent, the three of us watched the battle go down.

It was brief, as contacts with the enemy normally were in my experience. Once all of the troops were out in the open, they formed lines and waited for the frost giants to appear. They moment they did, the big bastards got raked with enfilading fire. They retreated quick-smart back into the entrance to the caves, where bullets kept them pinned in place. A few hatchets hurled out at the troops, but the throws fell short. It was more a gesture of defiance than a concerted offensive action.

Eventually the frost giants seemed to realise that, with their close-quarter weapons, they hadn't a hope of overcoming the long-range firepower arrayed against them, and they pulled back further into the caves, out of sight. Thor commanded a ceasefire and went galloping off into the glacier after them, hammer held high. This wasn't unexpected. As Paddy put it, "He hates the frosties with a vengeance. Can't think straight when they're around. If he didn't get a chance to give them a good pasting, we'd never hear the end of it. He'd be moaning and sulking the whole way home."

Ten minutes later Thor was back, with an air of satisfaction about him. His hammer was coated with blood-clotted fur. His right arm was splashed red up to the elbow.

As the punchline to the whole joke, grenades were tossed into the cavemouth. *Whump*, *crump*, *kerr-asshh*, the roof came down, a section of the glacier collapsed in on itself, and the frost giants were sealed inside.

Or maybe not.

"Ah, they'll dig their way out in a day or two," Paddy told me. "That's if they don't have an emergency back-route escape tunnel somewhere further up the glacier, which they probably do. They're not dumb, those big fellas, appearances to the contrary. Bit like Cyrus here. To look at him you'd think there wasn't a single thought going on in that head of his, but I know there's a brain buried somewhere deep within. Or at least, I'd like to think so."

"In't it Irishmen who are supposed to be thick?" Cy retorted. "Did you hear the one about the Irish pilot who crashed his helicopter? He got so cold he turned off the fan."

"Our reputation for stupidity is a terrible calumny against the nation that gave the world Yeats, Joyce and Wilde."

"And Riverdance," I said. "Don't forget Riverdance."

Paddy gave a sorrowful shake of the head. "There, I admit, we have much to atone for."

WE RECONVENED WITH the rest of the troops, and a quick head-count confirmed that no human lives had been lost in the course of Operation: Get Gid The Fuck Out. I was relieved and delighted. I'd have felt like shit if someone had made the ultimate sacrifice just to save *my* wretched skin. It was bad enough that a few of the guys had received injuries during the fighting, although luckily nothing more severe than cuts and scrapes, sustained mostly due to grazing themselves on rough ice.

A fresh set of clothes was found for me – snow-pattern gear like everyone else was wearing. Turned out my own kit was more or less in tatters, which in all the excitement I hadn't realised. Torn to shreds by frost giant claws and general abuse and wear and tear over the past day.

Dressed like the rest, I joined them on the yomp back to Asgard Hall. We hiked with the sunset at our backs, on through the dark, until around midnight Freya called a halt and proposed we bed down until daybreak. Sentries were posted on two-hour watches, bedrolls were produced, and rations of bread, beef jerky, salted cod, power bars and drinking water were doled out. Under the stars, I tried to sleep, but for once in my life couldn't. My mutant super power – the ability to nod off at the drop of a hat, any time, anywhere – had deserted me. My mind was full of racing thoughts, too many to process easily. Foremost among them was the knowledge that everything I'd agreed to myself must be absolute bollocks was, in fact, true. I'd been held captive by frost giants. Creatures from fantasy, from medieval myth, and they were fucking real. I'd seen them with my own eyes. Conversed with them. Had the shit kicked out of me by them. *Smelled* them, for Christ's sake. They couldn't have been more real if they'd had a factory stamp on their backs stating that they were a real product of Realness Incorporated, makers of real things that are, in reality, real.

In which case, how much else here was actual-factual? Were there truly trolls as well? Gnomes? Was that big fat oaf Thor over there, on his back snoring like a chainsaw, genuinely the Norse god of thunder? Was Freya a goddess? She sure as hell had the looks for it. Was Odin, all said and done, everything he claimed to be? *The* Odin? Was Asgard Hall *the* Asgard?

I still clung to the notion that there was, to coin a phrase, a rational explanation for all this. That, like in an episode of *Scooby-Doo*, the supernatural-seeming stuff could be accounted for by people wearing clever costumes or using trapdoors and mirrors and suchlike. But I knew this wasn't much more than a vain hope. I was thrashing around for a lifebelt to keep me afloat and all I could lay my hands on was a set of child's inflatable armbands.

"I see that look in your eyes, Gid," said Cy from next to me, in a whisper. "That stare. It's like that for all of us, the first time, when you finally twig what's what. Takes a while to get a fix on, know what I mean? Just try not to think about it too hard. Try to accept it. Simpler that way. It's not worth losing sleep over. This is just how things are from now on. This is the world we're in."

I lay looking up at a bunch of constellations I didn't recognise, and I waited to feel comforted by the advice.

TWENTY

Eventually I did fall asleep, and I dreamed I was back in the Astra.

I was back in the Astra, trapped upside down, and Abortion had burrowed his way out and was somewhere in the field outside, but he'd been gone a long time. Minutes, though it felt like hours. It didn't take that long to phone the emergency services, did it? What was he doing, giving them his life story?

"Abortion?"

Nothing. No answer.

"Abortion? Mate?"

Still no answer.

I tried it louder, almost a scream.

"Abortion!"

Don't flap, Gid, I told myself. *Bugger's strayed out of earshot, that's all. Trying to get to high ground to get a signal. Yeah, that's it.*

But it wasn't impossible that he'd wandered off. Abortion's brain had holes in it, which his train of thought often fell into and seldom chuffed itself quickly out of. Dazed and confused from the crash, he could easily have forgotten about me and trundled off back up to the road, maybe planning on heading back to the petrol station. By the time he got there, if he ever did, he might not even recall how he came to be out on a night like this in the first place. Meaning I was well and truly snookered.

I wriggled, struggled, but couldn't free myself. The cold was seeping into my muscles, my bones. I was constricted. Paralysed. Dying.

I woke up then, in Jotunheim, with my bedroll all twisted round me like a sweet wrapper. I got untangled, huddled tightly up and rubbed myself for warmth, and soon was dozing once more.

The claustrophobic car dream, I suspected, was destined to become a recurring nightmare.

Another one to add to the collection.

My tours in former Yugoslavia, then Iraq, then Afghanistan, had left me with a whole host of images that I could push to the rear of my mind and ignore while I was awake, but not in my sleep, when my brain was its own boss and did whatever it felt like.

The aftermath of a Sunni suicide bombing on a bus carrying Shiite militiamen in Basra.

An Afghan woman in the field hospital at Bastion, her face melted off by white phosphorus.

The charred corpses of British soldiers in a Snatch Land Rover whose armour hadn't protected them from an RPG attack near Kandahar.

Naked bodies piled high in the cellar of a house in Srebrenica, all males, the youngest of them a boy of no more than fifteen – Bosnian Muslim refugees slaughtered by a particularly vicious Serbian para-military death squad known as the Scorpions.

A British infantry platoon limping home to forward command, lugging several of their comrades behind them on improvised drag litters after a "friendly fire" incident when the joystick jockey operating a Predator drone a couple of hundred miles across the border in Uzbekistan opened up on them with Hellfire missiles, misreading his camera image and mistaking them for armed locals.

They came to me at night, these scenes and others. I lived them over and over, never able to escape them. Mental wounds, the kind that never heal. Bringers of night sweats and small-hours vigils that lasted until dawn.

The price we paid for being soldiers. The price of surviving warfare.

TWENTY-ONE

BEFORE DAWN WE were on the march again. My body had stiffened up during the night, a hundred separate bruises congealing, and I walked with all the grace of a horror-movie mummy, but I did my best to keep pace with the others. They'd come for me, risked their necks. Damned if I was going to slow them down or be any more of a pain in the arse than I'd already been.

Freya saw the ravens first, long before anyone else did. She made us halt without explaining why, until the two birds were visible to all, winging towards us from out of the sunrise.

"Oy-oy," said Cy. "Message from HQ."

"You mean those are Odin's?" I said, recalling the ravens that had been perched on his shoulders at the banquet.

"Huginn and Muninn," said Paddy. "And don't go asking which is which, because all ravens look the bloody same to me."

"And they're, like, carrier ravens? They'll have little slips of paper attached to their legs with Odin's orders on?"

"Not exactly," said Cy. "Wait and see."

The ravens circled above us for a while before descending. One landed on each of Freya's outstretched arms, and bugger me if she didn't greet them with a bow and a "good morning," just as if they were people.

"Huginn, Muninn," she said. "You have flown long and far, and I humbly thank you for your efforts."

The birds went "*cawww*" and "*arrrkk*" in turn, and flapped their wings and waggled their beaks, as though acknowledging and returning her courtesy.

Neither of them, I noticed, appeared to have brought any message container with it. I looked at Cy and Paddy. "So what now? She Dr Dolittle or something?"

Paddy just raised his monobrow in a way that said *keep watching*.

"You who are the All-Father's eyes and ears abroad," Freya said to the ravens, "you who go where he cannot and witness what he cannot and bring back news to him of all that happens, speak to me now in his words. Tell me his wishes."

"*Arrkk*!" said either Huginn or Muninn, and I thought we were in for a long morning if we were going to stand there until one of those birds actually started talking.

Of course, I ought to have known better by then, because one of them actually did. Both, in fact. They opened their beaks simultaneously, and out came the voice of none other than Odin himself. Odin, in bizarre avian stereo.

"Freya Njorthasdottir," the ravens said, "I see that Gid is among your number. He looks as well as can be expected. You have discharged your duty with your customary diligence."

"I did not do it for praise. To serve the All-Father is its own reward."

"Aye," Thor agreed.

"Nevertheless," said the ravens, "praise is due. I now have another job for you and your men to perform."

"Name it, Odin."

"Originally I dispatched Huginn and Muninn with the sole purpose of making this rendezvous with you and establishing mission status. On their way, however, they observed a disquieting sight. Trolls. Not far from the Asgardian border."

"How many trolls?" Thor enquired eagerly.

"Three. If you turn a few degrees northward from your current bearing, you will encounter them in two, perhaps two and a half hours."

"You wish us to kill them, All-Father?" asked Freya. I could tell the idea appealed.

"In days of yore I would have said yes," said Odin via raven walkie-talkie. "Trolls straying beyond the bounds of Jotunheim is not permissible, and these three look set to do just that. However, times are changing. New strategies are required to meet the growing threat of the true enemy. New allegiances too."

Thor gaped. "You mean...?"

"Yes, my son. I want them taken alive, not destroyed."

"Trolls – captive?"

"Annexed. Press-ganged. Recruited."

"Those brainless, lumbering –"

"– immensely strong, highly suggestible creatures, yes." The ravens stalked sideways up and down Freya's arms, canting their heads. "We discussed this. Several times. Were you not paying attention? If we can control a significant number of trolls, think what a blunt-force defensive unit they could make."

"I remember you suggesting something of the kind, father. I simply didn't –"

"Cousin," said Freya to Thor, butting in, "Odin's wisdom is not to be questioned. If this is what he desires us to do, we do it, difficult as it may seem."

"I'm not scared of difficulty," said Thor. "It's the notion of letting a single troll live, let alone making *pets* of the things, that I have a problem with."

"Is this a challenge you shrink from, my son?" the ravens asked, with a sly glint in their beady little eyes.

"Never!" declared Thor, and he beat his breast. Actually thumped himself in the sternum with both fists. If there'd been trees around, I wouldn't have been surprised to see him start swinging from them. "You want three trolls trounced and trussed and brought to you, father? Then that is what you shall have."

"Huginn and Muninn will lead you to their location," the ravens said, "and when you have overcome the trolls, transport will be sent to ferry them hither. Good luck, all."

The birds took off from Freya's arms, wheeling up into the firmament.

She turned to us. "You heard the All-Father, men. Is there any among you who would shirk the task Odin has set?"

As one, the soldiers yelled, "No!"

Even me. No idea why. The word just rushed out from my throat. It was as though someone else was speaking through me, much as Odin had spoken through the ravens.

"No!" I said, swept up in the moment, full of inexplicable enthusiasm, and thinking, *Trolls – how bad can that be?*

TWENTY-TWO

VERY BAD, AS it turned out.

In my head I had a vision of dwarfish, shrivelled things. Bit like Yoda. Shuffling along all hunched and wizened. Odin had said something about them being immensely strong and useful in defence, but to me it had sounded like pure hype. After the frost giants, which were surely the biggest, meanest bastards in the land, trolls had to be a happy hobbity lot by comparison, right? I thought back to the fairytales I used to read Cody when he was little. There was that troll who lived under a bridge in the story about the three billy goats. Couldn't be much of a threat, could he, if a fucking goat could sort him out with a head butt. Trolls. I mean, *really*.

But I was aware of Cy and Paddy both getting tenser as we tramped north-east after the ravens, so I asked if either of them had had a run-in with a troll and what I should expect, and they said no but they'd heard trolls were something to be steered clear of, and then another bloke, a ginge who I was pretty sure was called Allinson, or maybe Ellison, overheard and mentioned that he'd seen one while out on patrol a few weeks back. It was as big as a Challenger tank, he said, with long arms and sickly greyish skin, and the patrol's leader, Odin's son Vidar, had told them all to take cover behind some rocks while the thing passed because there was nothing to be gained by tackling a troll if it could possibly be avoided. The troll had lolloped by on a mission of its own without noticing any of them hiding, but what Allinson-or-Ellison remembered most of all was how the ground trembled beneath its feet.

"You could actually feel it through your boots," he said. "The vibrations from each step it took, and it was a hundred metres off at least. Arms the size of tree trunks. Fists the size of wrecking balls. And these two ruddy great blunt teeth sticking up from its bottom jaw, like tusks."

"But slow," said Thor, joining in the conversation. "Slow of wit and of limb. There was never a troll that was fleeter of foot than a snail, nor capable of out-thinking a worm. With our brains and speed, not to mention our weaponry, we shall make short work of the moronic creatures and fetch them triumphantly home."

"If you say so," I said. "Speaking of weaponry, though... Any chance I could maybe have a gun? Everybody else is packing, and I'm feeling a bit left out."

"Of course, Gid," Thor replied with alarming jollity, and within moments he'd commandeered a Minimi light machine gun, the best thing to come out of Belgium since waffles, and a Glock 17, the best thing to come out of Austria since, well, ever. Plus a day's worth of ammo. It said something for how well equipped these guys were that they had guns going spare, enough that they could afford to share them around. I was revising my estimate of the Valhalla Mission upward. Its aims remained murky to me, but somehow that didn't matter so much any more, now that I'd accepted I'd entered some Other Realm where the laws of science and nature as I knew them no longer applied.

"You will not shoot to kill," Thor warned me. "That said, mere bullets won't bring a troll down anyway. Their hide is too thick."

"What the hell are we supposed to use, man? Harsh language?" I said. An *Aliens* quote. Wasted on Thor. And pretty much everybody else. Sometimes I wondered if I wasn't too much of a sci-fi geek for this line of work.

"What we do is we use the guns to whittle down and weaken them," he said. "Whereupon I, with Mjolnir, rob them of their senses. That is how we will win."

HALF AN HOUR later, our raven scouts Huginn and Muninn swooped down to report that the targets had been sighted. They were making their way along a narrow, shallow valley ahead, which led directly onto Asgardian territory. The ravens recommended we proceed in parallel formation along both sides of the valley in order to catch the trolls in a pincer movement. Freya instantly divided us into two groups, her in charge of one, Thor the other. I was hardly astonished to find myself not in her group.

A dozen of us followed Thor's massive rolling shoulders upslope, onto the thin ridge that formed the valley's rim. The sky had greyed. An apologetic sleet was falling and one of those thin chilly winds had started up, the kind that drilled right into your sinuses like an ice cream headache. This was barren country, with little in the way of vegetation to afford cover or shelter. The valley's sides were a mix of shale and scree, interspersed with boulders and patches of coarse, long-lying snow. As scenic beauty spots went, it didn't. I couldn't think of a drearier, more miserable-looking place. Except perhaps my own flat. And Birmingham.

Thor called us to a halt with an upraised hand. He pointed down into the valley, and there they were. A trio of trolls.

The ginge had exaggerated, but only a little. Not a Challenger tank. Each was more the size of a Ford Transit laid on its end. Which, frankly, was big enough. They had loincloths on and leather caps with loops that fastened under the chin, plus furry boots on their feet, but the rest of them was bare naked, acres of skin showing, all of it the colour of the scum that sometimes collected on the surface of streams, white tinged browny-grey, and riddled with moles and liver spots and tufts of hair in odd locations. Massive muscles worked beneath as they hulked along, half hunched over, almost but not quite on all fours, their knuckles brushing the ground. Their brows beetled, shading tiny stupid eyes. Their jaws chomped, protruding tusk-like teeth all but poking into their nostrils. Every so often they'd grunt or croak to one another. It sound like language but not quite. Caveman-level, if not even more primitive. Mostly they just used gestures.

I felt nothing but disgust and revulsion as I watched them. Part of me advised leaving them well alone, shrinking out of sight. Another part wanted to stamp them out as you would a cockroach. They were intimidating and loathsome at the same time. I'd have taken the frost giants over them any day.

Thor signalled across to Freya on the valley's far side. She waved back, and began stationing her men along the ridge ahead of the trolls, downwind. Thor copied her. We crouched in wait. Guns were stealthily cocked, safety catches off.

Then the lead troll stopped, so sharply the other two almost bumped into him. He raised his head, sniffing the sleety air, then growled out a mangled syllable or two. He'd detected something... something he didn't like the smell of...

Thor cursed under his breath. "Son of a jotun whore! The wind has shifted. He scents us. Damn things have no intelligence to speak of, poor eyesight too, but fate has compensated by giving them extraordinarily sensitive noses."

"So?" I said.

"So," said Thor, "we take what little element of surprise we have left and we use it. Open fire!" he barked. "Fire at will!"

We did, strafing the trolls with bullets of every calibre. Freya's lot did likewise. The ground around the trolls erupted, becoming a frenzied dancing carpet of impacts. Most were stray shots, misses, but many were ricochets. Rounds bouncing off the trolls and spinning away in all directions.

Conventional bullets simply couldn't penetrate the trolls' skins. But they did sting, that much was obvious. Badly. The trolls flailed and thrashed about under the volley of gunfire, roaring and raving as though they were under siege from a swarm of angry hornets. Red welts appeared all over them, and the trolls hugged their heads and shielded their faces, and my

Minimi and everyone else's guns joined forces in a tumultuous symphony of bangs and cracks and chatters that rippled along the valley like thunder.

Empty mag. Eject. Fresh mag. Reload. Empty, eject, fresh, reload. It was second nature. Like riding a bike. I barely had to think about it. The Minimi juddered, nice and lively in my hands. My ears rang. Cordite smoke filled my nose, singeing my nostril hairs. I had my range. Every shot was made to count.

And in time, we brought the creatures to their knees. They couldn't take any more. They were wailing, pleading for relief in some guttural language that was all growls and vowels. And I felt not a shred of pity. When Thor gave the command to cease firing, I was the last to do so. And when he hared off down the slope, Mjolnir drawn, for some reason I was hot on his heels.

I ran, slip-slithering on the scree and crusty snow, again and again losing my balance and only just managing to stay upright, until we made it to the bottom, Thor and I, in time to meet Freya scrambling down from the other side. She paused to frown at me – what was I, a mortal, doing there, when this was god business? – while Thor didn't pause at all. He pounced on the nearest troll, straddling his back like a mahout on an elephant, and whanged Mjolnir repeatedly against his skull as though hammering an anvil. Freya tackled another of them, coming at him sidelong and wrapping both arms around his meaty neck. Grimacing, she tightened her grip, and the troll started to choke and splutter.

Me, I went for the third of the creatures with scarcely a thought. He was curled up on his side in the foetal position like some giant baby, trembling with pain and distress. I set about booting him in the head, hard as I knew how. It was like stamping on a huge lump of wax, solid but yielding. When my leg began to ache I switched to the hollow butt of the Minimi, with which I pounded the troll until a hand seized my arm, gently but firmly.

"It is done, Gid," said Thor. "The creature is insensible."

And lo and behold, he was right. The darkness cleared from my vision, and I saw that my troll was out cold, and looking in a pretty sorry shape too. What with the bullet hits and my blows, his head was all swollen and lumpy, raw as a tenderised cut of beef. Thor's troll was in no better condition, while Freya's had been throttled into unconsciousness. The breath wheezed threadily in and out of his lungs.

"Now I see why my father was so insistent that we retrieve you," Thor said to me. "I can understand Freya and myself being willing to take on a troll single-handed, but a mortal? One not gifted with the strength and endurance of gods? Truly that is the mark of warrior greatness."

"Or just plain foolhardiness," Freya commented. "Even when half subdued, that troll could still have killed you, Gid. All it would have taken was a heedless swipe of his arm, and every bone in your body would have been shattered."

"I'm touched by the concern," I said.

"I'm not concerned," Freya shot back. "Other than that I would have to face Odin's wrath were I to fail to bring you back to Asgard alive."

"All right then, but you must admit you're ever so slightly impressed by what I just did."

"So many people mistake madness for bravery."

"Never known the difference myself."

"And that," said Freya, "is why, whatever Thor may say, you are no warrior. You do not know fear. The true warrior understands that his greatest foe is his own terror of battle. It never pales and must be conquered again and again, and it keeps things in perspective. Whereas you, Gid, have either forgotten what fear is or never knew it in the first instance. That makes you reckless – a danger to yourself and, worse, to others – and *that* is why I am not happy to fight alongside you. And now" – she spun on her heel – "where are those ravens? Huginn! Muninn! Can you hear me? We have the trolls. Odin must send *Sleipnir* now, before they awaken."

Thor clapped me on the back, virtually knocking me off my feet. "Pay no attention to my elder cousin, friend Gid. Her asperity cloaks her true feelings."

"Which are?"

"Who can say? I'm sure she has some. Mine is the opinion that counts in these matters, and you can fight alongside me any time."

Flattered? I sort of was. I was definitely supposed to be.

Mainly, though, I was thinking, and not for the first time in my life, how fucking maddening women could be. Even goddesses.

No, especially goddesses.

TWENTY-THREE

"*Sleipnir?*"

"If I told you 'eight-legged horse that can fly,'" said Paddy, "what would you say?"

"A day ago I'd have said you might want to think about laying off the Guinness for a bit. Now, though..."

Paddy chuckled. Cy too. Tea had been made, and we were all sitting around waiting for the promised transport to arrive.

"Really?" I said. "An eight-legged horse? With wings? This I've got to see. Although" – having thought about it further – "it's going to have to be an enormous fucking horse to fit three trolls on its back. Or even one. You're pulling my plonker, aren't you?"

"Odin did have a horse called Sleipnir, back in the day," Paddy said. "Loki, his blood brother, was its mother."

"Hang on, did you say mother?"

"Bragi entertained us with a lovely long poem about it once. I think I can remember the basic gist of it. What happened was, this man, a stonemason, turned up offering to build a wall around Asgard, and the price he demanded was only the sun and the moon! And not just those, either, but also your lady over there, Freya.

The Aesir wouldn't agree to his terms 'til Loki suggested they set some impossible conditions. The stonemason had to build the wall single-handed and must do it within the space of one winter. If he defaulted, they'd have the wall for free. Bear in mind, this was going to be a vast fortification all the way around Asgard, so the Aesir never thought he'd have it done in time. The stonemason said, 'Fine,' and rolled up his sleeves and set to work. He was a right big strapping fella, with a huge black carthorse to help him, and he toiled hard as can be all through the winter, and it began to look as if he might just meet the deadline after all."

"Oh, this is terrific," I said, settling back against a rock, cradling my steaming brew. "Paddy does *Jackanory*. Carry on."

"So the Aesir were naturally a mite aggrieved," Paddy continued. He loved to spin a good yarn. "Thanks to Loki they were on course to lose the sun, the moon, and a very beautiful Vanir goddess to boot. So they bashed him around a bit, as you do, and told him to fix things. Now, in case you don't know about Loki, here's the salient point. He's a shifty little devil. And that's no mere figure of speech. He can change his shape to become anything he likes. And what he did was he transformed himself into a mare, a very pretty one with a nice mane and fine fetlocks and a long swishy tail and whatever else it is a lady horse has that makes her attractive to the men horses, and he went off prancing up and down in front of the stonemason's carthorse, which was a stallion in the full prime of life, no gelding, if you catch my drift."

"I very much do."

"And the carthorse went tearing off after Loki in his mare form, and the stonemason was obliged to down tools and give chase, because the horse had been doing a great deal of the work for him, hauling boulders and the like, which he couldn't do himself. He ran after them for a day and a night, and finally caught up with them the following afternoon. He dragged the carthorse back to Asgard but he was too knackered to do anything more on the wall that day, and would you believe it, spring arrived the very next morning, and basically he'd blown his deadline and forfeited his fee."

"Makes a change," I said, "a builder who overcharges not getting paid."

"Ah, but he wasn't just any builder. He was actually a frost giant in disguise, and when he saw that the Aesir had pulled a fast one on him he flew into a rage. He demolished the wall, then turned his attention on Asgard itself. Luckily Thor was on hand to clobber him with Mjolnir, and that was that."

"Or was it?"

"You've spotted that there's an epilogue coming."

"The carthorse managed to catch up with the mare before the stonemason reached them, and got busy. They did the deed, and Sleipnir was the result."

"Kee-rect," said Cy. "Give the man a medal."

"No thanks. Already got some, and I'm not quite sure what the point of them is."

"So, indeed," said Paddy, "Loki comes wandering back to Asgard a few weeks later, looking somewhat red-faced, and he's leading a colt on a rein. A colt with eight legs that seems to float in the air rather than walk – seems to glide like a bird, in actual fact. And he presents it as a gift to his blood brother Odin, and that's what Odin decides to call it: Sleipnir, which means Glider."

"Priceless," I said. "Loki's not only a transsexual but a transsexual in a different species, *and* he manages to get himself knocked up. There's the plot of the weirdest porn film ever made, right there." My next question seemed the obvious one to ask. "So where is he anyway? I'd like to meet him. 'How was it getting rogered by a carthorse? Still sore?'"

"Loki isn't at Asgard any more," Paddy said. "Something happened."

"Got himself kicked out," said Cy.

"How?"

"He was banished for the most heinous of crimes," a voice rumbled in my ear. I hadn't realised that Thor had sidled up to us during Paddy's tale and been eavesdropping. His expression was cold, his face as dark as, well, a thundercloud. "Loki destroyed the one, true, bright shining thing in all of Asgard. His trickery, his treachery, brought tragedy to our family, and for what he did my father consigned him to a dismal cave deep in the earth, where he was stretched across three sharp ledges, bound fast with iron fetters, and a serpent was hung above him, its fangs dripping venom into his eyes for all eternity. And no less a punishment did he deserve."

Thor's voice trembled with pure hatred. The anger radiating off him was almost a physical force.

"But what?" I said. "What did he actually do?"

Before Thor could answer, a low resonant thrumming started up from the north – a sound you felt as much as heard. The vibration seemed to bypass your ears and go straight to the bones of your skull. I knew straight away it was generated by a helicopter, but there was a particular shape to the sound, a pattern to the *whupping* and whirring, that was more than a little familiar. It had two layers, wavelengths doubling and overlapping, and it faded in and out of hearing as the chopper's position altered in relation to the acoustics of the landscape.

I stood – we all stood – as the aircraft finally hoved into view at the valley's far end, and glory be, it was exactly as I thought. A Chinook. A good old Wokka. Hauling itself through the sky, skimming just below the cloud cover, with that strange combination of majesty and ungainliness that only a Chinook had, like a whale in flight. Twin rotors savaging the air, running lights aglow in the gloomy greyness, exhaust hissing like a billion snakes – an aircraft I'd ridden in more than a few times and always been in awe of but never learned to love.

As it came close I saw that it had the name *Sleipnir* painted on the fuselage, just to the rear of the cockpit windscreen, along with a silhouette of a horse with four pairs of legs. I also saw by the lack of long-range fuel tanks on the sides that it was one of the older models, an HC2. Decommissioned, perhaps, once the HC3s came along in the mid-nineties, or else the MoD couldn't be arsed to spring for an overhaul and modifications and sold it off to the highest bidder, which in this instance was Odin Borrson.

The Wokka did a flyby, then put its nose down and pivoted smartly about on its front axis to come roaring back. The valley was just wide enough and flat-bottomed enough for the pilot to pull off a landing. Precision manoeuvring, clearance minimal, not a touchdown anyone would want to attempt too often, but he managed it, while we all crouched and turned away from the corrosive blast of dust and gravel the chopper's downwash inflicted on us.

Down went the cargo ramp and its extensions, revealing the grey interior of the cargo bay and the swathe of multicoloured cables that rimmed the doorway. At the same time up popped the starboard entry door and out stepped none other than Odin himself. His ravens flew to him the moment the Wokka's rotor blades fell still. With one balancing on each shoulder he went to inspect the trolls, then began supervising their loading onto the helicopter. It took fifteen men to lift each troll and cart him into the cargo bay. We squashed them in there one after another like sardines, making sure they were tied up tightly with the ropes Odin had brought. Then, soon, *Sleipnir* was taking off, even less balletic in the air for having a couple of tons of troll stuffed in its belly. It chuntered off over the horizon, lost from sight a full minute before it was lost from hearing.

Odin stayed behind. "The pilots know the way home without me," he said, "and the mood has taken me to accompany you on the rest of your journey."

For a time we all ambled along together in a straggling column, Odin using a forked staff as a walking aid, like some beardy old rambler. He chatted with Thor and Freya, and with the troops, but I could sense him working his way towards me. Every time I glanced round, he'd advanced a little further up the line, closer to where I was.

Finally he reached me.

"Gid. A word," he said, drawing me aside.

"Ooh, teacher's pet," said Cy, with a leer.

I gave him my middle finger.

Odin held me back until everyone else had gone past, and then we resumed walking, the two of us a good twenty paces to the rear of the others.

"Reports are," he said, "you slew a jotun in single combat. And you helped signally with the capture of the trolls."

"What can I say? I'm an all-round champ."

"You do see now, don't you, that your doubts were unfounded?"

I chose my words carefully. "Let's say I'm a whole lot more open-minded than I used to be."

"But questions remain."

"They do."

"Then now's your chance. Ask away. Anything you want."

His one eye gazed at me unswervingly. Huginn's and Muninn's eyes added to the scrutiny. I felt exposed, as though the whole world was looking at me, curious, prying.

"Okay then," I said, "for starters, let's take that helicopter of yours. I guess you have a landing pad for it not far from the castle."

"And a hangar. Not far but not near. Asgard is large. Plenty of acreage in which to squirrel things away. Even a Chinook."

"The thing here, though, is – assuming you are what you appear to be, one of the actual Norse gods, in the flesh, how come you have a helicopter at all? You've named it after your flying horse. Where is that horse? Have you got that stabled out in the grounds of the castle as well?"

"No," said Odin. "No, I no longer have Sleipnir. I had to give him up. Similarly, the Valkyries no longer ride steeds but use snowmobiles instead."

"You've moved with the times, is that it? You've updated. Upgraded."

He half smiled. "To a certain extent, yes. Gods are, after all, what men make them. A thousand years ago, when horses were the principal mode of transport, naturally we gods rode horses too. Anything else would have been strange. Nowadays, when people use mechanised conveyances, there's no reason why we should not too. By the same token, we wield guns now rather than broadswords and axes. Thor is the exception. He wouldn't be without his hammer. He's very attached to it. But the rest of us have embraced the physics of projectile and explosive. Why not? If nothing else it lends us an added edge over our traditional foes. The jotuns may be content to continue to use their ice weaponry, but little good does such a reactionary stance serve them in this day and age."

"Except when it comes to one-on-one duels."

"Their way of making a point. On their own terms, with *issgeisl*s and the like, they are formidable. It makes them feel better about themselves to capture a mortal every so often and demonstrate the virtues of their own old-fashioned battlecraft. It won't win them any wars, but it does prevent them from lapsing into utter despair. Poor things." Said with an almost fond chuckle.

"There's more to it, however," he went on, serious again. "Sleipnir is a very good example of the regrettable truth about being a deity in the modern age. Simply put, I don't have him any more because I lack the power to have him."

"Huh?" *Simply put* my arse. What the hell did he mean?

"I am, Gid, a mere shadow of the god I used to be. That's true of all of us Aesir and Vanir. In our heyday we were quite extraordinary beings. To stand in our presence would have been an overwhelming, mind-shattering experience for you. You would have reeled in awe before our splendour. You might never have fully recovered from the meeting, so dazzled and dizzied would it have left you."

"Blimey, talk about having a ticket on yourself."

"Whereas today, a man may walk beside me, close enough to brush my garment, and make flippant, derogatory comments, and neither is he cowed nor ashamed. That is how humbled we have become, how straitened. So much so that I cannot even lay claim to my horse. He is gone – lost. There was no tearful parting. I simply discovered at some point that Sleipnir had ceased to be one of my common appurtenances and would have to be replaced with some more prosaic equivalent. He was not to belong to me any more. Little does now. My ravens are perhaps the sole remaining legacy of my former greatness."

He chucked Huginn and Muninn under the beak with his thumb. They crooned softly.

"So, what, you're telling me you've had to downsize?" I said. "There've been divine budgetary cuts? Like the aristocracy, even gods can fall on hard times?"

"More or less," he said. "We are granted life by belief. Faith gives us form and vigour. Once, we were believed in fervently. The Norsemen worshipped and adored us. To the Vikings we were superstars, and every prayer sent up to us, every feast held in our honour, every battle waged in our name, every saga and folksong sung about us, filled us with ever greater power." He sighed, and the ravens let out odd little hisses that could have been sighs too. "Men gave willingly of themselves to nourish us and keep us. That is no longer so. Tell me, how many in Midgard these days even remember the Norse pantheon, let alone venerate it?"

"Er, not that many. We still know the stories, I suppose, but venerate? Nobody's really doing any of that."

"The stories help. They keep us alive. Whenever, wherever, someone commits a tale about us to the page or celebrates us verbally, it sustains us. It is an act of homage, whether it is done knowingly with that aim or not. It gives us credence. But the people of Midgard are largely secular now, or else in thrall to single, overarching gods who are all ideology and ideal."

"Like *the* God. Capital-G God."

"Yes."

"Have you met Him? What's He like?"

"We don't all get together at god club and compare notes, Gid," Odin said. "Besides, I don't believe in Him, and if He does exist, I don't like Him. His type of gods aren't gods who echo how mortals behave. They're gods who are held up as example of perfection to be emulated. They're not gods of the people. They're remote and inaccessible, and they demand blind, unthinking obedience from their followers. They're dictators. We Aesir and Vanir, by contrast, are mirrors. Other gods rule. We reflect and magnify. We are you, only more so. We share your flaws and foibles. We are as humanlike as we are divine, and I think we're all the better for that."

"Trouble is, that isn't the brand of god that's wanted in the twenty-first century."

"Hasn't been wanted for a very long time," Odin agreed, sombrely. "We are, I don't deny, superannuated. A throwback. It is, some might say, a miracle that we're still here at all. But we are. And like it or not, we still have a role to play in the affairs of men. As long as we continue to exist, we can't help but do."

"Any particular reason why you decided to decamp from, I don't know, Scandinavia or wherever, to the north of England? Was that part of the downsizing too? A forced relocation?"

"Ah, Gid, who's to say we have relocated?"

"Well, haven't you? Asgard Hall *is* in the north of England, right?"

"You're thinking literally. Like a mortal. Which isn't your fault, of course. How else could you think?"

"Where is it, then? Don't tell me Scotland. I haven't had my vaccinations!"

"Just the *north*," said Odin. "The frozen north. Everywhere has a north, and where that north is, where the snow tumbles and the winds blow icy cold and the nights are long and dark and the wolves cry, that's where you'll find us. That's our natural habitat. Anywhere north."

I pondered this a while, and decided it made sense. Not a great deal of sense, but as much sense as anything else around here was making.

"All right," I said finally. "I think we've covered pretty much all I need to know. Just one last question. You've talked about a true enemy. One you're gearing up to fight with. That's what you're recruiting for, why you're offering blokes like me employment, the reason for the training and the troll catching and all of it..."

"Who," said Odin, anticipating where I was headed.

"Yes. Who. Who is it? Who's the enemy?"

"Better than telling you," he said, "when we get back to Asgard I'll show you. Or rather, the Norns will."

TWENTY-FOUR

The Norns lived in a cottage on the opposite side of Yggdrasil from Asgard Hall. You couldn't see the castle from the cottage and vice versa. The World Tree blocked the view both ways. Odin and I headed straight there as soon as we got back on Asgardian soil, with a slight detour on the way so that I could visit Frigga for some running repairs. She changed my dressings, applied salves to my new injuries, dosed me up with some of that barely swallowable medicine of hers, and clucked and tutted a bit, telling her husband I was a man in clear need of rest. That wasn't on the cards, but I left feeling a great deal better than I had done. Right as rain and not as wet.

Cottage, as a matter of fact, was a generous description for the Norns' residence. *Tumbledown shack* would have been nearer the truth. Slates were missing from the roof, sometimes so many in one spot as to leave gaping great holes in its pelt of snow. Broken windowpanes had been patched up with rectangles of fibreboard. The brickwork was cracked and flaky and in serious need of repointing. Ivy and Virginia creeper had the building in their clutches and seemed to be doing their level best to pull it down into the ground. The whole place was sagging and lopsided from threshold to chimney.

A gate, leaning off a single hinge, opened onto an unruly, overgrown front garden. There was a well in the middle of the lawn, an olde-worlde wishing well type of affair with a small peaked roof on top and a rusty bucket hanging from the handle. Looked like no one had drawn water from it in ages. The path up to the front door looked like no one had walked up it in ages either. It meandered, a curving line of smooth, undisturbed snow to the porch.

Odin was not happy. His mouth was pursed. Nervousness was coming off him like a bad odour. Every step closer to the cottage, he seemed to have to drag himself that bit harder along.

"What's up?" I asked. "Somewhere else you'd rather be?"

"Anywhere else," he replied. "I don't dread much, but I dread the Norns."

"But you're Odin. The All-Father. The big kahuna. You're in charge of the show. What's the problem?"

"All Aesir and Vanir fear the Norns. They are the Pronouncers, the Three Fays of Destiny. They were old while we were still young. They determine the fates of all. Even gods must bow before them."

Three women you really don't want to meet, Freya had said. And Odin wasn't that keen on paying them a house call. Even Huginn and Muninn had chosen to give the event a miss and had fluttered off on some birdie errand or other. So, understandably, I was beginning to wonder myself whether this was such a good idea.

"We could come back another time. Or maybe you could tell me yourself about the enemy. We don't have to go to all this trouble if you don't want to."

"It's the best way," said Odin, grimly, gravely. "The Norns have skills that I lack. Their demonstrations of fact are more convincing than any mere words of mine would be."

He reached out to tug at the knob of a bell-pull. A bell clanged deep, unfathomably deep inside the cottage.

"Oh well, nobody home," I said before the ringing had even stopped. "Let's go."

"They're home. They're never not home. Hold fast."

We were on the doorstep for nearly five minutes, and I was starting to hope that Odin was wrong and the Norns were, for once, out. Nipped down to Asda or the bingo or something.

Then: light footsteps, stiff bolts being shot, a key creakily turning, and the door was opened by...

...not a wrinkly white-haired crone like I'd been picturing, but a girl, barely a teenager, blossom-cheeked and pretty. Reminded me very much of Sally Stringer, who I'd lusted after through most of secondary school, tried countless times to chat up at parties and discos without getting anywhere, and had my boyish heart broken by when she started going out with Brett Hughes. It had been an especially painful kick in the teeth because Brett's parents were well-off, had a large house, gave him a generous allowance, and Sally – the Sally I thought she was, the Sally I'd built her up to be in my mind – wasn't the kind of girl to have her head turned by wealth. Although apparently, at the end of the day, she was.

The girl smiled at us, coldly welcoming.

"Odin," she said.

"Urd," said Odin, and he had lowered his head, as if he could scarcely bring himself to look at her. He was even, I thought, shaking.

But she was just a *girl*. Simply dressed. Slender. Not tall. Slip of a thing. No threat to anyone.

"And Gideon Coxall," she said, turning to me.

"Gid."

"Your mother always preferred Gideon. Your father was the one who shortened it. It was a bone of contention between them – one of the few, all minor, until his infidelity. Afterwards, she wouldn't even let your friends call you Gid while they were in the house. 'Gideon,' she would insist. 'As in the Bible.'"

Me: eyes on stalks, jaw open to the neck.

But I recovered well, I thought.

"Okay, that trick isn't creepy much. What have you got back there, *The Big Book Of Gideon Coxall*, complete with illustrations?"

"Something of that ilk," said Urd. "I shall use Gideon too, because it was your mother's choice, and she is a significant factor in your past. What my sisters call you is their own business."

"Will you invite us in?" said Odin, having to force the request out. "I can't believe our visit was not expected."

"Nothing is unexpected to the Norns," Urd said, "and indeed we already know your motives for being here and have prepared accordingly. Come in, both."

She let us in, shut the door behind, and showed us along the hallway through to a lounge. The cottage's interior matched its exterior. Ripped and peeling wallpaper. Threadbare rugs and throws. Chairs well ventilated with holes. Moth-eaten, mildewed, mouldering curtains with hems so rotted away they barely touched the sills. The smell of dust, dense and peppery in the air. If the Norns were deliberately going for the shabby-chic look, they'd nailed it. Nailed it to the point of overkill.

In the lounge, two women rose to greet us. Both had a similar look about them to Urd. Same posture, same mannerisms, same colouring. In point of fact, they were exact replicas of her, just older. One by maybe twenty years, the other by a lot. One was Urd as she might be after childbirth, broader in the hips, plumper around the jowls. *Matronly* was the word that sprang to mind. The other was Urd as she'd become once menopause, osteoporosis, and the general withering of age had taken their toll: stooped, hair streaked with silver, lips shrivelled to a dog's bumhole with a sketching of moustache across the top.

"Verdande," Odin said to the mother version of Urd, and "Skuld" to the ancient version. There was a definite tremor in his voice. Oh how he did not want to be in a room with these three.

"All-Father," Verdande and Skuld replied. Usually a term of respect round these parts, but from their lips the title sounded sarcastic, even contemptuous. They were scornful of it, and of Odin.

The Norns gathered together in the centre of the room, and it was like a snapshot of three generations. Grandmother, mother, daughter. Which would have been charming if they weren't so eerily alike in every way. Triplets born across a span of several decades.

"We are busy," said Urd. "There is much work to be done."

"The tides in the affairs of gods and men are in full spate and reaching flood," said Verdande. "We must weave and divine as never before."

"Yet we have made time for your visit," said Skuld. "How could we fail to? We are the Norns. It was foretold."

"We are grateful," said Odin.

But they didn't much seem to care for further niceties. "Be seated," Urd instructed, and Odin and I did as told, finding places for ourselves on a settee between the sticking-up springs and the outbursts of horsehair stuffing. A one-bar electric fire buzzed hear our feet, shedding some warmth but no further up our legs than our ankles. Funnily enough, I couldn't see where the fire was plugged into. It didn't even appear to have a flex.

"What has Odin told you about us?" Urd asked me. "About how we work?"

"Little, I'd imagine," said Verdande.

"The All-Father is loath to acknowledge that we exist at all," said Skuld. "Or that, as we prove, there are things beyond his control."

"We see all."

"While he sees not nearly so much."

"Nor nearly so far ahead."

"One eye only."

"The other sacrificed in return for a drink from the Wellspring of Wisdom in Jotunheim."

"Plucked out and given to Mimir, the only wise jotun that ever lived. A poor exchange."

They were ripping the piss out of Odin, and he just stared at the middle distance and took it. I felt a bit sorry for him.

"For wisdom by itself is never quite enough," said Urd.

"Not when unaccompanied by foresight," said Verdande.

"Oh what it must be to understand all, but be able to predict the outcome of naught," said Skuld.

"How sad."

"How limiting."

"How short-sighted."

"Come on, girls, leave it out," I said. Someone had to stand up for the old bugger. He obviously wasn't going to himself. "So Odin's missing an eye. Never stopped Columbo, did it? Means he can't enjoy a 3D movie, but that's about the only drawback I can think of."

"Don't defend me, Gid," Odin said. "This... teasing is just their way. The Norns must be endured and never – I repeat – *never* antagonised."

"What's the worst they can do? Slag me off to death?"

The three women laughed in unison, a horrible sound, jarring and jangling like a bad guitar chord.

"Gideon has spirit," said Urd.

"Gid does," said Verdande.

"A hero born," said Skuld.

"No, whoa, what?" I said. "Hero? Oh no. That's enough of that."

"Modest?"

"Or ignorant."

"Or in denial."

"Denial of his future path."

"Shall we show him, sisters?"

"Show him the course we have set for him?"

"The thread we have selected?"

"Ought we?"

"He has come. We ought."

"He wants truth."

"We shall give him truth."

They were talking so fast now, I was having trouble keeping up with which of them was saying what. The three-way rota of Urd then Verdande then Skuld had been abandoned. They were all speaking at once, or finishing one another's sentences, or doing alternate words, I wasn't sure which.

"It is the price."

"The price of truth."

"To be shown the truth of himself."

"A truth for a truth."

"Does he wish to see what is to be?"

"As if he has a choice."

"In our house."

"On our terms."

"He cannot refuse."

Then, like that, they were gone, whisking out of the room in a flourish of skirts. I looked at Odin.

"What the hell was all that –"

And suddenly they were back, wheeling a TV set. It was sitting on a rickety hostess trolley, with a VCR on the shelf beneath. The telly was vintage; fake wood veneer, bulbous screen, loads of knobs and buttons. Mid 'eighties at the latest. The VCR was much the same. A top-loader the size of a kitchen sink, with clunky lever switches you had to press hard.

"Once, we spun threads," said Urd. They were back to speaking in turn, thank God. That overlapping dialogue of theirs had been freaking me out.

"One for every mortal," said Verdande.

"But so effortful," said Skuld. "So laborious."

"A grey thread for the common man whose life is never to amount to much."

"Occasionally a colourful thread for the freeman or the farmer, he whose lot is to provide for others and set a good example."

"And rarely, very rarely, a golden thread, for the chieftain, the king, the hero..."

"The uncommon man."

"The exception."

"The great."

"But that was then, and this is now." Urd produced a videocassette. It gleamed brightly. It looked for all the world like an ordinary plastic-cased VHS tape that someone had spray-painted gold. I glimpsed my name scrawled on the stick-on strip on the side.

"This is yours, Gideon," she said. "This is you. Your past..." She handed the tape to Verdande.

"Your present," said Verdande, passing it on to Skuld.

"And your future," said Skuld, slotting it into the VCR.

The telly, like the fire, lacked a plug cable. Still it came on when Urd prodded the main button. Verdande manually selected a channel. Skuld pressed "Play" on the VCR. The machine's drive motor whined and churned.

"Sit back."

"Watch."

"It will be instructive."

Out of the corner of his mouth, Odin said, "I was afraid this might happen. Those who come to the Norns seeking knowledge must pay for it somehow. In your case, the cost is submission to a demonstration of their power. If you weren't a hero, or so unintimidated by them, they wouldn't feel the need to flaunt their superiority. The greater your destiny, the stronger your character, the more they must try to belittle you."

"With a video?" I muttered back. "A Blu-ray disc, a sixty-inch plasma display, now that would impress me. But *this*?"

"They have modernised."

"Hardly."

"Nonetheless, I urge you, don't watch. Or watch for as long as you can bear, but close your eyes and stop your ears when it becomes too much."

"It's pre-digital technology," I said. "There aren't even remote controls. I'm not worried."

The TV screen flickered into life. A wash of static. Then...

TWENTY-FIVE

THERE IS A baby.

He gurgles.

He has a teddy. A woollen Rupert the Bear his nan knitted for him. It doesn't look much like the actual Rupert the Bear, but it had the yellow checked scarf and crude red jumper.

He loves that teddy. He sucks one ear so hard, it eventually comes off. Nan sews it back on, and the teddy is never quite the same from then on, but he still loves it.

THERE IS A toddler.

He hates tinned rice pudding.

His mummy is feeding him some. He knows he is going to sick it up. He tries to tell her to stop spooning it into him because it's just going to come straight out again, all over her. He doesn't have the words. She doesn't stop. It does come out.

He never can stand rice pudding after that. Even the smell of it turns his stomach.

THERE IS A little boy.

He has a bike.

It is a BMX, a Mongoose Supergoose with chrome frame and bright red everything else. He rides it over the pavements and through the underpasses and across the railway bridges. His father bought it for him second-hand and it's not in the best of nick, but still, it is the coolest bike ever. Then some neighbours' kids steal it. He sees them riding it a few days later, popping wheelies and giving one another backsies. He goes up and challenges them. They punch him and tell him to f-word off. Then they set about smashing up the bike in front of him, in a slow, sadistically methodical manner.

He lies to his parents about his swollen lip, saying he tripped and fell over and did it on a kerb stone. Crying in bed that night, he vows to himself he will never be robbed from or bullied again.

THERE IS A pre-teen at primary school.

He is tall for his age.

But not as tall as Mick McCulloch. Mick McCulloch is bigger than anyone, and knows it, and uses it. Mick picks on everybody in his year, and the year below, and even the year above. One day Mick makes the mistake of picking on the boy. He tries to trip him up in the school dining hall so that he'll drop his tray and people will laugh. He succeeds.

The boy stands straight up and starts whacking Mick in the face with the empty tray. And when the tray breaks, he uses his fists. And he won't stop, no matter how much Mick whimpers and begs. In the end a member of the catering staff pulls him off, and Mick is left sobbing in pain, bleeding, humiliated. But it's the boy who gets the bad reputation there after. No one dares hassle him. Everyone is a little scared of him. Even the teachers.

THERE IS A teenager at secondary school.

He isn't doing well.

His parents are in the throes of getting divorced. It's ugly. The atmosphere at home is sour, like curdled milk. He is failing in his exams. He is having to go and see the headmistress in her office far too often and getting put on report and threatened with exclusion far too often. His teachers are at their wits' end. He is obviously not stupid. He just isn't bothering. And his behaviour is disruptive. The class comedian, he always has a smart answer ready, just not the right kind of smart.

He crashes and burns academically. Further education is not an option. Then the careers advisor suggests the armed forces.

THERE IS A cadet.

He likes being a cadet.

He takes to basic training as though it were made for him. He doesn't mind officers yelling orders at him all day long. He doesn't mind having to get out of bed at ridiculous hours, being made to go on full-kit runs for mile after slogging mile, the endless drilling, the live fire exercises, the sleep-depriving night manoeuvres, the petty breaches of conduct or dress code that earn absurdly disproportionate punishments, any of it.

He is away from home. He is being treated like an adult, like a person with value. He feels for the first time that he belongs somewhere.

THERE IS A private.

He experiences his first taste of real combat.

He is in former Yugoslavia, peacekeeping after the NATO bombardments, helping implement the Dayton Accord. His squad comes under fire from a band of Croat guerrillas in Turanj, a suburb of Karlovac. The contact doesn't last more than two minutes – a ferocious storm of being shot at, shooting back, everyone scurrying about yelling their heads off. Two minutes of pure, hellish chaos.

And yet, when it's over, he can't be more exhilarated. His heart is pounding. His entire body tingles as though electrified. He is alive. More than that, he *feels* alive.

THERE IS A young man.

He is on leave.

He is jogging around the perimeter of Clapham Common. A girl comes jogging the other way. She is short, brunette, cocky-cute, with a marvellous bum which he stares at over his shoulder while he runs on, until he collides with a park bench, nearly unmanning himself. He continues on his way – sore, limping – hoping to encounter the girl again on the far side of the common, but she isn't there.

So he plans it like a military operation. He goes jogging at the exact same time the next day, and the day after that, following the same anticlockwise circuit the girl took. At last the strategy pays off. There she is. He pulls up alongside her. He says hi. Several hundred yards and some precision-targeted flirting later, he's acquired two objectives. One: her name, which is fancy and French-sounding, although she was born in Basildon. Two: her telephone number.

THERE IS A man.

He is getting married.

He stands beside his bride at the civil ceremony in hired rooms above a pub. His head is still spinning and his tongue sandpaper-rough from the stag night to end all stag nights. The celebrant asks him to take this woman, Genevieve Amber d'Aulaire, as his lawful wedded wife and to pledge to share his life openly with her, promise to cherish and care for her, honour and support her, et cetera.

It isn't the hangover that makes him feel as though his legs are going to give way. It's nerves. He thought he knew what fear was, but not until this day, not truly, as he makes his vows before friends and family. Gen's smile keeps him going. She looks hopeful, honoured, happy as can be, and that is his anchor.

THERE IS AN expectant father.

He is by his wife's bedside in the maternity ward.

He is saying stuff as she screams, trying to comfort her, insisting that everything is going to be okay. The bones in his hand ache from the crushing grip she is exerting. Her birth agonies make his soul cringe. Why is the miracle of bringing new life into the world such prolonged bloody torment?

Then the baby is placed in his arms, swaddled in a soft white cotton blanket patterned with rabbits. A son. He has huge, watchful, impossibly careworn eyes. He is studying his father's face, scrutinising it, as if to ask, *Are you going to look after me?* All the new dad can do is promise that he will, even as his vision swims with joy and relief.

THERE IS A corporal.

He is being discharged.

He has acquitted himself well, his superiors say. He has been an exemplary soldier, a credit to his regiment. His record is unblemished. He has given impeccable service to queen and country.

Well, if I'm so fucking big-balls wonderful, he wants to say, *why are you kicking me out?* But of course he knows why. Half deaf, with several ounces of his brain gone and a tin plate stapled to his skull, he is no use to them any more. He is a rifle no one makes ammunition for, an outmoded tank, an Operational Ration Pack, General Purpose that has passed its use-by date. He is excess to requirements. He is military surplus.

THERE IS A prisoner.

He is serving out his sentence as meekly-mousily as he can.

He gets on with his cellmates, a fraudster and a rapist. The two of them don't much like each other but he plays the middle man and repeatedly defuses the tension between them. He is a dab hand at this, and they all have to remain on good terms, don't they? Cooped up together for hours on end, smelling one anothers' farts and BO, hearing the creak of one another's bedsprings as they wank themselves to sleep at night – they're in a confined space, under pressure, and the last thing anyone needs is a blazing row.

That skanky, red-eyed crackhead, though, he's a different story. The prize arsehole of B Wing. He keeps getting into everyone's faces. Aggression pulses off him. If you don't move out of his way, if you look at him funny, he can flare up, lash out. He doesn't care about himself. He just hates. It doesn't matter who you are, he hates you, although he has a penchant for the weak. Hates the weak most of all. He noses them out and goes for them, viciously. Somebody has to sort him. Somebody eventually does, and forfeits the chance of early parole because of it.

THERE IS AN ex-con.

He is an ex-husband.

He is on his way to becoming an ex-father too. He's barely allowed to see his son these days, only on very occasional, heavily supervised visits. His wife has taken up with another woman, and they are providing the stability and nurture the boy needs. Cody is happy living with Gen and Roz. It's far more secure and normal than before, when he was living with a father who drank too much, smoked too much weed, and came home time and again with a bruised face and bloodied knuckles and a sorry tale to tell.

For his own sake the ex-everything stays in touch with Cody, phoning, emailing, keeping tabs on his progress at school, remembering birthdays and such. For Cody's sake, however, he remains as hands-off as possible. The boy will do better if distanced from him. The less he sees of his train wreck of a dad, the less compromised his chances in life will be. Failure is contagious, although hopefully not genetic.

THERE IS A man named Gid Coxall.

He is travelling in a car with a friend named Abortion.

They are heading north through the worst whiteout conditions the UK has ever known. Gid has nodded off in the passenger seat. Abortion steals a sideways glance at him, then produces his battered old rolling tin, the one he bought in Belize City, with the oh-so-subtle cannabis leaf design on it. He thumbs open the lid and starts to –

"Stop!"

TWENTY-SIX

VERDANDE PAUSED THE tape.

On the TV, the image froze in that flickery VHS way, wavering between consecutive frames. Abortion's hand fluttered up and down, placing a pinch of weed into one of his Bible page skins, then removing it, over and over. Just as he'd told me, he was steering the car with his knees. Stupid arse wasn't even looking at the road, concentrating on his rolling instead.

I stared at the screen, feeling shock. Anger. Incomprehension. All these things at once, and a kind of nausea too.

My life. I'd been watching *my life* on videotape, as though it were a rented movie. Me from the age of nought, through childhood and adulthood, right up to nearly now. All of the significant scenes, the meaningful moments, the narrative jumping from one to the next with a brief stutter of static in between. As if a film crew had been following me, making a biopic of Gid Coxall, and these were the highlights, the best bits cut together for the trailer. Every shot tidily composed. The lighting always right, the angle appropriate, the camera positioned to capture mood and feel. Some director had been toiling for thirty-odd years on this. Some Spielberg, some Cameron

– no, I was flattering myself; some journeyman hack – had made it his life's goal to create *Gid: The Movie*. Without the star of the show even realising.

At the beginning I'd not understood what I was seeing. Then, as the truth dawned, I'd gone through denial, fuck-me-rigid astonishment, outrage, before finally settling on acute distress. I'd had enough. I couldn't bear to watch any more. Did I want to relive the car crash? See Abortion getting torn to pieces by those wolves again? No I damn well did not.

Verdande was smiling. All the Norns were smiling. Not nicely.

"Why stop here? We were just getting to the interesting part," Verdande said. "Urd has had her turn, with your past. We've reached my realm, the fulcrum, the present. Skuld comes next, and I'm sure she has many things to reveal to you. Many extraordinary things."

"Why would I want to know my future?" I said numbly. "Bad enough to have to go through all the old stuff again."

"Why would any man want to know his future?" replied Skuld. "Because he is curious. Because he wishes to find out where he is going and be assured that it's the right direction."

"Mortals perceive their lives moment by moment," Verdande said. "They do not realise the course they are on as they travel it. They do not see how each decision they make is a crossroads on a long, winding journey."

"Except perhaps in hindsight," said Urd. "But even then, looking back, they may be aware only of a maelstrom of circumstance. It appears as if there is no design, just coincidence, random events, whims and missteps that have brought them to where they are today."

"To know your future," said Skuld, "is to appreciate how fixed and unavoidable your destiny is."

"Is and has always been," said Urd. "You will gain a greater acceptance of your life so far. You will know that what strike you as mistakes have all, in fact, been integral to your becoming..."

"...who you are," said Verdande.

"And who you are meant to be," said Skuld.

"But, look," I said, "I'm really not interested in what's going to happen next. That's assuming you can even show me."

"Oh, we can," Verdande said.

"If we can show you everything we already have..." said Urd.

"Then we can show you everything to come," said Skuld. "How can you doubt that, given what you have just seen?"

And of course, I didn't doubt it. Not for a second. These three weren't messing around. They weren't bluffing. That tape wasn't over. There was more on it. A lot more. Or maybe *not* a lot more. Which was one of the reasons I didn't want to take it any further. Who would want to know how many years they'd got left? When they were going to die, and how? Nobody. Nobody in their right mind.

"I'm happy with the state of things as they stand," I said. "'One day at a time, sweet Jesus,' and all that. Live for the now. Tomorrow can take care of itself. That's my philosophy."

"You aren't the slightest bit intrigued to learn what lies in store?" said Skuld, with a witchy leer and a rub of her gnarled hands. I'd thought people only rubbed their hands in story books, but she did.

"Nope," I said firmly. "Call me boring, but that's the way it is."

"The dear little creature," said Verdande to her sisters. "He acts as though he has a choice."

Cue smug laughter.

"I do," I said. "I do have a choice. I can get up and walk out. You un-press Pause if you like, but I won't be sticking around to watch. I'll be gone. I'll be dust. You see if I won't."

"Very well. Let's put it to the test, shall we?" Verdande clicked the switch, and the image of Abortion at the steering wheel jerked back into motion.

I stood up.

Or thought I did.

I kept standing up. Turning round. Walking out.

But somehow I remained stuck fast to the settee. In my head I was making good my bid for freedom. My body had other plans. Paralysed.

The Astra veered off the road. It bumped over the snowy verge, punched through the wire fence, and careened out into space.

I shut my eyes. Screwed them up tight. I could at least manage that, even if I was powerless to move in every other respect. I heard Abortion's heartfelt cry of *"Shiiiiiiiiiiiiiiit!"* I heard the crashing-crunching-thumping-dinging of the car as it bounced down the hillside. I heard my own grunts and helpless little doglike yelps as the rolling impacts jarred my body. Finally I heard... nothing.

Nothing except an empty, airy hiss.

It went on for a long time. I felt someone tap my knee. Odin.

"Gid," he said. "You may look now."

I opened one eye. Peeked.

All that was on the TV was static. It sizzled, white and black, like a night-time blizzard. Clusters of photons jostling against clusters of darkness, never-endingly.

The Norns looked mighty pleased with themselves, like they'd just pulled off a monumental practical joke.

"That's it?" I said. "That's all? I have no future?"

"Or," said Skuld, "the rest is for you to decide. You are free. Your options are unlimited."

"But you said –"

"The path of the hero," Skuld cut in, "has more branches than even Yggdrasil. Anything and everything is yours for the choosing. There is no certain route, no sure outcome. There is only what is right and what is wrong, and you yourself must be the constant judge of that. That's what being a hero is: freedom of choice. Death or glory. Fight or flight. Honour or shame."

"Coke or Pepsi. Look – stop me if I've said this already – but I don't reckon I am a hero."

"The evidence suggests the contrary," said Verdande, with a wave at the TV.

"The tape would not have ended where it did," said Skuld, "were you of a lesser breed, with more mundane prospects. What appears to be formless chaos is, in fact, endless possibility. Infinite opportunity. You are a rare, fortunate man, Gid Coxall."

I turned to Odin. "Do I trust them?"

"They are the Norns," he answered with a shrug. "Whether to trust them or not isn't really an issue. You simply have to accept everything they say."

"The All-Father may not be all-knowing," said Urd, "but he offers good counsel."

"This isn't some kind of set-up?" I said, suspicious. "Some plan the four of you have concocted together to make me stay?"

The Norns played innocent and offended. Hands to throats. Elaborately shaken heads. Deep frowns.

Odin, for his part, seemed bemused by the whole notion. "I and the Norns, collude? I don't think so, Gid."

"But you keep telling me I'm a hero. Are you trying to, how shall I put this? Seduce me, Mrs Robinson?"

"Aren't you staying?" Odin said. "Aren't you willing to fight on the Aesir's behalf? You appear to be. More so, certainly, than a couple of days ago. Thor's convinced you'll be a terrific asset. He told me you're positively bloodthirsty. You know no restraint."

"I... I've not signed on any dotted line yet."

"But you'd like to."

That solitary eye of his bored into me. I felt like an open book.

"I might," I said. "Maybe if I knew what we're going up against... I mean, that is why you brought me here to the Norns' lovely *Hello!* magazine spread mansion, isn't it? To clue me in on who the enemy is."

"And you have earned the right to be told," said Urd. She had another videocassette in her hands. A bog-standard black one this time, which she slipped out from a sleeve bearing the Sony logo.

Verdande ejected my gold tape and slotted the new one in.

Skuld said, "This was recorded just days ago."

"What, off the telly? It isn't somebody else's life story then?"

"A broadcast from one of the commercial terrestrial stations," said Urd.

"An episode of a popular documentary series," said Verdande.

"We've trimmed it down to the relevant portions," said Skuld.

I was baffled. They'd just shown me *me*, some kind of magical filmic compilation of events taken from my life, *Gid's Greatest Hits*

– and now we were about to watch an edited version of a programme off ITV or Channel 4? The contrast was almost surreal.

What the hell. Might as well play couch potato for a bit.

I leaned back, folding my arms behind my head and stretching out my legs.

"Don't suppose anybody's got any popcorn?" I said.

TWENTY-SEVEN

Transcribed excerpts from *Makepeace Meets... President Keener*

MAKEPEACE: [*in studio, to camera*] Good evening. I'm Peter Makepeace, and tonight on *Makepeace Meets...* we have a rare exclusive. For the past three weeks we've been granted continuous, unrestricted access to the subject of this episode. We've been following her every step, filming her while she handles her punishing workload, catching her on off-guard moments, interviewing her candidly one-to-one on several occasions, and also seeing her at home as she juggles the challenges of the most important and difficult job in the world with the arguably no less demanding role of wife and mother. She's a controversial figure, to put it mildly, much loved in her homeland, less so abroad, outspoken, gutsy, not afraid to stand up for what she believes in, intolerant of dissent, a strong advocate of libertarianism and individual responsibility who also implements draconian laws and espouses a hawkish foreign policy. There hasn't been a stateswoman of international standing to match her since Margaret Thatcher. She is, of course, the first female President of the United States, President Keener.

AUDIO DESCRIPTION COMMENTARY: There is a sequence of shots. We see President Keener going over papers in the Oval Office – climbing aboard *Air Force One* – meeting a delegation of African heads of state – listening attentively while her daughter practises the violin.

MAKEPEACE: Who is this woman who came from nowhere to seize the most powerful political post on the planet? How do her strong Christian principles influence and inform her decision-making? Why is America so in thrall to her that it has elected her twice, both times by a landslide? And what are her hopes and plans for the future? Over the next hour we are, I believe, going to answer those questions through our unrivalled fly-on-the-wall coverage of the day-to-day dealings of the USA's First Lady. This is *Makepeace Meets... President Keener*. Keep watching.

AUDIO DESCRIPTION COMMENTARY: Peter and the president are strolling across a snow-covered White House lawn. They are well-wrapped-up against the weather. She has her arm linked through his.

MRS KEENER: People claim I play up my Georgia roots, Pete. Some of the civil liberties groups say I shouldn't be so darn proud of where I come from. The South has a history, as you may be aware, not that charming a one. But, what, I'm supposed to be ashamed 'cause of stuff my forebears did? Ain't there a statute of limitations on that kinda thing?

AUDIO DESCRIPTION COMMENTARY: She continues over a montage of scenes of her hometown. Caption: "Wonder Springs, Georgia." We see a leafy street lined with antebellum houses – the sign outside a Baptist church – white and African-American children playing together in a schoolyard – an elderly couple in a swing chair on a front porch – customers in a diner eating pancakes – a pick-up truck driving down a lonely dirt road.

MRS KEENER: What happened back then happened. I can't change it. But if I open my mouth and all some folks hear is the voice of a segregationist or even, God forbid, a slave owner – well, I tell you, the problem ain't with me, it's with them. There's an urban intellectual elite in this country that'd like to think anyplace below the Mason-Dixon line is an embarrassment, an irrelevance, not the real America. But Pete, I beg to differ. They can't dismiss so many millions of Americans just like that. *They're* the minority. I believe I represent the honest, hard-working, dollar-earning, tax-paying majority. We're the ones who count, not them bow-tied, buttoned-up so-called smart guys in the college towns and the Manhattan high-rises. All they do is chatter and bellyache. The rest of us get out there and actually achieve.

MAKEPEACE: You're just a local girl who got extraordinarily lucky? Who was in the right place at the right time?

MRS KEENER: Pete, that's precisely it! I'm nothing special. How I got to where I am today is simple. I *am* the people who voted me in. I'm them, and they recognise that. I'm not some overeducated lawyer or some Harvard Business School type. I'm not someone who's spent her entire life in politics and knows nothing else. I speak the same language as most Americans speak. I may not have a pretty turn of phrase or use a bunch of fancy two-bit words, but what I am is someone who says what the average American says and thinks what the average American thinks.

MAKEPEACE: The people's president.

MRS KEENER: You said it.

MAKEPEACE: What about when someone calls you a redneck, Mrs Keener? I'm thinking of a recent *New York Times* editorial. What do you say to them?

MRS KEENER: What I say to them is there ain't nothing wrong with a bit of sunburn, if it means you've been outdoors working hard.

'Course, these days, we're lucky to see any sun at all, ain't we?

AUDIO DESCRIPTION COMMENTARY: The president is being given a guided tour of a munitions factory by its CEO and other executives. Caption: "Murdstone Dynamics Engineering Plant, Outside Louisville, Kentucky." Workers on a sheet-metal production line smile as she greets them.

MRS KEENER: You guys are doing such a great job here. Our forces on the frontline have every reason to be grateful to you.

AUDIO DESCRIPTION COMMENTARY: Mrs Keener breaks away from the group of executives to talk directly to one woman in coveralls and protective goggles.

MRS KEENER: Hey there. How're you doing?

WORKER: Can I just say, Lois – oh, may I call you Lois?

MRS KEENER: Of course you may. Your name badge says Darlene. May I call you that?

WORKER: I'd be honoured. Can I just say, Lois, we at Murdstone should be thanking *you*, not the other way round. You've given us so much work. Our jobs are secure. I can go home each night knowing I'm putting food on the table and a roof over my family's head, and I don't have to worry about defence budget cuts and factory closures and being made redundant, which I did with the previous president. You have no idea how much that means.

MRS KEENER: If it means a lot to you, it means a lot to me. No, don't cry, Darlene. You're gonna set me off too. Oh, there, see? You have. Come on, gimme a hug. There you go.

MAKEPEACE: [*voiceover*] It can't be denied she has the common touch, and I don't think it's just for show. She seems genuinely moved by her reception on the factory floor, and I can't think of another politician who would spontaneously and openly hug a person they'd just met like that, and share a tear with them. It's a remarkable sight. Truly unique.

MRS KEENER: I promise y'all are going to continue to have plenty to keep you busy. Here and at its other plants across the land Murdstone Dynamics has been working on a number of special projects for the Pentagon, which are currently being tested out west in places like Wright Patterson and China Lake and are almost ready to go. Some of you are probably manufacturing ordnance and spare parts for those right now. Keep it up. America's safety, and the safety of the free world, depends on you.

MAKEPEACE: Ted, not a dumb question I hope, but what's it like being the First Husband?

TED KEENER: I won't lie to you, Pete, took some getting used to, to begin with. At first I was thinking, "I can't do this." I had to give up my chain of car dealerships. I had to say goodbye to all my bass-fishing buddies and head off to DC, where I knew nobody. I was a mite anxious. How am I supposed to fill my time? What's the president's consort actually meant to do? But there's plenty here to be getting on with. Bryan and Carol Ann have become my priority. I look after them while Mom's off doing president stuff. Take 'em to school, fetch 'em back. Make sure they're eating right. It's a full-time job! Bryan's off to college in the fall, so maybe my life will get easier then, but I wouldn't bet on it.

MAKEPEACE: Does your wife find it hard finding time for you, with her schedule?

TED KEENER: Her schedule. Her *crazy* schedule. Well, we make time for each other. We have to so we just do. I'll admit I don't see as much of her as I once did, and that's a crying shame. But it ain't a surprise, considering. And it ain't for ever, neither. Three more years, and then she's out. So I can bear it. Grin and bear it.

MAKEPEACE: Would you say the job has changed her? Is she still the Lois you used to know? The woman you courted and married?

AUDIO DESCRIPTION COMMENTARY: Ted Keener spends a while pondering this, gazing out of the window.

TED KEENER: Well, sir, there ain't a simple "yes" or "no" answer to that. The Lord came to her, and that's gonna leave a mark on a person, you know what I'm saying? There's been distinctively two Loises in my life – the Lois she was before her vision and the Lois after. She's a more focused, more passionate woman since then. The old Lois wouldn't have recognised the drive the new Lois has. Sometimes I look at her and I think to myself, who is this lady? It's like I've had to discover, no, *re*discover...

AUDIO DESCRIPTION COMMENTARY: He gazes out of the window again.

TED KEENER: I don't feel like I've lost something, if that's what you're getting at.

MAKEPEACE: "More passionate." In her book she says you two have a hotter love life than ever before.

TED KEENER: Oh, now, sir, you're going to make me blush!

MRS KEENER: We have something in this country, I don't know if you've heard of it, Pete, but it's called *Manifest Destiny*. It's the belief that America ain't just the greatest country in the world, but that we Americans have a moral obligation to bring our way of life to every corner of the planet. It's what lay behind our forefathers' urge to push west during frontier times, hauling civilisation with them in their covered wagons, and it's been a cornerstone of our domestic and foreign policy ever since. All the great presidents have believed in it – Lincoln, Wilson, Reagan. Manifest Destiny. This nation has been chosen by God to be the pinnacle of all nations, the standard bearer for democracy, the greatest force for good the world has ever known...

MAKEPEACE: And that's the justification for all the military invasions you've instigated during your tenure as Commander in Chief.

MRS KEENER: You say invasions, I say interventions. *Tomayto, tomahto.* Yes, I've been sending our GIs into global trouble spots, and you know for why? 'Cause it needed to be done. Take North Korea. She was becoming a royal pain in the sit-upon, and our friends the Japanese were getting more and more alarmed by her behaviour, with good reason. So I bit the bullet and sent the boys in. Wasn't an easy decision, nor an easy victory neither, but it had to be done, and now there've been democratic elections just this year, the DMZ between North and South Korea is no longer a minefield, and we have a brand new ally in the Pacific Rim. Same goes for Taiwan. The islanders were kinda concerned about a certain neighbour of theirs across the Taiwan Strait wanting to bring them forcibly into the fold, as it were, but we've taken over the place and fortified it and shown that neighbour we mean business, and sure, there was some grumbling about that, but now everyone's pals again and we have one of the economic powerhouses of the Far East onside.

MAKEPEACE: That's quite some euphemism for threats of all-out war – "grumbling."

MRS KEENER: Grumbling, is all. There wasn't nothing going to come of it.

MAKEPEACE: How about the Ukraine? That was a, for want of a better phrase, bold gamble on your part.

MRS KEENER: Daring, I'd call it, but it paid off. There was a move there to go back to communist rule. Most Ukrainers didn't want that. We helped 'em resist the political pressure.

MAKEPEACE: By bombing Kiev.

MRS KEENER: Worked, didn't it?

MAKEPEACE: Cuba?

MRS KEENER: Just helping along an inevitable process. The regime there was on its last legs. Like a racehorse that couldn't run no more, it needed putting out of its misery. So we did that, and now Cubans are happier and better off they ever were, and what's more, any American can spark up a nice fat Havana cigar these days without guilt or shame.

MAKEPEACE: Beirut? Jordan? Equatorial Guinea? Kashmir? The Basque region?

MRS KEENER: What's your point here, darling? What are you trying to say?

MAKEPEACE: Nothing. I'm just listing all the sovereign nations which have been exposed to the Keener brand of, er, intervention in the past few years. It's quite a lengthy list. In fact, there hasn't been a single day since you took office when US military personnel haven't been engaged in active service somewhere or other in the world.

MRS KEENER: You say that like it's a bad thing. I know a number of five-star generals who'd think different. What's a standing army for anyway if it ain't for mobilising and deploying? It sure ain't there just to *stand*. Manifest Destiny, Pete. Manifest Destiny. It's like in my home. If I see some dirt somewhere, why, I'm gonna fetch my broom and sweep it away. It's called doing your domestic duty.

MAKEPEACE: I suppose one might reasonably ask, where's next? Who's Mrs Keener got lined up in her sights next? Have you spotted another patch of dirt that needs attending to?

MRS KEENER: Your country, of course. The motherland, the guys we kicked into touch back in 1776, the good old UK. I'm visiting next month, ain't I? And your Prime Minister Clasen has been pretty blunt about his dislike for me and what I get up to. He's forever running to the UN and griping about me like the preppy little schoolkid that he is. Maybe I'll use my state visit to Britain next month as an opportunity to launch regime change there. Clasen ain't so popular, is he? He's been trying to handle y'all's discontent over food shortages and the high mortality rate among the elderly and the hospitals not coping and the trains not running and all of that, and he ain't been making that great a job of it. I've heard his approval ratings are abysmal, like, the worst ever. Maybe I should come along and bump his sorry backside out of Downing Street. What do you think to that?

MAKEPEACE: [*voiceover*] She's joking. At least, I like to think she is. It's apparent that my line of questioning has irritated her. She told my producer originally that no questions would be off-limits, but I seem to have overstepped an unspoken boundary. Some sort of mollifying gesture is in order.

MAKEPEACE: I spoke to Ted earlier today. He told me he's looking forward to "date night" tonight.

MRS KEENER: Oh, that Ted! I tell you, we're like two teenagers sometimes, courting all over again.

MAKEPEACE: I get the impression he thinks you've changed.

MRS KEENER: For the better, I trust.

MAKEPEACE: He used the word "rediscover." In this context, what does that...? I'm not sure if I...

MRS KEENER: That's what I meant – two teenagers courting. Perhaps what he was saying is he feels he doesn't know me quite so well any more, on account of I'm so goshdarn busy all of the time. Just makes it all the more fun getting reacquainted, though, doesn't it?

MAKEPEACE: [*voiceover*] We're in *Marine One*, flying over the Potomac river to the Pentagon. The president is off to one of her regular meetings with the Joint Chiefs of Staff. I don't know if we're going to be allowed much further than the Pentagon heliport, but I'm going to try my best.

AUDIO DESCRIPTION COMMENTARY: *Marine One* sets down in front of the Pentagon.

MAKEPEACE: [*voiceover*] These weekly get-togethers are one of Mrs Keener's own innovations. Such is the intensity and frequency of American military operations overseas that they've become almost a necessity.

AUDIO DESCRIPTION COMMENTARY: President Keener exits the helicopter with her aides, heading towards a waiting limousine. Peter gets out too. Security men block the way, preventing him and the film crew from following the president into the limo.

MAKEPEACE: [*shouting above the helicopter engine noise*] That's as far as we get, apparently. It seems there are, after all, certain areas of the president's political life we're not going to be privy to. So... off she goes in that big black armour-plated car, to a room where the fate of American troops, and possibly of civilians of a foreign nation, is about to be decided. Like anyone else, all we can do is stand on the sidelines and wait.

MAKEPEACE: Bryan, Carol Ann, what would you say your mother's strongest attributes were?

BRYAN KEENER: She's a great mom and everything. I really, like, admire her. She's a role model. She doesn't take no BS from anybody.

CAROL ANN KEENER: Bryan, you can't say BS on television.

BRYAN KEENER: Yeah, you can. British television is like, they don't care. You can say BS, you just can't say bullshit.

AUDIO DESCRIPTION COMMENTARY: Bryan claps a hand over his mouth.

CAROL ANN KEENER: [*giggling*] Oh my Lord, Mom's gonna kill you. You said a cuss word.

BRYAN KEENER: It wasn't that bad of a cuss word. She won't get mad, will she? Will she? Not too mad. You won't show that bit, huh, Mr Makepeace?

MAKEPEACE: Does your mother get cross easily?

CAROL ANN KEENER: She's got kinda a temper, sometimes. Shouts a bit. 'Specially after she took this job. It's 'cause she's so stressed out and everything. She didn't use to be like that, before. Used to be much gentler with us.

BRYAN KEENER: But she never shouts 'less we deserve it. And she's got high standards, you know what I'm saying? For herself as much as for us. You promise you won't show that bit?

MAKEPEACE: I can't not ask. The big red button. How does it feel to have your finger on that? How does it feel to know that the power to destroy the world is in your hands? It must be – I don't know if exciting is the best way to describe it – exhilarating? Or terrifying?

MRS KEENER: It's a solemn responsibility that I take seriously, very seriously indeed. There ain't a day goes by that I don't wonder, am I going to have to make that decision today? Am I going to have to make that judgement call?

MAKEPEACE: That Judgement Day call, ha ha.

MRS KEENER: Ha ha, trying to trip me up there, ain't you, Pete? In that sneaky, snide English way of yours.

MAKEPEACE: No. No, I –

MRS KEENER: Maybe get me to admit I'm one of them religious fundamentalists, one of them, whatchemacall, End Timers, believing we're in the Last Days and Armageddon's waiting just around the corner.

MAKEPEACE: No, it was just a pun, a turn of –

MRS KEENER: It'd make for a good headline, huh? "Holy Wackjob Has Finger On Nukular Trigger." But you've got me wrong. I don't want to see the world end, Pete. Not that way. In a big ball of fire? That'd be just plain wrong.

MAKEPEACE: Do you think the world *is* ending? I mean, as we're on the subject. These snowfalls, the low temperatures, three years of almost constant winter... There are some who would say civilisation is teetering on the brink. We can't withstand many more years of this. We won't be able to maintain a stable society if the situation continues.

MRS KEENER: Pish and poppycock! Things'll pick up. They surely have to.

MAKEPEACE: And if they don't? Your critics have said you're being remarkably casual about what has the potential to be total environmental cataclysm. You haven't instituted a single policy to tackle it or even investigate the cause.

MRS KEENER: We know the cause. Volcanoes. What're we gonna do? Stop 'em all up with giant corks? Heck, maybe I *should* explode a few atomic bombs. Maybe that'd help melt all the snow away. Joshing, Pete, just joshing. The look on your face!

MAKEPEACE: But have you –

MRS KEENER: Let me say something, Mr Documentary Maker Man, just so's the viewers back home in the UK don't get the wrong idea. I've made plans to deal with what's going on. Contingency measures are in place. Things have been trialled which need to be trialled, and no, I'm not gonna tell you what I mean by that, 'cause it's top secret. If there's anyone out there doubts I have the grit or gumption to go through with my intentions – when appropriate – let them be under no illusion. I do. I very much do. Where's that camera? See my face. Look into my eyes. I am not to be rejected or ignored or trifled with. I am not the type to take any kinda challenge or insult lying down. I am here to respond to things as best I see fit, and you would do well not to underestimate my depth of feeling or my determination to act in the name of what I consider is right. Is that clear?

MAKEPEACE: [*voiceover*] As firm a reiteration of Lois Keener's presidential credo as there's ever been. And perhaps a hint as to her attraction to ordinary middle-class American voters. That forthrightness. That plain speaking. Although I can't help feeling she's strayed somewhat off-topic. When did the bad weather become an adversary needing to be faced down? I can't follow the logic.

MAKEPEACE: [*in studio, to camera*] So, what have I learned during my time with the president? She is not someone to be crossed lightly, yet she retains an essential charisma. She has a rigorous command of the facts of any given situation, yet she also relies heavily on her instincts, and her faith. She is fearsome and fearless. She is a woman who has undergone a profound spiritual metamorphosis, one that has taken her from smalltown Georgia anonymity and propelled her into the driving seat of Earth's last true superpower. There is steel beneath that courteous feminine exterior, yet warmth as well. She is a president of contrasts. Her true nature is elusive, slippery, tricky. Perhaps only she knows her own mind fully, she and one other, the God to whom she has dedicated herself wholeheartedly, believing implicitly in His plan, His mission for her, relying on His guidance. I've come away from making this documentary with a profound respect for Mrs Keener, coupled with a nagging unease. It's as if, for all that she's beguiled me, there's a part of me that recoils from that. The only way I can describe it is like being hypnotised by a cobra – the allure of something beautiful but dangerous. I'm hoping that her imminent visit to Britain will be as anodyne and uneventful as such state occasions normally are. And the very fact that I'm hoping that at all unnerves me. I'm Peter Makepeace. This has been *Makepeace Meets...* Thank you for watching, and goodnight.

TWENTY-EIGHT

THE TAPE ENDED. Skuld snapped the television off.

For a time no one said anything, so I felt pressure to break the silence.

"She's a foxy lady and no mistake," I said. "Not sure she's completely all there, up top." I tapped my temple. "But that's not necessarily a drawback. The more screws a girl has loose, the looser a screw she is."

Odin and the Norns just looked at me.

"What? I grant you, not the most PC remark ever made, but..."

Still looking at me.

"*What*? Am I missing something here? I am, aren't I? I thought I was going to find out who your Big Bad is, and then all you do is show me a programme about..."

Gid Coxall, king of the slowly dropping pennies.

"Oh no. You are kidding."

Their faces.

"You're not kidding."

I recalled the book Odin had lent me while I was recuperating from the accident.

"When you gave me her autobiography," I said to him, "I thought it was just... Well, at first I thought you must be a fan of hers. Admired her politics. I was halfway to thinking the Valhalla Mission was some kind of neo-Nazi outfit, and you approved of her views on gays and abortion rights and the rest. And then I thought, maybe not. Maybe you oppose her because she's big government. She's The Man. That was before I got the whole Norse gods thing clear, of course. But if you're against her, if she's the enemy... It is her, isn't it? You haven't got anything against Peter Makepeace? Because he's smarmy, yes, a bit of a prick and a know-all, but that's not a reason to set up an army. I mean, there are plenty of other TV personalities I can think of that deserve merciless hounding and execution. Simon Cowell and Piers Morgan spring to mind. Nothing wrong with those two that couldn't be solved with a Claymore mine down the underpants. But not Makepeace."

"It isn't him," Odin said.

"So – Keener. Christ. Shit. You really... Mrs Keener. You want to eliminate the President of the United States. The most powerful human being on the planet. Well, good luck with that."

"Don't you want to know why she's our foe?"

"No, Odin, I do not. What I want is not to know anything about any of this, not any more. Fuck, you nearly had me. I was thinking, 'Join the Norse gods on some military campaign? That could be cool.' But all you're after is assassinating President Keener. Bit tawdry, isn't it? And when's this going to happen? Her state visit, I suppose. You're going to bundle in with all your troops while she's on a tour of the Houses of Parliament or Buckingham Palace or wherever, take out her secret service detail, then take *her* out – and all because she's a warmonger, right? Forgive me, but that's not exactly very godly of you, is it? Or is it? Is that what gods do when they're at a loose end? Get in there amongst the mortals and create havoc? Throw their divine weight around, because they can?"

"Gid, you're coming at this from entirely the wrong angle," Odin said.

"Mortal," said Urd dismissively. Like someone else might have said *simpleton* or *moron*.

"Only seeing the superficial details," Verdande agreed.

"The broader picture eludes him," said Skuld.

I blanked them. Smug fucking bitches. "If you hate her so much," I said to Odin, "by all means feel free to. She's hardly my favourite politician, although her being a hot babe does take the edge off her for me. But what we Midgarders do in these situations is we try to vote the person out of office if we don't like them, or we go out on the streets and protest against them, or else we ignore them because if you do that long enough, eventually they go away. We don't just kill them. All right, sometimes we do. But not often, and only the real scumbags, the Ceauşescus, the Saddams, the tyrants, the ones who wouldn't know a free and fair election if it came up and bit them on the ballot box. And also – America. Come on. You don't launch an attack on the leader of fucking *America*. That's inviting a complete deluge of shit to come down on your heads. Gods or not, the USA is one nation whose bad books you truly do not want to get into."

I paused for breath.

"Finished?" Odin said.

"Only getting started, mate."

"I ask because you haven't let me put forward my side of things."

"You haven't got a side to put forward. At least, not one I'm willing to hear."

"Please just give me a minute to explain."

"Explain what? That you're trying to get Britain into deep shit with the States? Because, mark my words, you manage to bump off Mrs Keener and this country's going to take the blame. Clasen'll tell the Yanks we had nothing to do with it, but with his track record of complaining about her they won't believe a word, and the fucking cruise missiles will be raining down before you can even sneeze. And that's if we're lucky. I wouldn't put it past them to drop daisy cutters or even go nuclear. They'd be that narked."

"What if I told you Mrs Keener is the one who wants to destroy *us*, not the other way round?"

"That's pretty far-fetched. How's she even know you exist? There's only one god as far as she's concerned, the big daddy of them all, Jehovah. You lot are a pagan aberration. You're not real to her. That'd be like saying she wants to get rid of unicorns. Or dinosaurs, which she doesn't believe in either." It said so in her book. Dinosaurs were a lie invented by evolutionary scientists to prove that life on Earth had developed over millions of years when, as any sensible Creationist knew, the universe had been put together by God in just under a week. Must have come in kit form. Probably from Ikea.

"Unless," I went on slowly, "she does know you exist and wants to wipe you out precisely because you're non-Christian. Fuck. Is that it? Her game's heathen god genocide? The Man Upstairs has told her to do that for Him?"

Odin shook his grey head. "Would that it were that simple."

"But it doesn't bother her too much, attacking other countries. So why not pantheons as well? Your lot, the Greek ones, the Egyptian ones – I'm assuming they're all still around too."

"Not to my knowledge. As I told you before, I don't consort with deities from other faiths. I have no evidence to believe they were ever out there. Perhaps we are all isolated from one another in such a way that we can never meet. Perhaps, by cosmic design, every pantheon is an island, known only to itself and its worshippers. Every monotheist god too. This is not germane, anyway. Mrs Keener is not aggrieved with us on religious grounds, you have my assurance on that. Her hatred stems from a much closer, more personal source."

"He still hasn't fathomed it," Urd hissed to her sisters, with a nod at me.

"But he knows enough to make the connection," said Verdande.

"He is just about to," said Skuld. "It is due."

"Mrs Keener is holding a grudge against the Norse gods," I said. I was beginning to grasp the shape of something – a realisation that was immense and profound. The clues were all there. Principally I was remembering the tale Paddy had told while we were waiting for *Sleipnir* to arrive, and what Thor had said afterwards. Somehow I knew that was where the answer lay.

President Keener. Mrs Keener. Lois Keener.

Ping. Lightbulb popping on.

Oh no. No fucking way.

It couldn't be that straightforward, could it? That completely stupidly glaringly obvious?

I was about to speak again. Then there came an urgent rapping at the front door.

TWENTY-NINE

Urd went to answer it. I heard a woman's voice asking for Odin. We all went out into the hallway to see who it was. Skadi, the little skier goddess. She was on the porch, with her skis still on and her face flushed. She'd just hurried here from somewhere, *langlauf*ing straight up the Norns' garden path, ploughing ski tracks over Odin's and my footprints.

"Odin," she blurted out. "All-Father. I bear news from Heimdall. He has heard the distant advance of enemy troops. Artillery, he thinks, though he cannot identify of what kind. They approach from due west. Come quickly. We must gather our forces. Asgard is under threat."

Instead of answering, Odin merely closed his eye. I thought he was trying to pretend he hadn't heard what Skadi had said, or else was giving in to a moment of despair. Then he murmured, "Huginn, Muninn," and I realised he was communing with his ravens.

"Fly high, my faraway eyes," he said. "Higher, higher still. Soar to the apex of the heavens, where all stands revealed. Show me what you see."

He stood there for several minutes, turning his head this way and that as if scanning horizons, although his eye remained shut fast.

His body swayed slightly, buffeted by winds none of the rest of us could feel. Then, at last, the eye snapped open.

"Nothing," he said.

"You mean Heimdall's wrong?" I said.

"No, no. If Heimdall has heard something, then Heimdall has heard something. And on Asgard's western boundary lies dim grey Niflheim, the world of mists. Of all the Nine Worlds, the only one I cannot see into, the only one opaque to my gaze. Which, naturally, makes it an ideal location from which to mount an incursion."

"Who's attacking? Who lives in Niflheim?"

"It is the realm of Hel, loathesome goddess of the dead. But, though she and I are hardly allies, to launch an assault like this is not her way."

"So then it's *her*."

"Her forces, yes, I believe so."

"Or rather – his."

"His," Odin agreed.

"Your blood brother. The one you banished. The one who can change his shape to become anything he likes."

"That one. I will not say his name. I cannot bring myself to."

"Loki," I said.

Loki. Lois Keener. The first syllable of each of her names, like some awful crossword clue. Loki, waving his true identity under everyone's noses, knowing that nobody would catch on except those he wanted to.

"But," I said, "isn't he chained in a cave having snake venom dripped into his eyes?"

"No punishment is everlasting, nor any prison impossible to break out of. Not to a god, and especially not to one as guileful and elusive as him. He has been free for several years. He returned to Asgard immediately after his escape, but we gave him very short shrift and sent him packing. Thereafter he went to Midgard, where he has been ever since, at large, working his wiles and gaining himself a substantial earthly power base."

"Odin..." said Skadi impatiently.

"And now he's back, he's mad, and he's out for revenge," I said.

"Indeed," said Odin.

"In other words, he's a divine Steven Seagal. In drag."

"All-Father, I beg you," said Skadi. "The men are being rallied, but we need your leadership."

"Yes, yes, Skadi. I'm coming." Odin turned back to me. "So now you know what we're up against, Gid. Our enemy has marshalled the might of the most powerful nation on Earth. He has their armies and technology at his disposal. I believe he has been instrumental in devising new armaments designed specifically to combat us. You've seen the documentary. Seen how he has been pumping money into weapons research and development, to the detriment of the US economy as a whole. Seen how he has been sating his generals' lust for conflict in order to curry their favour and earn himself an unlimited say in their affairs. He has America's military-industrial complex eating out of his hand, and they've responded by innovating and manufacturing as never before, with his full connivance. Now is the time to throw in your lot with us and take up arms against the footsoldiers of the god of lies and deceit, if such is your wish."

"Lies and deceit. You really don't like the bloke, do you?"

"Nor he me," said Odin. "And his reasons for hating me are probably no less valid than mine are for hating him. Our feelings of antipathy are truly matched and mutual. His role was to commit the crime, mine to dictate the penalty, and he has resented me for it ever after. And we are seeing the first stone cast. The first battle of our war, long brewing. The first, I suspect, of many. Again, Gid – are you with us?"

"We're taking on the United States army." I was stalling for time, trying to work out which way I was going to jump on this one. "They have the latest weaponry, and by the sound of it some advanced, cutting-edge stuff as well. We're just a small bunch of has-been soldiers with conventional arms."

"I have done my best, given my limited means. And you have gods beside you, don't forget. The cream of Asgard and Vanaheim, famed for their prowess on the battlefield."

"But we're still going to be outgunned, outnumbered, out-everythinged."

"So?"

"Hopeless odds."

"So?"

"Its suicide."

Skadi was hopping from foot to foot, waving one of her ski sticks agitatedly.

"That's as may be," said Odin. "But the stakes are much higher than mere lives. Our enemy's wrath is such that, unchecked, it may shatter the Nine Worlds. Do you understand what I am saying? Thanks to him, all is imperilled. Not just Asgard and the Aesir. All. Including Midgard. Including your loved ones."

"My – ?"

"There's no time to go into the full story now. But you have to believe me, Gid. If my erstwhile blood brother is not stopped, it could spell universal doom."

"Oh," I said.

Cody.

"Well," I said.

My little boy.

"If it's universal doom that we've got to watch out for..." I said, and said no more.

Endless possibility, the Norns had told me. *Infinite opportunity*. I'd made my choice.

And the black rage inside me wasn't at all displeased.

THIRTY

WE WERE POSITIONED on high ground, overlooking a plain. About a hundred of us mortal troops, half the total of Odin's forces, plus a handful of Aesir and Vanir. Brought out in two batches aboard *Sleipnir* and now parcelled out along the curving ridge of a bluff, some of us still catching our breath from tabbing hard from the drop point. I was with Cy, Paddy, Chopsticks, Baz and Backdoor. I'd fallen in with the five of them en route, bumping shoulders with them in the Wokka's cargo bay. There was us together on the bluff and a handful of others, all under the command of Thor. This, I could tell, was now my squad. The team I belonged to. These things had a way of just clicking, of their own accord.

Facing us was one of the intersections between the Nine Worlds, the corridors where one world met and overlapped with another. Down below our positions there was nothing except a snowfield stretching westward, its far edge lost in a curtain of fog. The fog hung in an almost perfect straight line, as though held back by something you couldn't see, contained by a wall of glass. It hazed the setting sun, paling the scarlet disc to pink. It was utterly still. Not a breath of wind, not a hint of turbulence in its white depths.

Up to the fog bank was Asgardian turf. Beyond lay Niflheim.

"Where are they?" I murmured, mostly to myself. "Where the fuck are they?"

"They wait," said Thor. "They are well hidden. They wish us to grow uneasy and restless, so they wait. When they have waited long enough, they will emerge. Control of the battlefield is any army's priority, and that starts with control of the timing of battle. They know we would not dare venture into the mist, so the upper hand is theirs – the leisure to decide when to commence the attack."

"And in the meantime we lie here with our ball sacks turning to icepacks."

"Would you rather go down there into that impenetrable mist, where you can't even see the hand in front of your face, and try to root them out? I think not."

He had a point. Not that I wasn't tempted. I didn't much enjoy hanging around twiddling my thumbs before a contact. I wanted to get in there, mix things up. The black rage inside me wanted that too. This was what it lived for: moments of bloodshed and personal danger. What it craved, like a vampire craved blood or a zombie craved flesh. I was an addict, that was what it came down to. Violence was my drug, and for too long I'd gone without. It had been cold turkey for me ever since I left prison. I'd been straight for two years – straight and miserable. But I was well off the wagon now, and all the happier and healthier for it.

I glanced across at Cy, his eyes met mine, and I saw it in him too. Paddy likewise, and Baz. All of them. The same eagerness, the same unquenchable thirst. We feared it so much, yet at the same time needed it. We could die today. This could be our final few minutes, our last hurrah. We were shit-scared, skating along the edge of the screaming abdabs, and loving it.

Baz had the walkie-talkie for our unit, and now it squawked in his hand.

"This is Odin, to all."

"Here we go," I said. "Big pre-match pep talk from the coach."

"Hush!" snapped Thor. "My father speaks."

"Our foe's desire is to unsettle us," Odin said over the airwaves.

"Stand firm. It will not be long. Night is falling fast, and they will not want to fight in the dark. We have but minutes to go before battle is joined. Today is the culmination of all your work hitherto, your training, your dedication. The enemy intends to essay our strengths and vulnerabilities. Let us demonstrate our abundance of the former and absence of the latter. They have made this move earlier than anticipated, in hopes of catching us unawares, unprepared. Do not worry. We are ready."

The sun kept sinking, getting fainter and fainter, dusk deepening around it. Evening, and I'd had no lunch, and breakfast had been measly. I should have felt famished, but fear quelled the pangs. What a day it had been. What a twenty-four hours. From frost giants to trolls to the Norns to Mrs Keener – talk about having your world turned upside down.

"Any clue what's lurking out there?" I asked Baz.

He shrugged. "Intel hasn't been superb on this one. But then, what else is new?"

"Good point. Back in the army, I don't think I was in a single engagement where we didn't go in half-cocked, knowing next to nothing of what we should have known. Different situation, same old shit."

"American black ops guys, that's what I heard," said Backdoor. "With some kind of high-tech equipment. Who'd have thought we'd be going up against the septics, eh? So much for the Special Relationship."

"I think, seeing as who Mrs Keener really is, the Special Relationship's more like a Special Needs Relationship," said Chopsticks. "And we're the one in the wheelchair, being pushed around."

"Sure and that was a shocker, wasn't it?" said Paddy. "Ultra-conservative president turns out to be Norse god in disguise. Hands up who saw that one coming."

"And a male god and all," said Backdoor. "Makes me a bit sick to think I might have knocked one out over her a couple of times."

"Holy Mother of God, you didn't!"

"I only said might have, Pads. Never said I did."

"Oh, you did," I said. "You big divine-gender-bender fancier you."

I turned to Cy. "While we're here male-bonding with insults, and just in case I don't get another chance to ask – 'Coco Pops'?"

A grimace. "If I told you it was my favourite brand of cereal and that's all, would you leave it at that?"

"Nope."

"Thought not."

"Lad has certain tastes," said Baz, with glee.

"For...?" I said.

"Likes the white women, so he does," said Paddy. "By his own admission, prefers them to ladies of his own colour."

"And...?" I said. We were all grinning, even Thor. It was fun watching the youngster squirm. Helped take our minds off what was coming.

"Well, you remember the adverts, don't you?"

"This is so offensive," Cy muttered.

"'Turns the milk chocolatey.'"

I guffawed. Couldn't help it.

"Come on, seriously," Cy said. "It's borderline racist."

"Mate, you're blushing," I said to him.

"Am not. How can you tell?"

"I can tell. Is it true? White birds do it for you?"

"Nothing wrong with white birds, is there?"

"Nothing at all."

"You wouldn't believe how keen they are for a bit of brother, actually, Gid. Gagging for it. You lot obviously aren't measuring up. That's why they come to me, and man, are they grateful. I give 'em something they won't forget. You know the saying. 'Once you've had black...'"

"Hsst!" said Thor. "Enough. Look."

We looked, and there were figures in the fog. Dim, hulking outlines. Grey shadows that moved ponderously, purposefully. Coming towards us. Resolving. Getting sharper and clearer. Emerging. Revealing themselves.

I held my breath.

Mrs Keener and the Pentagon had, it seemed, been busy bees.

Very busy bees indeed.

THIRTY-ONE

I COUNTED NINE of them.

Not many.

But they were big. Each basically human-shaped but twice the size. They strode in a V formation, clomping cumbersomely over the snow. Five were dark blue, the other four jet black. Their sleek, rounded contours, backlit by the fading sun, gleamed dully. Giant mechanised suits of armour.

Each had an operator inside. I could see faces peering out through tinted plexiglass faceplates. Each moved a little stiffly, but with obvious strength and power. Servomotors in the legs swayed them along, and their arms swung, providing counterbalance. In place of hands the arms ended in flared nozzles which were connected by flexible metallic tubes to pod-like tanks on their backs. Vents, cowls and farings jutted out here and there from the bodywork, some obviously functional but the majority, as far as I could tell, for show.

Across their chests were strips of lettering. The blue suits of armour had JOTUN, the black ones SURT.

"JOTUN," I said. "The US army's built its own jotuns."

"No shit," said Cy.

"But what's a SURT when it's at home?"

"Surt is a fire demon," said Chopsticks. "King of Muspelheim, the World of Fire. Scary fellow, by all accounts."

"Oh yes," said Thor. "Very much so."

We watched them plod closer, those metal replica frost giants and fire demons, and if my own feelings were anything to go by, we were perturbed but also sneakingly impressed.

"What are we supposed to call 'em, that's what I want to know," said Backdoor.

"Robo-infantry?" Chopsticks suggested.

"Bit of a mouthful."

"Mecha-modules? Mytho-exoskeletons?"

"We'll get back to you on that one, Chops," said Baz.

The nine armour thingies – they really did need a name – halted some three hundred metres from our positions.

Within range of our rifles.

Odin gave the command.

"Open fire!"

And we blizzarded the tin-plated monstrosities with bullets.

And didn't put so much as a dent in them. The salvo of bullets churned the snow around the armour suits to mush, but left them completely unscathed. As their operators must have known it would. Why else stand there like that, inviting a pelting?

The shooting became sporadic, died out. My good ear singing a lovely high-pitched song, I squinted down onto the plain. What now? Surely the enemy were going to retaliate in some way.

As one, the nine resumed their forward march, fanning out. Soon they were less than a hundred metres away from the bluff, at which point they raised their arms, levelling those nozzles at us.

Over the walkie-talkie Odin barked, "Pull back!" Me, I was already beating a hasty retreat. I didn't know what was going to emerge from the nozzles but I had a hunch it wasn't going to be spangly fairy dust or showers of confetti.

There was a loud whooshing whine, and rocks exploded at my back. I hurled myself flat, feeling the thuds of other detonations all around, hearing cries of alarm. Baz crashed headlong to the ground beside me, with a yell of "Fookin' Nora!" I raised my head to catch a peek of the goings-on, and saw a huge, sizzling hole gouged in the bluff where we're been lying just moments ago. Snow had been turned to vapour. Shattered rock glowed orange at the edges. A man – I didn't know his name – was sprawled by the impact point. The left side of his body had been almost completely burned away. Incinerated. Smoke curled up from exposed cross-sections of charred muscle and bone.

Some kind of missile?

If so, it was like none I'd ever encountered before. And in fact I doubted it was a missile at all.

The sound came again, that kind of low, resonant hiss, and another section of the edge of the bluff disintegrated. Baz and I scuttled further away on our hands and knees as scorching hot debris rattled down around us.

"Did you see that?" he said.

"No."

"Exactly. It were nowt. Just a kind of... wobble in the air. Like heat. A beam of heat."

"A heat ray?" I said. "You're telling me those things fire a fucking heat ray?"

"The black ones, yeah. Must be a million degrees or something."

"Fuck me."

"Not while there are dogs in the street."

"What about the blue ones? What do they fire?"

"How the ruddy 'eck should I know?" Baz shot back. "I'm the expert on high-tech robot suits all of a sudden?"

I looked along the line of the bluff, and got my answer. I saw a soldier rise to a crouch in order to peer over the bluff at the enemy. He unclipped a grenade from his bandolier. A bolt of shimmering air streaked towards him from below, but this one brought intense cold rather than intense heat. He cracked in two. The beam engulfed his head and shoulders, flash-froze them, and then that section sheared off, sliding to the ground in a single solid mass, its departure lubricated by an abrupt gush of blood welling up from beneath. The rest of him crumpled in the opposite direction, torso spouting torrents of crimson.

Another soldier tried the same tactic, and this time succeeded in getting the grenade in the air before he too was freeze-zapped. The little steel egg spiralled through space, and full credit to the thrower, his aim was good. He'd surely have been pleased with himself, if he hadn't happened to be lying in two halves in the snow. The grenade landed within a yard of the JOTUN that had killed him, and exploded almost instantly, before the man in the armour had a chance to react.

Take that, twat, I thought.

But when the smoke cleared, the JOTUN was still standing. Its armoured shell was scorched, scratched, but essentially intact. Through the faceplate all I could see was an enormous fucking grin. The man inside was laughing his arse off, and who could blame him? Just been hit point blank by a grenade and emerged unscathed. If that were me, I'd be as happy as a dog with Bonio-flavoured bollocks.

A couple of the other guys tried to take out one of the SURTs with a Russian-made RPG-7. Same result. The impact staggered the thing but the rocket nevertheless failed to penetrate, and the reward for their pains was to get roasted on the spot – two men reduced to human barbecue in a split second.

I spotted Thor hunkered down nearby. He was scoping out the terrain from behind a boulder, trying to fathom a way of getting down into the fray without getting blasted. I scrambled over to him, Baz behind me.

"We're sitting ducks up here," I said. "Pinned down, and if we try to climb down to attack close-up, they'll just pick us off the slope like flies on a wall."

"What do you suggest?" said Thor. "Mjolnir itches to demolish."

"We go in from the sides." I motioned to either end of the bluff, where it descended in a shallow curve, flattening to meet the plain. "Take the long way round and hit them in a pincer movement."

"All well and fine, Gid, and I believe it workable. Two problems, though. I can damage those machines with Mjolnir, I am sure, but there is but one of me. Grenades do not appear to work, and bullets certainly do not. What do you propose the rest of you do?"

"I have a vague sort of idea, I think."

"Oh, that's encouraging, that," Baz muttered. "'A vague sort of idea.'"

"The other problem," said Thor, "is that our foes are doubtless expecting us to attempt just what you're suggesting, and will move to forestall it."

"So we need a distraction. A diversion."

"Of what sort?"

"Skadi."

BAZ RADIOED ODIN with the plan, Odin relayed it to Skadi, Skadi gave it the thumbs up, and we were in business.

Skadi had her little troop of skiers with her, maybe twenty of them in all, blokes she'd spent weeks coaching rigorously in the fine art of sliding along with two planks strapped to your feet. I watched them getting ready to move out, even as my squad started crawling along the bluff towards the north end. Two groups of men led by Odin's sons Vidar and Vali were heading off the other way, southward. The JOTUNs and SURTs, meanwhile, kept battering our positions with their beams of extreme temperature. You might say, ha ha, they were running hot and cold on us.

Skadi let out a long yodelling whoop, a kind of "ul-ul-ululul-luuu!" that reminded me of the sound crowds of Europeans make at ski races. And then she shot off down the face of the bluff, her boys following. It was a nearly sheer slope, just inclined enough that snow could lie on it, with the odd ledge projecting out here and there. They scooted down, twisting and mogulling from side to side, more bouncing than skiing.

The power armour operators naturally turned their attention on them, and one poor sod got hit by a JOTUN *and* a SURT simultaneously, before he could even reach the bottom. Half of him became ice cubes, the rest ashes. Another of the skiers took a tumble halfway down and plummeted the rest of the way, landing with the kind of impact you didn't get up from again.

The rest made it to the plain safely and started racing towards the enemy as fast as they could, weaving and winding across the snow, making moving targets of themselves.

I caught all this in over-the-shoulder glimpses as my squad scurried to the bluff's tip. Those skiers were as brave as hell. It was a kamikaze run, but they kept on going, with scrawny little Skadi leading the way. Christ, but that goddess could shift. She was skimming across the snow faster than was humanly possible, as though there were jet engines attached to her skis. Her arms were a blur, stabbing the sticks into the ground repeatedly. Jinking left and right, she drew the lion's share of the enemy fire. Beams shot past her, coming within a whisker but never quite finding their mark. The men following her were less speedy, and therefore less lucky. The JOTUNs and SURTs wiped out half of them in the time it took us pincer movement guys to reach level with the plain.

Then Skadi pulled off one of the craziest and classiest stunts I'd ever seen. She thrust herself straight into the gap between a JOTUN and a SURT, slowing down a fraction so as to make herself a more attractive target. The enemy took the bait, both of them rotating on the spot, arms extended, eager for what looked like an easy kill.

Big mistake.

Both of them fired at her at the same time. And both were directly facing each other as they did so. Skadi ducked beneath the beams, squatting so low her nose almost touched her skis, and the JOTUN shot the SURT and the SURT shot the JOTUN, and it was glorious. Mechanical frost giant burned. Mechanical fire demon got iced. A large hole was melted in the JOTUN's chest, the beam boring through to fricassee the man inside. The whole suit of armour just went stock still, inert, hot metal dribbling down its front. As for the SURT, a section of its front turned glossy white and cracked apart, suddenly as brittle as an eggshell. The operator himself wasn't hurt, but it was clear that some vital component in the suit had been damaged. The SURT started shuddering. Its arms flailed about like a body-popper doing one of those jittery breakdance moves. Then something went *ker-plof*, something else went *bang*, and the SURT toppled. Just keeled over into its back, and I had to fight the urge to yell, "Timberrrr!"

Two down, seven to go.

Odin's voice came over the walkie-talkie. "We have drawn blood. They are not unbeatable. You have been briefed on what Gid has in mind. Put his plan into action. Go!"

With Skadi and her remaining skiers still running interference for us, we set off at a sprint, us lot on one side, Vadir's and Vali's groups on the other, all zeroing in on the enemy.

I was pretty confident my idea for crippling those power armour suits would work.

I sincerely hoped I was right, though.

Otherwise this was going to be a short and exceedingly asymmetrical battle.

THIRTY-TWO

EVERYTHING HAS A weak spot.

It was one of the great undeniable truths in life that I'd seen proved again and again during my army days.

Everything, no matter how well guarded, well plated, well protected, had a point of vulnerability. A tank, for instance. The chink in its armour was its treads – exposed, necessarily thin and flexible. Take out one of them, ideally both, and that stonking great steel armadillo was going nowhere. It could still turn its turret and fire, but only in self-defence. As a mobile offensive weapon, it had been neutralised.

Same with a fortified building, a dug-in position, a sniper's nest. However many sentries had been posted, however inaccessible and impregnable the place seemed, there was always a way in. It could always be got at. Always.

If you didn't think that, you were fucked.

With the JOTUNs and SURTs, I figured the limb joints were the thing to go for. Specifically the knees.

The lower portion of each leg was conical, shaped much like bellbottom jeans, terminating in a large flat foot. Designed for stability.

Linking this portion to the upper portion of the leg was a ball-and-socket joint, and there was space between the joint and the top of the lower portion surrounding it. There had to be, so that the joint could move freely and the two halves of leg didn't grind against each other.

The gap wasn't much more than a few centimetres. But a few centimetres would do. Just the right size for lodging a grenade in. Just the right size for keeping that grenade in place 'til it went off. And the ball-and-socket joint was, surely, impossible to reinforce.

That was what I was banking on. That was my plan.

The only drawback – and it was rather a large one – was that in order to pop the grenades in we had to get right up beside the enemy. Close enough to count their nostril hairs.

And getting blasted full in the face by either a heat beam or a freeze beam was the sort of thing that could really ruin your afternoon.

The JOTUNs and SURTs were so preoccupied with polishing off the skiers that they didn't see us coming until we were almost on top of them. They quickly made up for the oversight, however, strafing us hard with their beams. At the same time they retreated into a defensive circle, covering one another's backs.

All we could do was keep running. We were committed now. No backing out at this late stage. All or nothing. Do or die.

The head of the soldier next to me disappeared in a burst of flame. He was that ginger bloke, Allinson, Ellison, whoever, the one who'd described to me his first encounter with a troll. One moment he was charging along. Next moment he was headless, the stump of his neck cauterised so efficiently that not a drop of blood came out. He staggered onward for several steps, sheer momentum carrying him along, until his legs buckled and he fell. Poor bastard. On the bright side, there was one less coppertop in the world going around frightening the kiddiewinks.

The SURT who'd killed him swivelled a few degrees, training its nozzles on me. I was staring straight down both barrels, and knew I was pretty much dead meat. There was less than five metres between us, and whether I switched direction, dived to the ground, or backtracked, no way could I avoid being hit. Gid Coxall was about to be flash-fried. Extra crispy. Done to a turn. Toast.

Then, just as the SURT fired, someone whizzed in front of me. Skadi.

She took the force of both beams, dead-on. I heard her scream. Saw her go down.

I didn't hesitate for a second. I'd been given a reprieve. A second chance. Mustn't waste it. I sprang over the smoking ruin of Skadi's body and ducked under the SURT's outstretched arms, pulling the pin on a grenade in the meantime. I slotted the grenade into the top of the lower part of the SURT's leg, which cupped it neatly and securely. Then I hurled myself flat into the snow and hugged my head.

Blammm!

Rolling over, I watched as the SURT teetered on one leg. The other leg had been shattered in two. The broken end hung uselessly down, showering out sparks and leaking hydraulic fluid. The thing then just overbalanced, collapsing to one side and slumping flat.

Yes!

No time to pat myself on the back, though. There were still six more of the fuckers to deal with.

I got to my feet, in time to see Cy knacker one of the JOTUNs using exactly the same method. Meanwhile Thor was doing the job his own way. He launched himself at one of the two remaining SURTs and brought Mjolnir crunching down on its head. This put a crack in the faceplate but did no other significant harm.

The thunder god was undeterred. Leaping up onto the machine's shoulders, he raised his hammer double-handed and began bludgeoning away at the tank on the SURT's back. The SURT lacked hands to pull him off with, and couldn't even bring its heat beam nozzles to bear on him because its arms were too long and didn't bend back adequately. Three blows and Thor had dented the tank. Another three and something began spurting out – liquid under high pressure, the fuel that powered the heat beam. On its next impact, Mjolnir struck a spark off the SURT's armour. Result: instant, massive fireball.

Thor was thrown clear by the force of the explosion, hurtling some twenty metres through the air, clothes alight, and I could have sworn he was chuckling as he flew. As for the SURT, its back was blown clean open, and inside, through a jagged hole fringed with flames, I saw the figure of a man writhing, burning, being baked in an oven of his own suit.

Served the bastard right.

Now it was open season on the suits of power armour. We had the measure of them. We had them licked.

Which wasn't to say that more of us didn't die. Each opponent we felled cost us at least two of our own, sometimes three. Somebody would come in from head-on, get obliterated, but his frontal assault meant somebody else could slip in from behind and plonk a grenade into place while the JOTUN or SURT was otherwise engaged. I saw Backdoor Kellaway do exactly that, with all the stealth and dexterity that his nickname implied. Then, when each bad guy was down, we were able to polish him off with a couple more well-placed grenades, dropped just by the faceplate. If the explosion itself didn't turn the operator's brains to soup, the percussion wave did. We swarmed around the enemy like hornets, and they swatted us, but we still managed to sting them. Fatally.

At last there was just a lone JOTUN left, and Thor went for it as though it was one of the real frost giants he despised so much. He clobbered it left, right and centre, so violently and enthusiastically that its operator was unable to draw a bead on him. Every time he pointed an arm at Thor, it was bashed aside by Mjolnir. Eventually Thor managed to knock loose both of the feeder tubes that supplied the freeze beam weapons. Detached, they dangled like limp dicks, gushing liquid nitrogen or some such all over the ground in a hissing glassy slick. The suit was now pretty much defenceless, and the operator knew he was fucked five ways to Sunday. His face was a mask of panic. He raised the suit's arms in surrender, but Thor wasn't having a bar of it.

"Clemency? Compassion?" he roared. "Mortal, you are sadly deluded. I am Thor, god of thunder, and I bear Mjolnir, whose name means lightning. A storm knows no mercy. It flattens all with its fury, and so do I."

He made short work of the JOTUN after that. Ultimately it was sprawled on the ground and he was hammering at it like a blacksmith working at his anvil. Every gong-like blow wrecked the power armour a little further. Parts came off. Fragments flew like shrapnel. The bloke inside was long dead before Thor finished trashing the thing. Organs liquefied by the impacts, I imagined. Bones reduced to powder.

All that the rest of us could do was stand around and wait for Thor to be done. He was drenched with sweat by the end of it. Steam plumed from his head. He straightened up, surveyed the mess he had made of the JOTUN, holstered Mjolnir, planted his fists on his hips, and heaved a deep and satisfied sigh.

"Remind me not to piss *him* off," I murmured to Cy.

"You already did once, remember?"

"Oh yeah. Well, remind me not to do it again."

"I won't if you won't."

"Roger that."

Victory secured, Odin arrived on the scene, accompanied by Freya and Tyr. It was near dark, the sun just a red ghost on the horizon. The ruler of the Aesir took stock, casting his eye over the nine ruined suits of power armour and the thirty or so of his troops who'd lost their lives defeating them.

I piped up, "Don't suppose that was it, eh? Loki's taken his best shot and lost?"

Sombrely Odin shook his head. "Far from it, Gid. My blood brother does nothing by halves. If I know him, and I do, this was merely an exploratory sortie, to give us a foretaste of the full mayhem and misery that is his to unleash. There will be more of this kind of thing. More and worse."

Freya came over. She'd just been to examine Skadi's remains.

"My aunt still lives, All-Father," she announced, much to my surprise but not, it seemed, the gods'. "Gravely wounded, but I can detect the divine spark still fluttering within her. We should get her to Frigga as soon as possible. Summon *Sleipnir*."

"It is already done," Odin said. "Huginn and Muninn have conveyed word to the pilots. Skadi will be in receipt of my wife's ministrations within the hour."

Which was the best news I'd had all evening. Skadi had taken a shot meant for me, and she was going to survive. I could kiss my guilt about that goodbye.

"You have done well today," Odin told us all. "You have fought with uncommon courage, cunning and valour. Some of our comrades have fallen. It was inevitable. But we will remember them. Bragi will celebrate them in verse. They will live on in our hearts. As for these others..." he said, indicating the enemy.

"They, All-Father, belong to me," hissed a voice.

The most horrible voice I had ever heard.

And its owner was no oil painting either.

THIRTY-THREE

"HEL," INTONED ODIN, and a definite shudder ran through him as he said it.

Not that I blamed him. Because the woman now stalking towards us across the battlefield was truly repellent. I'd seen some munters in my time, but this one was in a league of munterdom all her own. Although there was probably more to Odin's horror of her than just her looks.

She was gaunt, with a prominent cliff of a forehead, eyebrows so sparse they might as well have not been there, and lips so dark red they were all but black. Her face looked like she'd never known anything but nightmares all her life and had learned to love it. Haggard and forlorn, she seemed to embody utter despair, and this was echoed in her clothing, from the tattered black scarf that wreathed her head to the rough strips of black gauze that covered some but nowhere near enough of her emaciated torso.

Top half, bad. Bottom half, downright vile.

Because her legs weren't just bony like the rest of her, they were distended and misshapen. The flesh didn't hang on them right. It bulged and sagged and slid about as she walked, like raw dough that had been injected into a pair of sheer stockings. The skin on them was grey and marbled with blue veins. I'd seen legs like that before. On a decomposing corpse. But this was a living creature, wasn't it? How could she have a corpse's legs?

And then I thought, *Why the fuck not?* I was in a place where ravens could be used for long-range reconnaissance and communication, where there were such things as frost giants and trolls, and where somebody was gifted with the ability to hear stuff happening miles away. A part-living, part-dead woman? Big deal. Ho-hum.

Hel sashayed up to Odin, pleased with the effect her appearance had on everyone present. Men recoiled from her as she passed. Freya, even Thor, stepped back so as not to be within reaching distance of her. The smell she trailed in her wake was both sweet and foul. Rotting lilies. The fruity stench of shit. Soil and bitter almonds. The twilight air was cold, but the air around Hel was even colder.

It took everything Odin had just to stand his ground. But he waited for Hel to come, and barely flinched as she halted in front of him, close enough to place a hand on his cheek if she wanted. I knew somehow, without having to be told, that to touch or be touched by Hel was fatal. God or not, fatal.

"Brother of my father," she said.

"Daughter of my one-time brother," he replied.

"But not quite my uncle."

"Nor quite my niece."

"Hel's dad is Loki," Chopsticks whispered in my ear.

"I'd just twigged," I said.

"No fond words of greeting, Odin? No kiss for beautiful Hel?"

Beautiful? Had this bint checked in a mirror lately?

"You know I would be a fool even to shake your hand. And kiss?" Odin's mouth downturned. "I would rather kiss a dead dog's pizzle."

This wasn't bravado. From the way he spat out the words, I realised that what I'd taken for fear was actually something else: disgust. Odin wasn't scared of Hel. He simply detested her. With a passion.

"Yet one day you will welcome me," Hel said. "One day I will open my arms to you and you will sink into my embrace."

"I hope, for my sake, that that day is a long time hence, and that when it happens, I will be a plague upon you for all eternity. My groans of sorrow and sighs of regret will torment your ears and allow you not one moment's peace."

She looked mock-hurt. "How you spurn me, All-Father. Never forget, I can bring you rest. I can bring peace to that troubled heart of yours. Am I not famed as the purveyor of blessed oblivion, she who offers surcease to all woes?"

"I have no desire to lose myself in the misty greyness of your realm, Hel," said Odin. "Life, for all its pains and complications, continues to hold its lustre for me."

"But for how much longer?" Hel began to walk around him, like someone appraising a car. "You are old, Odin. Weary. A time of tribulation is coming, and even gods can perish. Why not let me take you now and spare you the effort and anguish of the coming days? Why not quit early and leave the struggle to these underlings and lesser gods?"

A claw-like hand waved dismissively at the rest of us.

"After all, with or without you they do not stand a chance against my father. Save yourself the distress of watching them stumble and fail. Come with me. Take my arm and walk beside me into Niflheim, and there let me entertain you in my palace, whose name is Sickbed, where the walls are a wickerwork of entwining serpents and where the black rooster sits, ever silent, never crowing. Let me lead you past Garm, my hound who howls at the gate, and let me carve food for you with my knife called Hunger and serve it up to you on a plate called Starvation."

"You're never going to win *Come Dine With Me* with a menu like that," I blurted out.

Hel rounded on me, whiplash-fast, and her eyes were black ice and the angry hiss she let out was a gust of arctic wind.

"Hold your tongue, mortal!" she snapped. "This is god business. Not for the likes of you to interrupt."

But, as Magnus Magnusson might have said, I'd started so I

might as well finish. "Ooh, I get it. 'Be quiet, the grown-ups are talking.'"

I wasn't sure quite why I was taunting her this way. Maybe I didn't want her to know how fucking terrified she made me, how even just looking at her turned my guts to water.

"One more remark out of you," Hel told me, pointing a gnarled finger, "and you're mine. Is that what you wish? When you've heard what's in store for those I take to my world?"

I caught a warning glance off Freya. But was that – could it be – a flicker of admiration in her eyes as well?

I was probably imagining it.

"Well, it's an appealing offer, love," I said regardless, "but I'm going to have to say no. Nothing personal. You seem nice enough and all, but I'm into more than just character. Looks count for a lot."

"Impudent insect!" Hel made a lunge for me, arm outstretched.

In return, instinctively, I raised my rifle. I didn't think a bullet would do much good, but it was all I had.

Hel took one look at the gun, stopped, and threw back her head and laughed, a sound like bones fracturing. Like the choking of someone being throttled. Like a blade stabbing repeatedly into flesh.

"Amusing. You truly believe I can be repulsed by a mere weapon?"

"It's worth a try. Look, you're here for the soldiers in those suits, right? Why not just take them, then, and fuck off out of it? Instead of hanging around making everyone feel queasy. Grab what's yours and go."

Hel laughed again. Her laughter was infectious. Infectious like the ebola virus.

"You scorn death. Fascinating."

"I've seen enough of it to know it *should* be scorned," I said. "Death's a joke. Big and intimidating, but when you get right up to it, not nearly as bad as it's cracked up to be. I died once, sort of. Death's just nothing. Unpleasant, inconvenient, but that's all."

"Perhaps death is like that where you come from, mortal, but here death is different. The afterlife in Niflheim is long and cold and dreary, a slow fade, a slow forgetting. Your spirit erodes over eons, worn to a nub by time. And all the while I preside over you, delighting in the sight of your prolonged, protracted withering. Does that sound like 'just nothing'? I think not."

Her words gave me a genuine chill.

"Not so quick with the repartee now, eh?"

"No," I said, and lowered the rifle. "Just that bit more sold on the idea of staying alive, actually."

"Sensible man."

"These nine souls," said Odin, indicating the scattered JOTUNs and SURTs. "They are the price for your allowing our adversary's troops access to Asgard through Niflheim?"

"Nothing is given for free, not even between my father and me," Hel said. "He told me if I permitted them safe passage, I could take back as many of them as died here. He anticipated all of them would, as did I, although not without cost to your side."

"Is it the first and last time he will attack via your realm?"

"Do you seriously expect me to reveal Loki's plans to you? What I can tell you is that this is only the beginning. A statement of intent."

"I assumed as much."

"Loki has more in reserve. Considerably more. And, from my point of view, these nine souls serve as a mere appetiser to the glut that will soon be coming my way."

All at once I realised there were grey shadows clustered behind Hel. Nine of them. I hadn't seen them appear. They were suddenly... just there. They were blurry, like figures seen through a shower curtain. I could just about make out the outline of heads, bodies, limbs. Nine dead American soldiers hovering obediently at Hel's back, and for all that they had no distinct features there was something horribly lost and inconsolable about them: the way they stood, the slumped posture. Helpless. Docile. Like kittens trapped in a sack, waiting to be thrown in the canal.

"Everything is arrayed against you, Odin," Hel said. "You cannot and will not win, certainly not with so pathetic and inadequate an army as the one you have mustered. It is over. The Fimbulwinter is here and all but done, and sure as night follows day, Ragnarök is coming in its wake. You know this. The pattern is set and cannot be altered. The pieces are in their right places. Ragnarök – the end of everything, the fall of the gods, carnage and catastrophe!"

She relished this last sentence, savouring the words like a fine wine.

"Fight, by all means," she concluded. "Resist. Scream defiance at the inevitable. In the end, the only one who will profit is me."

And with that, she turned and left, and the nine grey shadows trailed after her in a straggling line, like ducklings behind mother duck. Into the fog bank. Into Niflheim.

And the last faint glimmer of sunlight drained from the sky, and there was nothing but darkness.

THIRTY-FOUR

I COLLARED ODIN the next day for a chinwag. He was at the troll pen, checking up on the captives.

A large pit had been excavated not far from the castle and surrounded with a stockade of pine trunks sharpened to points. Here, the three trolls had been corralled and were being fed with whole deer carcasses supplied by Freya.

Odin was on a platform overlooking the pen. I scaled a wooden ladder to join him.

The trolls sat apart from one another around the edge of the pit. One was fast asleep, mouth slack, drool dribbling down his chin. Another had his arms folded and was distractedly scraping a furrow in the dirt with his heel while singing a repetitive, tuneless song to himself. The third was busy picking his teeth with the broken end of one of the many deer bones that lay scattered around the pen. I'd expected them to be raging against their captivity, trying to clamber up and batter their way out. In the event, all they were was bored and subdued. Gorillas at the zoo, resigned to imprisonment.

They reeked, too. The smell came not so much from the latrine hole that had been dug for them as from the trolls themselves, from giant bodies that had never known soap or a washcloth.

"Jesus!" I exclaimed, clapping a hand over my nose. It was like being downwind of a tramp, only multiplied by a hundred. "That's minging. You could stun an elephant with that."

"One gets used to it, if one stands here long enough," Odin said. "How are you, friend Gid?"

"You mean apart from slowly being choked to death by a new kind of bioweapon? Never better. Your missus has had a look at me and apparently I'm back to full fighting fitness. Everything's healed, rib, wrist, the works. It's incredible. Skadi's on the mend too. How does Frigga do it?"

"With love, skill, and a modicum of divine power. My question, however, was of a more general nature, pleased though I am to be apprised of the state of your physical wellbeing."

"I'm feeling okay, I suppose. About Loki and all that? Yeah, bring it on."

"So upbeat, even though the odds against us seem insurmountable?"

"Well, I've had a few ideas on that front."

Odin raised an intrigued eyebrow. "I'd be eager to hear them."

"One of them has to do with this lot." I pointed to the trolls. "Only, looking at them now, I'm not sure it's such a goer any more. You said they could be used as frontline shock troops, but on present form they don't look very shocking at all."

"Don't be deceived," Odin said. "They're passive now because their bellies are full and because they perceive no danger to themselves. Trolls are not at all bright creatures. When threatened, however, they turn savage. We harness that aggression, loose them against the enemy, and they will serve us well."

"Fab. Then why not let's get hold of more of them. Dozens if we can. Make it our priority over the next few days. Let's stockpile trolls like they're going out of fashion."

Odin flashed me his wolfish smile. "I like the sound of it. What else?"

"I've got a few more thoughts, some crazier than others. But before any of that, I want some background intel from you. I need to know what all this is about. Yesterday Hel mentioned a... Fimbulwinter, was it?"

"Yes."

"Now, my son used to like a TV show called *The Fimbles*, about some tubby, stripy creatures who lived in a magical garden with a talking bird with a Yorkshire accent. I'm guessing the Fimbulwinter's got nothing to do with them, right?"

"In so far as I have no idea what you're talking about, I'm going to hazard a guess and say no, it doesn't have anything to do with them."

"Shame, because the Fimbles are cute and cuddly."

"The Fimbulwinter is decidedly not. It is three years of the harshest, bitterest weather that has ever been known. Three years of snows, storms, hail, ice, darkened skies. And it comes as a harbinger of the end of everything. It forewarns that the time is nigh for a battle to end all battles, a final clash between the forces of righteousness and the forces of wickedness."

"And that," I said, "is Ragnarök."

He confirmed with a nod. "Ragnarök," he said, low-voiced, and repeated it, as though tolling a bell. "Ragnarök. A doom that I have long known was coming but been unable to do anything to avoid or prevent. Various factors have played out in the only way they could. I have watched events move towards this ineluctable conclusion, powerless to alter their course. Though a god, I have found myself as a mortal, a victim rather than a shaper of destiny. It has been... difficult, to say the least."

"What events? I'd like to know."

"Could you not ask one of your colleagues, perhaps? That Dennis Ling, he seems very well acquainted with Aesir lore. Or what about Bragi? He loves to spin a yarn."

"I'd rather get it straight from the top. And without lots of bad rhymes."

Odin sighed heavily. "Very well. I believe you have earned the privilege. Consider this a reward for your proven ingenuity and prowess in battle. But please bear in mind, recounting what happened – even simply recollecting it – is painful for me. Distressing in the extreme. It began with a malicious trick and a death. Not just any death, either, but a death of magnitude and great significance. Every death, one might aver, is such to the person who dies. Every death is an apocalypse. Yes. Every death is an apocalypse. Is it not, Gid?"

I shrugged. "Suppose you could say that."

"An apocalypse on a personal scale. Every death is the end of everything for the one dying. The end of their world. Their very own Ragnarök. This death, however, the one I'm about to relate to you, can truly be deemed apocalyptic. It set in train all that we are experiencing now. With it began the decline of Asgard and the ascendancy of Loki. It was the catalyst for the disaster presently facing us. Listen well. And should I shed a tear, understand that it is but a single drop from the ocean of tears that I have shed in the past and could yet shed over this tragedy."

THIRTY-FIVE

HIS NAME WAS Balder, *Odin said*, and he was my favourite son. One should not have favourites among one's offspring. One should love them all equally and treat them all equally, whatever their virtues or shortcomings.

Balder, though, was different. Balder was special. And it wasn't I alone who knew this. Everyone did. All among the Aesir, and among the Vanir, recognised that Balder was a cut above. He was handsome. Not just handsome; beautiful, exquisitely so. His hair shone like the sun. His eyes sparkled like a limpid stream. His voice was as soft and gentle as a warm summer breeze. Nor did he vaunt his looks or succumb to vanity in any way. He was modest and kind, with never a bad word for anyone. He was brave. He was forgiving. You couldn't think a cruel or unjust thought in his presence, let alone give voice to one.

I doted on him. How could I not? As did his mother. Frigga had only two children by me: Balder and Hodur, the latter of whom emerged from the womb as blind as an earthworm. Both we loved, Balder for his perfection, Hodur for his imperfection. My other sons... well, let's just say I haven't been the most faithful of husbands. In my callow early years I sowed my seed profligately. I have calmed down since, of course, and have become a contentedly uxorious individual. And I have never disowned or disavowed any of my children fathered on other mothers. Thor, Bragi, Vali and the rest, they are all flesh of my flesh and I am proud to acknowledge them as such. But the children one has with one's true love, one's forever wife, one holds in perhaps higher regard than the others. It cannot be helped.

The point is, Balder was universally adored. He was the best of us, the shining light of Asgard. Flowers would bloom in his footsteps. It's true. Even the gnomes, who are spiteful at the best of times, loved Balder. The jotuns too! Even them. He could do no wrong.

His only failing was no fault of his. Balder suffered from nightmares. Always they prophesied that he was going to die, and that his death would be murder, carried out by one of his brothers. The dreams tormented him in his sleep and also during his waking hours, with their memory.

Word spread among the Aesir about these nightmares, and the news brought gloom to all. An atmosphere of dread settled over Asgard, clouding our mirth. Were they merely dreams? Or an augury of a future event? Eventually a meeting was called at the foot of Yggdrasil to address the matter. At this council the Norns instructed me to visit a völva, a Midgardian seeress who had died many years previously. I mounted Sleipnir and rode to the völva's gravesite, a burial mound where on a wild and windy midnight I sang a chant and wove a spell to resurrect her. Those were the days when I had magic and plenty of it.

The völva clawed her way up out of the ground, groaning and shrieking. Her corpse stood before me, wreathed in rotted cerements, and in a voice as dry and crackly as fallen leaves she asked me what I desired to know. I told her: an interpretation of Balder's dreams. Her reply, instead of bringing enlightenment, served only to darken further the shadows that were already casting a pall over my soul.

She said Balder's days were numbered. Hel awaited him. And his murderer, she added, would not even realise he was his murderer until it was too late.

Then she sank back down into her grave and drew the soil over her like a set of bedcovers and resumed her everlasting slumber.

I returned with a heavy heart to Asgard, where I informed the Aesir there was nothing we could do. Balder's fate was sealed.

Frigga, however, refused to accept this. She was adamant that her beloved son would not die. So she set off and travelled across all the Nine Worlds, and in each one she exacted a promise from every living and unliving thing. She made them swear that they would not harm Balder. With her motherly charm and beauty she persuaded them all to keep to this vow, and then she returned home, content that Balder was now protected. For if all things were pledged to do him no evil, all animals, all plants, all the elements – the stones and wind and water – and all sentient beings besides, then surely he was safe and the portent of his dreams would not come to pass.

Now, around this time, my blood brother was making mischief worse than ever he had before. Recently, for instance, he had arranged for Bragi's wife Idunn, keeper of the Aesir's apples of youth, to be kidnapped by a jotun. The jotun, name of Thiassi, liked the look of Idunn, and Loki's assistance in her abduction was a condition of his release from Thiassi's clutches, into which he had carelessly fallen. Deprived of our regular diet of the apples of youth, we began to grow hoary-headed and dull-witted, and I only just managed to browbeat my blood brother into rescuing Idunn from Thiassi, else we all might have perished of old age.

Then he'd bamboozled Thor into paying a call on the frost giant Geirrod in Jotunheim without his hammer to protect himself. He convinced Thor he had no need of Mjolnir – he was formidable enough in himself. Thor foolishly fell for the ruse, and Geirrod did his utmost to kill the jotuns' sworn enemy, first by trying to drown him in a river, then by seating him on a stool that rose and nearly crushed him against the roof, and finally by flinging a red-hot iron bolt at him straight from the fire. He failed all three times, of course, but not for want of effort. More by luck than anything did Thor foil these assassination attempts.

My blood brother had also stolen a necklace from Freya – an incomparable piece of jewellery made specially for her by the gnomes. While she was in bed he buzzed around her ear in the form of a fly. She removed her hand from the necklace, which she was wont to clasp in her sleep in order to protect it, and swatted at the fly. In a flash my blood brother took on his usual form and pilfered the necklace. He would have got away with the crime had he not then chosen to turn himself into a seal and dive into the sea in order to hide his booty in the depths. Heimdall heard the splash and was immediately suspicious. He ran to the shore, caught the thief red-handed with the necklace in his seal mouth, and forced him to restore it to its rightful owner.

In other words, my blood brother – for the sake of convenience I shall use his name, distasteful though it is on my tongue – Loki had been doing little to curry favour among his peers. Quite the opposite. One by one he had managed to alienate the affections of all the gods and goddesses. It was simply in his nature to be like that, to sow discord, stir up trouble, foment dissent, earn enmity. He was born a jotun, you see, but unlike the rest of that race he was not large and shaggy and boorish and rough-mannered. Rather, he was good-looking, quick-witted and nimble-footed, for which reason when he and I met I felt an immediate affection for him and kinship with him. Hence we cut veins and swore an oath of blood brotherhood.

The longer he stayed with us in Asgard, however, the more he changed. Perhaps his jotun heritage was stronger in him than at first it seemed. He had forsworn it, rejected it, but it would not be denied and gradually asserted itself.

His misdeeds, to begin with, were harmless pranks, soon mended, easily forgiven. But then they became increasingly less do. He practised malice rather than mirth-making. Spite, not jest, grew to be his habit.

Hence he beheld Balder with ever more envious eyes. For Balder was all that Loki was not: universally adored, implicitly trusted, greeted everywhere he went with smiles and embraces and cries of delight. Loki's behaviour had gained him naught but suspicion and an ill-disguised resentment. He had only himself to blame, but did not appreciate that. In his mind the Aesir and Vanir had taken against him for no good reason. Balder symbolised all that we admired and aspired to. So he would bring down Balder.

I can but impute these motives to him. You would have to ask Loki himself if I'm right or wrong. I'm familiar enough with his character, though, to believe my assumptions are near the mark.

Now, you might think that because Frigga had got every object in the Nine Worlds to agree not to harm Balder that he was entirely safe. My wife, unfortunately, had overlooked one seemingly insignificant little shrub. The humble mistletoe. She felt that so small and feeble a plant was not worth bothering about. It was an oversight she rues to this day.

The Aesir decided to put her hard work to the test by standing in a ring around Balder and pelting him with various items. We attacked him with weapons, and all bounced off as though made of rubber. We threw rocks at him, and might as well have been throwing feathers for all the damage they did. We shot him with arrows which glanced off him as they would have a statue made of granite. He was truly invulnerable, and what sport we had proving it! How we laughed as we assailed him with ever larger and deadlier implements and he shrugged off the blows with scarcely a blink of the eye.

An ancient crone came hobbling up to my wife during all this and asked what everyone was up to. Frigga explained, and the crone expressed astonishment that every single thing in all of creation had acceded to Frigga's request. My wife let slip that she had neglected to include mistletoe in her inventory, thinking it unimportant.

The crone, needless to say, was the shape-shifter Loki in disguise, and armed with this crucial nugget of information he approached my son Hodur, who was standing aloof, alone, unable to join in the game of Balder-battering. Hodur, as I have said, was born blind. This was the first time that his disability had truly set him apart from the rest of us. Even sightless he was a tremendous warrior, possessed of immense strength. In battle he was always to be found in the thick of things, locating the foe by the sound of their voices alone. Once he laid hands on an opponent, that was it. They could not escape his clutches, or his crushing, lethal might.

Loki invited him to take part in the proceedings. Hodur asked him how he might do that, and Loki placed a bow and arrow in his hands. He would guide Hodur's aim, he said. All Hodur had to do was draw back the bowstring and let the arrow fly.

Hodur confessed afterwards that he'd had some misgivings about perpetrating this act, but he had so wished to share in the general merriment. It was a grievous misjudgement, and he paid a high penalty for it.

The arrow, you see, was crafted from a twig of mistletoe. And Hodur, with Loki's assistance, sent it whistling straight into Balder's heart.

Before our very eyes, the best of all Asgard died instantly – slain, as his dreams had foretold, by his own unwitting brother.

THIRTY-SIX

"That sucks," I nearly said, but didn't, because even I'm not that crass.

Instead I kept a respectful, dignified silence and watched as a lone, fat tear rolled slowly down Odin's right cheek, navigating the wrinkled valleys of his skin. I was thinking of Cody and imagining how I'd have felt seeing him die right in front of me. Some things were too horrible to even contemplate.

"It was..." Odin began, then stopped, then tried again. "It was as if that arrow pierced my heart too. And the hearts of all assembled. We all died a little in that moment. Frigga swooned and collapsed. I myself could not move. Then Hel appeared to gather up Balder's spirit. Though we entreated her to show mercy, to make an exception in just this one instance, she refused. Her transparent delight in claiming my son from me has guaranteed her my undying hatred. I have never seen anyone quite so elated as on that day. Hel considered it a personal triumph to lead Balder's mute soul away from us to Niflheim. It showed, more clearly than ever before, her supremacy over all. Even the noblest and greatest of the gods was, in death, mere grist to her mill."

"But you punished Loki," I said. "Nastily. At least there was that."

"For a time we did not know that he was the true guilty party," Odin said. "We blamed Hodur, and tragedy was heaped on tragedy, for Hodur had to atone for taking Balder's life and that could only be accomplished by surrendering his own. There is a balance that must be observed. Everything has a price. My wisdom, to take an example. Bought at the cost of an eye and nine days' suffering on a tree. The universe neither gives without taking nor takes without giving. For every action there must be a corresponding opposite action."

"Hodur killed himself?"

"As good as. Willingly allowed himself to be killed. Vali took the responsibility of striking the fatal blow with his sword, but it was suicide in all but name. Hodur put up no resistance. He offered his bare breast and Vali, sobbing, plunged his blade in. It was right. It had to be done. The scales were evened up, and none profited."

"Except Hel."

He laughed emptily. "Another soul to add to her ranks, yes. The only who ever truly gains from the deeds of gods and men is Hel."

"How long did Loki manage to get away with it before he was rumbled?"

"Not long. His own arrogance proved his undoing. There was a period when all seemed bleak and meaningless in Asgard. We went about our business glumly, feeling as though there was little point to anything. Balder was gone. Nothing mattered. Frigga took to her room and would not emerge. Whenever I spoke to her, I got little in the way of reply. She'd lost both of her sons, don't forget. I had others but she had none. It was a devastating, crippling blow."

"She seems to have come to terms with it."

"Ah, the creature that you see today – the Frigga who smiles and is kind and giving and patient and oh-so-obliging – is but a shell, a mask for the real Frigga beneath, a woman lost in the ache of perpetual bereavement, a woman with a void at the core of her. As for the rest of us, in the aftermath of Balder's death we went through the motions of living but were pale imitations of ourselves. Only Loki continued to evince any animation or zest, which should perhaps have alerted us to his guilt, but we were too lost in misery and too numb with grief to notice. In hindsight I can see how obvious it was. He feigned sharing our sorrow but he was laughing at us behind his face. His eyes ever sparkled with barely concealed joy. What a coup for him! How artfully had he pulled off this, his most audacious trick yet, his most vindictive act, the acme of treachery. None could question his superiority to the Aesir now that he had contrived the murder of the finest among us. But a successful deceit is no fun for the deceiver unless others are aware that he was responsible."

"Don't tell me, he owned up to it. Couldn't help himself."

"It was during a banquet. Time had passed, the wound of Balder's death was beginning to heal, life in Asgard was returning to normal, and we had recovered some of our vivacity and confidence. Loki sat at the table listening to us banter and laud one another, much as we had done in times gone by, and it stung him to the quick that everyone ignored his witty comments and no one would praise him for his achievements. Eventually it became too much. His resentment boiled over and he flew into a spiteful rage. He abused us all, calling us prigs and dullards and simpletons and many more vicious names besides. My family dared not respond in kind, out of respect to me, since Loki was my blood brother and therefore under my aegis. So I felt obliged to chastise him myself. This, though, only angered him further, until at last he could contain himself no longer, and out it all spilled. How it was he who'd been the crone who'd approached Frigga, he who'd convinced Hodur to loose off the arrow, he who's substituted the shaft for one fashioned from mistletoe..."

"Talk about stitching yourself up like a kipper."

"The Aesir rose up as one in fury, and Loki, recognising that he had gone too far and needed to save his neck, fled. With the aid of Huginn and Muninn I sought him out and found him in a house in a remote corner of the realm. There, by the hearthside, he was knotting lengths of string together in loops, something no one had ever thought to do before. As soon as he heard the Aesir coming for him, he threw what he was making into the fire, turned himself into a salmon and jumped into a stream. He thought we could never catch him in fish form, because he would be too wily to latch on to any line we cast into the water. He would not fall for a baited hook. Sadly for him, we recovered the mesh of string from the fire and used that to catch him instead. Too clever by half, Loki had been the architect of his own downfall. He had just fashioned the very device which trapped him – a net."

"Silly arse."

"Thor wrestled him out onto dry land and squeezed him back into his true shape. Together we then secured him in a cave with a poisonous serpent above him."

"Venom in the eyes. That's got to hurt."

"In ancient times our worshippers believed earthquakes were caused by Loki writhing in agony below the ground," Odin said. "Perhaps they were right."

He lapsed into musing. I didn't know what to say. One of the trolls broke the silence by lifting a buttock and letting out a tremendous, ground-shaking fart.

I wouldn't have sniggered if Odin hadn't sniggered first.

"An apposite comment from below," he said.

"Applause from the cheap seats," I said.

"Sometimes it takes the digestive tract of a troll to remind us what is important." Odin clasped my shoulder. "Go, Gid, and fetch me more of these malodorous lummoxes. Just try not to get yourself asphyxiated in the process."

THIRTY-SEVEN

The Taking Of The Trolls
by the bard Bragi

In ages hence, in lands afar,
This tale will oft be told –
How men and gods in unison
Went out collecting trolls.

Decree there came from Odin's lips
That none should dare relent
From capturing the ogreish things,
His forces to augment.

In Jotunheim, in Svartalfheim,
In Alfheim, all around,
Gods of Asgard, men of Midgard,
Ran those trolls to ground.

They baited traps with hapless goats –
Bleating, trembling prey.
The trolls could not resist the lure.
They took it, come what may.

From caves below, the beasts were rousted,
From dens on mountain slopes,
Then were steered and stunned with gunfire;
Caught and bound with ropes.

Some resisted, some fought back,
Some raised a fearful yammer.
None, however, withstood long
Once struck with Thor's dire hammer.

Sleipnir's pilots plied the skies
Flying to and fro.
Twice or thrice, e'en four times daily
Out and back they'd go.

And so it grew, and grew and grew,
The toll of captive trolls,
And more and more was Asgard pocked
With large empenning holes.

Until at last the All-Father
In voice unduly gruff
Announced the numbers did suffice.
"That's it," he said. "Enough.

"We've thirty now at least, I think,
Or forty – maybe more.
I've kept my eye on things, but still
It's hard to know the score.

"What's certain is the stench is bad,
And more will make it worse.
The trolls should be a blessing here
And not a nasal curse."

Their smell is rank, I can't deny,
Enough to make one wince.
Heimdall caught a whiff of it.
We haven't seen him since.

Huginn and Muninn overflew
The troll pens and – don't groan! –
They plummeted to earth just like
Two birds killed with one stone.

Still we must the bright side see.
We must remain firm-chinned.
The trolls will smite our foe ere long –
Not least if he's downwind.

THIRTY-EIGHT

SHAGGED OUT.

Done in.

Cream-crackered.

A fortnight we'd been doing our "bring 'em back alive" bit with the trolls. Day after day in-country, exploring their known haunts, with Freya using her tracking skills to find their lairs or stalk them on the move. Night after night under canvas listening to the lament of the wind, and occasionally the baying of distant wolves.

Alfheim: where the air was thin and the *aurora borealis* snaked greenly among the stars, and where I never saw a single elf despite Freya's insistence that they were watching our every move.

Svartalfheim: barren and grim, a lifeless lunar landscape of black volcanic rock and ancient lava flows, dotted with billowing geysers and patches of glassy obsidian.

Jotunheim: along the borderlands, the regions of intersection where it cold-shouldered Asgard.

The trolls were everywhere, but never in bands of more than two or three and more often than not solitary. Invariably they blundered straight into the traps we laid. They didn't always get to feed on the tethered goats we put there to sucker them in, either. Often Thor would leap out from hiding and cosh them on the head while they were still rubbing their tummies and smacking their lips in anticipation. It never once occurred to any of them to question why an animal was standing tied to a peg at the end of a blind canyon or next to an outcrop of rock large enough to conceal several soldiers. The prospect of a free, easy meal made the creatures even dumber than normal.

Winkling them out of caves was a mite more problematic. But again the nickering of a frightened goat usually did the trick, drawing them up from the depths as efficiently as a dinner bell.

Mostly we had to subdue them with gunfire, if Thor didn't get the chance to knock them out cold. We'd use tear gas as well, stun grenades, magnesium flares. Once, swear to God, a female troll got so disorientated and stressed out by all the noise and smoke, she wet herself. I felt strangely guilty about that.

Odin's ravens were with us the whole time. Radio didn't work across the frontiers between worlds, so Huginn and Muninn kept their boss updated on our progress. They also enabled him to guide *Sleipnir*'s pilots to our location when a troll was ready for retrieval.

By the end of it, when Odin decided we'd caught as many trolls as Asgard could handle, I could have done with a break. We all could have. But there was no time to rest. Mrs Keener's state visit to the UK was only a few days away, and we didn't know if this would coincide with another – maybe larger-scale – attack on us, but it seemed a fair bet. So on we pressed.

Thor was despatched on an errand to Svartalfheim, to request a favour off the gnomes. He took with him some sketches I'd drawn – "blueprints" would be overstating it, given the crapness of my drawing skills – and his wife Sif went along too, ostensibly as moral support but really because Thor wasn't big on tact and, according to Odin, dealing with grouchy gnomes required finesse.

I'd remembered Bergelmir saying how good the gnomes were at making tools. Odin had confirmed it, talking up their blacksmithing ability. "Masters of moulding metal," he'd told me. "They make it dance in their hands." He'd gone on to describe at length their underground forges, their furnaces that were heated by nothing less than the magma beneath the earth's crust, their vast cavern workshops that resounded deafeningly with the sound of hammered iron and hissing water.

If gnomes couldn't manufacture what I'd designed, no one could.

Not that it mattered much either way. That plan was something of a long shot, and the main purpose of it was to get Thor temporarily out of our hair. He couldn't come with the rest of us where we were going. We couldn't bring him along because we couldn't count on him to play nice and behave.

Not in Utgard, capital of Jotunheim and main hangout of the frost giants.

THIRTY-NINE

SLEIPNIR, A SET of snazzy ski fittings attached to its wheels, *whup-whupp*ed across Jotunheim. Ice fields glittered and winked below.

In the Wokka's cargo bay, with its familiar smells of grease, rubber and oil, Backdoor and Chopsticks played cards, Paddy frowned at a Penguin paperback with some kind of boring fine-art cover, Baz stared out of a porthole with the light slanting along his face, and the Valkyries kept to themselves at one end, crouched beside their snowmobiles, sharing silence and nips of something hard and clear from a hip flask.

Which left Cy and me going over strategy and comparing notes. The deep, concussive *thump-thump-thump* of the rotors meant we had to lean our heads together and shout.

"First and foremost," I said, "this is a diplomatic initiative. We're ambassadors from Asgard."

"And when it all goes tits up..."

"Don't you mean *if*?"

"No offence, bruv, but diplomatic? You?"

"Point taken. But I think I have some leverage here. The frosties should at least hear me out."

"And then when they've heard you out and start trying to kill you..."

"Then, and only then, the shooting starts. Just try not to get trigger-happy, Coco Pops."

"Oh for fuck's sake!" Cy exclaimed, exasperated. "My surname's Fearon. If I have to have a nickname, why can't it be something to do with that? No-Fear Fearon. How about that? Works, don't it? Or what about Cyanide? Get it? Cy. Cyanide. As in, deadly as... That'd be all right. I could live with that."

"Sonny, there's nothing you can do about nicknames. Once you've got one, you've got one and that's it. Tough, but there you go."

"What did they use to call you, then? In the army?"

Our RSM had come up with Cocks-Up. Gideon Coxall. Cocks-Up. See what he did there? He'd tried his very best to make it stick, but it hadn't. Mainly, I reckoned, because I wasn't the type who cocked up, not when it came to playing the army game at any rate. A nickname had to have a kernel of truth to it if it was going to work.

"Just Gid," I told Cy, straight-faced. "Nothing else."

I wasn't sure he believed me, not if the *Whatchoo talkin' 'bout, Willis?* look he shot at me was anything to go by. But he let it lie.

"I've got a question for you," I said. "You said you and the army life didn't get on."

"Yeah, so?"

"So why hook up with this outfit? Was it just the money?"

"Dunno. Probably. I'm a bit hazy on it myself, to be honest. Suppose I felt I was all out of other options, and fighting's the only marketable skill I have. I'd been on the dole for ages. Jobseeker's Allowance. Hah! There's a joke. Fifty quid a week doesn't *allow* you to do much except sit at home and watch daytime TV and eat tinned beans. And then I'd see all the dealers on the estate, how much they were making, the stuff they had, the cars with the thirty-two-inch subwoofers and the under-chassis strobe lighting and that... It didn't seem right, y'know? Didn't seem hardly fair. And there's soldiering in my blood. My granddad was a squaddie too, see. Mind you, it fucked him up good and proper."

"Second World War?"

"Nah, he missed that," Cy said. "Too young. But after. Did his National Service and liked it so much he enlisted. 'Took the Queen's shilling,' he used to say. He was white, by the way. My mum's dad. He married black, so that makes me, I dunno, eighth white or something."

"That might explain the –"

"Don't even start," he said, wagging a warning finger. "But the Queen's shilling wasn't worth shit, not after what they did to him."

"Which was what?"

"Christmas Island. Operation Grapple. The nuclear tests. Him and about a thousand other servicemen, the army just plonked them down on a speck of land in the middle of the Pacific Ocean, lined them up on a beach and blew up a fucking hydrogen bomb in front of them. My granddad said it was the weirdest thing he'd ever seen."

"His own bones visible through his hand?"

"Yeah, exactly. He had his back to the explosion and still his hand went all X-ray. There were no shadows anywhere, the light was that bright. And the noise... the noise was incredible. 'Like the planet splitting in two,' he said. And then a few days later his palms all blistered up, and so did the soles of his feet, and he got pretty sick. Then he got better again, and he thought that was it, end of. Only it wasn't."

"Cancer?"

"Funnily enough, not. He should've died from that. Plenty of the others did. And he smoked like a fucking chimney all his life. One way or another a tumour should've got him. But what happened was a whole lot more peculiar. One day, when he was in his sixties, he woke up and suddenly he couldn't remember who he was. No idea. Complete blank. He didn't recognise the woman lying in bed beside him. Didn't know her name."

"Well, we've all had mornings like that."

"Yeah, but she was his wife. They'd just celebrated their fortieth wedding anniversary. And he had no memory of who she was, or what his own name was either, or where he lived, what he did for a living, any of it. This is a true story. My gran took him off to hospital, and he stayed there for about three months while they ran tests on him, did scans, you name it. Some of the best brain specialists the

NHS had to offer came to examine him. Some private guys as well, because he was such a mystery and his case was getting famous in the medical community. No one could figure it out. My gran brought in old photos to show him, his medals, stuff like that. He looked at it and nothing rang a bell. His mates came and he hadn't the foggiest who they were. They told him about things they'd done together, hoping to tweak a memory. Not a flicker. Didn't recognise his own children, or me. It was bizarre the way he looked at me, studying me like he knew he should know me but just couldn't think how. Like when you see someone's face in the street and it's familiar but you can't put a name to it or figure out if you ever actually met them."

"And he stayed like that the rest of his life?"

"Pretty much. His whole memory gone, his whole life, apart from scraps, a few bits and bobs. All the major stuff – *fwoosh!*"

"Poor bugger."

"Him and my gran got sort of to know each other again, and they carried on living together, but they was like flatmates more than husband and wife. He adjusted, although of course he was never the same again. And we're sure the bomb tests were to blame. Couldn't've been anything else. The radiation planted this, like, time-delay computer virus in his head, and one day it went off and crashed his hard drive and he had to reboot from scratch."

"Don't suppose he tried suing the MoD."

"Yeah, like that ever works."

"Yeah. 'Bomb tests. What bomb tests?'"

"Or, 'You knew what you were getting into when you volunteered. You take the consequences.' I guess that's where my, like, ambivalent attitude to the service comes from. We give everything, they treat us like dogshit in return."

"Not here, though," I said.

"Seems that way. And Gid, don't worry. Seriously. We won't fuck this up. I've got your back, bruv."

I patted his scarred cheek. "Mate, I know you have. I've no worries on that score."

UTGARD LOOMED AHEAD. The pilots summoned me up to the cockpit for a squint. It was like some amazing dream-city, all shimmering spires and gleaming domed roofs. It rose sheer from the plain of ice, and it was ice itself, white and pale blue and in some places transparent but shot through with sparkling rainbow glints. There were layers to it, layers within layers folded together like the petals of a rose, and hundreds of cylindrical towers capped with spikes, reminiscent of minarets. In all it looked delicate and sturdy at the same time. Unshakeable. Unbreachable. Eternal.

Fair took my breath away.

"I'd never have imagined..." I said. "The frost giants are such honking great clodhoppers, but *this*..."

"Not bad, is it?" said the first pilot, Flight Lieutenant Jensen. Ex-RAF, and a decent enough bloke. Posh but not stuck-up like a lot of Blue Job flyboys were. Same applied to his co-pilot, Flying Officer Thwaite, who did insist on wearing the most annoying moustache in the world ever. Like a miniature bog brush fastened to his upper lip. He might as well have had I AM A BELL-END tattooed there instead. And he and Jensen were permanently deadpan, as though there was some massive private joke going on that only they were in on. But still, like I said, decent enough, the pair of them.

"Tall as Canary Wharf, some of those towers," Thwaite said. "And the whole thing's got to cover several hundred hectares, wouldn't you say, Jenners? For what's essentially a castle, that's pretty damn sizeable."

Jensen nodded. "Well-fortified, too. Only one way in or out, far as I can tell – that gate, with the bridge in front. Otherwise, rampart walls a couple of hundred metres high and a huge crevasse all the way round the perimeter. You could defend the place for ever and no one would get in."

"But we're not laying siege to it," I pointed out. "Just going up and knocking on the front door."

"Your funeral," Thwaite offered out of the side of his mouth.

"You'd like us to do a flyby, correct?" said Jensen.

"Make a meal of it," I told him. "They already know we're here. They'll have heard this crate coming a mile off. Let them have a good look at us, show them we're not making an effort to be sneaky or anything, it's all out in the open."

"'We come in peace.'"

"That's the general idea."

"These are frost giants, Coxall," said Thwaite. "I don't think 'peace' is in their vocabulary."

"Then today's the day they learn a new word."

Jensen yanked on the cyclic control column and took us in close to Utgard. We buzzed the jotun stronghold clockwise, banking steeply, and by the time we were halfway round, scores of frost giants were appearing on the battlements and on the balconies of towers. They gesticulated at us. They hopped up and down. I could see them yelling, and you didn't have to be a lip-reader to tell that they weren't showering us with warm words of welcome. Several of them, to get their point across, even turned, bent over and mooned us.

"A frostie's arse," I said. "Ugh. There's a sight I hoped I'd never see again."

Once we'd completed our circuit and made sure there couldn't be a single frost giant in Utgard who wasn't aware of our presence, Jensen stamped on the rudder pedals and we veered sharply off at right angles.

"How far out do you want me to set down?"

"Near, but not too near. A klick should do it. They're already spooked, so best not rub it in. Besides, I fancy a stroll more than a hike."

I went aft to inform the team that we were on standby to land, not that they didn't know this already.

To the lads I said, "Kindly fasten your seatbelts, return your tray tables to upright, and stop trying to fondle the stewardesses' bums."

Then to the Valkyries I said, "Ladies, you're here for emergency extraction purposes only. We come out of that place running, with a hod of frost giants up our arses, you swoop in and pick us up and get us back to *Sleipnir* ASAP."

The three of them looked at me as though I was the village idiot telling them how to tie their own shoelaces.

"We have trailer sleds fastened to the rear of our snowmobiles," one of them said. "What else are we likely to be wanting to do with them?"

"Just don't dawdle. You spot us coming, no hanging around, come fetch, fast as you can."

"We know how to drive these vehicles, mortal. Unlike some."

"Yeah, yeah, all right. I'm sorry. How many times do I have to say it? I stole your snowmobile and crashed it, and I'm sorry. It'll never happen again."

Apologies didn't wash with Valkyries, apparently. I wasn't ever going to be forgiven for my spot of twocking. They'd patched the snowmobile up, beaten out the dents and got it working again, but still. I'd sullied their "precious thing" with my grubby non-godly hands and that was an unpardonable offence.

Nonetheless, I didn't doubt that they would race to our rescue if need be, all guns blazing. According to Odin, the Valkyries were as dependable as rain at a picnic (although that wasn't precisely how he'd put it) and, moreover, they loved a good scrap. If we got into difficulties they'd be there like a shot. Trouble was something Valkyries hurried towards, not away from. They had a nose for it, Odin had said. Could scent it a mile off. Lapped it up.

Sleipnir bumped to earth, flinging up great billows of powder snow around it. The cargo ramp opened, letting in a burst of frigid air, and the Valkyries mounted their snowmobiles and roared outside, trailer sleds rattling along behind them. Each trailer sled seated two and, practising with them, we'd found that it was a safe ride, as long as you hung on for dear life to the handle grips on the sides. Otherwise you could easily get bounced off. The Valkyries parked in the lee of the chopper, whose fuselage screened them from direct line of sight from Utgard. The rest of us shouldered our weapons and, hunching against the bite of a bitter wind, began the march across the ice to the stronghold.

FORTY

THERE WAS A reception committee waiting at the gate. A couple of dozen frost giants in full ice-armour regalia, armaments galore, and not a friendly smile to be seen. I motioned to the others to hold back. Then, solo, I set a tentative foot on the bridge spanning the crevasse. A quick glance over the edge showed me a sheer and apparently bottomless drop. I felt a wobble of vertigo. No handrail, no barrier of any kind, nothing to stop you slipping off the side and falling if you didn't watch your footing. Health and Safety would have had a stroke.

I took another step forwards, and the frost giants firmed their grips on their weapons and growled.

One of them had a fancier helmet and a more ornately engraved breastplate than the rest, marking him out as the commanding officer present, captain of the guard or some such. He came out a few paces from the gateway to challenge me, *issgeisl* to the fore.

"Aesir!" he boomed. "Halt. You are trespassing on sovereign jotun territory. It is prohibited. Take one step further and perish."

"Two points, sunshine," I said, ticking them off on my fingers. "One: I'm not an Aesir, I'm just your bog-standard mortal. And two: it's not really trespassing if you come in an official capacity, is it?"

The frost giant just snarled, revealing blunt yellow teeth.

"All right," I said, "I'm willing to concede on that. You say I'm trespassing, then I am. But I have business here."

"With who?"

"First off, can I ask your name?"

He looked startled. "My name is no affair of yours."

"Hear, hear!" agreed one of the frost giants behind him. "That's the way, Suttung, give him nothing."

I nearly snorted with laughter.

The captain of the guard, Suttung, wheeled round and clouted the other frost giant with the flat of his *issgeisl* blade.

"Dimwit!" he cried. "Next time think before you open your mouth."

The other frost giant, rubbing his head, took a moment to work out what he'd done wrong, then cringed with shame.

"Well now... Suttung, is it?" I said. "I was wondering if Bergelmir's in."

"What if he is?" Suttung puffed out his chest, hoping to regain some of the authority his subordinate had lost for him.

"I want a word with him. I'd like to parley."

"Parley?" Suttung frowned. "You come here with guns, yet all you wish to do is talk? Forgive me if I find that hard to believe."

"I understand your suspicion, but the guns are just a precaution. Face it, you wouldn't turn up on the doorstep at Asgard unarmed, would you? But look at us. Only six of us, and there's three times as many of you guys here and thousands more within those walls. We're obviously no threat. We'd be crazy to think we were. Therefore you have to accept that what I'm saying is true. It stands to reason."

Suttung tried to look sly and knowing, which for the average frostie did not come naturally. "This could all be some trick. Some clever ploy. Odin is a cunning one."

"Nah, you're thinking of Loki there, mate, not Odin. But it is on the All-Father's behalf that we've come. I'd very much like an audience with Bergelmir, in Odin's name."

"And what if mighty Bergelmir does not desire an audience with you?"

"Oh he will," I said. "Just give him this message. Tell him, 'Hval the Bald's a lot shorter than he used to be.' Coming from a human, that ought to tweak his todger."

MINUTES PASSED. THEN the frost giant that Suttung had sent off with my message returned, and not long after that the six of us were being escorted through Utgard. The city guard formed a tight phalanx around us, and every so often there'd be a spot of jostling, an "accidental" jab with an elbow, an attempt to trip one of us up with a carelessly trailing weapon haft. None of us rose to it, we kept our cool, and soon enough the frost giants got bored of trying to provoke us. It was no fun if we didn't react.

Utgard really was a marvel. I hated to be so impressed by it, but I was. The place had everything you might have expected to find in a medium-size metropolis, all the amenities – shops, workplaces, plazas, accommodation – and every last bit of it constructed from ice. Ice walls, ice windows, ice furniture, ice tools. I saw a fishmonger's shop, his goods laid out in front keeping fresh on ice trays. I saw jotun kids, tall as me, playing with dolls of ice. I saw municipal statues, ice sculptures far larger and more intricate than any I'd ever seen made by human hands. A snowball was lobbed at me, chips of ice scraped up off the ground and compacted together by some frostie showing off to his mates how much he despised anyone from Asgard. It stung, but I shrugged it off.

Finally we reached a citadel, a palatial igloo-shaped building whose sides were studded with millions of ice crystals, creating a dazzling diamante effect. Liberace and Dolly Parton would have felt right at home here. Inside there was more of the frou-frou architecture and design: spindly columns carved in rising spirals, skeletal staircases that curved and arched and seemed to have no purpose other than just to be there, and ceilings with shapes suspended from them that resembled either snail shells or, if you had a mind to it, dog turds. There were also large numbers of...

"Chops, what do you call those carvings on the walls?"

"Ice friezes?" suggested Chopsticks.

"I know it does, but –"

"No, *friezes*. Ice *friezes*."

"Ohhh."

"Quiet, humans!" barked Suttung. "No talking."

Some of the friezes depicted great jotuns throughout history, heroes and leaders in suitably noble and dramatic stances. Others showed frost giants and Aesir in battle. Still others were unflattering portraits of Jotunheim's Public Enemy Number One, Thor. Thor, very overweight, with boss eyes, man-boobs, and a tiddly little Mjolnir held at crotch level. Thor going toe-to-toe with some frost giant or other and looking like he was getting the worst of the fight, even though I was pretty sure he'd never actually lost any of his legendary clashes with the jotuns. Thor lying face down, comatose, surrounded by empty drinking vessels, with a puddle of what could only be urine seeping out from under him. It was a crude, tub-thumping display of propaganda; part of me wished Thor could be here to see it, and part of me was relieved he wasn't.

A throne chamber at the heart of the building was where Bergelmir was waiting for us. He was perched on a dais with wife Leikn by his side, and I could tell he'd thought long and hard about how he should be posed when we were brought in. He'd settled on Broodingly Contemplative – legs akimbo, chin on fist, free hand toying with an ice dagger.

The room itself was packed with frost giants, and our escort had to shove through the crowd to get to the dais. More frost giants entered behind us, and even more stood on the gallery that ran round the chamber at first-floor height. The mood was distinctly hostile, which was no big surprise, but I tried not to let it faze me. In prison I'd been good at defusing tension. I could surely put that same skill into practice here.

"Ah yes, you," Bergelmir said, glaring at me. "Give me one good reason why I shouldn't gut you with this knife, right here, right now, and strangle you with your own innards."

To judge by the mutterings all around, the frosties could give him several good reasons why he should.

"Yeah, nice to see you again too, Bergelmir," I said. "Glad you survived that glacier getting blown up."

"Don't try your blandishments on me, human scum. There's no love lost between us."

"Okay, so I admit we didn't part as the best of friends last time. But that wasn't my fault, really, was it? I didn't ask to fight a duel with one of you lot, and I certainly didn't expect to win."

"That you did win is all that's keeping me from ordering your immediate execution. Yours and your associates'."

"I appreciate it. To be honest, I've been counting on it. I sensed – and if I'm wrong about this, please say so – but I sensed that in some strange way, in spite of everything, you quite admire me."

Bergelmir laughed, once, sharply.

"Maybe not admire, then," I said, "but perhaps respect? By frost giant standards I did well. You people put a premium on courage in battle and ruthlessness, and that's what I showed."

"True," said Bergelmir. "I would go further and say you have a callous disregard for your opposition, and not only that but an insanity inside you that comes to the fore in combat. A blind berserker rage. Would you agree with such a description?"

"I might, at a pinch."

"Which makes you exceedingly dangerous, not least since you've aligned yourself with our longstanding adversaries the Aesir. And now here you are, in our very midst, surrounded, at our mercy. Hmmm. Would I be wrong in thinking this is a perfect chance to dispose of a very irksome enemy combatant? Whatever your aim in coming here and surrendering yourself to us, it seems too good an opportunity to pass up, eh?"

"He must die," Leikn hissed at her husband's ear. "They all must."

"It's a reasonable point, Leikn," I said, "and a fella should always listen to his missus." I looked back to Bergelmir. "My main objection is that you have no idea what I've come offering. Aren't you just a little bit curious to know what it is I'm after? I would be, if I was in your shoes. If you wore shoes. I'd be asking myself, 'What's this bloke want from me? He's put himself and a bunch of his pals at risk, knowing that even with guns they wouldn't last long against this many jotuns – so why? What's he up to?'"

"Why should it matter to me what you're up to? You're only human. Insignificant. I don't even know your name."

"Gid Coxall. There, now you do. Pleased to meet you."

"It makes no difference," Bergelmir said with a casual wave of the dagger. "You could be called Arsecrack Walrusbreath for all I care."

That raised a titter from the home crowd.

"The fact is," he went on, "while your audacity is to be commended, and your personal courage not in doubt, I have no interest whatsoever in anything you might have to tell me. All that concerns me is the manner of your death, which will be of my choosing."

He stood and made a gesture.

"Seize him! Seize them all!"

And before any of us could react, we'd been grabbed by the frost giants, and our guns had been taken from us, and our arms had been pinned behind our backs, and all of a sudden the situation wasn't looking too clever any more.

FORTY-ONE

WITH A COUPLE of frost giants holding each of us in place and Bergelmir putting his dagger blade to my neck, the casual observer could have been forgiven for thinking we were well and truly fucked.

And we were.

And it would be a lie to say I'd anticipated this turn of events.

But all was not lost. So long as I could keep talking.

"Here's the thing, Bergelmir," I said. He'd bent down. We were virtually eye to eye. "You know as well as I do that there's big trouble brewing. Loki's on the warpath and he's got Asgard in his sights. There's going to be a major incursion any day now. It could even have begun already, in the time since I left to pop over to Jotunheim and have this lovely chat with you. Ragnarök's just around the corner. If the Aesir can't defeat Loki, he'll wipe them off the map. You know he will. He hates them that much."

"And in what way is such an outcome undesirable for us?" Bergelmir said. "If Loki destroys Asgard and all who dwell there, so what? He will have done everyone a favour. Are you not aware, Gid Coxall, that Loki was one of us, jotun-born?"

"Yeah, operative word 'was.' Isn't any more. He renounced his race, didn't he? Turned his back on you. Denied his roots. Became an Aesir in all but name. And he'd still be living as one of them now, all chums together, if he hadn't gone and overstepped the mark and got Balder killed. So you can claim he's your countryman if you like, a proud patriotic jotun, but you know and I know he isn't. The only side Loki's on is Loki's."

"You've heard the saying, though, 'My enemy's enemy is my friend'?"

"But is he? Is he really? Do you genuinely think that? After all, it's not as if he's come to you asking for your help in taking on Asgard. Where did he go when he escaped incarceration? Which of the Nine Worlds did he run to? Where's he been for the past few years putting together his special fancy-schmancy strikeforce? Not Jotunheim, that's for sure."

The effect this had on Bergelmir wasn't quite what I'd been after. He pressed the ice dagger even harder against my neck. The edge of the blade was so cold it hurt, a thread of fire on my skin. I wondered if it would feel any different when it actually sliced in, if I would even realise I was being cut.

Eyes on the prize, Gid, I told myself, *not on the penalty*. There were five other lives here at stake, not just mine. Cy, Baz, Paddy, Backdoor and Chopsticks had placed their complete trust in me. We were none of us getting out of here if I didn't somehow turn things around, and sharpish.

"He went to Midgard, didn't he?" I said. "Apparently it never even crossed his mind to look up his own blood relatives and ask if they might be willing to chip in and do their bit. What does that tell us, I wonder, about his feelings for you? To me it says he doesn't have any – except maybe shame. It's like he's embarrassed there's frost giant in him at all. He wasn't born looking like one of you, but he has the ability to turn himself into one of you if he wants, and has he ever done that? No. He prefers looking like an Aesir. He even prefers looking like a human woman. I mean, come on! He couldn't make it any clearer than that how he's pulled up his roots."

"So?" said Bergelmir. "It doesn't alter the fact that Loki wants what we want, which is an end to the Aesir. Were he to exterminate them all, especially the accursed Thor, there would be nothing but rejoicing throughout Jotunheim."

"But do you think it'll end there? Do you think conquering Asgard will be enough for him? He's doing his best to take over Midgard. Asgard's the next step. And after that? He's the power-mad type. One world, even two worlds, won't satisfy him. Not when there are nine of them available. I reckon after Asgard, Jotunheim will be third on his to-do list."

"You don't know that."

"No, I don't," I told him, in all honesty. "But you'd have to agree it's far from a remote possibility. He has such a low opinion of you, his fellow frost giants. What's a good way of demonstrating that? By coming here and crushing you. If he càn, he will."

"So what are you proposing?"

"Bergelmir, no!" said Leikn. "You're not falling for this, are you? I've never heard such claptrap in all my life."

"Hush!" Bergelmir snapped. "Stop talking, wife."

"But the human lies. With his every breath he lies. He will say anything to save his own wretched skin."

"I will be the judge of that, not you."

I buried a smirk. I was talking Bergelmir around, I knew it. Rejecting his wife's advice was a surefire sign that what I was saying was making sense to him.

"I'm proposing," I said, "an alliance."

"I thought as much," said Bergelmir. "It's out of the question, of course."

"Is it?"

"Jotuns fighting *alongside* Aesir? It'll never happen."

But the dagger was no longer pressing against my neck. That suggested it could.

"Separately, Loki's forces could beat us," I said. "Together, side by side, I doubt it. We could certainly give him a run for his money."

"And who would command this joint army?"

"You and Odin, equally."

"Has Odin consented to this?"

"I'm here as his spokesman. Anything I say carries his approval."

Bergelmir stepped back, making a thoughtful sound. The dagger was now pointing downwards. I wasn't in danger of a fatal tracheotomy any more. Hooray.

"I'm still not convinced Loki means us ill," Bergelmir said. "Blood is blood, and cannot be ignored. Forsworn perhaps, but it will always win out in the end. However..."

It was a substantial *however*, and it made Leikn fold her arms and go "Hmph!" while the rest of the assembled frost giants pricked up their ears, knowing their leader was about to make a statement of some importance.

"It would be foolish of me not to give this matter some consideration," he said. "The security of Jotunheim is paramount at all times. If we and the Aesir do share a common foe, then it isn't inconceivable that some sort of combined effort to repel that foe would be in order. I am not promising anything." This was directed straight at me. "Do not return to Odin telling him that the jotuns have agreed to some kind of pact with the Aesir. That is not so."

"What can I tell him, then?"

"That we will debate amongst ourselves, our wisest will apply their minds to the problem, and we will furnish him with an answer at some point."

"When?"

"We will not be rushed, Gid Coxall. It will be in our own time, when we feel ready."

"Can't say fairer than that, I suppose. Bergelmir, you're a star, and it's been a pleasure doing business with you."

I held out a hand. Bergelmir gave me a deep frown.

"Do you mock me?" he said. "A minute ago I was a whisker away from killing you. Now you wish to shake my hand?"

"Why not? You *didn't* kill me. That's as good a reason as any for some kind of friendly gesture."

Bemused, he wrapped his hairy paw around my hand, engulfing it.

"You," he said, "are a remarkable specimen. I find you hard to fathom. You aggravate me no end, yet it's hard to dislike you."

"You should get together with my ex. I think you and her would agree on every count. Except the not disliking part."

Bergelmir straightened up and clicked his fingers. "Release them all," he commanded. "Give them back their guns. They leave Utgard under my safekeeping. No one is to harm them. Anyone who causes them grief will answer to me."

MOMENTS LATER OUR squad was wending its way out of the citadel, encircled by guards as before, but more of them now. I was feeling double-dicked-dog pleased with myself, as I had every right to. The boys were looking pretty chipper too. It had been a close-run thing. I'd been one careless word, one slight misstep away from getting us all slaughtered. They'd held their nerve, and so had I, and it had paid off. The frost giants were going to come onboard, I'd have bet good money on it. It might take them a while to come round to the idea, but they would. Thor wasn't going to be overjoyed, but big deal. He'd just have to get used to it. It made sound strategic sense. We needed the sheer numbers the frost giants could provide. We needed their muscle. And now we could almost certainly count on it. A good day's work, done well. Trebles all round in the mess this evening.

Except, it was more likely to be an early night for me. I'd been riding an adrenaline surge, and now it was ebbing and exhaustion was starting to slug away at me once more. The prospect of my little bunk in the dormitory cabins was awfully enticing. I couldn't wait to turn in.

Trust me for thinking smug, cosy thoughts just when a huge consignment of shit was on course to hit a very rapidly spinning fan.

FORTY-TWO

THE SQUAD WAS strung out in a line, single file, with me at the head, so I didn't myself see what actually sparked off the whole clusterfuck. All I knew was that, suddenly, someone was firing shots, and a frost giant was screeching in agony, and other frost giants were roaring and gibbering, and all kinds of chaos had erupted.

I spun round, and there was a mill of bodies, big and small, frosties and humans. Glassy weapons shone in the sunlight. Guns sparked and spat. Suttung was ordering his guardsmen to stand firm and retaliate. They, for their part, weren't too keen on obeying. Two – no, three – of them were lying on the ground, blood pumping out through shattered ice armour. I glimpsed Paddy and Baz, both down on one knee, blasting away with their assault rifles. Cy and Backdoor were backing off towards the nearest wall, laying down suppressing fire. Chopsticks wasn't immediately in view.

We were in some kind of open-air marketplace, located in a square with an entrance at each corner. Frost giant civilians were screaming and running for cover. Vendors cowered behind their stalls.

Suttung at last got his subordinates marshalled. They mounted a concerted attack, and my lot redoubled their defensive efforts.

Me, I was still too stunned to react. I couldn't make sense of how things had gone so pear-shaped so quickly. I heard myself yelling for a ceasefire but nobody could hear me above all the hullabaloo and gunplay, and anyway there were frost giants now coming at us from all directions, so putting up our weapons was not a viable tactic.

Finally I spotted Chopsticks amid the mêlée. He was crawling towards an open doorway, leaving a huge smear of blood behind him on the ice like a crimson slug-trail. I darted towards him, but a frost giant blocked my way. He had a see-through broadsword in his hands, which he swung and whirled impressively. I unholstered my Glock and took out his left kneecap. I hurdled him as he collapsed, still beelining for Chopsticks.

Somebody else was heading towards him too, unfortunately. A frost giant, and he was much closer than I was. He was equipped with a kind of scythe. It had a reach of at least three metres, and the comma-shaped blade was as long as my arm. I loosed off a couple of rounds at him, but I was going full tilt and my aim was off. Chopsticks wasn't even aware that the bastard was looming over him. He kept on crawling, using elbows and clawed hands, every inch of his progress a hideous, agonised effort. He was half-paralysed, I guessed, his legs useless, some kind of spinal injury, and the doorway was broad and inviting, a promise of sanctuary, of safety...

And then the frost giant with the scythe took a powerful sideways swipe at him and sliced him clean in two at the waist.

"*No!*" I hit the frost giant running, slamming into him shoulder first. As he went down I double-tapped him in the face with the Glock, point blank range. Hollow-point Parabellum rounds; his brains hit the ground before the rest of him did.

I whirled and sprang to Chopsticks's side, but there were to be no groaned last words from him, no brave smile for his comrade-in-arms. The scythe had left him instantly, utterly, uncompromisingly dead.

I rose shakily. Took stock.

Frost giants were closing in on the other four, who were still in their pairs. Bullets picked off the frosties one by one, but as each fell another lunged in to take his place. We hadn't brought heaps of ammo with us. The guns had been meant for security and show. Nobody had reckoned on needing them for a full-scale ding-dong. I saw Baz toss his Minimi aside, having used up both the magazines he'd had on him. Out came his sidearm, a Browning BDM semiauto. Its clip held fifteen rounds, but after that was empty there'd be no more.

From the way Backdoor was conserving shots with his SA80, I guessed he was running low too.

And more frost giants were piling in from elsewhere. Civilians, unarmoured, were getting in on the act, picking up any handy object and bringing it to the fray.

It was hopeless. Only one thing we could do.

"Fall back!" I called out. "We can't hold position. Fall back!"

The lads heard me and understood, and I jabbed an arm behind me in the direction of the square's south-east corner, which is where we'd been headed before everything went tits up, and I supplied covering fire to allow first Baz and Paddy, then Cy and Backdoor to retreat to the exit there, and they in turned covered me while I joined them.

We scarpered out of the market square down a narrow passageway, with frost giants pursuing us in a howling, irate mob. Shots over our shoulders gave them something to think about but didn't deter them much. We weren't aiming, and mostly all we did was blow a chunk out of the side of someone's house or turn a windowpane into something you'd put in your gin and tonic.

We zigzagged left and right through a maze of side-streets and alleys. I'd no idea if this was the route we'd come in by, although I was 99% sure it wasn't. Our principal objective was putting distance between us and our pursuers. Beyond that, if we were lucky enough to find our way to the main gate or even just the perimeter wall, that would be a bonus.

"Anybody got a clue what happened back there?" Baz yelled. "Who the bloody fook started firing and why?"

"Save it," I told him. "We can post-mortem later. First let's make sure there's no more mortem to be post."

We rounded a corner and, would you believe it, ran headlong into another bunch of frost giant guards. This lot, four in all, had obviously been alerted by the gunfire that something untoward was up and were rushing to help. We despatched them in pretty short order, but it cost us precious bullets and the delay gave the frosties chasing us time to catch up.

A whirling object whistled past my ear, embedding itself in the wall to my right. One of those ice tomahawks. An inch to the left and I'd have been deaf on both sides; two inches and not being able to hear would have been the least of my concerns.

"Move!" I bellowed, and we moved, leaping over the frost giant bodies in front and scurrying pell-mell along the street. We were in anaerobic mode, like sprinters, sucking in enough air to meet our muscles' demand for oxygen but with nothing to spare. We couldn't keep up this pace much lomger. Cy, the youngest and by far the fittest of us, was racing ahead, but even he would burn out eventually. Flat-out, we were faster than the frosties, nimbler. But they took longer strides, and were generally stronger, with greater levels of endurance. In short, we were managing to stay ahead of them but only just, and we wouldn't be able to maintain our lead indefinitely. When we crapped out they'd be on us in a flash, and once our remaining bullets were spent and our guns were removed from the equation, we stood about as much chance of surviving as I did of sleeping with Jennifer Lopez.

Which might happen, but only in some parallel universe where J.Lo was blind and desperate and I was the last non-impotent man on the planet.

Then salvation appeared ahead, or at any rate a close approximation of it.

Utgard's outer wall.

All we had to do was follow it around, and we'd be at the gate.

Naturally, though, it wasn't going to be that simple. On reaching the wall itself we realised there was no convenient ring road that ran along the inside of it. Buildings butted up hard against its flank in either direction. The street we were on effectively dead-ended with it. Our only chance lay with the set of steep steps that projected out from the wall, leading up to the battlements that crowned it.

I didn't need to give any command. Cy started up the steps, Backdoor went next, and the rest of us were close behind, me taking the rear.

The steps were slippery. Each of us lost his footing several times, not helped by the mob of frosties, who bombarded us with weapons and anything else they could lay their paws on. That was if they weren't following us up the steps, which dozens of them did and which, with their sickle-claw toes gouging into the ice, they made a far better job of than we were making.

In fact, the front runner of them gained on me so fast, and was so close to snaring my heel with one outstretched hand, that I had to stop and turn and expend a bullet on him. His lifeless body thudded heavily into the frost giant behind, knocking him off-balance so that the two of them – one dead, one alive – toppled off the steps and plunged onto the roof of the house below and from there tumbled onto the street. It bought me a few metres' grace, although the Glock's slide had locked back, indicating that the pistol was now as much use as voting Green.

Cy reached the top, gunning down a couple of frosties who came charging towards him along the battlements. Then the rest of us were up there with him, and Paddy took it on himself to defend the steps, crouching with his SA80 set to single shot and planting rounds in the frost giants as they ascended. They could only come up one at a time, so that was fine as far as it went. Paddy could mow them down pretty efficiently, provided he aimed at armour-free parts of their bodies. He didn't have the luxury of missing; if he failed to account for each frost giant with the very first shot, the creature had a chance to get within striking distance, and then he'd be rogered.

Of course, he didn't have an endless supply of ammo, either.

But he stayed there, unhesitating, somehow able to steady his breathing so that each trigger-pull fell in the lull between exhalation and inhalation, and he whittled down the oncoming frosties.

Balls of fucking titanium, that Irishman.

He was only postponing the inevitable, though. He knew it, we all of us knew it. The frost giants would storm the battlements sooner or later.

I scanned both ways. There were watchtowers positioned at intervals all along the battlements, and other sets of steps that gave access up here. Already I could see sentries venturing out from the next watchtower but one, heading for us. There'd be more joining them before too long. I imagined Bergelmir had been informed by now that the delegation from Asgard had, for reasons best known to themselves, betrayed his trust and gone rogue. He'd be hopping mad and sending out every armed man he had with orders to bring back our cocks on sticks.

We had minutes left, if that.

I looked out over the battlements' sharp crenellations and saw a sight that gladdened my heart. But only a little.

The Valkyries were skimming towards us across the ice on their snowmobiles. They'd be at the stronghold's edge in seconds.

Thing was, we were two hundred metres up, and they were down there, and a crevasse yawned between us and them.

The Valkyries were coming to the rescue, but there wasn't actually anything practical they could do to get us out of this shitstorm.

FORTY-THREE

THE GOOD NEWS – there was some – was that *Sleipnir*'s rotors were starting to turn. Jensen and Thwaite must have clocked our predicament and recognised that an emergency airborne exfiltration was our best and probably only hope.

The downside of the good news was that it would take time to get the Chinook in the air. Wokkas couldn't just spring up from a standing start. Engines had to cycle, everything had to be running smoothly and all tickety-boo before a great goliath like that could lift off. The bigger the aircraft, the more of a warm-up it needed to get going. However frantically the pilots were prepping in the cockpit, *Sleipnir* could not be rushed.

Steady on, said those slowly speeding up rotors. *All in good time. I'm going as fast as I can.*

"Not fast enough, you bugger," I growled under my breath.

"Gid!" Paddy called out. "I'm dry. What're the options?"

"This way. We make for the gate."

We scuttled along the battlements, arriving at the first watchtower at roughly the same time as the sentries from the next watchtower along did. Basically it was a covered platform that jutted out from the wall, over the crevasse. There, we and the two sentries engaged. Backdoor's Browning burped its last, killing one of them. I snatched up the dead sentry's *issgeisl* and ran it through his mate, who looked startled, as if he couldn't work out how a human could handle a frost giant handweapon so well.

"I had practice," I told him, and the *issgeisl* made a great wet slurp as I yanked it out of his belly, taking some of his innards with it.

On we went. The Valkyries were directly beneath us, shadowing our progress on their snowmobiles. Rendezvousing with them at the gate was the only strategy that made any sense, but while they'd have no trouble getting there, we had a gauntlet to run. Plus, Suttung and his guardsmen were right on our tails.

Awesome.

But seeing as the only alternative was to surrender, and the frosties were hardly in a mood for taking prisoners, what else could we do?

Another pair of sentries blocked our path, and a quick check confirmed what I feared. Everyone was out of ammo. Backdoor's pistol shot had been our collective last.

I took point, meeting the first sentry with my *issgeisl* already swinging. He parried with his broadsword, then aimed a thrust at my chest. I sidestepped and brought the *issgeisl*'s axe end up between his legs.

His eyes bulged, his face registered stunned amazement, and then came a scream that would have made even Germaine Greer wince in sympathy. Frankly my next blow, using the spear end to slit his throat from ear to ear, was an act of compassion.

The second sentry was on me before the first had fallen. He chopped at me with his tomahawk, and I only avoided radical facial rearrangement by bending backwards like a contortionist. I collided with the rim of the battlements, completely off-kilter, in no fit state to block or duck his follow-up shot. His look said it all. *A-ha! I have you now!*

Then in an instant it changed to *huh?*

This was accompanied by the top of his head disintegrating in a red mist, and that jibed with the fact that a bullet from a high-velocity rifle fired from below had entered beneath his jaw and exited via his crown. A hell of a shot from an almost impossible angle, but one of the Valkyries had managed to take it, and I didn't pause to wonder who she might have hit if her aim had been just a smidgeon off, because the likely answer was me. Instead I gave her a quick wave of acknowledgement and let Cy grab me by the sleeve and hustle me onward.

Suttung and company were nearly on us by this time, and to add to our woes dozens of guardsmen cresting the set of steps ahead. We were sandwiched between two large groups of the enemy, with no way off the battlements except to leap over the side and plummet to certain death.

Paddy began murmuring a prayer. "Hail Mary, Full of Grace... Colm O'Donough here. If you're listening, now would be a fine time for a miracle. I know I've not been the best of Catholic sons and I may have said and done some things you wouldn't approve of, but if you could just see your way to helping us out..."

I felt like joining in. No atheists in foxholes and all that.

The frost giants slowed their approach, partly through caution but mainly through confidence. They knew they had us trapped. Suttung looked especially gleeful. He was itching to get his hands on the humans who'd done for so many of his guardsmen.

"Sell yourselves dearly, lads," I said.

Cy seemed on the point of speaking. There was something urgent on his mind.

Then – salvation.

Not divine intervention. Not a direct response from Him Upstairs to Paddy's prayer. But good enough.

Sleipnir bellied in from out of nowhere, with a roar like a thousand angry dragons. The Chinook swung about, presenting us with its huge rear end, and the cargo door was open and the ramp was extended down towards us, almost touching the battlements.

"Well, what are you waiting for?" I bawled at the boys. "An embossed fucking invitation?"

The downwash from the rotors was literally staggering. It pummelled and pounded from above. Even simply standing upright under it was an effort. Nevertheless Baz was able to crawl onto the crenellations and leap across to the ramp. Backdoor followed him, then Cy and Paddy in swift succession.

I saw Suttung howl with frustration, the sound swamped by the insanely loud cacophony from *Sleipnir*'s exhaust ducts. The humans were getting away! He urged his guardsmen forwards, and they tottered along the battlements, bent double, shielding their faces.

I abandoned the *issgeisl* and scrambled onto the crenellations to make the jump to *Sleipnir* myself. At that same moment the Wokka veered closer to the stronghold, too close for comfort, and Jensen had to make a correction. All at once the gap between battlements and ramp widened. It was now something like four metres, further than I could have managed even with a run-up. Baz and Backdoor were gesticulating at me from the cargo bay: *come on!* Cy and Paddy were crouched on the ramp, holding out their hands. The frost giants were seconds away.

Ah well, what the fuck. Damned if you do, damned if you don't. Who wants to live for ever? Et cetera.

I sprang.

Geronimo!

FORTY-FOUR

I WASN'T GOING to make it. Even as my boot soles parted company with the battlements I knew I was going to fall short of the ramp and start a long plunge into the crevasse. It was just the way it had to be. I couldn't have stayed put. Jumping and hoping was all I had.

So I was surprised as hell to thump chest-first against the lip of one of the ramp's three extensions, and just as surprised to find myself clinging on there, using hands, elbow and even chin to keep me in place. I bicycled my legs, trying to get a knee up onto the extension. Then hands fastened onto my uniform tunic, digging into its layers of padding, and I was hauled unceremoniously up and over like some item of baggage until all of me was on the ramp proper. I lay there, prone, gasping like a landed fish. I could hardly believe I'd done it. Still in one piece.

Someone else couldn't believe it either. Suttung.

As *Sleipnir* began to draw away from Utgard, he launched himself off the battlements, determined that his pursuit wasn't going to end here. He hurtled through space and hit the ramp with an almighty clang, flat on his stomach. Immediately he began sliding off and scrabbled for purchase. His talons found little they could dig into on the ramp's cross-hatched surface until, by chance, one hand encountered my ankle. He latched on, but his slide continued, and now he was dragging me with him.

The boys cottoned on fast that I was in trouble. It might have had something to do with me shouting out, "Fuck's sake, he's pulling me down!" They grabbed my arms and braced themselves. Suttung had slipped completely free of the ramp and was dangling off the end of it, between two of the extensions. The only thing preventing him falling was his hold on me. As my leg was halfway over the lip of the ramp, this was bending my knee the wrong way and causing me some considerable fucking amount of pain.

"Get him off! Get the bastard off me!"

Suttung clamped his free hand onto the ramp. That relieved the strain on my knee a little, but then he lost his grip and dropped back down again. The sudden shift caught everyone unawares, and I was tugged further out of the helicopter. Now I was hooked over the lip of the ramp, which dug excruciatingly into my midriff. The boys planted their heels in and attempted to bring me back up. Suttung hung on grimly. I'd become the rope in a life-or-death tug of war, and to be honest, I wasn't hugely enjoying it. I communicated this fact to the others in what I felt was, under the circumstances, quite a calm and reasonable manner. I might have used the word "cuntbags" once or twice but otherwise I was pretty restrained. Oh, and "shit-fuckers." And possibly "twatting bollockheads." Apart from that, though – a model of dignity and coolness under pressure.

Suttung just wasn't letting go, and to make matters worse his claws were spiking into my shin and Achilles tendon. It seemed likely he'd tear my foot off before he gave up his hold on me. *Sleipnir* was accelerating and he was getting swung in all directions, buffeted by the wind, a mad pendulum. I tried kicking at him with my other foot but he didn't stay in one place long enough for me to connect.

With all four of the lads pulling on me, they started to make some headway, and soon most of my body was back on the ramp. Cy thumped at Suttung's fingers hard as he knew how, but couldn't dislodge his grip. In fact it only made those talons sink in deeper. The blood was now streaking out over my boot, flecking the frost giant's arm and face.

One final heave, and I was safely in the cargo bay once more.

Unfortunately, so was my hanger-on. Suttung got one thigh over the lip of the ramp, then rolled himself the rest of the way in. He was up on his feet and raging in no time. He grabbed Backdoor by the head and threw him the length of the cabin. Backdoor collided with a bank of seats and went down hard. Then Suttung drew a weapon from the waistband of his armour, another of those fucking ice tomahawks. He lashed out at Cy with it, and the kid got a forearm up in the nick of time, which saved him from having a trapezoid-shaped blade embedded deep in his noggin. The downside was that his arm was slashed open clean to the bone. He fell, hissing through his teeth, clutching the wound.

Suttung made a big mistake in hurting Cy, for two reasons. First, I was fond of Cy and it pissed me off. Second, it meant he'd stepped close to where I happened to be lying. So close that I was able to scissor my legs around his ankle, twist, and bring him crashing to his knees.

I hadn't thought this one through too brilliantly, though, since he turned his attention on me. The tomahawk was up, poised, and Suttung's grin said he was looking forward to burying the hatchet with Gid Coxall – and not in a good way.

Then an Irish-accented voice said, "Hello there, frostie. You like cold? How about some dry ice?"

Paddy had the Chinook's fire extinguisher in his hands, and he sprayed the contents full-on into Suttung's ugly mug. Carbon dioxide jetted out from the nozzle in clouds, and Suttung shrieked. The stuff went in his mouth, up his nose, into his eyes, and he reeled backwards, frantically rubbing at his face with both forearms. Paddy gave him no quarter. Kept blasting away with the fire extinguisher. Driving him back towards the ramp.

I scrambled on all fours to help. Suttung teetered on the end of the ramp. His eyes were bloodshot and streaming. He was choking, flailing.

I gave his legs a good shunt, and all at once there was no more frost giant filling the cargo doorway. There was just a vista of Jotunheim, glinting ice fields, Utgard receding on the horizon, and the sounds of hammering wind and a falling, fading scream.

FORTY-FIVE

SLEIPNIR DOUBLED BACK and we picked up the Valkyries and their snowmobiles some two kilometres outside Utgard – a safe distance, and not far, in fact, from the splash of mangled red fur and flesh that had been Suttung. Then we began the journey home.

Five soldiers slouched together in sullen silence. Cy's arm was bandaged up, a nifty piece of field dressing courtesy of Paddy, and he had been fed some ace painkillers from the Wokka's first aid kit. He looked grey but okay. Backdoor was suffering from mild concussion but joked that it was only his head so no vital organs had been damaged. I'd staunched the bleeding from the gashes in my leg. We sat there and avoided one another's gazes. Each of the others wore a face like a slapped cock, and I'd no doubt I did too.

Someone had to skewer the sour mood. Guess who elected himself to do it.

"Well," I said, "that all went swimmingly, didn't it?" Which won a couple of weak smiles and not much else.

"Might as well get this over with," I went on. "What happened? Any idea? Somebody? Anybody?"

Shrugs.

"Come on, one of you must have seen *something*. Who fired first? Why? What at?"

"It was Chops, I think," Cy volunteered. "Not sure, but he was behind me and that's where the shooting started."

"Weren't you taking the rear?" I asked Backdoor.

He nodded. It was noteworthy that neither he nor anyone else sniggered at the phrase "taking the rear." Nothing, right now, was very funny.

"So you'd have been following Chops. Was it him? Did he open fire?"

"I don't know, Gid. I really don't. I wasn't looking his way when it all kicked off. First I knew about it was a couple of frosties were on the deck and so was Chops. It happened that fast. At a push, my guess would be a frostie made a move on Chops and he retaliated."

"Why would one of them do that, though?" I said. "They had specific instructions to leave us alone and not hurt us."

"Yeah, but you know how they was on the way in," said Cy. "All nudging us and giving it attitude and everything. Maybe one of them forgot what Bergelmir said and went back to how they was behaving beforehand, only he took the aggro too far and Chopsticks hit back. We was all on edge, bruv. I mean, Bergelmir, he'd been talking about executing the lot of us not ten minutes earlier."

The others echoed this with a round of disgruntled grunts. I'd not earned myself any Brownie points with the way things had gone in the citadel. Although I'd been able to pull our fat from the fire, the lads weren't happy that our fat had been anywhere near a fire in the first place. I couldn't blame them for that.

"No question, I take full responsibility for this mess," I told them. "My plan, my fuck-up. I just want to find out why things went south, so we can avoid a repeat in future."

"Maybe Chopsticks got careless," Baz offered. "Maybe his safety was off and he stumbled and pulled the trigger by mistake."

I shook my head. "I didn't know him as well as any of you did, but that doesn't strike me as like him. Chops was always measured and cautious. What's more, he'd know better than to march with his finger inside the trigger guard."

"Would he? He were only Territorial, after all. Saturday night soldier."

"Still."

"And accidents happen."

"And if guns are involved they're usually tragic accidents. Somehow, though, I just can't buy this as one of those."

"Maybe," said Paddy in a conciliatory tone, "we should chalk it up to experience and move on. What's done is done. Rehashing it isn't going to change anything and certainly won't bring Chopsticks back. I'll miss the lad because he was just about the only one around here with a bit of culture, unlike the rest of you philistine, pig-ignorant shites. But he's gone, and we should start coming to terms with that."

"And our chances of bringing the frosties onside have been scuppered too," I said bitterly. "We lost a man *and* screwed the mission, so you'll forgive me if I can't put it behind me quite yet, Pads."

"That's your prerogative. All I'm saying is, we're alive at least, even though it was touch-and-go back there for a while. That's worth remembering. It wasn't a total disaster."

"Irish eyes keep smiling, eh? Pot of gold at the end of the rainbow and all that."

"Those are meaningless insults, Gid, and with respect, fuck you."

"Fuck you too, Paddy."

That was the end of that conversation, and *Sleipnir* carried on to Asgard with some very surly and irritable passengers in its hold.

The thing was, an idea had started flitting around in my mind. It was a moth in the dark, flapping against me with its wings, and I kept batting it away but it kept blundering back, and I didn't like it. I didn't like the fact that it was even there, that some crack or chink that shouldn't have existed had allowed it to enter my headspace.

A single word, faintly whispering, bristling with unease.

Sabotage.

FORTY-SIX

I DREAMED I was in the car again. Back in that fucking Vauxhall Astra. Alone. Upside down. Cold. Numb. So numb, I felt I was floating. I didn't have a body any more, I'd slipped free of it and was just this shapeless entity called Gideon Coxall, an insubstantial thing in the darkness.

Then there was light.

It filled the tunnel Abortion had dug in the snow, highlighting every scoop and groove his hands had left. Bluish, coming from outside, it wavered, now bright, now less so.

A torch?

No. A mobile. The glow from a phone screen. Held in someone's hand. Someone who was approaching. Abortion. Had to be.

Maybe he'd found help. Maybe he'd got a phone signal and was coming to tell me the ambulance was on its way. Better yet, a search and rescue helicopter to airlift us the fuck out of here.

I tried to say his name but I didn't have a throat that worked properly. Didn't have a throat at all, it felt like.

The blue light brightened, whitened, rapidly. The end of the tunnel became a flaring dazzle that I couldn't look at any more.

I shut my eyes and opened them and I was in my bunk bed in Asgard. Around me were a couple of dozen men, snoring, snorting, turning over on creaky springs, mumbling in their sleep. A cabin full of slumbering bodies, restless and writhing.

Soldiers – a breed who seldom sleep soundly. Always unconsciously keeping an ear out for the enemy... or else grappling with nightmares.

FORTY-SEVEN

WE WERE NOW on a countdown to a deadline, it seemed. Mrs Keener's visit to the UK drew nearer day by day. Huginn and Muninn flew out over Midgard and sent Odin images of the preparations for her arrival. Odin spoke of city streets being cordoned off for security purposes, the Stars and Stripes being hung out on public buildings, and strenuous debate in the House of Commons over the wisdom and validity of asking her to come at all.

Prime Minister Clasen defended his decision on the grounds that Britain's business ties with the US remained strong, even if politically there were disagreements between the two countries. Besides, wouldn't it be better and more meaningful if he was able to challenge Mrs Keener on diplomatic issues face to face rather than via webcam?

Privately, in Cabinet – the ravens eavesdropped on a window ledge outside Number 10 – Clasen expressed misgivings about the visit, seeming to imply that rather than being invited, the President had more or less invited herself and he had been too intimidated to refuse. Mrs Keener was about to gatecrash, and she probably wasn't even bringing a decent bottle of plonk.

Protestors against American foreign policy were organising mass rallies, although the cops were going to see to it that they didn't get within a placard's throw of Whitehall or any of the other destinations on the presidential itinerary. Hence the street closures. Meanwhile, the TV channels were lobbying for interviews, although so far Mrs Keener's aides had turned down all the journalistic hard cases like Paxman and Dimbleby and approved on-air face time with only Alan Titchmarsh and Adrian Chiles. Real heavyweights who didn't flinch from asking the tough questions like, "What's your favourite colour?"

Our own preparations consisted of drilling like bastards, then drilling again, and then, when we'd had enough of drilling, drilling some more. In my spare time, such as it was, I went out in *Sleipnir* with the drawling RAFfer pilots and we scouted Asgard's borders looking for likely ingress points. Odin put the trolls on subsistence rations to make them less dopey and more aggressive, and it worked, although two of them became so hungry they had a fight and tore off and ate parts of each other, and had to be put down. The Valkyries, for their part, went about on their snowmobiles caching supplies and ammunition in various strategically useful places, mostly near the intersections between Asgard and the other worlds.

Either an attack was coming or it wasn't. Either Loki was going to make his move or he wasn't. That choice was his. Ours was whether to be caught with our knickers around our ankles or not, and we definitely wanted to avoid the "not" option.

I was still pissed off about the frost giants and losing Chopsticks, and I might have betrayed these feelings once or twice. For instance, when Bragi proposed reciting a poem about our recent trip to Jotunheim, and I told him he could stick his poem up his arse and shove that stupid beard of his up there too while he was at it. And another time, when Thor made some joke about being excluded from the mission to Utgard, saying it couldn't surely have gone any worse if he *had* accompanied us and had just started killing jotuns indiscriminately as soon as he arrived.

I suggested where he should shove his hammer – a similar place, funnily enough, to where I felt Bragi's poem and beard belonged

– and Thor looked all set to deck me, and would have if Paddy hadn't played United Nations and got between us and told Thor to go easy on me because I was taking Chopsticks's death very personally. Thor backed down, grumbling, and said that at least his visit to the gnomes had been a success and he'd brought back something of value rather than leaving a corpse behind. At which point I tried to deck *him*, and it took a combined Herculean effort from Paddy, Cy and Baz to keep me from doing so.

THE LAST PERSON I'd have expected to take me aside for a friendly "what's the matter?" chat was Freya Njorthasdottir. But that was exactly who did, on the eve of Mrs Keener's arrival.

Of course she didn't put a gentle arm round my shoulder and suggest we go for a drink. That wouldn't have been very Freya-like. Instead she came at me out of nowhere, thrust a hunting rifle into my hands – a bolt-action Lee-Enfield with fibreglass stock and thick rubber recoil pad – and loped off into the woods without a backward glance. It took me a moment to realise that, since she was carrying a hunting rifle as well, this meant she wanted me to go with her. At first I thought she was simply dropping a not too subtle hint. *Here's a loaded firearm. Go do the decent thing.*

I set off after her. I'd been out admiring a spectacular, rather ominous, blood-red sunset, and now dusk was falling, the trees slatting the purple sky. Shadows gathered, smudging the air beneath the pines. Freya set a formidable pace and I had to run full pelt to keep her pale silhouette in sight. Several times I lost her in the gloom and had to resort to following her footprints. They were shallow, often so faint as to be virtually undetectable; she must weigh next to nothing. I recalled Chopsticks informing me, not long before he died, that the Vanir were airy, spirit-like beings. Unlike their junior cousins the Aesir, who were all too physical and fleshy, the Vanir belonged to a loftier order of existence. The word he used for them was "evanescent." Freya's barely-there footprints proved it. That and the way she could move across snow with scarcely a whisper of sound. That time she sneaked up on me at Yggdrasil, I hadn't heard a thing. No wonder she was such a good huntress. Her prey never had a clue she was coming.

Finally – and I'd sort of begun to accept that this would happen – I lost her. Or she lost me. One or the other. Her tracks faded to invisibility, she herself had long ago sprinted out of view, and I was left panting in the depths of the woods, alone.

I leaned against a tree while I caught my breath. Silence descended around me – the utter silence of a snowbound forest. Nothing else like it in the world. Every noise, even your own breathing, deadened. Nature's soundproofed booth.

Which meant the snap of a rifle bolt being racked right behind my head seemed as loud as if the rifle was actually being fired.

I groaned. She'd done it again.

"Nice one," I said without turning round. "You got me. Don't I just feel like a clumsy mortal oaf."

"It was too easy," said Freya. "I couldn't resist."

"So are we going hunting or what?"

"It depends."

"On?"

"Your definition of hunting. And of prey. Look at me."

I did as I was told.

And gaped.

She was stark naked, apart from an amazing, intricate golden necklace. It had to be the one Odin told me about, the one Loki had tried to nick off her. Complicatedly braided.

Not that I was paying the necklace much attention, mind. Stark naked, remember?

"Ah," was all I said. Power of speech all but gone. A babe in the nuddy with a rifle pointed at your head could do that to you.

She was perfect. Not all inflated and plucked like a porn actress. Lean, curvy where it counted, everything in proper proportion, *real*. The cold air had done to her nipples what her nipples, in turn, were starting to do to my dick. And her skin was smooth and pale, like the snow her feet left hardly any impression in.

She lowered the rifle.

"Well?" she said.

THERE WAS HEAT. Burning breath. Skin flushed pink. Rough bark against my back, then against hers. A handful of hair, gripped so hard it hurt. Tongue thrust into wetness. The pressure of thighs around hips. Gasps rising to screams – cries to startle every animal within a three-mile radius and put it to flight.

She *did* weigh next to nothing.

AFTERWARDS WE MEANDERED back to the castle, rifles slung over our shoulders by their straps, and we talked. I wasn't normally a fan of postcoital chitchat. More the roll-over-and-start-snoring type. But we weren't in bed, and we had distance to cover, and not saying anything would have been awkward. More awkward than talking.

Freya revealed that she wasn't just a hunting goddess, she was a war goddess, a fertility goddess, a goddess of lust...

"In charge of nearly all life's essentials, then," I said. "Unless you're a goddess of pizza as well."

"My attributes haven't always made me popular among my own kind," she said. "I am frank about my needs and appetites."

"So I noticed."

"To earn my necklace" – she patted the front of her anorak, where the golden necklace lay beneath – "I slept with the Brisings, the four gnome brothers who owned it."

"All four at once, or one after another?"

"Does it matter?"

"Kind of. Not necessarily."

"They weren't terribly prepossessing individuals but they made up for it in other ways."

"How?"

"Do I need to spell it out? Let's just say attentive. And generously endowed."

"Gnomes are well hung?"

"Creatures of such poor physical grace and stature must have some redeeming features. It was... a memorable experience."

"Sounds like it."

"Odin was peeved at me, of course. He felt I'd debased myself. Which I had, I suppose." The corners of her mouth turned up as she said this. Here was a girl who didn't mind getting down and dirty every once in a while. As I myself was now well aware. "But if I see something I want, I go for it."

"Including me?"

"Don't think I haven't noticed how you've been staring at me ever since you got here. Particularly at my behind."

"Just appreciating a work of art."

"On the strength of that, I didn't think you'd be in any way unwilling."

"Bang-on there."

"And, in so far as I have a type I prefer, you're it. A warrior. A man of passion. Someone who seldom thinks before he acts. Callous at times. Rugged in manner as well as looks."

"I'll take all that as a compliment."

"It's meant that way. I had a husband once – a roamer, a faraway-eyed dreamer, poetically inclined. His name was Od."

"What was odd about it?"

"No. That was his name. Od. He disappeared one day. Just... wandered off, never to be seen again. I was sad that he went but it taught me that I wasn't suited to be with a man of that sort. My kind of man does not live too much inside his own head. He gets out there. He engages with life. He *does*."

"Like me. I do."

"I've seen it. We all have. Odin is especially impressed with your quick-wittedness, your decisiveness under pressure. He believes you might just make all the difference in the coming days. You might just tip the scales in our favour."

"Well, I'll try."

"And that's why he's concerned about this state of despondency you've fallen into since coming back from Jotunheim. You're still doing whatever's asked of you, but your heart doesn't seem to be in it any more."

"Hold it," I said, halting. "Before you go on, tell me – did he put you up to this?"

"What? Odin?"

"Did he ask you to get me out here and, you know, jump my bones? Has this just been some kind of sympathy shag to cheer me up? Because if so..."

She raised an eyebrow at me.

"If so..." I repeated, then said, "I don't really mind. It was great either way."

"Right attitude. And no, this was not the All-Father's idea. It was mine alone. And sympathy does not come into it. My own selfish desires aside, I simply wanted to bring you to your senses, remind you who you are, pull you out of yourself."

I leered. "That, you definitely did."

"Because, Gid, your comrade may have died, but you are still here. And we need you here. We need you fully with us when Ragnarök comes."

"Chops was a good man, though. When I think that Hel's got him now..."

"Has she?" Freya said, arching an eyebrow.

"She hasn't? But isn't that what happens when you die? Hel comes to collect you and drags you off to Niflheim?"

"Did you see her appear over his body?"

"No. I was kind of busy trying not to get killed myself."

"There is another world where the souls of the dead may go."

"What! No one told me that."

"Gimlé. High Heaven. The outermost of the Nine Worlds. Hel can claim sinners, those who have acted dishonourably or shamefully in life or have committed heinous crimes."

"I imagine that would include those American black ops guys."

"Yes. But a virtuous man, a blameless man, anyone who has been without taint, even a god, goes to Gimlé after death, there to spend eternity in oneness with the glorious light and majesty that lies at the heart of all creation. Was your comrade that sort of man?"

"Dunno. I'd say probably."

"Then there's every chance that that's where he is now – Gimlé."

It was a load off my mind, seriously it was, to think that Chopsticks hadn't gone to Niflheim and wasn't suffering a long drawn out erosion of the soul under Hel's cackling gaze. I felt suddenly about ten pounds lighter.

"So how come she got Balder, then?" I said. "Wasn't he, like, the ultimate Aesir? Asgard's answer to Gandhi?"

"It is the greatest of injustices," Freya replied. "She should never have had him. In the wake of Balder's death Odin despatched son after son to Niflheim, to remonstrate with Hel and get her to agree to send Balder on to Gimlé. She refused at first, but finally relented. She said she would do as Odin asked."

"'But.' I bet there was a 'but.'"

"There was. Odin, through his emissaries, had told her that every living thing was weeping with sorrow over Balder's death. Hel said if that was truly the case, she would let him go, but if not, he was hers to keep. And of course one living thing, and one alone, was *not* weeping."

"Let me guess. Loki."

She nodded. "Prior to his confession and imprisonment, he shed not a single tear for Balder, and any he shed afterwards sprang from pain and self-pity, nothing else."

"He's generally a big old tosser, isn't he?"

"He has been nothing but trouble to the Aesir since the day Odin took him in. Yet the All-Father used to have such a blind spot where he was concerned. He always managed to overlook Loki's misdemeanours or else dismiss them as mere pranks and japes. It was his greatest failing, and because it was wilful rather than inadvertent it is the reason he is destined for Niflheim when he dies, not Gimlé. If he can defeat Loki and prevent the destruction of Asgard, he stands a chance of redeeming himself. But given the relatively small size of the army he has amassed..."

I finished the sentence for her. "You wonder if he genuinely wants victory. He doesn't feel he deserves everlasting peace after death."

"Maybe he thinks he needs to be punished."

"Well, that's brilliant, isn't it? Deep down our gaffer's a ruddy masochist. He wouldn't mind if Loki trounces us. We lose and it's still a win for him."

"Let's not rush to harsh judgement. Odin is a complex and troubled soul, and it isn't easy to understand what drives him."

"I tell you what, I haven't signed up simply to see our side get its arse whipped," I said hotly. "I refuse to. So this is Man U versus, what, Charlton Athletic? There've been bottom-of-the-league upsets before. The underdogs have been known to have their day."

"Well said."

"Only..."

I hesitated. I'd spent half an hour giving this woman a knee-trembler up against a pine tree. Two knee-tremblers, to be strictly accurate. But did I know her? Know her well enough to own up to one of my biggest sources of anguish?

I wanted to discuss it with *someone*, however. Needed to. It was driving me nuts keeping it to myself, clamping a lid down on it.

We'd just shared saliva, semen, and Christ knows what else. Why not a secret too?

"What is it, Gid?"

"Listen, Freya, what I'm about to tell you, this stays between you and me, right? You don't breathe a word of it to anyone else. Especially not Odin. He'll either think I'm mad or he'll believe me and go off on one. I'd rather not burden him with it unless I'm a hundred per cent sure. Got that?"

"Yes."

"Promise you won't tell a soul?"

"I promise."

"Can I believe you?"

"If the solemn word of a Vanir goddess means nothing to you..." That was the old Freya talking, the ice maiden I'd been familiar with up until now. Nice to have her back, although I much preferred the warmer, randy Freya I was just getting to know.

"Fair do's," I said. "All right, here's the deal. I think we have a traitor in the ranks."

Her eyes widened, lids pulling well clear of the irises.

"One of my lads," I went on. "He wrecked the parley with

the frost giants, deliberately. It looked like we were on course to succeed, and he stopped that happening, and managed to pin the blame for it on Chopsticks."

"But... why?"

"Dunno. Simplest guess would be because he's employed by the other side. A sleeper agent or what-have-you. That or he just can't stand the frosties. It's not the *why* that's bothering me so much as the *who*."

"You don't know which of your men it is?"

"I have my suspicions, but that's all they are, suspicions. Nothing concrete. No hard evidence. A feeling, more than anything. A hunch."

"Why not confront him? See if you can get him to own up?"

"Because I could be totally wrong, this could all be just my imagination, and I don't want to wind the boys up needlessly and end up looking like a total paranoid prat. The only way to know for certain is to do nothing, act normal, and wait for the bastard to make his next move, if he's going to."

"Didn't all of you nearly get killed escaping from Utgard?"

"Yeah, so?"

"Well, if there's a traitor among you, his actions endangered his own life."

"Point taken. Where I come from there is such a thing as a suicide bomber, someone who's willing to martyr himself for his beliefs. But I'd wager that whoever-it-was was counting on me getting us out of there alive. Not only did he fuck everything up for me, the cheeky git then went and used me to save his own neck."

"A gamble."

"A calculated risk. Possibly he had some ace up his sleeve too, some get-out nobody else could know about. Trust me, I don't want to be thinking any of this. The whole idea makes me sick to my stomach. But it's gone and got itself lodged in my head, and try as I might I just can't seem to shift it."

"Then you must be vigilant at all times." Freya sounded surprisingly tender. Concerned, even. "Keep a close eye on the suspect. And if – when – he strikes again..."

"Castrate the fucker."

"I was going to suggest strangling him, but there's no reason not to perform your suggestion first, then mine."

All at once I was really liking Freya. She spoke my language. I was even tempted to kiss her, but I didn't think that would be welcomed at this moment. I didn't think we had that kind of relationship. Yet.

We ambled on, and the lights of the castle were just coming into sight when we heard a sound.

It started low, much like the lowing of a cow in distress. Then it grew, mounting in pitch and volume, until it reminded me of whalesong, plaintive and haunting. Loneliness in a vast ocean.

It kept rising. It kept getting louder. Freya and I had both halted in our tracks to listen, and her expression was a weird mix of dread and excitement, like someone about to embark on a rollercoaster ride. Me, I was uneasy bordering on nauseous. This was not a normal sound, not a good sound to be hearing.

Onward and upward it went, and there was a hint of shriek amid the blare now, a distorted top note – chainsaw, fuzzed guitar, dentist's drill going into molar. It was more than unpleasant, it was neck-hair-crackling eerie, and I wanted to put my hands over my ears, good and bad, to block it out. I did, and even so it still came in. It bored into my head. It reverberated through my teeth, the bones of my skull, my sinuses. It seemed to fill everything, the space between objects, all the gaps of the world, as though the sonic waves it consisted of were a solid substance, an invisible, all-pervading jelly. I found it hard to draw breath. I could barely continue to stand upright. My head swam. My vision blurred. The sound was inside me. The sound clogged my lungs and heart and arteries. I shouted against it, trying to drown it out with noise of my own, but I couldn't. It couldn't be fought or argued with. It wouldn't be ignored or resisted. I felt I was going to go deaf from it – the job begun by the roadside IED a few years earlier was about to be completed. Deaf, or possibly mad. If it didn't stop soon, if quiet didn't resume, the sound would rob me of my sanity, or what little I had.

Maybe it would never stop. Maybe this immense agonised wail would continue for ever and there would never be peace again.

From now on nobody would know contentment or tranquillity. Life would be rage and torment until the end of time.

The blackness inside me relished that thought. It was singing along to the sound, in dark discordant harmony.

Then the sound stopped.

I carried on yelling, unaware. I broke off only when Freya jabbed an elbow in my ribs.

The silence of the sound's aftermath was awesome, as if everyone in all the Nine Worlds was waiting with bated breath, head cocked, not uttering word.

Finally Freya spoke, and it was just a whisper, and even as her lips parted I somehow knew what was going to come out of them. What else could the sound have been?

"The Gjallarhorn."

FORTY-EIGHT

WE RAN TO Bifrost. We were joined en route by Odin, Thor, Frigga, Sif, Vali, Bragi, and a bunch of others. Everyone's faces were pale and etched in the moonlight. They knew. We all knew. This was it. The Gjallarhorn had been blown. Ragnarök had begun.

We converged on Heimdall's guardhouse, and there, in the doorway, we found Asgard's gatekeeper on his knees. The Gjallarhorn rested in his limp hands. Heimdall looked exhausted, as if the effort of blowing the twisty trumpet-like thing had been tremendous – had, in fact, nigh on killed him.

He couldn't speak. Too out of breath. All he could do was point a quivering finger in the direction of Bifrost.

Parked halfway along the bridge was a low-slung stretch limousine. Black, with blacked-out windows, and standing next to it was a woman dressed in a black fur coat over a long black dress. She had on a fur hat that matched the coat, and her knee-high boots were black leather. She also wore large, round sunglasses – black, of course – even though it was night.

She strutted into the aura of the limo's headlamps, swinging her hips like some Russian supermodel. Three-inch boot heels clacked on Bifrost's planks. Her smile was moon-bright and sickle-lean.

Mrs Keener.

"My family," she said to the assembled Aesir and Vanir, holding her arms out as if to embrace them all.

On the Asgard side of the bridge, nobody moved. Nobody so much as twitched.

"What, no greeting? No warm words of welcome? No 'hey, how you been'? I do declare, if this was Wonder Springs they'd be all over me like raccoons on a trashcan by now."

"Loki," said Odin, in a voice like stone.

"Oh no, don't be calling me that," said Mrs Keener. "That's a name I gave up going by years ago. There's only little old Lois Keener here these days. Loving wife, proud mother, not to mention President of the whole goshdarned United States of America."

"Drop this vile pretence," Odin said. "Be who you are, not who you are playing at being. It disgusts me to see you disport yourself in such a false and unbecoming manner."

"Stop being Mrs Keener?" She took a couple more steps forward, so that she was now near the end of the bridge, almost but not quite on Asgardian soil. "And why would I ever want to do such a thing? Adored, respected, feared – I've got it all. The people of Earth are on their knees before me, half a' them in worship, the other half cowering. I have power and influence beyond compare. Millions of mortals, maybe even billions, under my thumb. Being that other guy, that Loki you mention, it had its moments, I'll admit. But it ain't nothing next to being Lois Keener. Oh my Lord, the fun I'm having! Why did I never think of doing this before? I've got those Midgardians running around like ticks on a hog, hardly knowing what to do with themselves. I've thrown their strange, cruel little world into chaos, and ain't none of 'em even has an inkling who I really am. I used to enjoy messing with y'all's heads, but this is way, wayyy better. So thank you kindly but I'll stay just how I am for the time being. Why change what's working so well for me?"

"Why are you here?" Thor demanded. He brandished Mjolnir at her.

"Well now, Thor, my old sparring partner and patsy. Thor, god of *blunder*. You surely do like to get straight to the point, dontcha? I'm just making a quick stopover on route to Great Britain. A courtesy call, if you like. No harm in visiting the old folks back home, is there? See how they are, make sure they're how I remember 'em, remind 'em I exist..."

"Oh, we haven't forgotten you exist," Thor growled.

"And I am just so flattered to hear it." Mrs Keener fanned her throat. "A gal does hate to think she hasn't left a mark."

"Have you come to warn us?" said Odin.

"Warn you about what? You already know Ragnarök's a-coming. Maybe I'm mistaken but wasn't that Heimdall tooting on the Gjallarhorn just now? Sure sounded like it to me, and when the Gjallarhorn blows, that's when the fat lady starts singing. And besides, I think I tipped my hand just a few days back when I sent in those soldiers in the tanksuits. Which, by the way, nicely done. Y'all spotted a flaw in the design nobody else had, and you'll be glad to hear we've fixed that and given the tanksuits a major overhaul and an upgrade, so there'll be no more chinks in the armour."

"Then to gloat. Is that it? Is that why you're here?"

"Oh Odin, my old-time blood brother, my bosom buddy as was, would I do something so cheap and vulgar as *gloat*? A respectable Southern lady like myself? You wound me. I wanted to see y'all's faces one last time, is all. Fix 'em in my memory again. A quick refresher course, so to speak. So's I know once more who I'm about to destroy and why. And there you are, all lined up like crows on a picket fence. Thor Odinson, brainless as ever. Frigga – starting to look like the years are catching up with you, girlfriend. There's wonderful thangs they can do about that in Midgard. I can give you the names of ten cosmetic surgeons'd happily get to work on those laughter lines and those pouchy eyes of yours. And Sif... Well, you never were much to write home about, were you, honey? Pretty enough, loyal, empty-headed. Not the sort to set the world alight. Unlike me. Oh, and there, if my eyes don't deceive me, is Freya Njorthasdottir. Still hanging out with this bunch a sorry losers? The Aesir are beneath you as mud is beneath an eagle. Why wallow when you can soar?"

She'd neatly insulted almost everybody present, and no one seemed prepared to retaliate in any way, other than Thor, who confined himself to grumbling bad words about her under his breath. I couldn't understand why they were taking it so meekly. It was as if Loki had some hold over them and they were reluctant to antagonise him/her.

I, on the other hand, was carrying a perfectly good rifle.

And, I thought, I wasn't going to get a better chance than this.

I shot the bolt, chambered a round, raised the rifle, took aim, squeezed the trigger. All in the space of a couple of seconds. Why fuck around?

The bullet hit Mrs Keener dead in the centre of her body mass, passing straight through and ricocheting off the bodywork of the limousine. The range couldn't have been more than twenty metres. It would have been embarrassing to have missed at such close quarters.

She went down as though poleaxed. I considered putting a second bullet in her sprawled-flat body but decided not to waste the ammunition. She was dead. It was that simple. I felt a hiccup of weird excitement.

Holy fucking shit! I've just assassinated a President of the United States!

Put me up there with John Wilkes Booth and Lee Harvey Oswald. Gideon Jason Coxall, only the third ever member of history's most exclusive club.

Although, unlike the other two, each of whom had robbed the world of a much-loved leader, I'd done humanity a huge favour. It was like that thing about if you could go back in time and kill Hitler before the war, would you? Question answered. I would.

The reaction from the Norse gods was not at all what I was expecting. I'd thought they'd be pleased. I'd done their dirty work for them. Loki was gone. Ragnarök, therefore, would have to be called off. Hooray, surely? Happy finish. No more bloodshed. Yes?

Apparently not.

"Gid," said Odin. Kind of sighing.

"What?"

He looked resigned. Pitying. So did everybody else. "There are certain... protocols at work here. Formalities to be observed."

"But I just shot Loki. I mean, he's toast." I gesticulated at the corpse on the bridge. "He's out of the picture. That's a good thing, right? The bad guy's down and out. It's Bond killing Blofeld halfway through the film. There'll be no big confrontation now. The henchmen will all surrender. We won't have to blow up the volcano headquarters."

"Would that it were that straightforward."

I was finding this hard to believe. "He came – she came – and started nancying about in front of us. I had a gun. What else was I to do? Seemed a no-brainer to me. Still does. Would've been literally, if I'd gone for a head shot. And now it's all over. Isn't it? Ragnarök's off. Yes? No? It's off and we can all go home and eat choccy biccies and watch *Loose Women* in our pyjamas."

"We, Gid," said Odin, "are gods, but we are also creatures of myth. Of saga. Of story. How can I best explain it? Some things are just meant to be. Ragnarök has long been foretold. Its arrival is assured. From the moment of Balder's murder, events have unfolded more or less along a foreordained path. There have been detours, divergences, but always the basic course has remained the same, and cannot be altered. Believe me, if I'd thought killing Loki would change anything, I'd have done it ages ago. But I could not. It would not have been in accordance with the destiny that the Norns have laid out for us, the sequence of events that we are all part of."

"So you're saying –"

"What he's saying," said a loud, unfamiliar voice from the bridge, "is close, but no cigar."

It was Mrs Keener, and she was up on her feet, alive and well and looking, as might be imagined, somewhat narked.

"This coat is Barguzin sable and cost a fucking fortune," she snarled, and she wasn't speaking like a good ol' Georgia gal any more, she was speaking in waspish masculine tones. "And you've put a hole in it and the blood won't come out easily. It's ruined! Who are you anyway?"

"I'm..." was all I managed. Mrs Keener's on-the-spot resurrection had, unusually but understandably, left me at a loss for words.

"No, wait," she said. "I recall Hel telling me that one of Odin's tame monkeys was a bit smarter and feistier than the rest, and I'm guessing you're him. It's Gordon, is it? Gudgeon? Something like that. Well, I suppose I should applaud your initiative, but as Odin's trying so dismally to put into plain English, you can't fight fate. There's a time and a place for me to die, as there is for everyone. It just doesn't happen to be now and here, with me getting shot in the chest between my slightly sagging yet still remarkable breasts. Otherwise do you think I'd be so crass as to turn up at Asgard all on my own, without even so much as a CIA bodyguard to leap into the path of a bullet? Or arrow, or hammer, as the case may be? Typical human thinking. Du-u-*umb*. Just not realising the scale and scope of what you've stepped into."

I raised the rifle and sighted along the barrel. "I can always stick another one in you if you'd like. You might not die but I'm sure it'll hurt."

"Fire away." Mrs Keener spread her arms, making herself an even easier target. "I can take it. All it'll do is ensure your death will be even more truly horrible. I've marked you out now, mortal, you see. You've just earned yourself a position high up on my shit list, right near the top. You'll live to rue the day you ever laid eyes on me."

"I'm already rueing it, shemale," I retorted. "Now you're using your real voice, you're pretty creepy. Makes my skin crawl even looking at you."

"Whereas when I spoke like this" – she'd resumed her breathy, high-pitched Southern lilt – "you found me kinda attractive, huh? Well, ain't you just the predictable male lunkhead, thinking with those there gonads of yours. They'll be the first things to go when the time comes, by the way. I'm looking forward to having you in my clutches and separating you from them slowly using just my little old fingernails. Wouldn't that be just dandy?"

"It'll be a bigger job than you think."

"You are just the cutest! Takes some kinda guy to boast about the size of his parts when he's being threatened with emasculation."

Her smile, false as it was, tightened into a purse-lipped sneer. "I ain't just whistling Dixie here, mister. You shouldn't make the mistake of thinking that. What I say I'm gonna do, I do."

"Still got this rifle, sunshine," I said. "Smack dab between the eyes, and you'll have the mother of all headaches to deal with."

She glared at me through those footballer's wife sunglasses. You couldn't see her eyes but you could sense the fury in them. I'd goaded her good and proper. How to win friends and influence people, the Gid Coxall way.

"Well. That's plenty enough of *that*," she said. One of the limo's rear doors sprang open, seemingly of its own accord. Mrs Keener bent to climb in. "It's war from here on in. Y'all are gonna suffer and die for what you did to me. The centuries I spent in that cavern, my eyes sizzling and burning and growing back only to sizzle and burn some more. The torture and humiliation you put me through. Payback's a bitch, and that bitch is me. Asgard's end is coming. We've had the Fimbulwinter. Now it's Ragnarök's turn to step out onto the pitcher's mound. Three strikes and you'll be out, all of you. Bottom of the ninth, and there ain't no way you're saving the game by stealing a home run."

The door slammed. The limo revved and reversed rumblingly along Bifrost. At the far end of the bridge it U-turned and tore off down the road, snow spewing from its tyres. We watched its taillights fishtail into the dark, two red eyes shrinking 'til they were gone.

"Baseball metaphor," I said, as the echoes of its engine noise faded. "Anybody here speak baseball? Because I'm drawing a total blank."

The Aesir and Vanir, however, weren't up for a laugh. They turned and wandered away in dribs and drabs. Freya was one of the first to go. As she passed me, she said in a conspiratorial murmur, "Pity. It would have been a good, clean kill."

I winked, but she pretended not to notice.

FORTY-NINE

Soon there was just me left, and Heimdall. I went and checked on him. He was sitting in the doorway of his guardhouse and looked better than he had a few minutes earlier. Starting to recover from the effort of blowing the Gjallarhorn, which was now back hanging on the wall.

"All right?"

Heimdall gave a weary nod. "In a way, I'm relieved," he said. "Ragnarök has begun. Finally it's begun. The onus of knowing that it was coming, knowing that one day it would fall to me to announce it – this sat heavily upon my shoulders. But now the moment has come and gone, and I feel... uplifted. How strange."

"It's not so strange. Nothing worse than the wait before an action. You're dreading what's ahead and you're glad when it all finally goes off."

"True."

"So what happens next? What's the order of play? When do the actual hostilities commence? Any idea?"

Heimdall shrugged. "Loki will marshal his forces and attack at some point in the near future. I'm listening out for it even now.

As soon as I detect enemy activity, however faint and remote it is, I will raise the alarm. As yet, I've heard nothing untoward."

"Well, he's only just left, hasn't he? Let's give the bloke a chance to get his act together. You're sure you're going to be okay?"

"I think so."

I said goodnight and made my way back along the drive towards the castle and the cabins beyond. Bed beckoned. Some kip was definitely in order. There wouldn't be much of it in the days ahead, I imagined.

Along the way I caught up with Bragi, who was straggling behind the rest of the Aesir. He was a slow walker, the head-down, trudging type. I fell in step.

"Few days back, that thing about the poem..." I said to him. "Sorry about that. I shouldn't have slagged you off."

He gave a not-to-worry shrug. "I have a thick skin, Gid, as a poet must. How else can he survive the jeers and insults that sometimes greet his work? If there's anyone whose feelings you should be concerned about, it's Loki. You were unwise to antagonise him, you know. He is not one to be trifled with."

"Who was trifling? I meant to kill the fucker stone dead. How was I supposed to know a bullet in the chest would only piss him off?"

"Perhaps no one anticipated you would take such precipitous action."

"Even so, it's like there's a bunch of rules here I don't understand, probably because nobody's seen fit to tell me what they are. I mean, you're gods, but you're not immortal, but you can't die 'til the time comes for you to die. Have I got that right?"

"More or less."

"Well, how does that make sense?"

"It makes sense if you stop thinking of us as deities as such."

"And what do I think of you as instead?"

Bragi frowned deeply, looking inward. "Odin would explain this far better than I."

"Have a go."

"We are... myths. Do you understand what I mean by that?"

"Stories."

"If you like. Bigger than that, but yes, basically stories. We are created things, fabrications, and we're aware of it. We know full well where and how we originated. We are incarnations of the tales that the Norsemen told around fires on long, cold nights, the sagas that entertained them and enlightened them and helped keep the dark at bay. We were given form and substance by oral tradition, licked into shape by it just as the first Aesir were themselves licked into shape by the cow Audhumla from the salty rim of the Ginnungagap. The storytellers assigned us our personalities and patterns of behaviour in order to help their people understand the universe and their own environment. Vikings were all about fighting with their neighbours or trading with them. No wonder, then, that the storytellers dreamed up a cosmos in which gods are engaged in constant border disputes with their enemies and rely on certain allied races to supply goods they can't manufacture themselves. Through us, our tales, our deeds and feuds, the Norsemen affirmed and justified their place in the grand scheme of things."

"This is nuts," I said. "You're saying you *know* you're not real?"

"Not at all," he replied. "We're real. The storytellers' imaginations *made* us real – as real to every member of their audience as the person sitting beside them. Granted, they bestowed us with power, made us capable of superhuman feats. A bit of exaggeration there. Poetic licence. But real all the same. Our squabbles, our rivalries, our passions – nothing about us, deep down, was unintelligible or 'godlike' to the Norsemen. To them we were ordinary people with a few added extras. Gods made in mankind's image. I expect this is hard for a modern, rationalist mortal like you to comprehend."

"Yes. No. Maybe a little. Not being funny, but TV soap operas – you know what those are?"

Bragi smiled lopsidedly through his lush beard. "I've heard of them."

"Not a fan myself, but my ex is. She follows a couple of them religiously. To her, the characters are like people she knows. I mean, she's not retarded. She knows it's just actors working from a script. But on some level I think she believes the characters exist. While they're onscreen, at any rate. That's why viewers, millions of them, get so absorbed in the shows and watch them week in, week out. Waste of time if you ask me, but if it makes them happy..."

"It's life, but a heightened version of it."

"Yeah."

He waved an index finger in the air. "And so are we. And we, too, have certain plotlines we must follow. Our lives, and deaths, have already been dictated and mapped out by the storytellers long ago, and preserved for posterity in the *Eddas*. We know how things are going to turn out for us. We all have predetermined roles to play and destinies to fulfil."

"But that's..." I groped for the right phrasing. "Isn't that, well, a bit depressing? You're called gods but you're actually – no offence – puppets."

"'Puppets' is putting it too strongly. It makes us sound as though we lack free will. We have free will. We merely choose to act in the manner that's been established for us beforehand. Take Thor. He couldn't bring himself to befriend a jotun if he tried. But that's fine, because he has no great desire to befriend a jotun. He's happy to want to bash in the brains of every one of them he meets. So there's no inner conflict there, no angst. We all accept who we are and what is expected of us."

"Hell of a way to live."

"But what's the alternative? Not to live?"

"When you put it like that..."

"It's difficult to grasp, I appreciate," Bragi said, "but we Aesir have these existences that have been bestowed upon us, full of extraordinary events and lasting longer, far longer, than any mortal's – so why not make the most of them? Enjoy them, rather than moan about the few modest limitations that have been imposed on them? For most of us, it's not something we allow ourselves to be troubled by. Only Odin seems to take it hard. He alone feels woe over our lot and frets about it. Thinks too much, that's his problem. Wisdom takes its toll. But the rest of us, we're content to cherish and relish what we have."

"And now it's all coming to an end."

"Without wishing to sound too fatalistic, what must be, must be.

All tales reach a climax. At some point the bard must tire and say 'enough.' What good is a story without a finish?"

"Soaps never bloody finish," I said. "They just grind on and on. But that's the nature of them."

"Indeed. They give the illusion of progress without offering any form of resolution. Somewhat like a mortal life."

"Except mortal lives do have a resolution, if you can call it that. They all end eventually."

"And maybe that's the crucial difference between a mortal and a god – between you, Gid, and me. I am a living story, an element of a larger overarching narrative. My tale has been told over and over in the past. Doubtless it will continue to be told over and over in the future. Maybe *that* is immortality: to recur and recur. Even now, perhaps someone is writing or speaking about me, putting words into my mouth, generating afresh the essence that is Bragi, bard of Asgard and enshriner of the doings of the Einherjar. I am embedded deep in the Midgardian psyche, below the surface but ever present. All the Aesir and Vanir are. We survive within you from age to age, as ideas, stories, archetypes. And every time we are remembered, every time our saga is retold, we are re-created whole and live out a brand new lifespan."

"You reckon?"

"Why not? If gods are fictions, then we are brought to life wherever there is a bard by a hearthside or, if you prefer, a writer at a desk. They think of us, therefore we are."

"Shit..." My head was starting to throb. It was a lot to take in. Who'd have thought school dropout Gid Coxall would be standing discussing this kind of metaphysical bobbins with Asgard's very own poet in residence, while waiting for the end of the world to start?

We'd arrived at the castle.

"Well, here's where our paths divide," Bragi said. "Goodnight, Gid."

He walked off one way. I walked off the other, only to stop after a few paces and turn and call out: "This does work out okay, doesn't it? Ragnarök? There's a happy ending?"

"For some, yes. For others, no."

"But ultimately the good guys win, the bad guys lose. Yeah?"

"It's a work in progress," Bragi said after a moment, then added slyly: "Aren't we all?"

And that was as much as I could get out of him on that subject.

Bloody creative types.

FIFTY

THE FIRST INCURSION came the next morning. A hit-and-run. No contact, no casualties. They took out one of our ammo dumps, situated near an intersection with Svartalfheim.

We inspected the damage – Thor's team, with Huginn and Muninn monitoring for Odin. Nothing much to see, just a smoking crater and a few strewn, charred trees that had once been a copse.

"C-4 plastic explosive," Backdoor opined. "About twenty pounds of it."

"No shit, Sherlock," I said. "And here was I thinking those trees fell over all by themselves."

"They must have been conducting surveillance from across the way," said Paddy, gazing towards Svartalfheim. "Saw the Valkyries stash the ammo. Marked the spot for future reference."

"Is this state-the-fucking-obvious week or what?" I snapped. I turned and eyed the undulating barren badlands of Svartalfheim, wondering if Loki's commandos were still out there somewhere. Bedded down in black camo gear and watching us through binoculars. And chortling.

"The gnomes," I said to Thor. "I thought they were on our side. Friends of Asgard."

"The gnomes are nobody's friend," he replied. "They do business with whomever wishes to do business with them but they owe allegiance to none but themselves."

"So how come they've given safe passage to Loki's troops?"

"They haven't," said Huginn and Muninn in tandem, speaking in Odin's voice from their perch on Thor's shoulders. "What you must understand is that the gnomes dwell perpetually underground. Sunlight turns them to stone, so they daren't venture up onto the surface. Even starlight makes them unwell. Their home is their caverns."

"Meaning anyone can wander across their world if they want to."

The ravens gave a synchronised nod. "The terrain above is no man's land, yes. The gnomes have no use for it, and care little who crosses it. Enter their caverns unannounced and unbidden – that is a different story. Then you'll find yourself facing red-hot pokers and tongs, wielded by some very irate little beings."

"Who have no respect for one's dignity," Thor said, rubbing his buttock in memory of some wound inflicted once upon a time.

"Then we need to patrol this crossing-point," I said. "We site a round-the-clock watch here."

"You think they'll come over again?" said Cy.

"Maybe not. It was a precision strike, a one-off. If I were them I wouldn't hit the same place a second time. But they're not *me*. They're probably a lot swankier and cockier than me, and they might think if they've got away with it once they can get away with it again, and come in deeper this time. Let's play on that. Let's give them an incentive. Commit a dozen men, and one of Odin's sons – Vali, say – with one of the special pieces of kit the gnomes made for us. Let's see how that pans out."

It PANNED OUT pretty well – for us. Two days later the commando unit sneaked in over the border again, at dawn. We'd set up the appearance of basic guard duty near the intersection, a pair of two-man tents whose occupants kept watch on four-hour rotating shifts, not varying their routine one iota. Loki's men tiptoed through the grey light, combat knives drawn. Throat-slashing was on their minds. Easy kills.

Then they were strafed with gunfire from a secondary encampment hidden on high ground further into our territory, and while they were scrambling to their fall-back positions Vali came stomping onto the scene.

The gnomes had provided us a half-dozen suits of armour made of iron, according to the specifications I'd provided. These were no match for the enemy's tanksuits in terms of firepower, mainly because they had none, but they were at least their equal in bulk and density. Each of the contraptions weighed an ounce or so shy of a ton and stood nine feet from boot to head, with a barrel body some fifteen feet in circumference. Only a warrior god could wear one. Only a warrior god had the strength to move the legs with his legs and manipulate the arms with his arms.

Vali, strapped inside the armour, bore down on the startled commandos. They rattled away at him with submachine guns but couldn't put a dent in his inch-thick ironclad hide. Then he was on top of them and started side-swiping them with the armour's fists, which were solid, cannonball-like clubs. Bodies flew. Skulls were crushed.

The remaining commandos saw sense and beat a hasty retreat towards Svartalfheim, but treetop snipers picked them off as they ran. Not one of them made it safely out of range.

"And that, ladies and gentlemen," I said, from an obs post overlooking the kill zone, "is how you do *that*."

IT WAS A good start. We'd field-tested the gnome-built armour and it worked. Slow and clunky, but it did the trick. And we'd convincingly repulsed a covert attack. Score one for the home side.

But other cross-border raids came from Niflheim and Muspelheim. Commandos darted in and blew shit up. Our painstakingly laid ammo dumps went up in smoke one after another, and there were low-level skirmishes all round the perimeter of Asgard, often costing us lives. We were being pinpricked left, right and centre. We could sustain it for the time being, and gave back as good as we got. But it was obvious this repeated harrying was all part of a softening-up process, designed to wear down our reserves little by little, and our resolve.

One thing we learned about the bad guys. With any we killed, inspection of the bodies consistently revealed no uniform insignia and no dogtags. These, then, weren't legit soldiers; they were mercs. We weren't fighting GI Joe but Blackwater or ArmorGroup or some other private military contractor, and somehow that made it better. Rather than being ordinary, straight-arrow, regular-army types who'd enlisted with the noble intention to defend their homeland, these were men who'd signed on the dotted line specifically to take part in war. Just like us. Level playing field, as it were. Each side as dirty as the other.

THE SIEGE WORE on, and what really got on my tits was that, being as it was a siege, we had no real way of taking the fight to the enemy. We could only react, not act. A full-on assault by Loki would have been something we could deal with directly – meet and grapple with – and it was surely coming. Until then, we were perpetually on the back foot, fending off and playing catch-up. Not my idea of fun.

Meanwhile Odin, in spare moments, was following events in Midgard via raven-cam. Mrs Keener's state visit was turning out to be a surprising success. It was a charm offensive of epic proportions, the President glad-handing and back-slapping and generally winning round her UK detractors. The London protest march coincided with her first chat-show appearance, and that may have accounted for the low turnout on the streets of the capital. The organisers surmised that people had stayed home to watch her on TV so that they could fuel themselves with indignation and come out afterwards all fired up and ready to demonstrate.

They must have been disappointed, then, when a second London protest march, hastily scheduled for the next day, was even more poorly attended than the first. The public, it seemed, didn't dislike Mrs Keener as much as it had been assumed they did. After having seen her on telly, where she'd defended her policies, dismissed the climate doomsayers and their fears about the neverending winter, and gone on at length about her family and her love of the Good Lord Jesus, they were coming to the conclusion that she really wasn't as bad as everyone made out. And with each subsequent interview broadcast, British opinion of her rose. This had the result that, when she began a tour of the regions, the marches intended to dovetail with her itinerary never materialised. They had to be called off due to lack of interest.

The papers even started talking about a "Keener effect." One editorial described her as "an all too rare ray of sunshine" and another "an antidote to the dismalness of the times." Even *The Guardian* admitted she had a certain something.

It drove me into a frenzy to hear Odin report all this.

"She's Loki!" I yelled. "Fucking Loki! Why doesn't anyone see through her? I thought only Yanks were gullible, but us lot are just as bad. Worse, even. We shouldn't be falling for any of this guff. Are we not British? Naturally cynical? Don't we laugh when we see sincerity and Christian faith?"

Not any more, it seemed. Not in these dark, difficult days. Mrs Keener was offering hope and simple answers, something Clasen had been failing to do. Loki had honed his craft over centuries of misleading and hoodwinking the Aesir and Vanir. Frightened mortals were easy marks for him.

"And thus his might increases," Odin said. "In the guise of President Keener he makes them love him, or fear him, and are not love and fear both forms of reverence? Are they not both the prostration of the lesser before the greater? He said it himself – he has billions under his thumb now, either through intimidation or enthralment. They celebrate him. They speak of his deeds, and whether approvingly or not doesn't matter, as long as they're speaking of him at all. Their words augment him. He becomes more puissant with every mention, more energised, capable of ever greater, ever bolder feats of wickedness and mayhem. He feeds off their expressions of adulation and detestation. Millions of your countrymen, Gid, are adding further to his stores of power."

"Simply by feeling strongly about him and talking about it?"

"It's a kind of worship. As his reputation grows, so does his divinity."

"Gods are stories, Bragi told me."

"And my blood brother's tale is now being retold millions of times a day," Odin said with a sad, sage shake of the head. "He is on countless mortal tongues. Not realising it, they imbue him with significance whenever they praise Mrs Keener, or criticise her. They lend him their belief and that enhances the myth of him and armours him. Oh, it's a grand deceit he's practised this time, a hoax of unparalleled proportions. I almost admire him for it."

"Personally, it makes me wish I could have another crack at killing him."

"That is not your role, Gid. You are a hero."

"Isn't it the hero's job to take down the archvillain?"

"Sometimes," said Odin. "But sometimes the hero is simply the man who makes the right decisions. He enables what should be to be."

THE PHONY WAR lasted another four days or so. The guerrilla-style sorties became more frequent and nudged further and further into Asgardian turf. We were stretched thin trying to cover and defend so many of the intersections at once. Our troops were getting tired and discouraged, and the major assault hadn't even started yet. Loki had us chasing around all the time, shoring up our forces at each intersection, repelling attacks. Barely did we have a chance to catch our breath before we had to tackle the next incursion somewhere else along the borderlands.

Physically it was gruelling. Psychologically, too. Relationships within the ranks began to fragment. In my own squad, Paddy and Backdoor were getting on each other's nerves, and Cy and

Backdoor as well. Backdoor, in fact, was pissing just about everybody off, even mild-mannered, affable Baz. A bit of needling and ribbing was par for the course in army life, but in Backdoor's case the name-calling had started to take on an edge. He flung "bog-trotter" at Paddy twice and got away with it the first time but not the second. It was the way he said it, more than anything, that put the Irishman's back up. The "fucking" he stuck in front of it the second time didn't help.

They'd have come to blows if I hadn't stepped in and managed to pacify them. I even persuaded them to shake hands manfully. This was for their benefit but also for the benefit of everyone else in our cabin. There was a score of spectators to this bedtime fracas, keen to see a punch-up. *None of that shit*, I was telling them. *Not on my watch*.

It happened again the very next morning during the wee small hours. Me and the team – minus Thor, who'd drunk too much the previous evening and couldn't be got out of his bed for love nor money – were yomping towards a Niflheim intersection. That was where, according to Heimdall's ultra-sharp ears, yet another raid was about to take place. It was our turn to take care of it.

Backdoor was whingeing about lack of sleep and the futility of seeing off one attack only to have to deal with another one a few hours later somewhere different. I was about to tell him to stow it but Cy got in before me.

"Will you just put a fucking sock in it, all right?" he hissed.

Backdoor retorted using the most unpardonable word for a black person there is. Cy, understandably, went ballistic and laid into him. I let him give Backdoor a pasting for a little while, because the fucker deserved it. But when I weighed in and hauled Cy off, what did the kid do but turn round and lamp *me*.

That could not stand. I lamped him back, then while he was reeling I grabbed him and put him into a compliance hold. Wristlock, twisting the hand round, followed by rotation of the entire arm. This forced him down onto his knees, head bent. I put a knee in the small of his back for good measure. He writhed but couldn't get free. All he could do in his helplessness was swear at me. I bellowed at him to shut the fuck up, then launched into a big long rant about everybody not arguing, not sniping at one another, not using racial slurs of any kind, just keeping all their shit in one bucket and pulling together and playing as a team, because if this was what we were like now, imagine how bad it could get when the *proper* fighting started.

"So stop bitching, start behaving like you were born with some balls, all of you," I finished off, "or else!"

We continued on our way in silence. I'd asserted my authority and felt I'd made my point, but I was still fuming inside. We shouldn't be in-fighting and falling to pieces. That was exactly what Loki wanted.

And once more, suspicion was flitting through my mind. We had an infiltrator, an *agent*-fucking-*provocateur* in our midst. And I was growing more and more certain that I knew who it was.

One good thing came of the incident. When the enemy emerged from the mists of Niflheim, we were all so keyed up that we didn't hesitate. We gave them what-for, venting our frustrations in a hail of bullets. Bastards didn't know what hit them. We roared like lions as we fired, and I was roaring loudest of all.

FIFTY-ONE

A LULL.

The raids ceased.

A hush settled along Asgard's borders.

We caught up on lost sleep, scoffed plenty of scran to replenish our strength, and enjoyed the downtime while it lasted. Because we knew it wouldn't last long.

The calm before the shitstorm.

FREYA AND I were out on one of our, ahem, "hunting expeditions." These we fitted in as and when we could, always at her instigation. With her tracking skills she'd find me wherever I was, hand me a rifle, and off we'd trot. Sometimes, once the fun and games were over, we'd even go and bag a token deer or rabbit to bring back, just so's no one would suspect we were up to anything other than what we said we were up to.

She was the fiercest sexual partner I'd ever had. Silent and intense while we did the deed. Hardly ever crying out in pleasure, but bucking and shuddering so violently when the moment came that I was never in any doubt I'd hit the spot. She'd claw me, often bite. It was fighting as much as fornication, each of us wrestling for dominance, demanding a submission from the other.

Something in me responded well to this. I'd lose myself while shagging Freya much as I'd lose myself during combat. It was primal and animal, us out in the woods, in the snow. None of your candlelit lovemaking with rose petals on the bed and Barry White grunting in the background. Just body thrusting and grinding savagely against body. Bare skin getting smeared with a mush of snow, soil, flakes of bark and fallen pine needles. Very few words exchanged beyond "turn over" or "try this" or "there."

It was how people fucked when there was a war on and a world was at stake and lives could end tomorrow. Urgently, no grace or ritual to it. Raw, raw, raw.

On this particular occasion we were on our second go-round, or maybe third. It was easy to lose track. One bout of rampant shaggery shaded into another, with little recovery time in between. Then all at once Freya said, "Stop."

I said, "Stop as in we're changing position, or...?"

"Just stop. And be quiet."

I froze. We listened. Me on my knees, her on all fours.

"I don't –"

"Hssst!"

Then I detected it. Sensed it through my legs rather than my ears. Vibration.

Rumbling.

The earth moving, but not in *that* way.

"What *is* that?"

"I don't know. We need to go and see."

Abrupt withdrawal. Clothes flung back on. Charging through the woods towards the sound.

It was being made by an engine of some sort – a massively horsepowered motor that propelled something wheeled and huge. The closer we got, the more resonant and ground-shaking the sound became. The snow on the forest floor danced. The trees themselves shivered.

We began to hear crashing noises and splintering creaks. Pines falling, being shoved over.

Finally we caught our first glimpse of the machine. It was a wall of grey metal moving among the tree trunks ahead. There were caterpillar tracks as thick as my thigh, wheels several feet in diameter. Whatever this was, it barged the trees aside as though they were nothing. Old-growth pines shattered into toothpicks in front of it, toppled over like ninepins either side of it.

A tank.

But the biggest ruddy tank ever. Like twelve double-decker buses bolted together, three abreast, in two tiers of six. Just steamrollering through the forest, butting aside anything that got in its way.

As it passed us by and trundled off, leaving a cloud of black fumes, I looked at Freya. "How do we stop that?"

"No idea. We just do. Someone has to. It's heading for the castle. It mustn't get there."

"We need to raise the alarm."

"I'd be surprised if Heimdall hasn't already."

She had a point. The mega-tank might have caught the two of us with our pants down, but Heimdall napping? Not a chance. Especially not when it was setting up such an unholy row. Heimdall, who could hear an ant breaking wind in the Brazilian rainforest, knew full well this monster was on its way.

"Odin will already be mounting a defence," Freya went on. "We should get back there and join in. That's where we can be the most useful."

So we belted off in the direction of the castle. Freya led the way unerringly, and we soon overtook the mega-tank, which was going at little better than walking pace. It must have weighed several hundred tons, and no engine, however large, could move that much bulk at any decent speed. On foot we outstripped it easily, and we were back at the castle well before it got anywhere near.

As Freya had predicted, preparations were under way to meet it. Everyone was out, and armed. The Valkyries were gunning their snowmobiles. Skadi was on her skis, fully recovered now and looking as sprightly and agile as she'd ever done. Odin was marshalling the troops to form a defensive perimeter, with secondary and tertiary lines behind.

Freya and I went straight up to him and told him that men and guns alone weren't going to cut the mustard.

"Have you seen this thing?" I asked.

"Not yet. Huginn and Muninn are aloft, but..."

"Trust me, it's not going to be bothered by bullets. Not even an RPG'll pierce its armour, I don't think. It's just... mammoth. I don't know if it's got firepower. Didn't see. It probably has. But even without, it could roll right over us and we'd be nothing but roadkill."

"What, then? What do you suggest?"

"There's only one possibility. Is *Sleipnir* prepped?"

"It can be."

"Shit. Then we'll need a delaying tactic as well. Can you spare some trolls?"

"Of course. How many?"

"Let 'em loose. As many as possible. While they're, hopefully, holding that machine up, we get a small unit to tackle it from the only direction no one'll be expecting."

"Which is?" asked Odin.

"Above."

FIFTY-TWO

THOR BEGGED TO come with us.

"Gid – friend Gid – you need me."

Sleipnir's pilots had been scrambled. We were expecting the Wokka to arrive at any moment to pick us up. In the background there was a low, ominous growl. The mega-tank was now no more than a mile from the castle, according to Odin's ravens, who'd just returned from their scouting mission.

"No, you belong here on the ground," I told Thor. "Best place for you."

"But I can help."

"Help by being the backup, the Plan B if Plan A fails, which it might well. You're one of our heaviest hitters, mate, if not *the* heaviest. Together with your brothers you can hold the line, if necessary pick up where we leave off."

"Surely –"

"You just can't be spared," I insisted. "A few mortal troops, on the other hand... Well, if we fuck up we won't be missed, will we?"

"Besides," said Odin, "someone has to wrangle the trolls."

"Is that not your job, father?"

"It's now yours, Thor. I shall be accompanying Gid and his men."

This was news to me, but I took it in my stride. He was the All-Father, after all. The guv'nor. What he said, went.

"I may be old," Odin continued, "but I remain a warrior. My heart still beats to the drum of battle."

"Father, no," said Thor. "If I can't be spared, then you certainly can't."

"My son." Odin laid a hand on his shoulder. He had to reach up to do it. "I must go. I have no choice. What Gid calls a 'mega-tank' is, I believe, an ancient enemy of ours brought to life in another form. In which case, it is incumbent upon me to fight it and defeat it, not you. This is what I am fated to do. It is written. So be it."

Thor puffed himself up, then deflated. The look in Odin's eye said argument was futile. His mind was made up.

"If this is really your wish, father, it cannot be gainsaid. I am your loyal, obedient son and have submitted to your will at all times."

Odin laughed, shaking his head. "No, you haven't. You have been the most wayward and headstrong of all my children, Thor."

Thor laughed too. "That is true."

"But you have also," Odin said, "been one of my proudest accomplishments. Every inch the fighter. Courageous to a fault, and a staunch protector of Asgard. Look after the place in my absence, Thor. Keep defending it to the last breath in your body. That is all I can ever ask from you."

"Father..."

"You have loved our home as I do. Continue showing it that love."

They looked at each other, and I saw a bond between them, a mutual respect, as strong as any I'd ever seen. They weren't just father and son. Not even just clan chief and heir. They were brothers in arms too. And this was their hour, their shining time, when they would prove themselves against the severest odds they had ever faced.

"I shall," said Thor. "And so, always, will you."

In reply, Odin smiled – somewhat sadly, it seemed to me – and then the Chinook came racketing in over the treetops.

WE WERE ABOARD, a five-strong squad plus Odin, and ascending. We checked our weapons as *Sleipnir* humped us into the sky. We also checked the abseiling equipment I'd sourced from Skadi's stock of outdoor gear. Anything skiing- or mountaineering-related, you name it, Skadi had it. By the bucketload. I loved that little minx. Not only had she taken a shot meant for me, she was just so insanely fucking focused.

"This is going to be a walk in the park," I reassured everyone. "We lower ourselves down onto the top of the tank, find an access hatch, blow it, get in, plant some high-ex, bundle out, bish-bosh, the job's a good 'un."

Paddy rolled his eyes. "'Walk in the park,' the man says. Suppose it is, if by 'walk' you mean 'suicide mission' and 'park' you mean 'two-hundred-ton armour-plated enemy transport.'"

"You chicken, mick?" Backdoor sneered. "Me, I live for this shit."

"Can the backchat, both of you." I tilted my head towards Odin. *Top brass on deck.*

They clammed up.

Sleipnir circled, gaining altitude. I'd asked the pilots for a fly-past first so we could all get a squint at the mega-tank and assess the feasibility of my plan, if it had any. The Wokka came over it at five hundred feet, and Flight Lieutenant Jensen banked to starboard. We lined the portholes on that side, peering down.

The mega-tank had left a tremendous swathe of devastation behind it, a clear-felled path through the forest as wide as an A-road. This led the eye straight to the tank itself. Moonlight and its own running lights outlined it amid the trees. In shape, it was basically a rectangle with outcurving flanks. There were projecting structures at each corner – gun turrets, swivel-mounted and fitted with multiple-barrelled rotary cannons. I'd not been able to see those from ground level when Freya and I first encountered the tank. There was also a pod perched at the front like a head on a neck, shape of a flattened sphere. The control cab, if I didn't miss my guess.

A pair of searchlights beamed forward from the cab. On top of it rose a pair of triangular fins. I couldn't figure out what those were there for.

"Are they, like, ears?" Cy wondered.

That was how they looked to me. "Some kind of radar array?" I suggested.

Backdoor agreed. "They're curved. Could well be parabolic antennae."

"No," said Odin. "Purely decorative. Ears."

"How do you know?"

"I know, Gid, because this mechanical beast is a representation of a real, living beast. In much the same way that those so-called tanksuits purported to be jotuns and fire demons, here we have a man-made mimicry of a creature known to all in Asgard. My blood brother has been having fun. What we are looking at is Fenrir."

"Fenrir?"

"Those 'ears' confirm it. It's meant to be Fenrir. The giant wolf. The devourer. One-time scourge of the Aesir. We captured and muzzled him a long time ago. My son Tyr permanently wedged his maw open with a sword – and lost a hand in the process. As far as I know, the real Fenrir is still chained to a rock in far Muspelheim."

"And Loki's come up with his own version."

"Rather than go to the trouble of freeing the original and releasing him upon us, he has manufactured this instead."

"A high-tech stand-in," I said. "Well, nice to know, but it doesn't alter the plan. In fact, I think I'd prefer to take on a big-arse tank that looks like a wolf than a big-arse proper wolf. It's slower, for one thing."

"It's also training its guns on us," Baz warned.

Jensen had spotted this himself. His voice came over the intercom. "We're about to take incoming. Evasive action. Hang on tight!"

We grabbed onto whatever we could – seats, bulkheads, the webbing on the walls. Next instant, there was the judder of heavy calibre fire from below. Flashes of tracer fire lit up the Wokka's interior.

Sleipnir pirouetted gracelessly. A few bullets raked the hull. One shattered a porthole.

"Fuck fuck fuckfuckfuck," I breathed as broken glass flew.

The engines bawled, the entire chopper groaned and shuddered from stem to stern, as Jensen poured on the speed and threw us into a steep climb. We clung on for dear life as the cargo bay canted, rapidly reaching 45° from horizontal and getting closer to perpendicular by the second. He was trying to present *Fenrir*'s gunners with as narrow a profile as possible, and at the same time shrinking the size of the target with distance. The comfort and safety of his passengers was a minor consideration. Getting the Wokka out of range of the rotary cannons was the prime directive. If the six of us stayed intact in the interim – bonus.

Soon *Sleipnir* was near vertical, straining hard against gravity. All at once Paddy lost his grip and started slithering down the bay. He'd have broken an ankle colliding with the closed cargo ramp if Baz hadn't managed to catch him by the arm as he tumbled past. The rest of us kept ourselves attached, though we were dangling around like demented marionettes.

Finally the tracers stopped their mad strobing around us. Jensen powered down a fraction and levelled *Sleipnir* out.

"All okay?" he asked over the intercom, before adding one of those typically droll RAF apologies. "Sorry for shaking you up like that, but crisis situation, you understand."

A quick glance round showed me no one was injured. Paddy was massaging a sprained shoulder, but winked to say *no harm done*. I went forward and popped my head into the cockpit.

"Good job, fellas."

"If we go in again, Coxall, those guns are going to rip us to shreds," Jensen said. "This ship isn't built for dogfighting. She handles like a brick shithouse, and even the best pilots can't do anything about that."

"And we are the best pilots," Flying Officer Thwaite chipped in.

"Of course you are," I told him. "And with a cock-duster 'tache like yours, I bet you're pretty popular with the boys down the nightclub, too."

Thwaite's eyeballs bulged in indignation.

"Now," I went on, ignoring his splutters, "we *are* going in again and you *are* getting us over and onto that fucking tank. Thor should be running the trolls in any moment. They're our diversion. The tankies will be so busy with them, they won't be concentrating on us. That's the big idea so let's make it happen, shall we?"

Thwaite looked fit to deck me. Jensen, on the other hand, just eyed his instrumentation, glanced out the windscreen, and gave a grim nod.

"Roger that," he said. "We can do this."

"But –"

He cut his co-pilot off. "We can do this."

I clapped them both on the helmet and went back aft.

Guiding *Sleipnir* into position ought to be relatively straightforward.

Abseiling safely onto *Fenrir*'s back without getting massacred by those rotary cannons – now *that* was going to be the tricky part.

FIFTY-THREE

THOR AND HIS brothers held up their end of things just fine. They freed a dozen trolls from the pens and chivvied them in *Fenrir*'s direction. The trolls would normally have turned on the Aesir the moment they had a chance, but the looming mega-tank was bigger, noisier, scarier, altogether more of a threat. So they focused their aggression on it instead.

Fenrir had just broken through the treeline when the trolls attacked. I saw them swarm around it and start clambering on. One of them managed to haul himself onto a gun turret and immediately received a blast full in the face. At a hundred rounds per second, the rotary cannon didn't leave much of his head behind. His decapitated body slumped back to earth.

This did nothing to deter the other trolls. Soon they were all over *Fenrir*'s sides, hammering and battering with their fists and yowling in gruff indignation. One of them, still on the ground, attempted to stop the mega-tank by grabbing hold of one of its caterpillar tracks. His hands got drawn into the mechanism. His arms swiftly followed. Between them, wheels and track munched up the troll all the way to the shoulders. He stumbled back, screeching horribly, the stumps of his arms spouting blood by the gallon.

More trolls died, chewed to pieces by the rotary cannons as they were scaling *Fenrir*. This approach wasn't serving them well, and the remainder of them saw sense and leapt off to fetch weapons. These included tree trunks and boulders. They mounted a fresh assault, frothing and gibbering in their fury as they battered away at the tank.

A female, shrewder than the rest, took a big, pointed rock and jammed it between two wheels. Next instant, a gun turret flayed her to shreds, but she'd achieved what she set out to. *Fenrir* slewed round as one caterpillar track seized up while the other continued turning. The driver braked, then began rocking the tank back and forth in the hope of jolting the obstruction loose.

While he was doing this, *Sleipnir* came down from overhead, descending plumb-line vertical, at speed. The cargo ramp was out like a cheeky kid's tongue, and me and my squad, with Odin, were poised on the tip of it. Climbing ropes hitched us to the Wokka's interior, looped through karabiners attached to harnesses around our waists. We had gloves on our hands and dogged determination on our faces.

"Ready?" I yelled.

Some nods. A couple of thumbs raised.

"You sure you still want to do this?" I asked Odin.

"No," he said, white hair whipping about like mad under the brim of his hat.

"Feel free to bail."

"Never."

"But you're not even packing."

"I'll cope. I'm more resourceful than I may appear."

Sleipnir slowed to a halt ten metres above *Fenrir*.

"Go!" I cried out. "Go! Go! Go!"

We unspooled the free ends of our ropes behind us and launched ourselves backwards off the ramp. Friction-braking with our hands, we touched down five seconds later. *Sleipnir* was already rising even as we unclipped our ropes. Jensen wasn't hanging about. The Chinook was a big, tasty target – even more so than the trolls – and *Fenrir*'s gunners weren't slow to cotton on to that fact. All four turrets erupted around us, firing upwards as *Sleipnir* beat an extremely hasty retreat. The helicopter rode brilliant, sinuous columns of tracer into the sky.

The gunners might have hit it, too, if *Fenrir*'s driver hadn't been trying so hard to dislodge the boulder. The mega-tank jerked and lurched, throwing off their aim, and also throwing us off-balance. It wouldn't be long, I thought, before the rock was worked free and *Fenrir* was able to resume its course towards the castle.

And, now that I was actually on top of the tank, I could see that it had a pair of stubby forward-facing gun barrels emerging to either side of the control cab. Each was tipped with a hollow, breezeblock-like muzzle brake, suggesting the barrels were much longer than they appeared, if they needed recoil compensation. Probably they telescoped out when firing commenced. The bore was 125 millimetres, give or take. Serious artillery. *Fenrir* could lob shells that would make mincemeat of the castle's defenders and rubble of the castle itself.

Time to shit or get off the pot.

"Baz! Backdoor! Stick some plastique on that control cab, see if you can't make a hole in it and scramble this thing's brains. The gun turrets have got limited a range of traverse so they don't accidentally open up on each other. We're in a kind of blind spot here, but for fuck's sake watch out for them anyway."

I turned to the others.

"You three, on me. There's what looks like a hatch back that-a-way, near the rear. I want to be through it in the next ten seconds."

I was bossing Odin about as if he was just one of the team, but I didn't really notice I was doing it and he didn't seem to mind. He scrambled across *Fenrir* with the rest of us, pretty spry for an old geezer. Somehow, through everything, that hat of his was staying put, still shading his absent eye. Must be a godly talent, I thought, the ability to keep a hat on at all times, in all circumstances. Either that or the thing was glued in place.

What had appeared to be a personnel hatch proved to be just that, when we got to it, and eminently blowable. Paddy wedged a blob of C-4 under its lip, inserted the detonator, unreeled the wire, and lay down flat with the priming assembly in his hands. Cy, Odin and I joined him on our bellies, and I invited Odin to clamp his hands over his ears. Backdoor triggered the explosive.

The *whump!* was deep and satisfying, and it was barely finished before I was back on my feet and sprinting for the hatch. The lid had flipped open on its hinges, what had been a plain domed disc of steel now a blackened, twistily fanlike thing. I fired a couple of shots with my Minimi down into the hatchway just in case there happened to be anyone immediately below. Then I pounced onto the ladder inside and slid down it, hands and feet on the uprights rather than the rungs, in time-honoured windowcleaner style.

I was in a narrow axial passageway, same dimensions as a coffin stood on end. Everything was lit blood-red by battle stations lighting. The passageway ran the length of *Fenrir*, with paired crawlspace tunnels leading off, two ahead, two behind. Access to the gun turrets. A second ladder awaited at the far end, going up the "neck" into the control cab, and also down. To the engine room, was my guess.

Odin appeared beside me, then Cy and Paddy.

"In, we're fucking in," Cy breathed. "We done it, man."

"Not yet," I cautioned. "We haven't done anything 'til the bastard stops rolling."

"It in't rolling right now, bruv."

Famous last fucking words. That very moment, *Fenrir* gave an almighty lurch, and suddenly was moving freely once more. The rock was gone and the driver had full control back. I felt the tank pivoting on its axis and pictured those twin artillery barrels being brought to bear on the castle and the lines of defence around it. The gun turrets were still rattling away, too, slaughtering trolls.

There was a shallow rise ahead. We had three minutes, I estimated, maybe less, before this travelling nightmare crested that and had the castle bang in its sights.

FIFTY-FOUR

THE GOOD NEWS was that the forward ladder did, indeed, go down into the engine room.

The bad news?

Fenrir wasn't just an all-terrain assault vehicle.

It was a bloody troop transport as well.

Next door to the engine room there was a hold containing fifty-plus American mercs, all tooled up and ready for some action.

How did we find this out?

Because the bastards were lying in wait for us.

They knew we were aboard. They knew we'd breached the roof hatch. They knew which way we'd be likely to head.

And no sooner had we arrived at the engine room than they laid into us.

They rushed in via a short passageway in single file, carrying KA-BAR knives with 7-inch matt-black blades, which they brandished as they greeted us with cries of "Hostiles!" and "Kick their asses!" and "Hoo-ah!"

Five of them were in the confined space of the engine room with us before we got our shit together to respond. There was every chance they would have obliterated us, too, if they'd only decided to sneak up on us rather than go for the gung-ho, yelling-their-heads-off option.

My simple solution to the problem was to let them have it with the Minimi. The difference between us and them, at that moment, was that *Fenrir* was their ride and they had no desire to damage it. Hence the knives, a prudent precaution. Us? We didn't care. Damaging was what we were there to do, one way or another. It didn't much matter how.

The five went down, victims of a mixture of overconfidence (theirs) and ruthlessness (mine). Others behind them backed off down the passageway, suddenly appreciating the fact that we had little to lose and they had lots. I heard some frantic debate as they retreated, stuff about bringing knives to a motherfucking gun fight, and what were they supposed to do now, huh?

We couldn't allow them time to come up with an answer.

"Paddy. Cy." I pointed to two diesel turbines the size of Transit vans. They were churning away deafeningly as they bullied *Fenrir* along. "You know the drill. Fifteen-second fuses. When you're done setting the charges, follow me out."

"Which way you going?" Cy asked.

"Which way do you bloody think? Through the septics. There's got to be an exit at the back for them to pile out of during an assault. That's our way out too. I make a hole through them. You follow."

"All on your own?"

I unhooked a couple of grenades from my belt. "Nope. I'll have some help from Mr and Mrs Pineapple here."

"And me," Odin added.

I was through second-guessing his participation, through querying his combat readiness. He wanted in? Fine by me. I'd no idea how much cop he'd be in a scrap, but hey ho, the more the merrier.

Three steps into the passageway, Odin said, "Gid, my ravens."

"What about them?"

"Someone must look after them, feed them."

"You're worried about your birds at a time like this?"

"If I don't survive..."

"Let's not go there, eh?"

"And Frigga. I want you to tell her –"

"Listen, Odin," I said firmly. "If you're not getting out of this alive, then I'm definitely not. So I'm not about to start promising to tell anyone anything. There's no point."

"I've been a poor husband."

"She knows that. She also knows you love her anyway. Poor husband? I wrote the book on it. But at least you and her are still together, unlike me and Gen. You stuck it through. That counts for a great deal. Now, there's a fuckload of mercs about twenty feet away from here, and every second we spend having this heart-to-heart is another second we give them to figure out how to deal with us. So let's forget the what-ifs and focus on the right-nows, yeah?"

"Blunt as ever, Gid," Odin said. "And in your own fashion, wise."

"Cheers."

I turned with a grenade in each hand and plinked out both pins with my thumbs, keeping the striker levers nice and flat with my fingers. Loki's men had withdrawn behind a steel door ahead. They'd gone quiet, which to me said they were braced to launch a counterattack. Charging down the passageway with guns blazing, two-by-two formation, one of each pair shooting high, the other low – that would be how I'd tackle it, in their position. Small arms rather than anything high velocity. Trying their utmost to keep casualties high and collateral damage to a minimum. Make each bullet count and for fuck's sake don't hole the engines.

Sure enough, the door swung open and two pistols poked out. High and low, just like I'd predicted. The men holding them emerged as I lobbed the grenades along the passageway and in through the doorway. I grabbed Odin and hurled him and myself to the floor.

"Oh fu –" one of the Americans managed to get out, and "Holy Mother of –" the other.

Then: *BOOM! BOOM!*

The near-simultaneous detonations of two fragmentation grenades in a confined metallic space. Like gigantic gongs being rung in Hell.

Before the smoke had even begun to clear I was inside the hold, Minimi to shoulder. Odin was hard on my heels, and I briefly wondered what he was going to do, seeing as he was bare-handed. *His problem, not mine.*

The grenades had killed over half of the Yanks outright, injured plenty more, and stunned the rest. There were maybe a dozen left who were battle-worthy. They staggered to their feet as Odin and I burst in, and while they were groping for their sidearms I began putting them down with the Minimi. Nice and surgical.

But I couldn't neutralise every one of our opponents before return fire became a reality. Pistols started to spark, and I took shelter behind a heap of sprawled bodies.

I signalled to Odin to join me behind my gory barricade. He didn't see. Admittedly I was on his blind side, but it appeared he had his own tactic for handling the enemy fire, and that was to run straight into it.

Crazy? Oh yes. But somehow it worked for him. Not one bullet found its mark as Odin rushed the soldiers. He moved surprisingly fast, and doubtless none of them had anticipated a full-speed-ahead frontal assault like this. They'd expected he would dive for cover – like any normal person, such as me, would – and gauged their aim accordingly.

He seized his nearest opponent, a corn-fed, freckle-faced farmhand type, and smashed him backwards against the hold wall, knocking the wind out of him. While Farmhand wheezed for breath, Odin rammed a fist into his sternum. I heard the sound of his ribcage caving in – a splintery *crack* like a piece of fibreboard getting stamped on.

Odin swung Farmhand's huge frame round just as another American, a Mike Tyson lookalike, opened fire on him from the side. The body took the bullets, jerking with the impacts. Odin then flung Farmhand at Tyson-alike, who wasted precious seconds wrestling the corpse off. By the time Tyson-alike had disentangled himself from his dead comrade's limbs, Odin had his throat in an chokehold. He wrenched, and the American's atlas bone snapped, spine and skull parting company. A professional hangman couldn't have done it better.

I was impressed as hell. Who knew Odin had it in him? His name meant "war fury," that was what Bergelmir had said, and he was living up to it. White-haired and age-withered he might be, but when necessary he had the speed and vigour of someone far younger and better built, not to mention the killer instinct of a true warrior. The Americans, for their part, were open-mouthed with shock. An old guy, dressed like a civilian, not a gun to be seen on him, and he was taking them apart? No way. How?

Odin kidney-punched another of them, then used the man's pistol – while he was still holding it – to eliminate two of his own colleagues. Both head-shots, one through the eye, the other ripping off its victim's entire jawbone. For the *coup de grâce* Odin twisted the soldier's arm up, lodged the pistol barrel under the chinstrap of his helmet, and pulled the trigger a third time. The man had a chance to choke out half a scream, but that was all. The helmet kept the top of his head from flying off but everything else got very messy.

Me and my Minimi were starting to feel redundant. Odin was a tornado, swift, remorseless, brutal. I foresaw a time when he and Loki would finally have it out between them, just the two of them, man to man, blood brother against blood brother. It would surely have to happen, and when it did, I didn't rate Loki's chances. He could shape-shift into the Incredible Hulk, and Odin would still pound him into the dirt.

At the very moment I had this thought, Odin glanced my way. His eye widened.

"Gid! Behind you!"

I rolled round to find a soldier looming over me. It was hard to know how his face looked, whether he was black, white, Asian, whatever. He had few features left, just a tarry, sticky mess of burnt skin and cartilage where lips, nose and cheeks had been. Shrapnel hedgehogged him from forehead to neck. Only his teeth, exposed by the melted O of his mouth, were intact. Straightened, bleach-white gnashers, clenched in a rictus of rage. And his eyes – bulging, aglow with the thirst for vengeance.

If this man with the mushed mush was still in pain, he wasn't aware of it. He was somewhere way beyond that sort of concern. All he wanted to do, all he *could* do, was kill me.

The semiautomatic pistol levelled at my face was poised to make his desires a reality.

FIFTY-FIVE

THE GUN, A chunky Desert Eagle, was so close, I could see right up the barrel, along the curved grooves of the rifling, all the way to the bullet snug in the breech. Or so it seemed. Maybe I would see that bullet as it came out, watch it corkscrewing towards me during a final, precious microsecond before it hit with a white thunderclap and there was nothing more.

It was an instant of clarity that lasted far longer than it should, stretched out like a holidaymaker on a sun lounger. Somehow I couldn't lift the Minimi, draw a bead on Pizza Face here. There was all the time in the world, and none. Surreally serene, I was able to think, *Oh well, this is how it happens, this is how you die.* I felt no animosity towards my would-be killer. Just a grunt doing his job, same as I'd done my job dozens of times before, killing to earn a wage. He was so badly injured, so far gone, he probably didn't even register me as anything human. I meant as much to him as a paper target at the shooting range.

His finger squeezed. I saw the gun's hammer nod forwards.

Then something slammed into him sidelong. The Desert Eagle went off and I felt the peppery sting of powder burns on my left cheek, and my left ear when absolutely silent from the percussion of the gunshot – but I wasn't hit, I wasn't dead...

The gun went off again, and yet again. Odin and Pizza Face were grappling on the floor, the weapon between them. The soldier was pulling the trigger over and over, a reflex, while Odin dug both thumbs into his throat, strangling with all his might. I heard a click – the Desert Eagle's magazine running empty – and another click – the hyoid bone at the base of Pizza Face's tongue breaking. He gave a rattly gurgle and went rigid.

Grimacing, Odin eased himself off the body.

"Done," he gasped.

We helped each other up to our feet. I scanned the hold. Soldiers lay everywhere, a few of them moving but none with any active purpose. The writhing, spastic throes of the terminally wounded.

Also terminally wounded, it turned out, was Odin. He sagged to his knees, and I realised the front of his overcoat was riddled with bullet holes and sodden with blood. His opponent's shots hadn't gone wild, as I'd hoped – prayed – they had. Odin had a good half-dozen rounds in him.

The All-Father was a goner.

I knelt by him. "We'll get you to Frigga, that's what we're going to do," I said. "We'll get you to her and she'll fix you. All you have to do is hang on. We'll be out of here in a jiffy."

"No, Gid," he rasped. "Noble of you, but no. I've sustained harm beyond even my wife's power to mend. I can feel..." He coughed, and blood dribbled out over his beard. "I can feel how much is... broken inside me. I've not got long."

"Bullshit. You're a god. The All-Father. Come on, you hung on a tree for nine days. You can pull through *this*."

His hat had lost its rakish grip on his head, and for the first time I could see his left eye. The lids were puckered over the empty socket, sealed and sunken like lips with a secret they would never tell. His right eye still glittered, but its lustre was fading.

"I knew going in," he said, "that this was to be my end. Swallowed by Fenrir the devourer... never to return. My fate. I am not sad. I regret leaving life... but it has been a long life... and a good one too. My wife, my lovers, my sons, my family... even my blood brother..."

He coughed again, and this time gouts of blood bubbled up.

"And you, Gid... It has been a privilege to know you... even if only for such a brief span of time..."

He fell against me, crimson-bearded.

"I saved you," he said. "Gimlé. Not Niflheim. Gimlé!"

And that was his final word, a cry that left his body forcefully and took all his remaining strength with it. Slack, limp, he died in my arms.

FIFTY-SIX

I HAD ABOUT a fifth of a second to digest the fact that the All-Father was no more. Then two things happened.

First, *Fenrir* reverberated to an immense explosion, rocking back on its caterpillar tracks.

Second, Cy and Paddy came haring in from the engine room.

"Fucker's started bombarding," Cy yelled, over the ringing in my head.

"And we've ten seconds to get clear before the charges blow," Paddy added.

I was still holding Odin – couldn't move. Paddy took stock of my situation. His face fell. Then, barely missing a beat, he grabbed me by the arm and wrenched me upright. Together he and Cy hauled me through the carnage that Odin and I had created in the hold. There was an exit at the rear, as I'd guessed. Cy punched a release lever, and a segmented garage-door type of affair rolled upwards in front of us. We scuttled out under it on all fours and sprinted away from *Fenrir*.

The tank was now perched on the brow of the rise overlooking the castle, with the scattered corpses of trolls around it and behind. It sent a second shell scudding through the air towards the building. I heard the whizz-shriek of the projectile coming in to land, followed by the chunky wallop of masonry shattering.

Then *Fenrir* itself was the one to suffer. The C-4 in the engine room did its stuff. The tank lurched upwards and bulged outwards at the same time, slumping straight back down onto the snow. It came to rest at an angle, both tracks askew, wheels out of alignment like bad teeth. Its armour stayed largely intact, but many of the rivets had popped and the steel plates didn't mesh as neatly as before.

A second, louder explosion, this one external, saw *Fenrir*'s head shear sideways off its neck. The control cab came to rest canted at a forward angle, like a sleeping drunk's.

All four gun turrets were still operational but the mega-tank itself was driverless and going nowhere. Its artillery barrels were fully extended, but without anyone to fire them they were as useful as a eunuch's dick.

Thor appeared moments later, leading Skadi, Freya, and his brothers. Between them they mopped up the gunners, whose fighting spirit had pretty much deserted them now that they were stuck defending a dead duck. Mjolnir cracked the turrets open like steel piñatas, and Freya mercilessly despatched the men inside.

A cry of victory went up, begun by the Aesir and echoed by the mortal troops over by the castle.

Knowing something they didn't yet, I was in no mood for celebrating.

I felt even less like it when Backdoor emerged from the woods.

Alone.

FIFTY-SEVEN

WE BUILT A funeral pyre through the night and set it alight at sunrise.

Odin's body was laid out on a raised wooden platform, a bier, and beneath it logs and branches were stacked up and doused with engine oil.

He looked at peace, lying on his back, hands clasped on his chest. His hat was placed over his belly to hide the bullet holes. Frigga lovingly arranged his hair so as to cover his lost eye.

"He was always so self-conscious about that," she said, to anyone and no one. "He didn't like it being obvious, what he'd sacrificed in order to gain knowledge." A bitter laugh. "I can't see why, since we all knew. But vanity was among his shortcomings. The least of them, but there nonetheless."

To Thor fell the honour of igniting the pyre. There was no squabbling about this among the sons. All were aware that their father had had a favourite. It couldn't be helped. That was just how Odin had been – not always fair, not necessarily impartial – although none of them had ever for a moment doubted his love.

Thor carried a flaming torch to the pyre, and it was awful to see him weeping. So huge in stature, but stooped now, shrunken, humbled by grief, his beard silvered with tears. He touched the trembling torch to the wood, and fire leapt from the stacked lumber.

Huginn and Muninn had, until this moment, been stationed on the bier. I wouldn't have said they were actually in mourning for their master. They'd just hung about near his body, shuffling up and down beside it, as if at a loss for anything else to do. Sometimes they'd arch their wings and let out a doleful *awwwrrkk!* or preen each other as if for comfort.

Once the fire started, the ravens took to the air. They flew away like two black souls, disappearing into the redness of the cold, bloated new sun. I doubted we'd ever see them again. Odin had been concerned about who would feed them after he was gone, but they would fend for themselves. Without him animating them, lending them his voice and mind, they were nothing special now, just birds. Nobody else would have the same rapport with them as he did, so it was right that they go off and spend the rest of their lives doing whatever ravens normally liked to do.

The flames coiled up the logs, sparking and spitting. In no time at all they were crowding around the base of the bier. They surged onwards and upwards as though jet-blasted, roaring through the wooden latticework on which Odin lay and latching greedily on to his clothing. As his corpse began to roast, Frigga fell to her knees with a hoarse sob of anguish. Sif and Freya went to her side and caressed her shuddering shoulders. Everyone else dropped their heads, and embers and smoke rose spiralling into the sky.

SOME TIME LATER, when the fire had begun to ebb, Bragi announced he was going to recite a memorial ode. Nobody groaned, as was usually the case when a Bragi poem was in the offing. A respectful hush fell.

Eyes red-rimmed, he began. The poem was short, to the point, and rather touching.

As the sun rises, another sun sets.
You shone a light. Now a darkness descends.
Odin, All-Father, in woe and regret
Your soul to High Heaven we humbly commend.

You were the sly one, the wily one, wolf.
You learned and, in learning, learned pain –
A pain that you shared with none but yourself.
Your wisdom you put to good gain.

You were the war god, the furious cry,
The patron of warrior lust,
Looking with favour on those who would die
For causes both noble and just.

Your judgement might waver, your temper might flare,
You were often aloof and apart,
But never in doubt – and beyond all compare –
Was the stoical strength of your heart.

O father, my father, All-Father, you fought
With bravery here, and you won.
And now we whose lives your self-sacrifice bought
Will continue the work you've begun.

This, as your body succumbs to cremation,
We solemnly, dutifully, fiercely maintain –
That Asgard, our home, our snow-fastened nation,
Shall never be conquered while Aesir remain.

"And Vanir!" Freya shouted.

"And us!" added one of the troops, and others agreed. "Yeah! And us!"

All at once a great massed chorus of devotion and loyalty rose up. I would have joined in, except for the fact that Odin wasn't the only one who had died defending Asgard last night and this rankled with me. Baz's body still lay out there with *Fenrir*, and was he getting the state funeral, the poetic oration, the pomp and circumstance, the standing ovation? Not a bit of it.

Baz wasn't Odin, of course, and his death wasn't nearly such a big deal, certainly not as far as the Aesir were concerned. Odin had been the main man, the commander in chief, the guiding light, top of the pyramid. Baz had been just another footsoldier; a pawn, not a king.

But he would still be missed, and in a way it was even worse that he'd lost his life stopping the mega-tank, because Asgard wasn't *his* native soil. There'd been far less at stake for him personally, meaning he'd given up more.

Backdoor'd told me how it had happened.

"Stuck his neck out too far," he'd said. "We were placing the charges on the cab of that thing, and I told him to be careful, keep low. I *told* him. But he just didn't listen. Leaned out. Got just inside the arc of fire from one of the turrets. Got ripped apart."

I looked over at him now. Last night, spattered freshly with Baz's blood, he'd seemed shellshocked by the experience. Said he couldn't remember much after Baz bought it. He'd set the fuses, scrambled off *Fenrir*, run for the trees, all on autopilot, numb.

He looked okay this morning, however. Everybody around him was chanting and cheering, reaffirming their commitment to the cause. It was a collective declaration of defiance, a way of coming to terms with the momentous blow we'd received, and Backdoor was giving it as much welly as anyone.

And that just did it for me. Something inside went snap.

I didn't believe Backdoor's account of events. I didn't believe a word that came out of that muttonchopped gob of his. Not any more.

It wasn't the time or place to have this thing out, but I couldn't wait a moment longer.

I stormed over to him, butting people aside.

"You!"

He blinked at me. "Gid?"

"You – you self-satisfied little turd. I've had it up to here with you."

Around us the crowd started to go quiet. Fire-bright gazes turned.

"What is this?" Backdoor said. Captain fucking Innocent. "What's the matter?"

"*What's the – !?* I'll tell you what the matter bloody is, sunshine. You. You're the fucking matter."

"Gid, I've no idea what's got into you, but –"

I lunged closer to him. Our noses were almost brushing. "I wasn't sure it was you, at first. Utgard. Chopsticks. I reckoned it could all just have been a terrible accident. I thought I'd give you the benefit of the doubt. No proof, no witnesses. Maybe Chops did just discharge his weapon by mistake. But then, with Baz... I should've known better. I shouldn't have left you alone with him in a combat situation, but I wanted you off *my* back. The engine room job was too important to have you come along and wreck it for us somehow."

"Gid, please, why don't you calm down?"

"Calm down!"

"This is an emotional time. For all of us. You're tired, you're not thinking clearly. I'm not even sure what you're getting at."

"You!" I bellowed. "You, is what I'm getting at."

Now nobody else was talking. The only sound, other than Backdoor's and my voices, was the snap-crackle-pop of the pyre.

"You," I went on, "have been fucking with us all along. You got Chops killed and the rest of us nearly as well. You also got Baz killed. I don't know how you did it, but my bet would be you shoved him in the way of those guns."

"Shoved him... Why the hell would I do that?"

"Because you're here to sabotage us. You've been sent by Loki. You're his inside man."

"Loki?" And he laughed. The nerve of him. Fucking traitor. Laughing in my face. "I've got nothing to do with Loki. Never had. Never even seen him, except on telly when he's, you know, her. This is absurd, Gid. I can't believe I'm hearing any of this."

"Believe it, you tosser. You even admitted you fancy Mrs Keener."

"So what? Who doesn't? Okay, yes, I did fancy her, but not after I found out who she really is. If *that's* your basis for all this shit you're accusing me of doing, it's pretty flimsy, I've got to say."

"Also, when I first met you, you described yourself as sneaky."

"Well, I am. It was hardly a confession."

"Blatant. Rubbing our noses in it."

Backdoor laughed again, this time for the benefit of our audience: *Are you hearing this unmitigated bollocks?* "You know what? You're insane. That's what you are. Going around saying I've murdered my own teammates. Insane. That IED that put a hole in your head, it's done a complete number on you." He reached out and tapped my skull where the titanium plate was. "Inside here, it's all clowns and monkeys."

He shouldn't have done that.

"You shouldn't have done that," I told him.

"You shouldn't be calling me a traitor," he replied.

I swung for him. But Backdoor knew me well enough by now. Knew what I was like. The punch was predictable and he saw it coming and got up a forearm block. I craned back my head, planning to nut him on the bridge of his nose. Something nudged against my groin, and I froze.

"Ah-ah-ah," Backdoor said, shaking his head and grinning.

I didn't need to look down. He had a gun to my balls.

"Bastard," I hissed.

"What part of 'sneaky' do you not understand? You could take me in a fair fight, Gid, no question. Cream me. So why would I be so stupid as to let this be a fair fight?"

"Put it away. Let's deal with this like men."

"Isn't that what we're doing? Just as different kinds of men. You your way, me mine."

I tensed. "I'll –"

He jabbed the pistol firmly into my crown jewels, and I tried not to wince. "You'll do nothing, unless you'd like to be singing soprano for the rest of your life. Just stand still and give me what I want, which is an apology and a retraction. You don't go around calling somebody a traitor unless you have evidence. You don't have any, only a couple of half-baked theories. You've just false-accused me and you need to take it back."

"Not going to happen. I know what I know. And being the guy

who's threatening to blow my balls off is hardly helping your case, is it? Sign of guilt, to my mind."

"I'm defending my reputation," Backdoor said. "Surely if I just let you beat me up, wouldn't that be more suspicious? Whereas this" – he ground the gun harder still into my nethers – "is me publicly and robustly telling you I deny everything and you can go fuck yourself."

"And this," said Freya in his ear, "is me telling you to put the gun away or you'll be the one singing soprano."

She'd crept up behind him silent as a panther, and her hunting knife was between his legs. Backdoor didn't realise it at first, until she nodded her head downward and he followed her gaze to find the blade poking out from under his crotch.

"You wouldn't," he breathed.

"Try me."

Backdoor went up on tiptoes, and the knife rose with him, blade keeping light contact with the zipper of his trousers. He searched Freya's face, and something there told him she wasn't fooling around. He hesitated. Then I felt the pressure of gun against genitalia ease. He raised the pistol with his finger outside the trigger guard, showing Freya he meant no harm.

"I'd never really have done it," he said. "I was only bluffing."

"That makes one of us," she replied. She withdrew the knife.

"But the fact remains, I'm not what Gid says I am. He's lying."

"For what it's worth, I agree. Not about the lying, but I think he's mistaken. You're not acting like someone with something to hide. Your declarations of innocence have the ring of truth."

"There," Backdoor said to me, and to everyone else. "One of the Vanir believes me. I reckon that's enough to clear my name." Smug triumph was written all over his face, which made me yearn even more to plant a fist in it.

I probably would have, but Freya saw what was brewing and held up a hand to me like a policeman stopping traffic. "Gid. Back down. You've embarrassed yourself enough as it is. No need to add idiocy to the list of offences."

"But –"

"It is the All-Father's funeral," she said tightly. "You shame his memory with these boneheaded melodramatics of yours."

"But Backdoor –"

"– deserves the apology he's asked for. Give it to him now." She leaned close and whispered so that only I could hear: "One pair of balls is much the same as another to me. I don't value yours *that* highly."

She wasn't joking. The knife was still in her hand.

"Backdoor," I said. "Sorry." I didn't mean it.

He shrugged. "Bygones." He didn't mean it either.

"I jumped to conclusions." *I still think you got Chops and Baz killed.*

"Easily done. We're under stress." *You fucking wankstain.*

He moved off. I'd be watching him closer than ever from now on. He knew that. I'd make sure, too, that I never turned my back on him. And he'd damn well better make sure he never turned his back on me.

Slowly the crowd started to disperse. The pyre was a heap of blackened, twisted wood, licked here and there by pale flame. What was left of Odin lay amongst it, indistinguishable.

I turned to Freya, who was sheathing her knife.

"Okay, maybe I could have timed that better," I began, "but..."

"Don't expect forgiveness," she said, head averted from me. "I'm not that kind of deity."

"I've never assumed you are. Still, you stood up for me just now. That's something."

"No. I helped you out only so as to end an impasse and defuse an awkward situation. Don't read anything more into it than that."

"You saved my bacon – by threatening to cut off his."

"Humour won't redeem you," she said, stony-faced. "Especially when it's as inappropriate as yours always is. Do you not appreciate the seriousness of our predicament? Odin is dead. We've lost our leader. And Loki will have plenty more surprises up his sleeve."

"More *Thunderbirds*-type machines like the tank?"

"Oh, undoubtedly. And without Odin to marshal us, exhort us, maintain morale and focus when the going gets tough –"

She was interrupted by a cry.

Someone nearby had just collapsed. Heimdall. Grief-stricken, it seemed, just as Frigga had been. He rolled on the ground and his hands were pawing at the sides of his head. It looked like he was tearing his hair out.

Then I realised. Not grief. Agony.

"My ears!" he gasped. "My... they... *aaaarrrghh!!*"

I frowned at Freya. Her expression was as perplexed as mine.

"I can't hear a sausage," I said.

"It's coming!" Heimdall yelled. Blood oozed between his fingers. "It's... I can't bear it! Help me! Help! It's coming! Screaming. So low... So loud..."

And then he fainted.

FIFTY-EIGHT

CONFUSION REIGNED. FRIGGA took charge of Heimdall, instructing two of the men to carry his unconscious body to the castle. Meanwhile the rest of us milled about, all of a tizz because we knew an attack was imminent but had no way of telling where it was coming from or what form it would take.

"Fuck," I said to Paddy and Cy. "First we lose Odin, our eyes in the sky. Now Heimdall, our long-range radar. We're being crippled bit by bit."

"What was that, some kind of sonic weapon?" said Paddy.

"That knocked Heimdall for six? Yeah, sonic weapon'd be my guess."

"But where's it positioned?" said Cy. "How far off?"

"Wouldn't have to be close by at all, given how extraordinarily acute his hearing is. Look, we've got to get on top of this. Pads, go scare up Jensen and Thwaite. Tell them to get *Sleipnir* in the air, pronto. We need some idea of what's approaching and where from."

Twenty minutes later the Wokka was up and on patrol, ranging outward from the castle in an expanding spiral sweep. At intervals Thwaite radioed in. "Nothing to report," and "Still nothing to report." No fresh penetration of Asgard's borders. No visual confirmation of anything out of the ordinary.

"You don't think maybe Heimdall got it wrong?" Cy wondered. "Whatever it was they blasted him with, it messed with his head? Made him imagine something that in't there?"

"Possible. As long as he's out cold, he can't say. But my money's on him being right. Face it, Loki's hit us once already in the past twenty-four hours, hard. He knows we've got to have sustained losses. Maybe he even knows about Odin. Naturally he's going to want to press home the advantage. Catch us while we're still reeling."

"Second bite of the cherry, type of thing."

"Only, we're a cherry that bites back. So let's make damn sure we're ready to."

I soon had Thor, Vali, Vidar and Tyr taking command of their units and organising them into a defensive position. Once again, three concentric lines were set up around the castle. I was reluctant to dish out orders to Odin's sons – it felt like an inversion of the proper chain of command – but there was drift there. Understandably. They'd just lost their dad, for fuck's sake. They were bereaved, distraught, not thinking straight. Somebody had to gee them up. Nobody else was volunteering, so the role fell to me.

The sun climbed. The morning wore on. It started to seem that perhaps Cy was right and Heimdall had been confused, misled somehow. He'd said, "It's coming!" so urgently. So why wasn't it here by now?

There was grumbling in the ranks. Apprehension spawned annoyance. The lads were impatient for something to happen, and as their tension mounted, so did their tempers. Thor and his brothers kept a rough discipline, barking at anyone who got out of line. It was not a good day to piss them off.

Noon arrived, the sun at its zenith and shedding as much weak winter warmth as it had to give. By now even I was coming to the conclusion that this was all a false alarm. Poor old Heimdall had had his senses overloaded by some long-distance weapon of Loki's. His thoughts had been scrambled and he'd not known what he was saying.

I was on the point of telling Odin's sons – or rather, gently but firmly suggesting to them – that they order the troops to stand down. Everywhere, tired and drawn faces. Frayed, ragged looks. The boys needed a break.

Suddenly, the trolls started howling in their pens.

It was a terrible sound, rough-edged with fear and panic. They babbled and hooted, repeating hoarse almost-words in their coarse almost-language. There were only ten of them left after the assault on *Fenrir* but they made enough racket for three times that many. The air around the castle echoed with it and with the thumping that accompanied it as the trolls pounded agitatedly at the pens' wooden stockades.

"Something's got them spooked, all right," Cy said.

"Quite," I said, and executed a quick weapons check. Others did the same. All at once, exhaustion was gone, swept aside by a flood of adrenaline. We were alert, on our mettle. The wait was over. We were in business.

I stole a sidelong glance at Freya, who like me was stationed in the second defence tier. She hunkered just over a hundred metres away with Skadi and what remained of Skadi's ski-troop unit. She turned her head my way, gave just the tiniest of nods, and resumed looking straight ahead. There was no smile, and I hated myself for hoping for one. What was I to her? Just some mortal she was boffing, a convenient booty-call buddy, a piece of scruff she'd picked up on a whim and could just as easily drop. I fulfilled her needs in some ways, mostly in the jiggery-pokery department, but in other ways I was hopelessly lacking. She made me feel like the gamekeeper who was allowed to give the lady of the manor a right old seeing-to but would never be invited to the high-society balls.

But then, I supposed, that was what you got for shagging a goddess. Mortals and deities – it clearly wasn't a recipe for long-term relationship bliss.

Focus, Gid. Priorities.

The trolls went quiet. That, in a way, was worse than the howling.

Then the ground began to shake.

At first it was just a mild vibration, a tingle in the trouser legs.

It developed gradually into a low, deep-seated throb, like someone was playing one of the bassiest, bottommost notes on a cathedral organ. We all looked around. Nobody could pinpoint which direction the sound was coming from.

It grew and grew. Soon the earth beneath us was actively juddering up and down, as though it was a trampoline some giant was leaping on. My vision blurred, and all I could think was that *Fenrir*'s sound signature was nothing compared to this. The mega-tank had been big. We were about to be visited by something bigger still. A fuck sight bigger.

Abruptly the ground cracked open near the foot of Yggdrasil. Stones, soil and snow erupted, a geyser of solid matter, and showered down around us. We ducked and hunched. Someone screamed.

The jagged split in the earth broadened and deepened. Debris continued to burst out, propelled skyward from below. Rocks bubbled up like champagne fizz. Something, some massive machine, was tunnelling up from the depths, churning towards daylight, violently displacing vast amounts of mineral as it went. Yggdrasil trembled to its highest branches. Huge cracks and splintering were audible, the sound of the World Tree's roots being bored through and torn asunder.

The tumult reached an apex, and for once I was glad of my dud ear. I wasn't suffering as badly as anyone else. I was only hearing half as much of the cacophony. It was only half deafening me.

Up through the hole came the nose of the thing – like the end of an enormous steel pipe, blunt but with a rounded rim. It grew like the shoot of some vast plant, rising in a column that rivalled Yggdrasil itself for size. It was roughly cylindrical, its surface pitted with countless scrapes and gouges. Rows of serrated-edged wheels fringed its lower section, spinning and screaming like circular saws.

When more of the machine was out of the earth than in, it slowly tipped over under its own weight. As it slumped forwards, sinking into a furrow of its own making, a pair of panels slid open on either side near the nose, to reveal panes of thick, ultra-toughened glass. They were oval – sort of eye-shaped – and lit from within. I glimpsed the silhouettes of people in them: the vehicle's crew, moving with brisk, businesslike purpose.

The wheels stopped spinning. For a moment the now-horizontal machine appeared to be pondering, making up its mind. Then some of the sets of wheels started up again, the ones on its underside, and it swivelled, got its bearings, and tore across open ground towards the castle with a fantail of dirt and snow jetting up behind it a hundred feet in the air.

Between the castle and the snakelike, burrowing vehicle stood us and our guns.

Not much opposition at all, relatively speaking.

FIFTY-NINE

"JORMUNGAND," SAID THOR.

"Jormun-who?"

"Jormungand. The Midgard Serpent."

"Loki's tech version. What's the real Jormungand do? What's it capable of?"

"Killing. Killing with its breath alone."

I looked back to the massive tubular behemoth barrelling towards us. Men in the front ranks had already opened fire on it, and their bullets were bouncing off like grains of rice. An RPG arced towards it, trailing smoke. The explosion left a star-shaped scorch mark but made no appreciable difference.

"Its breath..." I said, wonderingly.

And then *Jormungand* was within spitting distance of the outer defence perimeter, and it let rip.

The noise was indescribable. Beyond loud. Staggering. Gut-wrenching. An immense booming blare that sprang from its hollow front. The sound radiated outwards in a visible cone, a warped, white-tinged shimmer extending perhaps twenty metres ahead of the beast. And anyone touched...

...burst.

No other word for it.

Humans became patches of red fog. Clothing was shredded. Bones were pulverised. Even guns were shattered into components and fragments of components. One moment, a living, breathing person. Next, a thinning spray of popped organ and vaporised blood.

Jormungand was fitted with some kind of audio generator, massively amplified, and used soundwaves to drill a path for itself through the earth, pummelling rock to dust. Up above ground, those same soundwaves could be employed as a weapon. Nothing – organic or inorganic – could withstand a volley of such sheer *volume*. It was instantaneous destruction by decibel.

There was nothing else for it but to retreat. No point holding the line when the enemy could carve through so easily. The outer defence perimeter broke. Men scattered and ran. *Jormungand* ploughed onward, propelled by those serrated wheels. It was on a direct course for the castle, and I doubted there was anything we could do to divert or waylay it.

The radio on my belt crackled.

"Ground forces, this is *Sleipnir*. I see you're, ah, having a spot of bother down there."

"Too bloody right we are, Thwaite," I said. I scanned upwards and spotted the Chinook zeroing in over the treetops. "Any ideas?"

"Flight Lieutenant Jensen's had one. Can't say I'm mad keen on it myself."

"Right now I'll take any suggestions you've got."

"We're, er, we're going to ditch the chopper."

"Ditch...?"

"On top of that thing. See if we can't stop it that way."

"Are you sure about this?"

"Christ, no. Jenners reckons there's a one in ten chance we'll make it out alive. My own estimate's somewhat more conservative. But needs must and all that sort of thing."

I didn't think I could talk them out of it. Didn't want to, truth be told. There weren't a whole lot of other options available to us.

"Fair enough," I said. "Thwaite? About your moustache?"

"Yes, Coxall?"

"It's a pretty nice one, actually. Lush. I'm just jealous."

"Acknowledged," said Thwaite. "Over and hopefully not out."

I watched *Sleipnir* pick up speed. It swooped in behind *Jormungand*, its rotors two discs of grey blur. Jensen was keeping its nose up, so that when the crash came – and it came jarringly hard – the Wokka's underside took the brunt. *Sleipnir* bellyflopped onto the back of the unsuspecting *Jormungand*, a dozen tons of aeronautical engineering colliding at speed with Loki's crawling serpentine vehicle.

The force of the impact smashed *Jormungand*'s rear end deep into the ground and crumpled part of its topside inwards. It also split *Sleipnir*'s fuselage in two, and I saw the forward section of the helicopter, cockpit and all, shear off and roll down *Jormungand*'s flank. It hit the earth head-on, bounced, and came to a halt.

The aviation fuel in *Sleipnir*'s tanks ignited. The fireball engulfed fully half of *Jormungand*, and the vehicle jolted, then shuddered to a complete standstill.

The explosion flung chopper parts far and wide. One of the rotors hurtled into the woods, scything through trees. The other shot over our heads, falling apart as it flew, each of the three blades separating from the rotor head mechanism in weird slow motion. One blade struck the castle, embedding itself in the side of a turret. The other two sailed lazily over the top of the building to land somewhere on the far side.

As the smoke cleared and the flames subsided, it became apparent that *Jormungand* had been halted in its tracks for good. Jensen's possibly suicidal ploy had worked. The burrowing machine's back had been broken and a significant number of its serrated wheels damaged beyond use, including the crucial underside ones, crushed by the falling Wokka. *Jormungand* was disabled.

Not entirely, though.

It might not be able to move but its soundwave drill remained intact. Its nose was pointing straight at the castle, but I judged that the building was safe; *Jormungand* had been stopped a hundred metres short of it, well outside the drill's range.

What I hadn't counted on was that the focus of the drill could be narrowed and elongated. The aperture at *Jormungand*'s front began to contract like the iris of an eye un-dilating. Metal plates slid inwards from the circumference, screeching against one another as they tightened the drill's scope to a circle just a couple of metres in diameter. They were honeycomb-patterned, sound-deflecting.

Then the metal beast roared, and a beam of pure bludgeoning sonic power leapt from it, pounding into the castle like some huge spectral lance. Stones and mortar imploded. The whole building groaned and seemed to recoil. Ripples spread outward from the initial point of impact, solid three-foot-thick walls quivering like jelly. Windows detonated, spraying out shards. Flakes and fragments of masonry tumbled down in a kind of landslide, leaving jagged gaping views of the rooms within. Sections of roof fell in on themselves. The castle from end to end seemed to be losing cohesion, shaking itself to bits as though in the clutches of a Richter 10 earthquake. No doubt all this demolition would have been as noisy as hell, if *Jormungand* hadn't been drowning out everything with its drill's devastating howl.

"No!"

This was Thor, and I saw him mouth the word rather than heard it. His face was aghast, a mask of disbelief.

"No!" he exclaimed again, and then without any further ado he turned and charged at *Jormungand*, tugging Mjolnir from his belt as he went.

I followed him, for no good reason other than that somebody needed to cover his back, just in case. Also, I wanted a piece of that machine almost as much as he did, although I wasn't sure there was a great deal I personally could do.

Thor leapt up onto the front of *Jormungand*, right into its gaping maw. His only thought was to destroy the device that was destroying his castle. Hammer in hand, he set about beating the metal plates that served as a focusing lens for the drill. They began to crack and splinter.

It occurred to me that this wasn't a wise move. Thor hadn't thought it all the way through. Or maybe he had and just didn't care. Ending *Jormungand*'s attack was his sole ambition. The likely consequences of the method he'd chosen to achieve this were neither here nor there.

One of the plates broke away, and the quality of the drill's sound changed. It became less steady, with a shrill edge. Thor continued to chip away at the plates, and I saw the sleeve of his tunic fly off in tatters. His left arm was exposed to the soundwaves and the skin started to wrinkle and tear.

I yelled at him to give up, that he was going to kill himself. Of course he couldn't hear me. Teeth clenched, jaw set, he rained hammer blows on the plates. The skin of his arm was curling off in ribbons and bloody loops. Either he was so intent on what he was doing that he didn't notice or, more probably, the pain was of no importance to him. Only subduing *Jormungand* mattered.

Another plate shattered and fell free. The drill was now making a hideous, irregular droning noise. The soundwaves needed a circular, symmetrical outlet to function properly. By ruining the funnel, Thor was disrupting their pattern of emergence. De-optimising the drill's efficiency. Already – a backward glance showed me – the castle was shaking far less violently, although deep fissures were still appearing in its walls. One entire buttress crumbled away, as though cut loose. Roof tiles slithered off in cascades.

Thor himself wasn't faring much better. His left arm had been flayed to the muscle and hung useless at his side. Flesh dangled off it in grisly tatters. Blood poured down in rivulets.

He didn't let up, though. One-handed, he pounded with Mjolnir, relentless. The more damage he did to *Jormungand*, the more damage it did to him in return. The vehicle's "breath" was butchering him, peeling him, rending him to pieces. His left leg was starting to go the way of his left arm. His chest was bared and reddening. The drill ate away at him layer by layer. It was as though he was being sand-blasted to oblivion. And there was little else I could do except stand and watch. If I climbed up there with him, I'd be gone in a nanosecond. It was only because he was a god that he could withstand the drill at all. Divine strength and durability were buying him the time he needed. Those and his own sheer willpower.

Would it be enough?

It *had* to be enough.

Rib bone glinted. Muscle glistened. The hammer beats slowed but didn't stop. Thor had cleared a hole in the plates that allowed him to step through. He did so. He staggered into the full hurricane force of the drill, which cleaned the hair off his head, the beard from his face. I had no idea how he was able to keep going, how he could even put one foot in front of the other, but nonetheless he somehow managed to stumble on into the throat of the machine. Mjolnir was suffering too, its head turning to dust, its handle to splinters. Both it and its wielder were losing integrity before my very eyes.

Finally Thor raised Mjolnir above his head and delivered an immense, devastating blow to something inside *Jormungand*. I didn't see precisely what he hit. I was at the wrong angle, not close enough. Whatever it was, though, it must have been vital to the operation of the drill because in an instant the sound died and a silence fell. A silence shot through with the screaming of tinnitus.

Thor, what was left of him, tottered backwards. He took nine steps. He was a ghastly, gory scarecrow version of himself. Barely alive, ruined beyond redemption. He sagged to his knees on the rim of *Jormungand*'s front end, and then slipped off onto the ground. When his body hit the snow it splashed rather than thudded.

I hurried over for a closer look. Was he – could be conceivably be – still alive?

No. Not a hope.

What lay in front of the vehicle was only just recognisable as physical remains, a fractured skeleton in a soupy puddle of blood and organs. Nothing apart from the half-eroded hammer still clutched in one hand would have told you that this mangled mess had once been the god of thunder.

SIXTY

VALI, VIDAR AND Tyr got inside the incapacitated *Jormungand* and wrought havoc on the crew. As reprisals went it was neither swift nor gentle. They took their time exacting revenge for the death of their brother. Screams came from within the vehicle – raw, pleading, protracted. The windows that were its eyes were spattered with red.

It wasn't unsatisfying to know that this was being done.

THEN THERE WAS an interval of numbness. A period in which to take stock. Regroup. Lick wounds. Drink. Eat. Tally up how much we'd got left.

Our inventory of assets went something like this:

- a dozen Aesir and Vanir
- the Valkyries
- ten trolls
- just over one hundred and fifty mortal troops

We'd lost our head man, our strongest warrior, our one and only transport helicopter, and most of our castle. Heimdall was out of action for the foreseeable future, lying comatose in bed, blood still leaking from his traumatised eardrums. Frigga was tending to him and to the injured men, most of whom were suffering from wounds inflicted by falling debris, bone breaks, severe contusions, concussion, that sort of thing. One of the intact wings of the castle was now a field hospital. Thwaite was there. He'd been pulled from the wreckage of *Sleipnir* in very bad shape, and Frigga had promised to do what she could for him, but she wasn't optimistic about his chances. Jensen, unfortunately, was past saving.

The respite lasted, in all, a little under three hours.

Then the frost giants arrived.

A DELEGATION OF them appeared at the castle gate. Three in all, led by Bergelmir himself. They requested an audience with Odin, but didn't seem surprised to learn that he wasn't around any more. Nor Thor either.

In the event, they got lumped with me. I went out to meet them, taking Cy, Paddy and Vali along for backup and moral support.

"Gid Coxall," Bergelmir said, almost affectionately. "Well, well, well. What a state Asgard finds itself in, eh? That it should come to this. And your poor castle. An impressive edifice once, although hardly the rival of Utgard."

"We're redecorating," I said. "Once we're finished, you'll love what we're doing with the place. It's going to add hugely to the value when the time comes to sell. Kirstie and Phil would be proud."

"You speak in riddles, as always," Bergelmir said. "Familiar words put together in incomprehensibly strange ways. It's one of the things that makes you so intriguing and so maddening."

"All right, so what's the deal here? Let's cut right to it. I'm not in the mood for fannying around. Have you come to a decision on my offer? Us and you, in partnership. Because I'll be frank, we could do with reinforcements. Loki's got us on the ropes and there's surely more to come from him. Frost giants and Asgardians together, the dream team, what do you say?"

Bergelmir's contemptuous laugh was an answer in itself.

"Oh no! Dear me, no. That bird has definitely flown. In the light of your treacherous behaviour in Utgard, an alliance? I think not."

"It was an accident," I argued, not convincingly because I wasn't convinced myself that it had been. "A slip-up. I wish it had never happened."

"And well may you, but it doesn't change anything. Jotuns died, among them Suttung, a much feared and respected figure among our race. And after I'd granted you immunity from harm, too. I took that as a personal affront. A blatant slap in the face. No, any charitable feelings I may have harboured towards you, Gid, are long since vanished. Now I desire only your painful demise."

"Well, that's good to know. I mean, at least I'm clear where I stand. So you're here to tell us any deal's off, yes? Is that all?"

"In a manner of speaking. This is us doing you the courtesy of informing you that there now exists a state of all-out war between Jotunheim and Asgard. Ragnarök is upon us, and it is beholden to us as jotuns to assist as energetically as we can in the complete and utter destruction of the Aesir and all their collaborators."

"So you're siding with Loki. That's it. Non-negotiable."

"Yes."

"And if at a later date he turns on you?"

"We will act accordingly," said Bergelmir. "But I doubt it will ever come to pass. Especially not if we prove ourselves to be diligent aides to him in this instance."

"Right now I'm looking at three frost giants," I said. "Forgive me if I'm not exactly quaking in my boots."

"Ah, but observe."

Bergelmir turned, put a hand to his mouth, and let out a long, loud, hooting call that echoed across the landscape.

And frost giants appeared. They came out from the woods, stomping into view, kitted out in a glittering array of ice armour and weaponry. There were hundreds of them. Maybe even thousands. Everywhere I looked, frost giants.

"We have the castle fully surrounded," their leader said. "Every able-bodied jotun of fighting age, male and female, has taken up arms and come. We will grant you one hour in which to rally your forces and prepare. One hour and not a minute more. Think of it as a vestigial mark of the esteem in which I once held you. Then we attack. No mercy. No quarter. We will fight you until the very last of us is dead – or the very last of you. Good day, Gid. When we two next meet – and I'm sure we will, and soon – you will find me altogether less congenial."

Bergelmir smiled, bowed, and left with his companions.

SIXTY-ONE

HE WAS AS good as his word. One hour later, almost to the second, the frost giants moved on the castle.

I'd used the grace period to assess where the building's weak points were – and there were plenty of them – and make sure they were as well defended as they could possibly be. *Jormungand* had inflicted the most damage on the west-facing aspect. One major hole and several minor ones. Rubble formed convenient ramps, and I'd predicted the frosties would concentrate their efforts on using these to storm the breaches. That way they could establish a beachhead within the castle walls.

Which was exactly their plan, and we hit them with a withering crossfire as they came. We had to shoot from reasonably close range since we couldn't afford to waste too much ammo. Ice armour was effective at deflecting bullets at a distance, so we kept it down to fifty metres or less, which didn't leave much room for error. A few of the frosties got through and the combat turned dirty and hand-to-hand. The majority didn't make it past the slopes of rubble, however. The bodies began to pile up in the breaches, two, three, even four high.

The first wave of the attack lasted nearly forty minutes before a horn sounded the retreat. Bergelmir's troops withdrew to the trees, to retrench and steel themselves to start again.

By that point I'd had an idea. "A brilliant one, even if I do say so myself."

"Go on then," said Paddy, and when I'd outlined it he twisted his mouth up and said, "That could work. Maybe. Can't hurt to try, at any rate."

"Oh give over, it's genius!"

"No, *Finnegans Wake* is genius. You've come up with something that might make a difference and equally might not. Which is hardly the same."

"Sour grapes. You just wish it was *your* idea."

"If it makes you feel better, then to be sure, I do."

We got down to business preparing a – ho ho! – warm reception for the frost giants. No sooner were we done than they came at us once more, a fresh wave of them scrambling up the rubble, yowling and bellowing all the way.

"Fire!" I yelled into the walkie-talkie, but I wasn't referring to guns. All along the castle's western flank, men threw flash bombs onto the stacks of frostie corpses, which we'd laced with every kind of combustible liquid we could lay our hands on – fuel oil, lamp oil, diesel, petrol, even cooking fat. The bodies quickly became a great flaming barrier, a fiery screen with a dual function: it drove the attacking frost giants back, and the heat affected their weaponry and armour. Some of the ice-smiths' handiwork melted outright. Some of it held together, but was severely compromised – blades blunted, helmets and breastplates thinned.

Steaming, sodden, more vulnerable than before, the frost giants fled for the safety of the trees. Snipers on the battlements took them down as they ran. Freya was up there, leading the shooting, and her Lee-Enfield cracked rhythmically and repeatedly. I'd known she was a top-notch markswoman, but this was something else. No frostie she aimed at made it back to the forest. She would ratchet the rifle's bolt, sight, pull the trigger, and that was another of the big buggers flat on the deck. Reloading the five-round magazine took her next to no time, too.

The stench from the burning corpses was atrocious. All that fur and fatty flesh. And as the flames subsided and the acrid smoke cleared, out of the woods the frost giants came yet again. Now, though, they were closing in on the castle from all sides evenly, and I could tell they weren't going to converge on the breaches, not this time. Tried that twice and got nowhere. They went straight for the walls instead, and started to climb.

Boy, could they climb. The long talons on their hands and feet dug deep into the mortar and the cracks and crevices in the stonework, as effective as a mountaineer's ice picks and crampons. The frost giants swarmed up the walls like the biggest, ugliest, whitest spiders imaginable. We shot them down as they clambered, but there were masses of them and we weren't able to pick them off quickly enough. They began cresting the battlements, unslung their *issgeisl*s and other weapons, and engaged with us in earnest.

All along the castle's rim, men and gods grappled with towering, shaggy monsters. Odin's sons were at the forefront. Vali, Vidar and Tyr despatched frost giants in all directions, sending bodies tumbling to the ground. The Valkyries were in the thick of it too, whooping high-pitched battlecries as they gunned frosties down. Skadi was there.

Sif too. Thor's missus hadn't struck me as the Xena Warrior Princess type. I'd written her off as pleasant but mousy, and assumed she would stick with Frigga, helping to care for the injured, but not a bit of it. She was Aesir, and that meant getting down and mixing it with the enemy at a time of crisis. The death of her beloved gave her added impetus. She was a little hellcat, eyes bloodshot, taking out her very considerable anguish on her late husband's favourite punchbags. Any frost giant who strayed into her path didn't live long to regret it.

Freya, of course, performed sterling work, and I did my bit. Gave a pretty good account of myself, in fact. Just let my inner berserker have free rein and went along for the ride. Up on the battlements, I forgot everything. I didn't feel anger or hatred or fear or regret. I didn't have any petty problems any more. Nothing bothered me or distracted me. I was pure purpose. I existed to do one thing and that was kill frost giants. They appeared, I did away with them. Some I shot, some I stabbed, whatever suited. I had my Minimi in one hand and an appropriated *issgeisl* in the other, and ploughed through their ranks, cold, unfeeling, inexhaustible. I could have gone on for ever. Time had no meaning; I measured my progress through the world in terms of enemies exterminated. The only clock that counted was the one that registered the racking up of dead frost giants.

This was what I did best, what I was made for. I wasn't a good husband. I wasn't a good father. Nature hadn't designed me to hold down a McJob and be Mr Domestic and live the cosy life. It had designed me to fight and slay. I had no other function. This – wading headlong into the enemy and mowing them down – was me.

And the blackness at the core of my being exulted. It screamed with a joy that was beyond happiness, beyond ecstasy, inexpressibly sweet and mindless. You couldn't get a high like it from any other source. Drink, drugs, unbridled sex, they paled by comparison. Poor substitutes. *This* was the real deal. Uncut. Raw. Mainline. Heavenly. The utter, unutterable bliss of not having to think, not having to feel, having only to recognise, react, and move on. See enemy. Kill enemy. Find next enemy. Repeat ad infinitum, or until the supply of opponents runs out.

The sun set. The sky greyed. There was that greenish glow on the western horizon that signified the last of the light. And when it was gone, that was when Bergelmir decided his troops had had enough for the day. Once again, the retreat was sounded, and the frost giants pulled back. Any that were still scaling the castle walls leapt back down to the ground and scurried off; any that were still on top of the walls did their best to make a getaway, and many succeeded. White silhouettes, they ghosted across the snow to the dark sanctuary of the woods.

We watched them go, knowing we hadn't won, knowing they'd be back tomorrow, but knowing too that we'd done as well as we could have hoped and better than anyone might have expected. After all, we were still holding the castle, weren't we? And as long as we had that, we had something.

SIXTY-TWO

I WAS KEEPING lookout in the ruined hollow that had been one of the castle bedrooms. Nothing was happening outside. Campfires winked in the forest, but there'd been no sign of any overt hostile activity. Bitterly cold air whistled in through the caved-in outer wall. The stars were out in their millions, each a fleck of ice. The moon was as round and hard as a cannonball.

Freya brought me a mug of tea. She knocked on the frame of the shattered door first, before entering.

"Didn't want to startle you," she said. "I know how easy you are to catch unawares."

I murdered that drink. Hot, milky, delicious. "You're a godsend," I told her when the mug was drained.

"Soldiers love their tea. If I've learned anything these past months, it's that. They can't function without it."

"An army marches on its stomach, but only if its stomach's got a brew inside. So, what's the news? How's everyone holding up?"

"Reasonably well. Thwaite, however..."

"How is old Face Fungus?" I asked, although her tone of voice had already told me.

"He didn't make it. Frigga gave him all the attention she could, but she's been run ragged, her power is stretched thin... and he just didn't have the strength."

"Bugger. Anything else I should know about?"

"Nothing much. I did come across two of your teammates arguing."

"Backdoor and who?"

"Not him. Cy and the Irishman."

"Paddy? Arguing with Cy? What about?"

"That I don't know. I came in at the end of it. They were in the banqueting hall. Paddy called Cy a name and walked out fuming. That was all I saw."

"Huh. Well, they're both big boys. They can sort themselves out. It's a pressure situation. There's bound to be some friction. I'll maybe have a chat with them later, but it's probably just them getting on each other's nerves. Nothing to worry about."

Freya sat down beside me at my vantage point, near enough that our thighs were not quite touching. She stared out into the darkness. "Quiet out there."

"I'd say 'too quiet,' but that'd be a movie cliché. Frosties seem bedded down for the night. Doubt they'll attack before daybreak."

"Agreed. They're re-equipping themselves. Their ice-smiths will be busy repairing weapons and casting new ones. Normally it's a week's work to shape a decent blade, but they can put together something makeshift in under an hour."

"Let 'em. Makes no difference. Whatever they throw at us, we can handle it."

"From anybody else I would call that bravado. From you – you really believe it, don't you?"

"Why not? It's the only way to think. Otherwise, might as well just give up and go home."

"Why haven't you?"

"Why haven't I what?"

"Gone home."

"Don't understand the question."

She nestled in close to me. We were definitely touching now, her body firm and tight against mine. Knowing Freya, this was purely pragmatic. Compensating for the freezing temperatures, shared physical warmth, all that. And yet, it wasn't. It was more.

"This isn't your fight," she said. "You're a soldier of fortune. You're here only because money is involved. But still, you're going to see this through to the end. You're happy to."

"Loki has to be stopped."

"Is that all?"

"Isn't it enough? Nobody on Midgard seems able to stand up to him, but *we* can."

"Can we? We've taken such dreadful losses."

"Still here, though, aren't we? Still standing."

"I'm just saying I wouldn't blame you if you wanted to quit."

"I wouldn't forgive myself if I did."

"Asgard isn't your world."

"It isn't yours either, lady from Vanaheim."

"True, but I have a blood connection to it. The Aesir are family."

"And I feel like I have a connection to it too. I liked Odin a lot. I even liked Thor, the great big buffoon. And..."

I almost said something about her. About liking her. More than liking. Her being the strongest of my connections to Asgard. But that might have spooked her. Worse, she might have just laughed scornfully, and I simply didn't want to take that chance. I wasn't scared of much but I was scared of Freya rejecting me. Better that she and I have this exclusively sexual thing going, keep it at that level. I could gamble on making it more than that, but I might well wind up broke if I did.

"And," I said, "I'm a bloke who finishes what he sets out to do. I don't leave a job half done. Especially this sort of job. It's just who I am, Freya. I've come to realise that. I'm not cut out for much except combat. It's my thing, what I'm built for. Which is pretty sad, when you come to think of it – that I'm not really a well-rounded person, that I'll never be content as a civilian, that fighting is all I have. But as Detective Harry Callahan famously once said, 'A man's gotta know his limitations,' and I now know mine.

"For a while, after I got dropped from the army, something was missing. Not the piece of my head that I left in Afghanistan.

Something deeper, essential. A purpose. I lost that and had nothing to replace it with. Coming here was about getting a second chance, but turns out it was also about reconnecting with who I am – who I'm supposed to be."

She didn't comment, didn't tell me to stop droning on and shut up, so I carried on.

"I fight. I kill. I'm a man of war. I'm not particularly proud of it, but I'm not ashamed of it either. Plenty of soldiers *hate* war. Most, I'd say. It scars them, fucks them up for life. But they fight anyway, because they're brave and because it's expected of them. And I'm no less fucked up than anyone. You should see some of the nightmares I have. Wouldn't wish them on my worst enemy. But my one advantage is that I know that, come what may, I have an aptitude for soldiering. I know I do it well, better than anything else. That – what's the word? – mitigates things for me. Makes it easier to put up with the rest of the shit that comes with the profession. Life hasn't given me a better alternative, so grin and bear it, eh?"

Her head snugged into the contours of my neck. Her shoulder pressed against my pectoral. Her hair smelled faintly, deliciously, of pine forests and ozone.

"And I'm not scared," I said. "Even if we lose to Loki – which we won't – I can accept it. I won't mind dying if it means I've done my bit trying to foil his plans. Bullying bastards like him can't be allowed to go unchecked. They have to be challenged, faced down, given a damn good slap if that's what's required. And above all else I know that this is the upside of me being such a full-on battlefield hardcase. I can use it in the name of what's right. Cloud, silver lining. I've been gifted with the ability to kick arses and the good sense to know which are the arses needing to be kicked. And that's... Freya?"

My only answer was a soft snore.

I smiled to myself. A Vanir goddess needed her beauty sleep as much as the next person.

I did something then that I never thought I'd do with Freya. Tenderly, I kissed the top of her head. She stirred, mumbled what might have been a complaint, then settled down again.

The wind hissed.
The castle slumbered.
It was a good night.
The best.

SIXTY-THREE

SCREAMS BROKE THE dawn hush.

I snapped awake and was on my feet in a moment. Freya was up too, and already at the room's empty socket of a window. She was staring out towards Yggdrasil, where the commotion was coming from. Low grey cloud carpeted the sky, hazing the World Tree's uppermost branches. There'd be snow soon, lots of it.

"What's going on?"

"Deserters."

"What! No fucking way."

"Look."

Over by Yggdrasil, frost giants were milling about in a cluster, very busy. There were men among them. Uniformed. Ours. They were the ones screaming. Protesting. Pleading.

"Shit," I breathed. "How can you be sure they're deserters? Couldn't the frosties have just captured them?"

"Without a firefight? Without any of us hearing gunshots? I don't think so. And why else would anyone have left the castle, if not to desert?"

She was right, damn her. I gauged the range from us to the

World Tree. Too far. The frost giants were armoured. Our rifles were no good. We couldn't help. All we could do was watch as a couple of the frost giants picked up the first of the men by his arms and raised him high. Then in a series of quick, brutally decisive movements they pinned him to Yggdrasil's trunk, skewering ice daggers through his wrists and calves. He howled and roared in hopeless torment. The other men were dealt with in the same way, until all of them, eleven in total, were impaled on the tree.

Their grisly task completed, the frost giants disappeared back into the forest. One of them turned towards the castle before he left. Even at a distance I recognised the posture, the air of pompous authority. Bergelmir.

"They came to us in the night," he called out, in no doubt that there was an audience to be addressed. "They came without weapons, seeking peace and the freedom to return to Midgard unmolested. They said they'd had enough of fighting. They were sick and tired of it. With Odin gone, they said, their cause was lost. Battling on would be futile. The odds against them were hopeless." He gestured at the squirming, crucified men. "This is our response. We jotuns do not let our enemies go unpunished. Nor do we know the meaning of mercy."

Then he was gone, while the men fixed to the World Tree screamed on.

"He mocks us," Freya snarled. "He mocks the All-Father's time of trial."

"Let's get out there. Get them down."

"No. We can't risk it. Bergelmir will be waiting for us to do just that. Those men aren't only an object lesson, they're bait. Besides, it will take us several minutes to organise a rescue party and reach them. Shock and blood loss will have already done for them by then."

"So we just leave them hanging there, is that it?"

"There is another way." She raised her Lee-Enfield. "Jotuns may not understand mercy, but I do."

"No."

"Yes, Gid. You know this is the right course of action. The only course of action."

"Freya, don't."

"I'm not asking your permission. If you're squeamish, look away."

But I didn't.

Eleven rifle reports. Eleven shots straight through the heart. Eleven suspended bodies twitching, falling silent and still.

IT WASN'T UNTIL an hour later that I discovered that Paddy was one of the eleven. Their ringleader, in fact. Cy told me over breakfast, after I'd asked where our tame Irishman was.

Absolute gut punch. Left me gaping.

"Paddy?" I said. "But..."

"You didn't realise?"

Numbly I shook my head. "I couldn't make out any of their faces. Haven't checked since. Paddy? You're sure?"

Cy nodded.

"Fuck. Fuck the fucking fucker."

"I know. I can't believe it either."

"But he was, you know, one of us. One of the gang. He was probably the last person I'd have expected to wimp out on us. Wait. Didn't you and him have a bit of a barney last night?"

"Yeah. Who told you?"

"Little dicky bird. What was it about? You piss him off somehow?"

"No. Well, yeah, a little. But it wasn't like that. That wasn't why he went out. He came to me, and he was well fed up. Said some stuff about nobody being in charge any more, this was turning into a slaughter, the frosties would just keep coming at us 'til they'd polished us all off. Asked me if I'd join him in a walkout. I told him not to be so defeatist. It got heated. I may've even called him a coward. Paddy got the hump and flounced off. That was it. I honestly didn't think he was going to go through with it. I thought it was just talk, him letting off some steam."

"He thought he could negotiate with the frosties? Persuade them to let him through their lines?"

"Apparently."

"For such a smart man, he was a stupid arse, then, wasn't he?"

"Smart was Paddy's problem, if you ask me. Overthinking things. Trusting the frosties would listen to reason. Assuming they'd act honourably under the circumstances. Those are mistakes a smart person makes."

"Yeah, we're well past the honourable stage with them. It's just about winning or losing now. Living or dying." I sighed. "Paddy... you big Irish twat."

"Suppose we should be grateful he only managed to get ten men to go with him," Cy said. "Could've been worse. Could've been more."

"Is that the general mood? Could there have been more?"

"Honestly, bruv?"

"Go on," I said, knowing I wouldn't like what he had to say.

"Yeah. There's a lot of unhappy fellas here, Gid. Lot of people wondering if it's worth it any more, if we in't on a hiding to nothing. Odin's gone. So's Thor. We're down by our two biggest players, and no disrespect to Vidar, Vali and Tyr but they're none of 'em in the same league. Strong all right, but they don't fill the hole. Don't carry the same weight. And there's however many frosties out there, not to mention Loki. Fuck knows what he's still got in the pipeline, but it's bound to be something big and nasty if what we've seen so far is anything to go by. There's men here who reckon Pads and the others had the right idea."

"Yeah, and look how far it got them."

"Which only makes it worse, dunnit? Now everyone's feeling even more trapped. Rats in a cage and that. No way out."

"How come this is news to me?" I said. "You've have thought I'd have picked up on it, wouldn't you?"

"Mate, no offence, but you're not exactly 'man of the people' these days. You're not in touch with the vibe. You hobnob with the Aesir, you give orders – whether you realise it or not, you've become officer class. So naturally no one's going to tell you the truth to your face now."

"Apart from you."

"Apart from me. And then there's laying into Backdoor like you did, tearing a strip off him at Odin's funeral…"

"Officer class again?"

"Well, that and you came across as a bit, sort of, I dunno…"

"Be gentle."

"Nuts."

"How nuts?"

"Nutty as squirrel shit."

I sat back and peered around the banqueting hall. People were hunched over their food, eating mechanically, subdued. Nobody looked like they'd slept much. Hollow eyes, taut faces. A few of them caught my gaze and glanced away immediately. Resentment I could have coped with, but they were just blanking me, as if there was a barrier between us and nothing to say that would penetrate it, nothing they could express in words.

It was time to take matters in hand.

I stood up.

"What're you doing, man?" Cy asked.

"Grabbing the initiative," I said, and strode to the top table, where the handful of remaining gods sat.

I rapped the table with a spoon until the already near-silent hall was completely quiet.

"Listen up, everyone," I said. "Going to keep this short. Short and as sweet as possible. Last night some men did a very foolish thing. One of them was somebody I considered a pal. If I'd had any inkling what he was about to do, I'd have talked him out of it. Failing that, I'd have beaten some sense into him. I realise what many of you are thinking. 'We're screwed. There's no point carrying on. We're all going to wind up dead. If the frost giants don't get us, Loki will. Might as well give up.' I'll tell you what. Not only is that bollocks, but if you allow yourselves to think that way, then we *are* screwed. Yes, we've had setbacks, and yes, I'll admit that the enemy do seem to have the upper hand. But I know something they don't and probably even you yourselves don't, and it's this. When the blue team has something worth defending and the red team doesn't, the blue team wins, hands down. Every time.

Doesn't matter how many of them there are, how well supplied or not, how well armed or not, they always win. And we have something worth defending."

"Yeah?" shouted someone. "Such as what? A fucked old castle?"

There was a ripple of bleak laughter.

"Nine worlds," I said. "Not one. Not two. Not even three. Nine of them. And Loki will stomp all over the lot of them in his stiletto heels unless we stop him. You know what Earth's been like since Mrs Keener got elected. Tearing itself apart, conflict on top of conflict, and her lording over it all, looking all kitten-cute and butter-wouldn't-melt. Imagine that times by nine. *That* is why we've plonked ourselves down here in this 'fucked old castle.' *That* is why we're going to keep holding it come hell or high water. Just to wipe the grin off her – Loki's – smug fucking face. So let's do this. Let's get out there and fight like we mean it. Let's Ragnarök and roll!"

No great rapturous surge of applause greeted the end of my little speech, but then I was hardly Winston Churchill and it was hardly "We shall fight them on the beaches..."

As I looked around the banqueting hall, however, nobody was avoiding my gaze any more. People were sitting up a little straighter. I'd knocked some of the despair out of them.

I prayed it would be enough.

Really, it had to be.

BEFORE GOING OUTSIDE to face the music once again, I paid a call on Frigga in the field hospital to find out if any of the injured was in a fit state to hold a gun.

Odin's widow shook her head sadly.

"Anyone who's here is too severely wounded even to walk," she said, nodding at the rows of mattresses on the floor and the men sprawled on them. She looked wrung out, empty, like a used juice carton. "I have helped them all I can, and now rest is the best cure they can hope for."

In one corner there were several bodies lined up head to toe, under blankets.

"And that lot aren't going anywhere," I remarked.

"Alas, no. Them I can do nothing further for."

"Heimdall? What about him? Any change?"

"See for yourself."

Asgard's gatekeeper lay with a bandage round his head covering wadding on both ears. He was so still, he could almost have been one of the nearby corpses. His chest moved up and down lightly, infrequently.

"The trauma is as much to his mind as his ears," said Frigga. "Sensory overload on an unimaginable scale. He ought to recover, but when, how soon – who can say?"

"And you?" I asked. "How are you bearing up?"

"I have never been so tired."

"I mean about Odin. Losing your husband."

"You are kind to worry, but I cannot think about that right now. Cannot afford to. I must be strong, for all our sakes. My own concerns must wait. Besides, I am accustomed to bereavement. It's become almost a way of life for me."

"I'm finishing this," I told her firmly. "I'm seeing it through right to the bitter end. For Odin. I owe it to him. If it wasn't for him I wouldn't be alive. He died saving me."

"That's my husband," she said. "That's him through and through."

"I just wanted you to know that."

"I'm grateful. And I wish you luck, Gid." Doubt clouded her wan, genial features. "I fear, though..."

I stopped her. "Uh-uh. None of that."

She stiffened, understanding, steeling herself. "Of course. There is always hope."

"That's the spirit," I said. "Always hope."

Because, I thought, when you're completely fucked, when your back's to the abyss and the hordes of Hell are closing in, when everything's stacked against you and you're down to the last dregs of your strength – hope is the only real weapon you've got.

SIXTY-FOUR

THE FROST GIANTS started their next round of assault not long after. They opted to go for the breaches again, charging at them in dense packs, flying-wedge formations, putting everything into it, hoping that sheer weight of numbers would carry the day. They threw themselves through the jagged gaps, often tripping over one another in their urgency and haste. We used grenades to hold them back, but they just kept on coming, some with half an arm blown off, others with their armour shattered and blood pouring from dozens of wounds, all undeterred. There was fire in their bellies. They were unstoppable. They waded among us, lashing out with their handweapons, taking bullets until they could no longer stand upright. Even when brought to their knees they refused to give up. *Issgeisl*s and tomahawks swung and swung until the hands holding them were too weak to maintain their grip.

A Valkyrie copped it right in front of me. She was reloading her pistol when a frost giant reared up behind her. I didn't have a clear shot or I would have taken him out. The frostie clamped his hands either side of the Valkyrie's head. Whole chunks of him were missing. It wasn't clear how he could still be alive. Yet he was, and he still had enough strength in him to crush the Valkyrie's skull. She kicked out, raked his arms with her fingernails, but it was no use. The frost giant pressed his palms together, and her head was distended, impacting to a red-and-yellow pulp.

I emptied a whole magazine from my Minimi into the fucker's heart. It wouldn't bring the Valkyrie back, but it did make me feel a whole lot better.

Snow began to fall. The overcast sky had grown so dark grey it was almost black, and a first vague flurry of flakes became, in no time, a thick deluge. Snow fell on mangled frost giant corpses, and settled. Snow fell on Aesir and Vanir as they fought, and settled. Snow fell on soldiers firing guns and throwing grenades, and settled. Soon we were all whitened, hoary with snow, and the only real way of telling Asgardian defender from jotun was that they were so much larger than us. The castle walls grew deep crusts of snow. Courtyard flagstones were buried under it. The air itself seemed a solid mass of the stuff, saturated with it, hard to breathe. Eyes stung. Clothes grew cold and heavy. The roar of battle was dulled.

The frost giants didn't let up. The blizzard conditions seemed to favour them. They were used to this kind of weather. Thrived in it. Eventually we had to concede ground. They drove us back from the very largest of the breaches, and having gained a toehold there, they came flooding into the castle in ever greater numbers. Soon we found ourselves defending an archway the frosties had to enter one at a time. We clogged it with their bodies, but they just hauled the dead aside and pushed on into the cloistered courtyard beyond.

Sif was the next significant casualty. A frost giantess – Leikn, no less – managed to clip her with the axe end of her *issgeisl*. Sif reeled, bleeding from a deep gash in the meat of her shoulder. Before she could gather herself, Leikn had flipped the *issgeisl* and run it through her torso from behind. The weapon's spear end jutted out through Sif's sternum. She looked down at its blood-smeared tip incredulously. Leikn yanked it out and shoved it in again. Sif coughed, vomited a stream of pure glistening crimson down her front, and sagged forward. A third thrust from Leikn sent a galvanic shudder through her entire body as she lay prone on the floor.

It so happened that I'd just emptied the magazine currently in my Minimi, but that didn't matter. I sprang at Leikn, swinging the gun two-handed like a club. A bullet would be too clean, too quick. I wanted to punish the hairy great bitch, and I wanted her to *feel* her punishment.

She roared as I pounded on her. Her *issgeisl* whirled. But I wouldn't stay still. I darted around like a monkey, sneaking in hits as and when I could. Finally I got what I was after, an opening, a clear shot to one of her vulnerable points – her knee. The Minimi's stock struck with a pleasing *crunch*, shattering the joint. Leikn shrieked and staggered. I immediately brought the rifle butt up between her legs, hard. Sexual discrimination? Not me. When it came to low blows, I was strictly equal opportunity.

The frost giantess fell, whimpering, clutching her privates, leg twisted at an ugly angle. I discarded the Minimi, now bent to all buggery, and snatched up her *issgeisl*, which she'd dropped. I didn't pause. A sliver of furry midriff was exposed between segments of her armour. I rammed the axe blade home there, burying it deep in her guts, all but chopping her in half. Entrails scuttled out in slick, purple-grey coils.

Nearby a voice screamed, "LEIKN!"

Next thing I knew, Bergelmir was hurtling towards me. He did not seem any too happy. In fact, it would be fair to say he looked murderously insane. Which, given what I'd just done to his missus, he had every right to be.

We fought, *issgeisl* against *issgeisl*. Our weapons clashed and clashed, each impact sending vicious shockwaves up my arms. Bergelmir was in a frenzy. Spittle frothed his lips. He growled in a completely subhuman way, through bared teeth. There wasn't a trace of civilisation to him any more. He was maddened beyond reason, an animal. I blocked and parried his frantic attacks, all the while waiting for my moment. Any second now there'd be some let-up. Bergelmir would overstretch himself, swing wildly, miss, and as he was recovering his balance I'd be in like Flynn. A maiming stab, and he'd be done.

A burst of bullets raked his helmet, ricocheting off, stunning him. Then somebody grabbed my arm, pulling hard. Cy.

"Gid! We're out of here. Fall back, fall back! The frosties have overrun the area. We need to go."

A swift look around confirmed the truth. The frost giants were pouring through the gateway, and the courtyard was theirs. Most of the soldiers around me were dead and the few of us that were left would be in that category too if we didn't retreat, pronto.

"*Human!*" Bergelmir bellowed at me as Cy and I became part of a ragtag exodus from the courtyard. He was rubbery-legged, hand clamped to head. "*I will tear out your liver and eat it before your eyes! I will cut a dozen wounds in you and shit in them all! I will drive this* issgeisl *up your arsehole 'til it comes out through the roof of your skull!*"

"And for our second date...?" I shouted back.

Then we were behind an inner gate, which was hastily slammed shut and barred. The frost giants began hammering on it from the other side. The gate's timbers creaked and shuddered, the hinges groaned, but it held fast.

For now.

I snatched up my walkie-talkie and thumbed the Push-To-Talk button.

"All units, this is Gid. Sitrep?"

Vali's voice: "We're keeping them out, but not for much longer, I fear."

Vidar: "Same here. There are just too many."

Tyr: "They've broken through. Nothing we can do."

Freya: "Ammunition's starting to run out." She was up on the battlements, taking potshots. "I think I can last another quarter of an hour or so."

Skadi: "The Valkyries and I are doing what we can, but..."

The "but..." said it all.

Our situation was bleak and turning bleaker by the minute.

And then, just when it seemed things couldn't get any worse, they did.

SIXTY-FIVE

THE SNOW AND the din of battle prevented us from hearing it until it was almost on top of us. It descended through the cloud cover, pushing out a great grey blister in the overcast's underside before bursting through. The size of a naval frigate, it was suspended in the air by ten gimbal-mounted fans, each at least twenty metres across. Its prow was peaked and its aft bulbous, and its hull boasted dozens of multidirectional automated machine guns which swivelled and traversed impressively. The name *Nagelfar* was painted along its keel in ten-foot-tall capitals, and as it swept overhead, passing across the castle, its fans chopped spirals in the falling snow, leaving white vortices in its wake.

Everyone stopped in their tracks and stared up at it. You couldn't not. For a time the battle halted as the immense vessel sailed over. Its shadow brought temporary respite from the blizzard, although the downdraught from its fans kicked up so much of the fallen snow that a whiteout followed immediately afterwards. When that had cleared, the thing could no longer be seen, although the dizzying drone of its engines could still be heard.

I dashed for the battlements and sprinted around to get a view of where the aircraft had gone. Freya met me as I stood gazing out.

Nagelfar was coming to rest beside Yggdrasil, not far from the slumped hulk of *Jormungand* and the scattered wreckage of *Sleipnir,* and within sight of the gutted *Fenrir*. It dwarfed them all, even the World Tree. It settled on its undercarriage like some leviathan queen taking her throne. The fans slowed and the fog of loose snow they'd thrown up from the nearby trees drifted down to earth.

Doors slid open all along its hull and ramps unfurled, telescoping out to touch the ground. Familiar shapes appeared in the doorways: the bulky outlines of tanksuits. They started down the ramps, and as they emerged into the daylight I saw they weren't quite the JOTUNs and SURTs I remembered. They trundled rather than walked. In place of legs they now had wheels, three on each side in triangle formation, yoked by caterpillar tracks. The heads were better armoured, sunk into the humps of the shoulders so that they protruded less, and instead of faceplates there were now visor slits. I recalled Mrs Keener on Bifrost saying that the tanksuit designs had been given an overhaul and an upgrade. Here, then, were the Mark II versions. Looking even deadlier and more fit for purpose than the originals. Oh happy day.

They rolled towards the castle, a good fifty of them all told, swishing through the slush and mud left behind by the frost giants' tramping feet.

I looked at Freya.

"You know I said Loki won't win?"

She nodded.

"I may have changed my mind."

Luckily, she thought I wasn't being serious.

I totally was.

QUICKLY AS THEY could, Vali, Vidar and Tyr clambered inside our low-tech tanksuits, while Skadi was tasked with the mission of going to the troll pens and letting the unsanitary beasts loose.

Odin's sons battered their way through the frost giants to engage with the oncoming JOTUNs and SURTs outside. At the same time

Skadi abseiled off the battlements on a rope, snapped on her skis, and scooted off. The frost giants, meanwhile, redoubled their efforts. The appearance of *Nagelfar* on the scene gave them an added boost, not that they really needed it. They'd already been shitting on us. Now, with Loki's third big monster-machine freshly arrived, they were shitting on us from an even greater height than before. Our forces were divided. We were taking flak on two fronts. The frosties scented just how badly we were in trouble and fought harder than ever to take the castle.

Vali, Vidar and Tyr did their very best out among the tanksuits. The JOTUNs and SURTs took a pasting. Improved or not, they met their match in the form of three righteously pissed-off gods in gnome-made iron outerwear. The tanksuits bundled in with their freeze rays and flamethrowers firing full throttle, and the Aesir knocked them back. It was a thing to see – a tanksuit spinning helplessly through the air, whacked clean off its wheelbase by a swipe from a clunky, metal-sheathed arm. One JOTUN got pounded into the ground, almost literally. Bashed on the bonce repeatedly until its wheels were submerged in the muddy soil. A SURT ended up so dented and misshapen, it was barely recognisable. The man inside was presumably no better off.

Then the trolls entered the fray. At least, most of them did. A couple showed more sense than I'd have credited a troll with and hurried off into the forest, avoiding the battle altogether. The rest, however, true to form, headed right into the midst of the fighting. Because the JOTUNs and SURTs looked to be the nastiest players on the pitch, naturally the trolls went for them rather than Odin's sons. Bursts of flame scorched the trolls' bodies, and subzero beams zapped them, and some fell, but the others piled on into the tanksuits, batting them aside, clobbering them, picking them up and tossing them around.

For a few minutes – a few brief, precious minutes – it looked like the battle outside the castle might just go our way. Between Odin's sons and the trolls, the JOTUNs and SURTs had their hands full. They were taking casualties by the truckload. Their superior firepower (and icepower) wasn't getting them anywhere. They'd come on like a tsunami, only to crash against a granite cliff of resistance, that shuddered from the shock but withstood.

Their actions became hesitant, unsure. I could imagine the operators inside yelling like crazy into their comms sets, asking one another what the hell was going on, how come these motherfuckers weren't *breaking* like they should, why were three low-rent Iron Man knockoffs and a bunch of jumbo-size caveman-type goons getting the better of the might and majesty of US military knowhow? On paper this should have been a rout. So how come the tanksuits were taking all the punishment instead of dishing it out?

I allowed myself to believe that we did stand a chance after all, that Vali, Vidar and Tyr – with the trolls' help – were going to swing things in our favour. The blizzard was dwindling, too, which was also to our advantage. Maybe, maybe...

Then *Nagelfar* itself got involved, and that was the tipping point. The decisive moment. The final, fateful turning of the tide.

The automated machine guns on its hull swung into play, strafing the battleground. Their accuracy wasn't pinpoint, but damn well as near as. The trolls were first to take the brunt of it. Laser dots suddenly speckled them, like a fluorescent dose of the measles, and then pieces started flying off their bodies. They jerked and flailed, disintegrating under a hail of sabot-cased flechette rounds.

"Christ..." I groaned.

The guns then turned their attention on Vali, Vidar and Tyr. The gnomes' suits of armour stood up to the onslaught. The iron shells became peppered with pockmarks. The flechettes weren't penetrating, but the guns fired so thick and fast, and their volleys were so fiercely concentrated, that their targets were scarcely able to move. In fact, it was all the three gods could do just to stay upright.

This allowed the dozen remaining tanksuits to close in and blast away at them point blank, unimpeded. Ice and flame together battered the gnome armour's surfaces. Superheated and supercooled in several places at once, iron cracked and ruptured. Tyr was the first to die. The tanksuits peeled his armour off him in fragments, exposing him bit by bit to their weapons. It was dismal to watch, and just as dismal to see the same being done to Vali in turn.

Vidar managed to stumble away while his brothers were getting the freeze/burn treatment. He made it back to the castle with the armour falling off his body at every footstep, crumbling away in chunks and flakes until it was just a trail of scrap metal behind him in the snow. His strength was nearly gone as he threw himself across the threshold of one of the breaches. Almost immediately he was in the clutches of frost giants, who hauled him off somewhere, recognising him as a prize, a captive worth taking while he was in no fit state to resist.

Freya and I were still up on the battlements, and by this time I was becoming resigned to the inevitable. So, it seemed, was she. I didn't even bother checking via the walkie-talkie to see how the fighting was going in the castle itself. I didn't want to know. Besides, I could tell by the sounds of battle, or rather the increasing lack of them; gunfire was becoming sporadic and petering out. And now frost giants could be heard singing. An unholy racket, more football terrace chant than actual melody, drifting across the roofless turrets and tumbledown walls. I couldn't make out the words but their sense couldn't have been clearer: *face it, losers, we've won.*

"Freya..."

"Gid." She gripped my arm, tight. "You did your best. Never doubt that. No one could have done more." Her eyes sparkled like frost under lamplight.

"But we –"

"We tried. But it is Ragnarök. It isn't called the Doom of the Gods for nothing. Victory was never going to be easy."

She was planning on saying more, but frost giants had found us. They approached from both sides along the battlements, much as had happened at Utgard. Freya and I checked how much ammunition we had left – enough for a last little burst of mischief – and then turned back to back.

"Meet you in Gimlé," she said over her shoulder.

"Sure thing," I replied. "I'll be the one with the red carnation in my buttonhole and carrying a copy of the *Times*." Then to the frost giants I said, "All right, boys. Come and have a go if you think you're hard enough."

They sneered, snarled, and charged.

They were just metres away when clusters of brilliant little laser dots painted the battlements between them and us, swirling on the snow-capped stonework. Wisely, they halted. The laser dots then swept upwards to mark Freya and me.

I braced myself, but no flechette rounds came. The message was clear. *Don't move a muscle, or they'll be cleaning you up with a mop and bucket.*

As we stood there pinned in place, a fur-clad figure exited *Nagelfar* and strode towards the castle, passing briskly between the last few JOTUNs and SURTs, which backed away respectfully.

"Well, howdy there," the figure called up, reaching the base of the castle wall. "And how're you two doing this fine day?"

"Smashing," I said. "And you?"

"Oh now, let me see. Almost all of the folks I hate the most are now dead. Me and my jotun buddies appear to have conquered Asgard. And Midgard's official biggest pain in the bee-hind is currently stuck with more laser sights trained on him than a sow's got teats."

Mrs Keener beamed at me, happy as a bride on her wedding day.

"All in all, I'd say I'm just peachy, wouldn't you?"

SIXTY-SIX

WE STOOD HUDDLED in the shadow of *Nagelfar* – everyone from our side who was still alive and not bedridden in the field hospital. Shockingly few of us. We looked bedraggled and downcast. Beaten. Hollowed by defeat and humiliated by surrender.

EPIC fail, as Cody might have said.

It sickened me. Not just that we'd lost, but that we'd lost so thoroughly. I wanted to believe there was some way we could reverse the situation and still pull off a victory, but frankly that wasn't looking any too likely. We'd been disarmed, and frost giants surrounded us in throngs, and beyond them the tanksuits were loitering, along with *Nagelfar*'s guns. Some kind of last-ditch comeback was just too tall an order.

Mrs Keener was having a high old time. Strutting up and down in front of us, looking all preeny and disdainful.

"So this is it, huh?" she said. "All done and dusted. To be honest I'd been expecting more of a challenge. All this time, knowing Odin, I was thinking I was gonna be in for some serious opposition. I went to a whole heap of trouble having these here heavy-duty vehicles built, and turns out I hardly needed 'em. Talk about disappointment. I feel as let down as a pussycat with an inflatable mouse."

"All right, all right," I said testily. "We get it. You've won. No need to rub it in."

She snapped round to look at me. "No need? Oh, there's every need, big guy. I've waited a long time for my revenge on the Aesir. Tucked away underground for ages – *ages* – suffering the torments of the damned, I dreamed of nothing else. This is my moment and I am determined to wring every last drop of enjoyment out of it I can."

"Look, Mrs Keener... Loki?... No, I'm going to stick with Mrs Keener... Look, Mrs Keener, nobody here is in a position to do you any further harm. Let your prisoners go. There's no question that Asgard is yours. The decent thing to do now would be show some compassion."

She seemed astonished. "Let them go? The very idea! Who do you take me for, sir?"

"The men at least. The mortals. What else are you going to do with them? Mass execution?"

"It had crossed my mind. Are you trying to plead for your own life?"

"Not mine specifically. Everyone's."

She stepped closer to me, and in spite of everything I couldn't help thinking how flat-out ravishing she was. Someone this beautiful and this bewitching, it was easy to see how she could have enslaved a world.

"What if I offered you a deal... Gideon, is it? What if I agreed to what you're asking, but at a price?"

"The price being...?" I said, suspecting.

"What do you think?"

"Just say it."

"You." Almost a purr. "You've sure been a tick under my saddle and I'd like to make an example outta you. And it occurs to me you might try and get yourself killed tryin' to escape, or something like that. So you promise to come meekly, in exchange for the lives of all these other guys."

"What by you mean by 'example'? Would this be a sex thing by any chance?"

"Oh, you! You know full well it ain't. I mean you peacefully submit to a big old spectacular execution, and the rest go free, just like you want. You have my word on that."

My throat was crackly-dry. My stomach felt like I was both constipated and about to pebbledash my Y-fronts at the same time. A voice in my head was screaming *No!*

"Okay," I croaked.

To my right there was a soft sigh. I didn't look round. That was where Freya was. There were also murmurs from the other prisoners – surprise, hope maybe.

"But they live," I went on. "I want your guarantee on that. They live and they go home safe and sound."

"You have it."

"Gid, Loki is a trickster," Vidar croaked from amongst the crowd. "You cannot trust him."

"Oh hush up, you," Mrs Keener said. "Don't you pay him no mind, Gid. Whatever anyone might say, I do possess a sense of honour. Shake on it?"

We did. Her hand cold in mine, and slender, but strong. Then Bergelmir stepped up and grabbed me roughly by the collar. His *issgeisl* was raised and ready.

"It will not be swift, human," he said in a voice thick with emotion. "A hundred cuts or more. By the end I will have you pleading to be put out of your misery."

Mrs Keener caught his arm. "No, Bergelmir. Not now. Not like this. I reckon Gid deserves something a little more... exotic. And I have just the thing in mind."

"He is mine," stated the frost giant leader, towering over her. "Mine by right. He killed my Leikn."

She was not intimidated. "And you can officiate at his death, I promise. The job of executioner's yours. But I'd like it to be elaborate – ceremonial – and that's something we have to prepare for. It won't take long to build the apparatus we're gonna use. Once that's set up, he's all yours."

Bergelmir considered this, finally nodding. "A pleasure deferred is a pleasure increased."

"Attaboy. Now, haul his sorry carcass off to *Nagelfar*. Stick him in one of the troop cabins, and make sure he's well guarded. As for the rest of this crowd, back to the castle with them. And make sure they're well guarded too. I'm not anticipating any misbehaviour, but you can't be too careful."

As Bergelmir frogmarched me past her, I said, "You'd better keep your promise, Loki. Or..."

Mrs Keener arched one plucked-to-a-perfect-comma eyebrow. "Or...? You ain't got an 'or' to threaten me with, Gideon. You ain't got jack spit. But," she added, "when I make a deal with somebody, I always keep my end of it. Well, pretty much always."

It was all the assurance I was going to get.

It would have to do.

SIXTY-SEVEN

THE CABIN WAS deep within *Nagelfar*'s bowels. It had a hard bunk, no porthole, a dim lightbulb, a solid metal door. A snapshot of a toddler was Blu-Tacked to one wall. A pair of size 12 Converse trainers sat on the floor, waiting for an owner who was in all probability not returning.

No less than four frost giants were posted outside. I paced. I was going nowhere; pacing was all I had. Back and forth, back and forth. Seven steps one way, seven steps the other.

More than once the phrase *What the fuck have you done, Gid?* jangled through my head. Sacrificing myself to save everyone else wasn't something that came naturally. One of the first rules of soldiering: never volunteer. A motto which surely applied to executions more than anything.

The decision, however, had seemed logical at the time, and still did, just about. Nobody else could have struck the same deal, because nobody else had pissed off Mrs Keener quite like I had. In that sense, I hadn't had a choice. I hadn't been trying to be big and clever, I'd simply played the one measly bargaining chip I had left – myself.

I racked my brains over and over. Not long from now, a few hours perhaps, maybe less, I was going to die. Horribly. There was no either-or about that, no debate. But was there possibly some way I could use it to turn things around? Was there still a chance of redeeming the situation to some small extent?

After a while, when I'd paced enough and thought enough, I banged on the door. I demanded at the top of my voice to see Mrs Keener. The frost giant guards told me to go and perform some very uncomfortable acts. I persisted. Eventually they got tired of me making a nuisance of myself and one of them went off to fetch her.

"What's going on?" Mrs Keener said as she entered the cabin. "There a problem with the accommodation?"

"Not as such. The place smells like old jockstraps, but apart from that, no real complaints."

"Well, I am just so sorry, Gideon. Soldiers ain't always that big on their hygiene. I'd've lent you the use of the stateroom, 'cept that's mine. 'Course, you'd have even more to complain about if this was the real *Nagelfar*. Sides and decks of *that* ship are covered with fingernails and toenails, like fish scales, and the crew's all ghosts."

"I should count myself lucky, then, when you put it like that."

"Me too. I didn't take a fancy to travelling about in something quite so ghoulish. Wouldn't suit the way I am now. Same way I wasn't keen on wrangling proper monsters like Fenrir and Jormungand to attack Asgard with. I'm a fine, upstanding Southern lady. Don't need to be consorting with low, savage beasts, not when I can have stylish vehicles made for me that do the exact same job but with far less of the fussing and griping and cajoling."

"You actually believe you're Lois Keener, don't you?"

"Most of the time, yes," she replied, with casual frankness. "I've been wearing her skin so long, she and me have become one. That's a figure of speech, by the way – wearing her skin. I ain't Ed Gein or that queer fella outta *Silence of the Lambs*. I've adopted her form and I'm so at home in it now that sometimes I can scarce recall how I used to look."

"And she's dead, I suppose, the real Mrs Keener."

"As a doornail. I killed her with my own two hands in her kitchen and buried the body in the woods out behind the yard before the kids came home from school. I'm not sure why I chose her outta all the people I could have. Other than her name, 'course. Couldn't resist that. I suppose the reason was 'cause she was so attractive and unassuming and I just liked the idea of taking some nobody from nowheresville and rocketing her up the ladder to the most powerful position in all Midgard. It appealed to my sense of irony, as well as presenting a challenge to my wits and my silver tongue. Could I do it? Could I make the biggest of all somethings outta nothing? Turned out I could, no sweat. The people of Earth – so easy to manipulate, so malleable. Such sheep. All I had to do was give 'em a vision of integrity and steel willpower, wrapped up in a physically appealing package, and they just fell in line. Piece of cake."

"And she never had a visitation from God, did she? You made that up after."

"Well, from *a* god, yes. Me. Nice little twist of the facts, that. Cover story to explain any changes in personality folks might notice. This fella came to her door, pretending to be a preacher, newly arrived in town, all steeple-fingered and pious as you like. And Mrs Keener, so trusting, invited him right in. My smiling face was the last thing she ever saw."

Mrs Keener said this with such a broad grin, I thought her head was going to split in two.

"Anyhoo, much as I'd love to stay and chat, Gid, I am on a schedule here. Lots to oversee – mainly the nice little doohickey we're busy building to kill you on. So what can I do for you? Why'd you want to see me?"

I tried not to imagine what the "doohickey" might be. Those kinds of thoughts were not helpful.

"I have a favour to ask. Two, actually."

"Really? You're haggling? You know you ain't in any position to do that. Not at this late stage in the game."

"A condemned man is entitled to a last request or two, isn't he?"

"Maybe in a Midgard prison, on death row. But we ain't in Midgard any more, Toto."

"Still," I said. "You've got me all lined up for a spectacular, messy death. I'm going to be putting on a big show for you. Consider this my fee."

"Your fee is the lives of those folks at the castle."

"Then I'm after a small raise. Honest, it's not much. At least hear me out."

She planted a fist on her hip and cocked her head. "All right then, I'll listen. I ain't guaranteeing I'll say yes, but I'll listen."

I outlined what I wanted.

The first thing I asked for brought a mildly puzzled frown and a cry of "Aww, cute."

The second, a crooked, wicked smile.

"Let me think about it," Mrs Keener said, turning to go.

An hour later: "Visitor."

The frost giants ushered Freya into the cabin. They hulked there with us, all four of them, heads bent under the ceiling. It was a hell of a squash. Freya and I had virtually no room to ourselves.

"Little privacy maybe?" I said.

"Orders," said one of them. "Neither of you is allowed out of our sight while you're together."

"We can barely breathe. How about you back off outside? Leave the door wide open. You'll still be able to see."

Eventually they agreed.

Freya and I sat side by side on the bunk. The silence simmered between us.

Finally she said, "You're an idiot."

"Not quite the words of condolence I was hoping for."

"How dare you do something so... so..."

"Brave? Self-sacrificing?"

"Selfish."

I bristled. "Buying other people's lives with my own is selfish how, exactly?"

She looked away. When she looked back, her eyes were brimming, and I felt bad for snarking at her.

"Loki might have let everyone go free," she said.

"I doubt it."

"But he might have. If you'd just kept your peace, there's every chance..."

"You know that's not true. Besides, hello? It's Gid you're talking to. I open my mouth and crap comes out before I can stop it. It's the curse of being me."

"Why couldn't one of the others have done it, though? Why did it have to be you?"

"I dunno," I said. "I suppose I've become the leader, by default. No, that's too grand. The spokesman. The mouthpiece. So it sort of had to be me. Tall poppy syndrome. You rise up, you have to expect to be cut down. But also..."

I thought hard. I'd been doing little else but thinking hard since getting locked up in this cabin.

"I should probably have died in that car crash. Or if not then, immediately afterwards, thanks to those wolves. I was damn lucky. I got a second shot. So everything since has been gravy, as far as I'm concerned. A bonus life. Which makes the idea of losing it that much easier to adjust to. I've had fun. These past few weeks have been baffling, painful, intense, sometimes fucking awful – but what a laugh! I've done shit I'd never in a million years have dreamt of doing, and I've been a warrior again, and fighting a fight worth fighting, what's more. Nothing questionable about working for Odin and defending Asgard. This wasn't some spurious war cooked up by civil servants and businessmen to keep the oil flowing and the rebuilding contracts flooding in. This had *meaning*. It was clear cut – like the Second World War and unlike any of the conflicts since, except possibly the Falklands. A definite bad guy with nefarious ambitions, and us the last, best and maybe only hope against him. A soldier couldn't ask for more than that."

"So at least *you've* got something out of it."

"Don't be like that."

"Like what?"

"All bitter and twisted. I was going to go on to say something else. One of the most amazing things about this entire situation is that I've met... well, you. Bear with me here, because I'm hellish clumsy when it comes to this sort of stuff. But... I don't know what you think of me, Freya, but I think you are pretty incredible. And incredibly pretty. But mostly pretty incredible."

I spotted the guards making stupid, leering faces through the doorway.

"Oh fuck off, you," I snapped. "This is difficult enough as it is, without cockfaces like you getting involved."

"Concentrate on me, Gid," Freya said, taking my hands. "Ignore them."

I tried. "I'm a hard-shelled bastard, I know it. I come across like nothing bothers me, nothing gets to me. I love my son, but that's about it as far as finer feelings go. Otherwise, all front, no depth. That's the impression I give, and that's more or less how it is. But you, Freya... I can't get over the fact that you're *you* and you chose me. You could have anyone, you could go out with gods, but it was humble little mortal Gid Coxall who got the nod. I'm not pretending I don't realise that it's chiefly been about humping one another senseless. I get that. Any port in a storm, and so on. And I'm not against shaggery for shaggery's sake. Far from it. Bring it on, I say. But if there was more to us than that, if I've been more to you than just a convenient booty call, I have to know. You have to tell me."

"You choose now to ask this? When you're moments away from dying?"

"It's that close, is it?"

"They're nearly ready. Your 'audience' is being gathered."

"Shit. Then yes, this is precisely the time to ask. When better? And don't just tell me what you think I want to hear. Be honest. Straight from the heart. Is it possible for a goddess – I'm going to use the word *love* – to love a mortal? Can it happen?"

There was a pause. A long one. Then, gaze averted, in barely a whisper, Freya said, "It can. Yes. It can."

I sat back, contented. "I think I can go to my grave happy now."

"Truly?"

I nodded. "I mean, let's face it, I've loved a goddess and she loved me back. Doesn't get much better than that."

The frost giants were bombarding us with mocking "ooh" and "wooh" noises, but it hardly registered.

"If I could help you in any way," Freya said. "As I helped those men they pinned to Yggdrasil..."

"You would, I know, and I appreciate the offer, but you can't, can you? Not from out of the crowd. You won't have a gun."

She lowered her voice. "I could slay you now. Spare you that way from what's in store."

"With your bare hands?"

"You know I could."

"And then the frosties would kill you too."

"So?"

I smiled at her, sincerely. "I don't want that. And more to the point, if I die here now, Mrs Keener won't need to keep her half of the bargain. Much as I hate the idea, I've got to go through with this. It's shit, but there's no other way."

"Time's up," one of the frost giants announced.

"Loki promised us half an hour."

The frost giant shrugged. "We jotuns don't run our lives by clocks like you do. I don't even know what an hour is. Your ladyfriend's been here long enough by my reckoning, so say goodbye to her."

I muttered something uncomplimentary. The frost giants just laughed.

"Gid..."

Freya took my chin in her hand and guided my face towards hers, and we kissed.

Our first ever real kiss.

And our last.

Sweet, and firm, and deep, and over all too soon.

But a kiss I would have remembered for all my life, even if I were to live to a ripe old age.

SIXTY-EIGHT

My lips were still tingling from the kiss when, not much later, Bergelmir came to collect me.

Outside they'd built a scaffold out of wood. The timber had come from Yggdrasil itself. Several lower branches had been lopped off and sawn into planks. The stumps wept a sap so dark orange it was almost the colour of blood, and I could sense somehow that the World Tree was in agony. Just something about the way its other branches drooped, the way the breeze shivered its leaves. It was sacrilege, to dismember Yggdrasil like this – I sensed that, too. I glimpsed the squirrel Ratatosk scurrying this way and that along boughs in an absolute frenzy, squealing with rage, his tail a furry exclamation mark. There was nothing the little rodent could have done to prevent the frost giants from desecrating his home. He was doubly pissed off for that reason.

The scaffold was large and crudely put together, but sturdy-looking. It consisted of a platform with a simple framework built on top, a rectangle with cross-braced corners. Wooden pegs had been used for nails. Short ropes were attached to all four cross-braces.

Everyone had been mustered in front of it. Frigga was there, dragged away from her patients. Vidar, Bragi, Skadi, Freya of course, Valkyries, plus Cy, Backdoor and the couple of dozen other surviving mortals. Frost giants. Some men I took to be the tanksuit operators, out of their machines and looking quizzical and bloodthirsty – executions like this clearly not an everyday occurrence for them, but something worth experiencing nonetheless. And, waiting on the platform itself, Mrs Keener. She watched me approach with the air of a society hostess about to welcome her guest of honour. She even clasped her hands together as I climbed the scaffold steps, with Bergelmir prodding me from behind.

"I am so glad you could make it!" she exclaimed.

"Wish I could say the same," I replied.

"Come now, don't be like that. It's your big moment, Gid. In some strange way I think you even want this. A grand finale." She pronounced it *fin-ayl*. "An ego like yours, it wouldn't be satisfied with you just dying along with everybody else. It had to be public and splashy and meaningful, didn't it?"

"What can I say? I'm a fame whore."

"Plus it gives you one last chance to show off how goshdarn down-home courageous you are. Quipping and wisecracking, a wiseguy all the way to the end. We'll see how it easy it is to keep the jokes coming once Bergelmir's started in on you." She looked over my shoulder. "First, though, if my eyes don't deceive me, I see that we have some last-minute arrivals."

Everyone followed her gaze. From the shadows beneath Yggdrasil a trio of female figures emerged, walking out into the thickening afternoon light. One strode gracefully, one waddled, and one hobbled along with the aid of a walking stick.

The Norns halted at the scaffold's edge. I found it oddly consoling to see them. In some weird way it seemed to confirm the rightness of what I was doing. It was as if they'd come to give my death their seal of approval.

"The Three Sisters," said Mrs Keener. "How generous of you to grace us with your presence. We are honoured. Tired of one another's company, huh? Decided to leave your cottage and actually witness events for a change, 'stead of viewing them through your scrying well or whatever it is you're using these days?"

"It is Ragnarök," said jailbait Urd.

"The end of all things," said motherly Verdande.

"The cutting of many threads at once," said bent-backed Skuld.

"We Norns have long foreseen this time."

"And anticipated it."

"And dreaded it."

"Now it is upon us."

"All destinies converge."

"The spinning ceases."

Once again the three of them were doing that thing where they spoke one after another so flowingly and seamlessly, it was as if they had a single voice.

"We have come because there is no more to predict."

"The past has tightened to a knot."

"The future is unclear."

"It is a pivotal point, the moment of all moments."

"We must see it as it unfolds, with our own eyes."

"To learn the outcome as others do, while it happens."

"Without foreknowledge."

"Without foreshadowing."

"Without foreboding."

Mrs Keener chuckled delightedly. "I couldn't have asked for more. The Norns themselves, curious to know how everything is gonna turn out. Know what that means? Means I've done it. I've truly won. I am greater than destiny. If I have brought matters to the point where the Three Sisters are half blind now, only able to see what's in front of their eyes, then I have overcome all limitation, and anything is possible." She was almost hugging herself with glee.

"Do not exult just yet, Loki," Urd warned.

"Wheels turn," said Verdande.

"An end may yet be a beginning," said Skuld.

"You don't scare me," Mrs Keener retorted. "That's just sore loser talk. Wheels? Nothing's turning today 'cept me, sisters, and that's 'cause I'm on a roll."

She fixed her attention back on me.

"Now, let's not get ourselves distracted any more," she said. "Betcha eager to get this over with, huh?"

I made a yes-and-no noise.

"Then we'll have you tied up and screaming in no time. Bergelmir...?"

Just as the frost giant was about start attaching the ropes to me, Mrs Keener slapped her forehead.

"Wait just one cotton-picking moment! What on earth am I thinking? You asked two favours off of me, didn't you, Gid?"

"I was wondering whether you'd remember."

"Conjugal visitation rights with Freya, and... oh heck, what was the other one? Clean slipped my mind. No, wait, I've got it. You asked if I'd give up my 'inside man' – assuming I have one, of course. That was it, wasn't it? Let you have him and let you decide how he should be dealt with."

"Yup."

"Well, I said yes to your first favour, and so happens I'm inclined to say yes to this one too. Nothing pleases me – or amuses me – quite like seeing one man getting his satisfaction on another who's done him a bad turn. I know all about slights and injustices and how they can make you feel. Story of my life, some'd say. So, you asked me to reveal who the guy was, the double-crosser, the one you reckon was throwing spanners in the works and was responsible for getting a couple of your buddies killed. I said you describe who you think it is and I'll say if you've got your man. You did, and the result is... Boys?"

She was calling out to the nearest of the frost giants who were policing the crowd of onlookers.

"Him." She pointed. "Fella with the walrus whiskers. Yeah, him. Fetch him up here willya?"

The frost giants homed in on Backdoor, who looked aghast and dumbfounded. They grabbed him and strong-armed him onto the scaffold.

"What the – ?" Backdoor spluttered. "Gid, what the fuck is this? What are you doing?"

"Obvious, isn't it? You screwed us, mate. You've been Loki's bumboy all along, just like I said at Odin's funeral. I want to show you what I think of that. Worst crime of all – betraying your own side."

"But I didn't!"

"You fucking did. You can deny it all you want, but I know."

"But I don't know Loki. I've never seen him before in my life. Never seen *her*." He gesticulated at Mrs Keener. "Never met her, never made any kind of deal with her. This is crazy! Why are you doing this to me? I fought next to you. I put my balls on the line, just like you. I'm not a traitor!"

"Sounds pretty convincing to me," Mrs Keener commented. "Swearing blind he ain't the one."

"Well, he would, wouldn't he?" I replied.

"Tell him," Backdoor said to her urgently. He was starting to panic. Maybe he'd guessed what I had in mind for him. "Tell him I'm not working for you. I'm nothing to do with you."

"Ain't down to me, pal. This is Gid's call."

"He's got it all arse about face. I'm good. I'm loyal."

"Gid?"

I eyed Backdoor coolly. "No," I said. "You're a conniving bastard, no doubt about it, and for that, you're getting the same treatment I am."

His eyes swivelled towards the rectangular frame. "No..." he gasped.

"It's only fair," I said. "I'm being punished for doing everything right, so you should be punished too, for doing everything wrong. That way, it all balances out."

"Gid..."

"Do him first," I said to Mrs Keener. "Whatever you're planning on doing to me, he gets it first. I'll watch."

"Very well." She nodded to Bergelmir. "This must be your lucky day, Bergelmir. You're gonna have your fun with *two* of them."

The frost giants' ruler laughed from way down in his belly. Couldn't quite believe his good fortune.

"No! Please, no!" Backdoor yelled hoarsely as the frost giants bound him to the frame by his wrists and ankles. They strung him inside it with his limbs outstretched so that he formed an X shape, like a vote in a ballot. He bucked and struggled, but it was no use. "This isn't right! This isn't fair! Mrs Keener, you can stop this. Please, for God's sake, stop it!"

Her response was a nonchalant shrug. "If you're what Gid says you are, then you've outlived your usefulness to me. The game's over. What's one player less on the field?"

Bergelmir produced a short ice knife with a half-serrated blade. In a few deft strokes he slashed off Backdoor's clothes, leaving his top half bare. Backdoor yelled even harder and writhed against his bonds, but spread-eagled as he was, he had no leverage, and the knots held fast.

"There is," said Mrs Keener, having to raise her voice to be heard above Backdoor's protests, "an old Viking method of execution. You may have heard about it. Many of the kings and chieftains of the Norsemen's enemies died in this way. It ain't pleasant in the least. It's known as the blood eagle."

I dimly recognised the name, although I couldn't recall the details of what a blood eagle actually involved.

Luckily, Mrs Keener was happy to explain.

"It's very simple. The executioner – in this case, Bergelmir – severs the victim's ribs one by one, right close to the spine. Then he grabs the two halves of the ribcage and yanks them back and outward so's they look like wings. Next he hauls out the lungs, leaves 'em dangling. Finally, as the coop de grass, he packs the wounds with salt. Might be overkill, that last bit, and we may not bother with it. Depends on the victim still being alive, and after all the rest you've got to think that's gonna be a mite unlikely. But we'll see. People have an amazing capacity to endure even the most extreme ordeals, so you never know. Y'all get the gist of it, anyway. This is what we're gonna do to our buddy Backdoor, and then to our buddy Gid. Blood eagling them. And you folks get to watch."

She turned to Bergelmir.

"Any time you're ready, big guy."

Bergelmir gave a yellow grin and brandished his knife.

Backdoor had gone limp. He hung from the ropes, his breath coming in fast, sharp pants. He was in shock. He couldn't believe what was about to happen to him. Didn't want to. I could see it in his eyes – they were glazing over, his mind was going elsewhere. He was retreating inside himself, trying to escape the here and now, vanishing into tunnels within.

Wherever he went, though, however deep he dived, he would never be quite lost enough.

And as Bergelmir got to work on him, all I could think was that was going to be me next. In a few minutes' time, that would be my back getting hacked open, my blood spilling out in steaming slicks, my bones being sawn through, my body wrenching and twisting hopelessly, helplessly, my throat hurling out those soul-searing shrieks and howls...

SIXTY-NINE

IN THE END, they didn't need the salt. Ian "Backdoor" Kellaway was dead by the time Bergelmir delved into his chest cavity, eased out the two wet pink sacs of his lungs and draped them down his bare lower back. Backdoor's head hung slackly. His eviscerated body, with its rack-of-rib wings, looked like some demonic angel's. Bergelmir was steeped in blood from the butchery, his forearms solid crimson, as though he was wearing elbow-length evening gloves.

"He can come down now," Mrs Keener said, and the frost giants untied Backdoor and dumped him unceremoniously over the side of the scaffold. "It's Gid's turn."

Every instinct I had was screaming at me to resist, to fight, to do everything I could to escape. The berserker blackness inside me strained, wanting desperately to be allowed to cut loose. Reining it in took every ounce of self-control I had. This wasn't about me any more. This was about all those soldiers out there at the foot of the scaffold, hugging themselves, stamping their feet in the battle-churned snow. My survival no longer mattered. Theirs did.

The ropes were tied chafingly tight. I hung suspended above a puddle of Backdoor's blood, which was congealing swiftly in the cold. It had poured onto the scaffold's planks like rainfall. Mine would soon be added to it.

I wanted desperately in that moment to be able to see Cody again, one last time. Tell him I wished I'd been a better dad and I was sorry I hadn't tried harder to make things work with his mother.

That not being possible, I searched out Freya in the crowd and locked gazes with her. I would keep looking at her throughout what was coming.

"And thus we arrive at the main event," said Mrs Keener. "Gideon Coxall has got his own back on the man he reckons was a traitor, and now he himself is gonna suffer and die in the exact same way. If I were a betting woman, I'd wager money on him lasting a good sight longer than the previous fella. Made of tough stuff, this Gid. Pure rawhide."

"Enough of the showman bollocks," I said. "I'm ready. Just give the order and let's do it."

"You don't want me bigging you up? Very well. Oh, but there is one thing I feel I oughtta mention. In the spirit of full disclosure and such."

"Go on, then," I said impatiently.

"You were definitely right about me having a man on the inside. I like to think of him as my mole. Not in the sense of someone who passes on secrets but in the sense of someone who digs holes in the ground and undermines people."

"So?"

"Well..." She drew the word out: *way-ell*.

Then she dropped the bombshell.

"Weren't him."

She was looking towards Backdoor's corpse.

"Weren't him at all."

I thought I'd lost the power of speech.

"Just felt you should know," she said, "seeing as you went to so much trouble fingering the fella and getting him executed and all. You were so certain you had your guy, I really didn't have the heart to tell you you were wrong. 'Sides, it was more fun this way, going along with you, giving you your head like a wild Appaloosa, seeing how far you'd take it. And you took it all the way, Gid. Right as far as you could. My, but you're a cold, hard son of a gun. Anybody gets the wrong side of you, whoa nelly, they better look out! You have no qualms about terminating them with extreme prejudice."

She stroked my cheek.

"And I have to say, I find that kinda attractive. Sexy, even. I can see now what Freya Njorthasdottir sees in you. You're as forthright and ruthless as she is. It's a match made in Gimlé."

I managed to stir my lead-weight tongue. "I don't believe you. This is bullshit. You're trying to trick me. It *was* Backdoor. It fucking was."

"So you've persuaded yourself. But I swear, hand on heart, I never clapped eyes on the man before today. He wasn't lying either when he said the same about me."

"But..."

"It's the most delicious thing watching you squirm like this, like a worm on the hook. It's the gravy on my biscuits. You just put an innocent man through the most obscene, brutal torture imaginable. Not wishing to get all Oprah on you, but how does that make you feel?"

Gutted. Appalled. Shattered.

Livid.

"You – you fucking bitch!" I roared. "You could have said. Any time, you could have said."

"And why would I have done that, when stringing you along meant I could have this moment of exquisite tormenting? Psychological pain can be far harder to bear than physical pain, and far more rewarding to inflict."

I lunged at her, although the ropes made it a useless gesture.

"Now, now, none of that," Mrs Keener chided, wagging a finger. "Don't be getting mad at *me*. If you should be mad at anyone, it's yourself."

"Who, then?" I said thickly. "Who was it?"

"Don't you know?"

I had an inkling. There was only one person left it could have been. But I'd trusted him. I'd considered him a friend.

"He's right over there." She motioned towards the onlookers. "Looking kinda shifty, it has to be said. No need for that, honey," she called out to him. "Don't have to pretend it ain't you I'm talking to. It's all right. It doesn't matter now if folks know who you are and what you did. You're safe. You're under my protection. In fact, why not come up here and take a bow? You've done good work, far as I'm concerned. You deserve your moment of glory."

The man she was addressing broke free from the crowd, passed through the cordon of frost giants, and made his way, a little sheepishly maybe, up onto the scaffold.

He stood beside Mrs Keener, and she placed a friendly, conspiratorial arm round his broad boxer's shoulders.

"Wotcher, bruv," Cy said to me. "How's it hanging?"

SEVENTY

THERE WAS A twinkle in Cy's eye as he spoke.

"Yes, I was the one fucking with you, not Backdoor," he said. "It was me. Me, the black guy. Just because someone's black don't mean he's above suspicion. In't we supposed to be colour-blind these days? Positive discrimination's as bad as the negative kind. No reason to think my skin tone makes me whiter than white."

He chortled at his own wit.

"Mrs Keener hired me to be an agitator," he went on. "To be a – how'd you put it, Mrs K?"

"A destabilising influence."

"That's it, a destabilising influence. Just to make her victory that bit more likely. Sow a little uncertainty here, start a little infighting there, classic psy-ops stuff. It wasn't hard to get recruited to Odin's army. No one was exactly vetting us, were they? You turned up, you were in, that was more or less it. Odin was grateful just to have the warm bodies. My job, my real job, once I'd joined up, was to gain someone's confidence, someone influential. Get close to them, then keep them off-balance, off their game."

"If the head's unsteady, the whole body wobbles," said Mrs Keener.

"Me," I croaked. "I was the head."

"Got it in one," said Cy. "I wasn't going to try for Odin himself. Too big a target, and too remote. Hard to get his trust, harder still to manipulate him. So I started on Thor. Kept challenging his authority, antagonising him, pissing him off. Not a painless tactic on my side, but it seemed the way to go... until you came along. Soon as I met you, I knew you were the one. You had that take-charge look about you. You were a newcomer, but you were going places. Plus, we had similar backgrounds, we were on the same wavelength. We had a bond going from the start. You liked me. That made you the perfect mark."

"The perfect chump, more like."

"Same difference. Look, d'you really want me to spell out everything I did, how I made it all work? Because it feels like I'm monologuing here, and I know you've got stuff you'd much rather be getting on with."

I was about to tell him that he could happily shut up because I wasn't interested in hearing anything more that came out of his lying fucking gob.

But then I spotted something out of the corner of my eye.

Movement.

On top of one of the castle turrets.

A figure making stiff, halting progress across the damaged roof up there.

A man, searching for a vantage point, a direct view of the scaffold.

A man with a rifle.

I directed my gaze back on Cy. Kept my expression as straight as I could. Poker face on.

"No, you go right ahead," I said. "Spill it all. I know you're dying to. Explain to everyone how clever you are and how stupid I've been."

Bergelmir gave a growl. "Must we do this? The day's wasting, and I yearn to plunge this blade into the killer of my wife."

"Just a few minutes more," Mrs Keener said to him soothingly.

"My boy Cy hoodwinked Gid in fine style, and it's only right he gets his chance to gloat."

"Yeah," Cy agreed. "Why not? So I made myself your right-hand man, Gid. Your sidekick. Robin to your Batman. We had those chats about my childhood and my poor old granddad getting irradiated and losing his memory. Which, by the way, was all true. I might have embellished the tough-upbringing stuff a little, for added authenticity. But the basics is all real."

"You were never in the army, though, were you?"

"Nope, that I did make up," he admitted.

"You referred to your granddad as a squaddie. That should have tipped me off. No one who's actually been a squarebasher uses the word *squaddie*. Only the tabloids do."

I darted a glance to the castle. The man with the rifle was settling himself down on a flattish section of the roof, taking a sniper's prone stance. Nobody but me appeared to have noticed him. The crowd had their backs to the castle, and their attention, anyway, was focused on the drama unfolding on the scaffold. And everyone on the scaffold had their attention focused on me and Cy.

How long this state of affairs would continue was unclear, but I would try and keep it going long enough for the rifle man to line up his shot and take it.

I knew who he was now. I'd recognised him by the white bandage around his head.

Heimdall.

Risen from his sickbed. Recovered from the injuries inflicted on him from afar by *Jormungand*. Tooled up and out for blood.

He'd been overlooked. Mrs Keener had presumed he was out of action for the duration and had not bothered to post a guard over the field hospital. She'd been overconfident. It was a lapse, and now she was going to pay the penalty.

"Okay, so I did slip up there," Cy said. "But not too badly, and in every other respect I was flawless. Starting the firefight in Utgard, that was my first big win. Chopsticks died, and your plans for an alliance with the frosties were scuppered."

"You could have got yourself killed too, though," I said.

"No chance. Mrs Keener had given me an emergency code phrase, something I could say that'd let the frost giants know I was under Loki's protection so they wouldn't touch me. An oath sworn on Ymir's bones. Whenever a frost giant hears 'by Ymir's bones,' he's got to pay attention and respond."

"It's true," said Bergelmir. "A jotun must always attend carefully to any plea that invokes my father."

"Then by Ymir's bones, cut me down from here," I said.

"Within limits," Bergelmir added with a grim laugh.

"That was my Get Out Of Jail Free card," Cy said. "Only, I didn't have to play it because *Sleipnir* turned up in the nick of time. Chopsticks's death started the rot. You were rattled, and the other guys began to wonder about your leadership abilities. So I just had to keep needling and gnawing at them. Poor old Backdoor was the easiest to get a rise out of. Closet racist. You learn to recognise the type. They don't need to say anything. You can just tell. I knew he'd blurt out something nasty eventually, and I knew it would piss you off and drive a wedge further between the two of you. You already had him in the frame for what happened to Chopsticks. Now you were completely convinced he was the bad banana in the bunch. It meant you were constantly looking over your shoulder at him and your head wasn't fully in the game."

My arms had begun to ache from taking the weight of my body. My head was aching too, with the knowledge of how Cy had played me and used me. The fucker. He'd get his.

I dared to check on Heimdall again. He was sighting carefully. I hoped he was as good a shot as Freya. I suspected he might be.

"Baz buying it on top of *Fenrir*, that was just my good luck," Cy went on. "You blamed Backdoor for that when he hadn't done nothing. It was just like he said: Baz's own fault. An accident. Casualty of war."

"And Paddy. Your argument with him. You weren't trying to talk him out of deserting, were you? You were talking him *into* it."

"Give the man a big hand. Paddy was in two minds about quitting when he came to me. Wanted my opinion. Wanted to be given a reason to stay. He was surprised when I told him I thought bailing was a good idea."

"But he left angry at you."

"Only 'cause I wouldn't join him. I said I respected you too much to abandon you in your hour of need."

"Ha ha."

"Yeah. He didn't like being made to feel more ashamed of himself than he already was."

"Didn't stop him going, though."

"I told him I thought he had a fair chance of making it. It was the encouragement he needed. He went and rounded up some others, some kindred spirits. He believed me when I said the frost giants would definitely let them through. We all know how well that went."

"Right under my nose all along," I said. "You. It was you. I could kick myself."

"Yeah, you could, if your legs wasn't all tied up."

"Don't be upset, Gid," said Mrs Keener. "There's a noble tradition in Asgard of people being blind to treachery in their midst. Odin held me close to his bosom far longer than he oughtta have. It was his fatal flaw."

"Plus," said Cy, "I'm good. I have a knack for subversion, it seems."

Mrs Keener was beaming with pride. "Yeah. I wish I could say I taught Cy everything he knows about fifth-column work and deviousness and being the joker in the pack, but I can't. The kid's a natural. Soon as I found him I knew he was my guy."

"How *did* you find him?" I asked. "Want ad? Open audition?"

"Weren't hard. I'm Loki. I have an instinct, an affinity, for shady characters. I can sniff them out a mile off. Washington's full of 'em, I don't need to tell you that. I'm in my element there, like a hog in a wallow. But I'm drawn to them wherever I go, and Cy so happened to be visiting the States not so long back. Florida, wasn't it?"

"Disneyworld," said Cy. "Orlando in the snow in't much fun, but they're offering great package deals. Not enough people going through the turnstiles, 'cause of the weather."

"And there I was too, shilling for the Sunshine State's tourist board. 'The citrus fruits may be frozen on the trees, but come to Florida anyway. The attractions are as great as ever.' Cy was there when I was doing a press tour at the House of Mouse, in the crowd. I was shaking hands with Mickey and Donald, but I was aware there was somebody nearby who I felt could be very useful to me. I had my secret service detail take him to one side, and the rest is history."

"What did she bribe you with?" I asked Cy. "Please don't tell me it was just money."

"'Course it was money," he sneered. "What else is there worth having? Masses of money. Tons of it, taken from some billion-dollar black budget slush fund. Money that means I can get my mum off the estate and have a car that'll make the drug pushers' cars look like Volkswagen fucking Beetles. Money that'll make me better than them, better than types like the bastard who gave me this." He gestured at his scar. "Money that'll give me a decent life and keep the authorities off my back and stop me ending up just another broken-Britain waster with no prospects and nothing to show for myself. Lottery-win money, in return for a few weeks' work, a bit of play-acting. 'Hell yes,' I said. Didn't even have to think twice about it."

"A condo in Miami too, don't forget that," said Mrs Keener.

"Yeah, my very own place in the sun. For when the Fimbulwinter's over and the climate goes back to normal. US citizenship thrown in as well. Everything, Gid. The total package. The boy from Bermondsey, all set to start a new life as a high-roller in America, a player. Sweet."

"You must be so proud of yourself."

"Oh, I am, mate, trust me."

"But it's tainted money. Blood money. You'll never enjoy spending it."

"Who the fuck are you to judge me?" he spat. "What'd you come here for, if it wasn't to earn cash for killing? If that in't blood money, I dunno what is."

"I'm a soldier. It's what I do. You're a bottom-feeding scumbag. There's a difference."

"Yeah? Well, if so, I'm a scumbag who's standing here a free man, on the winning side, while you, soldier boy, are stuck there like a fly in a web, waiting to have your fucking lungs pulled out. So much for principles, eh? Where's that got you?"

"Really!" said Bergelmir with an exasperated grunt. "Isn't it time the bickering ended and we got down to business?"

"Bergelmir has a point," said Mrs Keener. "Much as I love the sight of two grown men waving their manhoods at each other, I think we need to carry on with the show. There's folk here standing in the cold who want this to be over with. Let's not keep 'em on tenterhooks any longer."

"At last!" Bergelmir took up position behind me.

I peered up at the castle.

Come on, Heimdall, get a bloody wriggle on. Now or never.

"You're the famous chatterbox, Gid," said Mrs Keener. "No parting words? No last pearls of wisdom before the knife goes in?"

"Yeah." I was looking at the Norns. As one, Urd, Verdande and Skuld turned their heads towards the castle and back again. They knew. Their shared secret smile told the tale.

"Go on, then. Enlighten us all."

"Don't miss, Heimdall."

I didn't say it loud. If his ears were back to their usual, ultra-sensitive selves, he would hear me, and if they weren't, it didn't matter.

Lines of puzzlement creased Mrs Keener's forehead, rapidly morphing into ridges of surprise as the truth dawned and her eyebrows went up.

Then a bullet smacked into her face, and she had no forehead at all.

SEVENTY-ONE

EVERYTHING HAPPENED QUICKLY after that.

Even before Mrs Keener's body hit the scaffold planks, Heimdall loosed off a second shot. This one had a dual function, zinging through the rope that secured my right arm and hitting Bergelmir behind me. I heard him give a squawk of agony and drop the ice knife with a clatter.

With my arm suddenly free I swung sideways, twisting within the frame. I held my left arm rigid to stabilise myself, then started trying to undo the knot around my left wrist.

Heimdall saved me the bother by severing that rope as well.

Next thing I knew, I was on my knees on the platform. Doubling round, I began fumbling with the knots at my ankles. I knew I hadn't much time. I needed to release myself before someone collected their wits and made a move to stop me. All around, there was consternation. Frost giants yelling, babbling. Stunned expressions everywhere. Mrs Keener was dead. Loki! They couldn't believe it.

The human onlookers couldn't either. I sensed, more than saw, a surge of astonished delight within the crowd. And something else – a swell of activity, motion, a sharply rising floodtide. They had an opening, right now, while the enemy was still in shock and disarray. A window of opportunity. If there was ever a time for a violent insurrection, this was it.

Success! I got one of the knots undone.

Then a shadow loomed over me. Bergelmir. His right arm hung limp, blood from a bullet hole in his shoulder mingling with the pints of Backdoor's blood already matting his fur. He growled in pure bestial fury and swung at me with his left paw.

I ducked under the blow and scrambled away from him on hands and knees. The rope still tethering one ankle caught me up short. Bergelmir threw himself onto me flat out, like a wrestler doing a body slam, and I rolled out of his path. More by luck than anything I found myself within reach of the dropped ice knife, and snatched it up. The freezing cold of the handle seared my palm.

Bergelmir was on his feet too. He'd removed his armour for the execution, which made my life easier. I lashed out at his leg, slicing the shin open to the bone, and he reeled back, hissing, but was on the attack again in an instant. I struck again with the knife but missed, and his foot made contact, kicking me full in the jaw. My head snapped back and two molars were knocked clean out of their gum sockets. I had never been kicked so hard by anyone. I fetched up lying on my side, the world seesawing sickeningly around me, blood bubbling out over my lips.

Bergelmir charged, intent of following up the first kick with a second one, this time to the kidneys, and a bullet whanged into the planks in front of him, sending up a spray of splinters. Heimdall had no doubt been aiming at Bergelmir himself, but now that his targets were moving he wasn't so accurate.

The shot made Bergelmir hesitate, at least. Briefly, but long enough. I roused myself. *Shift your arse, Gid!* I sprang to my feet, knife hand extended, using the momentum of the action to carry the blade forwards. It sank into Bergelmir's thigh up to the hilt, and I yanked it out. Blood geysered; I'd got the femoral artery, just as I'd hoped. Bergelmir attempted to stem the blood flow, but it just welled out around his frantic hand. He gave up, and turned on me. He took two steps, and I retreated. He grabbed for me, futilely, his eyes clouding. Another step. His blood was hosing all over the platform, forming a small lake. His giant body sagged visibly as the life was decanted out of him.

One further step brought him within reach of me, but he tottered, and then slumped to his knees.

I contemplated slashing his throat, making it quick for him. I decided against.

He saw it in my eyes. He settled back on his haunches, both arms dangling now, knuckles to wood. Words rattled out of his throat.

"You... damn you..." he said. "A mere human... I do not yield..."

And then his head nodded forwards and he was gone.

A SWIFT ASSESSMENT of the state of play beyond the scaffold told me that the Asgardian uprising was going well. Encouraged by Vidar, men and gods alike were grappling with the frost giants in a fervour. *Issgeisl*s and other handweapons had been wrenched from their owners' grasps and were being put to use against them. The frosties had the numbers but our side had the advantages of surprise and determination. It helped that the opposition were doubly leaderless now, what with Mrs Keener and Bergelmir both having been scratched off the score card in swift succession. All at once they had no one to rally them, no one to inspire them. Too many unexpected events were taking place at once. The reversal in their fortune was cumulative, like an avalanche, gaining impetus as it went.

A few of the frost giants went for the better-part-of-valour option and fled the scene. When others saw this, they panicked and copied them. Soon it was a mass exodus, a thundering stampede for the forest. The frost giants were thoroughly routed. Those that remained – and there weren't many – stood their ground bravely, but our lot swarmed over them, Vidar, Skadi and Freya to the fore. Heimdall contributed from up on the castle turret, sniping until his ammo ran out. Before long, there wasn't a single living frostie to be seen from the castle.

Our human enemies had observed which way the tide was turning and were beating a hasty retreat of their own. I saw them making for *Nagelfar* in an unruly herd. Among the bobbing heads was one with a set of peroxide cornrows.

The blackness in me snarled.

Cy.

I sprinted for the scaffold steps, hurdling the near-headless remains of Mrs Keener. My own bullet hadn't been capable of killing her, but Heimdall's certainly had. It was a case of right time, right place, right assassin. The look on the Norns' faces immediately before he fired had said that this was how it was supposed to be. Loki's life was meant to be ended by Asgard's gatekeeper. No one else but Heimdall could close the book on the great trickster. Loki's fate was written that way.

Freya hailed me as I ran past. I gestured towards *Nagelfar*, and it was then that I realised I was still holding Bergelmir's knife. My hand was clamped round it, and it dawned on me that I couldn't actually let go even if I wanted to. My skin was stuck fast to the handle.

Nagelfar's fans started whirring and the ramps began to retract. Airborne dreadnought had just become refugee vessel. I leapt onto the nearest ramp as it rose and scurried up it like a rat up a drainpipe. The door ahead of me was closing, and I heard Freya shouting from the ground below, telling me to jump off, I wasn't going to make it. But I was. I fucking well was.

I reached the door. It had very nearly slid to. Elongating my body, I daggered through the narrow gap. The door clanged shut.

Nagelfar then gave a shudder and a lurch. Its entire frame shook mightily as it hoisted itself off from the permafrosted earth.

There was me aboard, its crew, and a handful of American mercenaries.

I wasn't bothered about any of *them*. They could live or die, I didn't give a shit.

There was only one person on that ship I cared about.

It was me and Cy now. I was going to find him and kill him, and God help any bastard who got in my way.

SEVENTY-TWO

I HEADED FORWARD to the bridge. It seemed the likeliest place to start looking.

By the time I got there I'd already run into a few of the bad guys. I couldn't recall precisely what had happened during these encounters. All I knew was that the ice knife was even bloodier than it had been before.

The bridge was a kind of gallery affair with a broad, curved windscreen overlooking *Nagelfar*'s prow. The five-strong crew were busy arguing as I arrived. One man, clearly the captain, was demanding that a course be set for Svartalfheim. Two pilots, seated at computer-controlled flying stations, disagreed. They were in favour of attacking the people on the ground with *Nagelfar*'s guns. It was too good an opportunity to pass up, they said. There'd never be a chance like this again.

Voices rose. The captain wasn't managing to assert his authority. The chain of command had broken down, a sure sign of a retreat turning into a shambles.

I slit the captain's throat in mid-sentence. He was so involved in the argument that he never heard me approach.

The navigator went next. By that point the two pilots had realised they were in the shit, and decided to go on the offensive with *Nagelfar* while they still could. Maybe they thought they could hold me to ransom by turning the ship's guns on my comrades. Maybe they thought this would deter me somehow.

When I was finished with them, I rounded on the fifth man. He was young, a subaltern or some such. Completely bricking it.

"Can you fly this thing?" I asked.

He shook his head. "N-no. I'm only a j-junior rating. You n-need two men anyway."

"So I've effectively crashed us then?"

He nodded. "Y-yes sir."

The blackness in me wasn't bothered. The blackness didn't have much interest in self-preservation. That wasn't the way it worked.

"Oops," I said.

Thwunk!

That was the sound of a punch coming out of nowhere, connecting with my skull. My head whiplashed sideways. Neck tendons cracked.

THWUNK!

A second punch, even harder than the first. The whole of my right cheek went numb, then suddenly seemed to expand like a piece of popcorn in the microwave, puffing out with pain. I said goodbye to another molar.

"Whoof!"

That was the breath being driven from my lungs by a fist ramming into my stomach with the force of a steam piston. The tooth was expelled along with it.

"Cunt."

That was Cy, looking down on me as I crawled on all fours at his feet. I was wheezing, and my head was a squall of sirens, my vision wavering as though I was underwater.

He booted me in the midriff, spinning me over onto my back. I tried to lift the knife. He stamped on my wrist, crushing it to the floor.

Alarms wailed on the bridge. Red lights whirled and flashed. The deck began tilting beneath us, and I could hear *Nagelfar*'s engines churning asynchronously. The ship was fighting to keep itself in the air, and failing.

If Cy was at all worried that *Nagelfar* was going down, he didn't show it.

"I've been itching to give you a good going over," he said. "Just to prove I'm the better man."

"Jury's still out on that," I managed to mumble through swelling lips.

Cy leant down and belted me full in the nose. I felt the *snap* of bone breaking, an electric jolt all the way up into my sinuses.

The alarms were getting louder and more strident. The deck was tilting ever more steeply. I could just see the windscreen, and filling it was the bulk of Yggdrasil, canted at a crazy angle. *Nagelfar* was heading for the World Tree. A computerised voice added itself to the cacophony of warning sounds. "COLLISION IMMINENT," it intoned, loud but calm. "COLLISION IMMINENT."

Cy set about pummelling me methodically and relentlessly. In his eyes there was nothing. Only blackness. The same blackness that was in me, the berserker rage that could take you beyond reason, beyond sense, make you fight and want to fight and only ever want to fight.

Then *Nagelfar* gave an abrupt lurch, and all at once the deck veered to almost vertical. Cy and I started sliding. We rolled helplessly, limbs tangled. I tried to latch onto something with my free hand on the way down but couldn't. We thumped up against a bulkhead, Cy taking more than his fair share of the impact. I wasn't sure but I thought I heard, above all the ruckus, one of his ribs crack.

I still had the knife. Had no choice about that. Soon as I'd got my bearings, I stabbed down with it. Cy caught my forearm with both hands and held me off. The blade of the knife had become oddly distended, mottled. Hot blood had melted its surface and then become frozen to it, adhering in blobs and greasy swirls. As far as I could tell, though, the thing was still sharp enough to do what it was supposed to.

I drove down with all my strength, spare hand pressing on the pommel. Cy continued to resist. The knife point quivered above his mouth, which was wide open in a rictus grimace of strain. I could see all of his teeth, his tongue, even that dangly bit of flesh at the back of his throat. *Nagelfar* was tipping over even further, not even on its side any more but starting to turn turtle. Yggdrasil's trunk filled the windscreen.

"Collision Imminent. Collision Imminent."

"*You* got Backdoor killed," I growled at Cy. "It wasn't me. *You*. But know what? Him getting executed bought Heimdall the time he needed. If Backdoor hadn't been blood eagled first, I wouldn't be here now to stick this down your fucking gizzard."

The knife descended, slowly but surely. The tip was now framed by Cy's teeth. The blackness in his eyes began to be replaced by something else – bright terror.

"Collision Imminent."

I put a knee on his chest and dug in with it, managing to locate the fractured rib, or near enough. A noise came out of Cy's throat, a cross between a grunt and a shriek. His grip slackened, just for a split second, and I rammed the knife all the way home. I felt the soft pressure of the blade slicing meat, splitting his tongue down the middle. Then the firmer pressure of the top of the blade grinding against his palate.

With the pain of his mouth being carved open came a sense of inevitability. Cy knew he couldn't win any more. He couldn't survive this.

Resignation entered his gaze, and now the knife point was piercing the back of his throat, sinking in deep. Blood frothed up. His body started to go into convulsions. His eyes rolled up in their sockets.

"Collision –"

No longer imminent.

Nagelfar, all but upside down, plunged prow first into Yggdrasil. The crash sent me somersaulting rearwards. My hand was torn from the ice knife, which was firmly embedded in Cy's jaws. Skin ripped free, but that was the least of my concerns. Huge branches punched through the windscreen, shattering it to smithereens. An immense hollow groan was either metal tearing or the World Tree crying out, I wasn't sure which. *Nagelfar* bore down on Yggdrasil, and there was a profound, resonant *cre-e-e-eak* like nothing I'd ever heard, the sound of timber splintering, magnified a thousandfold, as though an entire forest was being flattened in one fell swoop. All I could do was lie in a helpless heap against an inner wall as the inverted ship rode the breaking Yggdrasil, the two massive objects toppling together like exhausted wrestlers in a clinch.

When they fell, all was darkness.

After they fell, all was silence.

IN THE DARKNESS and silence, I was alone.

There was nothing.

Only me.

Adrift.

Isolated.

Enclosed.

And then...

...LIGHT.

A tiny glimmer of it. A twinkle, like a distant blue star.

And someone saying my name.

"Gid."

Someone I knew.

"Gid. Wake up."

Someone who was dead.

"Listen, you've got to wake up."

Abortion.

"They're on their way. I got a signal. Had to go all the way back up to the road to get it, but I got one. They said keep you conscious, don't let you nod off. They said they won't be long. I think it's a chopper that's coming."

The light, a mobile phone screen.

"That's it, keep those eyes open. We're going to be okay, Gid. They're coming. We're going to be okay."

SEVENTY-THREE

So THERE I was, in hospital, in a corner bay in a six-bed ward, woozy with super-strength painkillers but too wired to sleep, waiting for the dawn to come and with it, hopefully, some enlightenment, some certainty.

All I had to keep me company through the dark was the mumbling and snuffling of the other patients in the ward, and my own confusion. Questions swirled, and questions within questions, and I struggled to make sense of them.

I was prepared to accept that everything I believed had happened, hadn't. I could live with the idea of it all being just a delusion. Asgard, Odin, Thor, Loki, frost giants, trolls, the battles, the lot – just events conjured up in my brain during the time it took for Abortion to leave the crumpled car, climb the slope, make the 999 call and come back down. What had seemed to be weeks of my life had taken place in a few minutes, a full-length narrative unfurling at lightning speed in my head while I'd been suspended upside down inside the Astra. I'd been hovering in and out of consciousness, perhaps even on the verge of slipping into a coma, and my mind, prompted by various cues, had chosen to play out a complex fantasy of war and death amid the snow and ice of other worlds.

A dream, in other words. A vivid hallucination I'd lapsed into, somewhere in the depths of myself, somewhere where I no longer had control over what I was thinking. I'd created an action movie featuring the Norse gods, with myself as the star and a major supporting role for one very famous real-world personality. It had been exhilarating, scary, sometimes far-fetched, sometimes illogical, like any good action movie. There'd even been a romantic subplot, the leading man winning over the gorgeous love interest in spite of her initial frostiness towards him. All the elements that made for an entertaining couple of hours down at the local multiplex, or perhaps an evening in with a rental DVD.

I could happily go along with writing it off as nothing more than a figment of my imagination.

Except...

How come it had felt so real?

There had been pain. Lots of it. There had been danger that had had me sincerely fearing for my life. And that wasn't all. The biting cold. The trolls and their noxious smells. The angst of watching people I liked getting brutally killed. All experiences that were too harsh, too diamond-sharp, to be purely imaginary. I could recall, without any difficulty, the sensation of the wolf's teeth sinking into my wrist, the way the *issgeisl* shivered in my hands when Hval the Bald struck it with his, the feel of my skin tearing off on the handle of Bergelmir's ice knife... How was it possible I knew exactly what it was like to undergo such things, in the finest detail, unless I really had?

So, what if it hadn't been a dream? What then?

Suppose I'd died in that car, just for a few moments, and my soul, spirit, essence, call it what you will, had travelled *elsewhere*?

It wasn't the least bit plausible. But just suppose.

There were a few clues to support this theory. Bergelmir had mentioned the *Einherjar*, Odin's army of "heroic dead." Say I'd been one of them, if only briefly. Say I'd transmigrated – fancy word I remembered from RE lessons at school – and found myself caught up in an escalating battle between good and evil. It made a kind of sense, if you believed in that sort of stuff.

Another possibility was that, while out cold, I'd tapped into some hidden motherlode of mythology. Bragi had talked about the Norse gods being embedded in all human psyches, implying that their adventures were a part of our core programming, hardwired into us whether we realised it or not. More than merely dreaming, I'd accessed some inner database and discovered a whole bunch of stories there, which I'd then interacted with, writing myself into the narrative and even giving myself a pivotal role because, well, because why not? Like David Copperfield, we all wanted to be the heroes of our own lives, didn't we?

Or – how about this? – what if it had been a combination of the two? On some level I'd been aware that I was dying, or near death at any rate, and come up with a lucid, fictional way of visualising my struggle not to give in, my fight to live. It would explain why the Norns' videotape of my life stopped at the car crash. It also would account for Odin's comment about every death being "an apocalypse on a personal scale," for each of us our "very own Ragnarök." My characters making subtle, sidelong hints at my true predicament.

The bloke in the bed next to me moaned in his sleep and asked someone called Sonia if she'd remembered to put the cat out.

The night wore on. I longed for some kind of definitive answer to my musings. I wished I could know for sure, one way or the other, whether I'd genuinely fought alongside gods at the Viking end-of-all-that-is or simply been an accident victim having a bit of a funny turn.

Whichever way I looked at it, I did have one major regret. I hadn't had the chance to say a proper goodbye to Freya. I'd met my ideal woman, had had to abandon her, and had no way of getting back in touch with her. It was a terrific shame. If I thought about it too hard, I began to feel an ache inside, a yawning sorrow. So I tried to put it out of my mind.

If anything good was to come from the whole episode, it was the realisation that I should try harder with Cody. Face it, who had I been thinking of – the only person I'd been thinking of – when I was about to be blood eagled? He and I were estranged, but we needn't be strangers. I resolved to make an effort, try and see him more often, not just leave the raising of him to Gen and Roz. It wasn't too late to re-establish myself in his life. I'd have to be patient, take it one step at a time, but if he was willing, I'd gladly meet him more than halfway. I wasn't the All-Father but I could still be a father.

Next Bed Man was now muttering about whose turn it was to do the dishes. Such prosaic dreams the man was having. I should be so lucky.

In the crack in the curtains the night sky began to lighten, turning oyster grey. I could hear the hospital stirring and waking up – hushed voices, squeaky footfalls in corridors, things being placed clatteringly on trays. Soon, daylight was silvering the snow-laced branches of the tree immediately outside the ward window – some species of evergreen. The zigzag redbrick horizons of a northern city stretched beyond.

At about half past seven, as breakfast was being brought round, Abortion came skidding into the ward, all flushed and excited.

"Gid! Gid! You're awake. Good. You've got to see this."

"'How are you doing, Gid?' 'Oh, fine, mate, thanks for asking. Not too badly injured in the crash you caused.' 'Yeah, sorry about that. A thousand pardons.' 'That's all right. You came out of it unscathed, that's all that matters.' 'Yeah, that was pretty lucky, I thought.'"

"Later," Abortion said blithely. "You can have a go at me later, any time. Right now, you have to see the news. I was watching in the waiting lounge, where I've been all night, incidentally, sitting up while you've been all cosy in bed."

"You can't guilt me, so don't even try."

He grabbed the bedside TV set, swung it round on its arm, and switched it on.

"Whoa, steady," I said. "They charge a fortune for that."

"I know, but this is big."

And it was big. Every channel was carrying the story. All other programming had been suspended.

"...and once again, our breaking news this morning," said a sombre newscaster. "Lois Keener, President of the United States of America, has suddenly and unexpectedly died. Mrs Keener was at work in the Oval Office when she suffered what appears to have been a massive stroke. In a statement, Vice-President Bennewitz – now acting president – has confirmed that this was the probable cause of death, pending an official autopsy report. Beyond that, few details are known."

I watched with widening eyes... and a strange sensation in the pit of my stomach.

"Mrs Keener, a colourful and controversial figure on the world stage, had shown no previous signs of ill health. In fact, at the age of forty-two, she appeared to be in the prime of life, making her death all the more surprising. We can cross over now to our Washington correspondent for the latest."

"America is in shock and mourning," said the Washington correspondent. "It's the early hours of the morning here, but nobody has gone to bed. People are up and about. Many are glued to their TV sets. Nobody can quite believe it. I've seen strangers hugging one another in the street. Grown men weeping. There's a sense of... numbness, I suppose you could say. It's surreal. Comparisons could be drawn with the shooting of John F. Kennedy."

"What do we know about the circumstances of Mrs Keener's death?"

"Very little so far, beyond what the vice-president revealed in his statement earlier. Yesterday afternoon, at approximately three p.m., Mrs Keener was in discussions with military advisors and the Joint Chiefs of Staff when all of a sudden she slumped in her chair and collapsed to the floor. Paramedics were on the scene within minutes and applied emergency resuscitation methods, but without success. She was pronounced dead on arrival at George Washington University Hospital thirty-five minutes later. The cause of death is reported as 'catastrophic intracranial haemorrhage': in effect, a blood vessel in her brain ruptured, resulting in a build-up of fluid that ravaged vital brain tissue. Messages of support and sympathy for her family have been coming in from other world leaders, including our own Prime Minister Clasen. However, there have also been jubilant public celebrations in certain countries, people taking to the streets to express their joy that someone they regard as a national enemy, an oppressor, is no more."

"Fuck," I breathed.

"I know!" said Abortion. "Who saw that coming?"

"Not her, that's for sure," I said.

And a thought flashed into my head.

Heimdall's bullet.

Could it have been...? Was it conceivable...?

The newscaster droned on – a moment in history, a terrible tragedy for Mrs Keener's husband, son and daughter, an abrupt end to the remarkable rise to power of the self-professed "soccer mom from Wonder Springs," blah blah blah. Abortion plumped himself down on the end of my bed and helped himself to my breakfast, starting with the carton of orange juice. I turned away from the TV and stared out of the window.

She'd died at almost the exact same time I was tangled up in the car.

Coincidence, surely. That was all. A case of life imitating "art." To read anything more into it than that would be a great mistake. That way madness lay.

The tree outside, I noticed, had honeycomb-like bark. An ash.

Coincidence too, of course.

I was about to turn back to the TV and rescue my breakfast from Abortion's clutches when, all at once, a grey squirrel popped out from amongst the tree's foliage. It scampered to the very tip of a branch, until it was level with the window ledge. It stopped there, peeping around inquisitively, then swivelled its head and looked straight at me through the glass. Beady black little rodent eyes met my gaze, held it for several heartbeats. A brush of a tail twitched and fluffed. A nose quivered.

And then – swear to God – the squirrel raised one ratty-clawed forepaw in the air, level with its ear.

The fucking thing saluted me.

And then it was gone, dashing back into the snowy darkness of the tree's heart.

In that moment, I knew.
Not a sliver of doubt in my mind any more.
I knew.
And, knowing, wise at last, I smiled.

ACKNOWLEDGEMENTS

HUGE GRATITUDE IS due to David Moore for nursing my Norsery and Gary Main for checking my Chinookery.

ABOUT THE AUTHOR

James Lovegrove published his first novel at the age of twenty-four and has since written more than fifty books. He has been shortlisted for numerous awards, including the Arthur C. Clarke Award, the John W. Campbell Memorial Award, the Bram Stoker Award, the British Fantasy Society Award and the Manchester Book Award, and his work has so far been translated into fourteen languages. He is a regular reviewer of fiction for the Financial Times. In 2011 he became a *New York Times* best selling author with *The Age of Odin*.

www.jameslovegrove.com